"*Wings Unseen* is an enthralling female-driven fantasy debut. The world, magic system, and terrific characters—with two complex, multi-layered heroines along with the male protagonist—drew me in and kept me rapt. The romantic set-up goes sideways in a delightful way, satisfying me entirely. The characters truly grow and change over the course of their epic quest, including a heroine who begins in a dark place and rises above it. An initially unlikable heroine, Vesperi is deftly handled and won a place as my favorite character. Compelling, entertaining, and enlightening, *Wings Unseen* is a fantastic read!"

-Jeffe Kennedy (Author of The Twelve Kingdoms trilogy)

"War, treachery, and star-crossed lovers abound in this high fantasy novel. . . . Farrell's (*Maya's Vacation*, 2011) book is imaginative, filled with detailed worldbuilding, but rarely bogged down in exposition. Each of the protagonists' stories is engaging in its own way. . . . Vesperi is the most intriguing of the three protagonists, despite being the most morally questionable, since she is the only one who appears to have agency from the very beginning. Janto and Serra spend a large portion of the novel following cryptic prophecies from the Brotherhood instead of making their own choices. But they're still likable enough, and these faults don't remove the tale's fun. This inventive epic about two kingdoms soars above its faults."

-Kirkus Reviews

Hi East Bay Neighbor!
I hope you enjoy Book 1 in
My Wings Rising duology!

Rebecca Yancey Farrell
March 2024

WINGS UNSEEN

REBECCA GOMEZ FARRELL

Meerkat Press
Atlanta

ISBN-13 - 978-1-946154-00-2 (Paperback)
ISBN-13 - 978-1-946154-01-9 (eBook)

Library of Congress Control Number: 2017907727

Printed in the United States of America

Published in the United States of America by
Meerkat Press, LLC, Atlanta, Georgia
www.meerkatpress.com

For those with the courage to see.

CONTENTS

PART TWO: THE CULLING

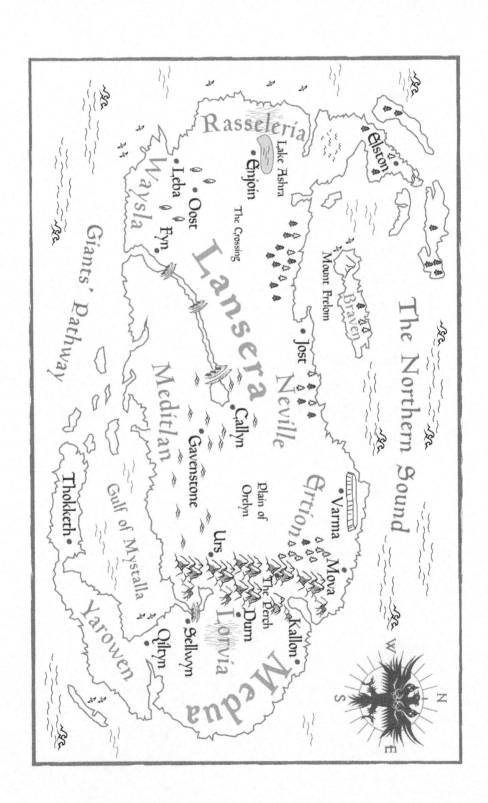

PART ⊕NE

BREEDING SEAS⊕N

CHAPTER I
VESPERI

He was an enticing prospect, Vesperi had to admit. Candlelight enhanced his muscle's curves where they strained against his black tunic. Fluffs of dark feather down stuck to the material, one of the reasons Vesperi knew he was a Raven, a spy from Lansera. The other was the cloak hooked on his pointer finger, its shade the luminous purple of a sunset over Mandat Hall on a cloudy night. A cloak that audacious declared his ambition for Vesperi's hand the moment he rode through Sellwyn's gate. Maybe the spy had chosen it for that effect; her father was drawn to power like a priest to intrigue. But Vesperi doubted Agler had the wits for that deception. Doubtless, the fool simply lacked subtlety.

He stared at her, waiting for an invitation to speak from her bedroom doorway. She let him wait. Meduan men rarely waited for anything. Vesperi constantly had to, especially for her brother Uzziel. She'd cursed the day he was born, and he returned the favor with every contemptuous look he gave her. Not that her curse could have made his life worse than it already was. He'd flown out of their mother's womb with his birth cord tangled multiple times around his neck, his lips and nails deep claret. He should have been put to death—if a girl, he would have been—but Lord Sellwyn longed for an heir and wouldn't hear of it. So the whelp lived and spited her with every breath from his sick bed.

"Lady Sellwyn?" Agler broke the silence with a cough. His muscles tensed appealingly. The man's form *was* extraordinary.

"Oh, please, *Ser* Agler, come inside," she drawled. "Do take a seat."

She shifted on her side, careful to tug her blouse down an inch. Then she fluttered her lashes.

He blushed and slid into the chair farthest from her bed. She laughed. "Such chivalry from a Lorvian, for a *lady* like me." This spy had no idea how Lorvian men behaved. With words that fine, he could never have been raised a distant northern noble, no matter how long he claimed to have been at court. She patted the bench next to her. "Why don't you come closer?"

He considered it, uncertainty evident in his downcast eyes. But his voice was stern. "Your father is home. I know he gets . . . angry . . . on occasion." He paused. "I wish to give him no reason to dislike me."

Vesperi grew weary of his manners. This man—this spy—was a waste of her time. She iced her tone. "What do you want with me, Agler?"

"To marry you, of course."

"Of course, of course. So many men come here with that same idiotic idea. I am not the marrying type."

Agler narrowed his eyes. "Are you mocking my proposal, wench?"

Vesperi laughed again. At least he was attempting to be a man now. "No, Agler, I am not mocking you. I am letting you know precisely where you stand."

"I'm a better match than any of those buffoons who've paraded through your father's hall." He spoke faster now, hiding his nerves. "I could offer your father a thousand souzers tonight if you agree to the marriage."

"Yes." She crossed her legs slowly. "But what could you offer *me*?"

His face flushed, but he had the forbearance to pretend it was anger. "Offer you? That's preposterous, woman. I do not have to offer you a thing. Why, I ought to call the guards this instant to . . . to . . ."

How precious. He couldn't say the words.

"To beat me?" she finished for him. "Spare yourself the embarrassment. I have taken beatings from the guards since I was old enough to talk. I don't feel the fists anymore." She rose, planting her feet on the carpet. "And you do need to offer me something. My father has agreed I may choose my own husband." A lie. Her father had asked her opinion on the matter once, but that hardly qualified as handing her the decision. He would never do that; no man of Medua would. But Agler did not realize it.

"I have yet to meet a suitor who was man enough to impress me. You certainly do not." Agler may have mimicked the swagger of Medua's courtiers with his garish colors and quick temper, but it wasn't in his blood. She wondered whom he had been over the mountains before becoming a Raven. A field worker from Wasyla? Certainly not one of those disgusting frogmen from Rasseleria. She had seen one once in the convent, wearing the bone-studded robe of the advers, Medua's priesthood. The frogman had felt her staring and trained his yellow eyes on her while his tongue flicked out between his lips.

"Vesperi, tell me then. How can I win you over?" Agler's voice revealed only a hint of the exasperation he must have felt. The Raven was a fish thrown into a pool of sheven here, sharp rows of teeth gleaming from their opened mouths. She almost pitied the spy.

He changed tactics. "You are ravishing. And more clever than any other woman I have met—you would make a good advisor for a man like me. I'm going to rise fast, you'll see, and you should be the lady on my arm. You belong at King Ralion's court, not wasting away in a hovel like Sellwyn Manor." His voice hinted at tenderness. The emotion was a ludicrous possibility, but his bargaining chip was not. If she had to take care of her brother much longer, she would do something completely insane, poison Uzziel's porridge or inflict him with her talent the next time they were alone. By Saeth's hammer, she wanted to be rid of her brother.

Agler breathed heavily, his wavy, sandy blond hair shifting. It begged to have fingers run through it. The spy offered Vesperi an easy escape, but she didn't want it, not in truth. She wanted Sellwyn Manor.

Vesperi sighed then waved her hand toward the door. "Go. We're done here."

"I'll say when we're done, woman, not a whore like you."

Agler almost choked on the words as he spit them out. Did the Ravens think this boy fully trained? He would not last two seconds in a camp tavern, much less at court. Luckily for Agler, Lord Sellwyn saw only what he wanted. In this case, the substantial pouch of coins tied around the spy's waist.

It was fortunate she had convinced her father to let her speak with Agler before saying yes to the mummer's proposal. Vesperi would have been a complete laughingstock after his inevitable discovery, forced back into the convent so Lord Sellwyn need never lay eyes on her again. A man who addressed her as "Lady" wasn't one on whom she could hang her future. The more she considered it, the more his pathetic attempt at winning her hand angered her . . . and it had been so long since she had used her talent. She had to hide it until she was ready to show Father how important it could be for him, how invaluable *she* could be . . . But a little play could be explained away well enough.

Agler sputtered on about teaching her to be a respectable wife or some such nonsense, but he never raised a hand toward her like a true Meduan would have. That final mistake sealed his fate. Vesperi gazed out the tiny window high above her nightstand. Three of the four moons clustered close that night, and she focused on the biggest one—silver-hued Esye. With her middle finger raised, she imagined squeezing the moon by its halo, draining the light from it. Energy flowed into her body and churned within her palm like a hound chasing after its tail.

"Vesperi, what are you doing?"

There was fear in the question—*I must be glowing.* His rounded eyes reminded her of a lizard's, and then his face went white. She wondered what he saw. The last time, the nun had screamed something about fish scales, and she'd been desperately curious to know how she appeared when channeling the talent ever since. Her hair writhed with the force of strengthening energy, and she breathed in sharply, jabbed her raised finger toward him. A single bolt of silver flashed into his chest, and in seconds, she was alone.

A lick of flame lingered over the pile of ashes then vanished. She was disappointed to see she had burnt the chair to a crisp as well as the man. At least there were no marks left on the wall. Vesperi could summon her talent, but she did not know how to control it.

She yelled down the hall. "Servant. Come clean up this mess."

A young girl with bronzed skin scurried inside, keeping her head low.

"Those ashes." Vesperi pointed at the remains. "Sweep them up."

The girl hurried back into the corridor to fetch a broom, deftly side-stepping the incense-shrouded altar to their god, Saeth, that dominated the hall.

A flash of inspiration made Vesperi call after her. "Bring a box with a lid and a quill and paper also." *This will be fun.*

The girl nodded as she disappeared down the hall, blending in with the shadows.

Vesperi knelt, sticking her hand in the warm ashes. A waterfall of them slipped through her spread fingers. *Such a waste. He had been so handsome.*

CHAPTER 2
JANTO

Jory's iron-tipped quarterstaff hit Janto's left shoulder guard with a resounding clang. He fell onto the grassy plain with an *oomph*. Eyes closed, Janto willed the pain to stop. *Why did I agree to quarterstaffs?* He glanced longingly at his sword, discarded on a nearby patch of mud.

"Did I hit too hard?" Jory's nasal voice acted as a new, excruciating weapon of torture in an already ringing head. Nearly as burly as his father, Cino Xantas, liege-lord of Ertion, Jory resembled a monolith more often than he did a young man. His voice had not caught up to his bulk.

Janto rolled over, letting the distant sight of Callyn—the capital city of Lansera, which straddled the tempestuous River Call—soothe him. A quartz-encrusted bridge connected the city's east and west sides and sparkled so bright, mothers told their children to turn away for fear they'd go blind. It wasn't the shine that caught Janto's eye, however, but the horse and rider bounding through the city's westward gate, barely more than a speck on the horizon. Still, Janto's gut clenched. All members of the council had arrived by midevening yesterday. He knew that too well, recalling the hours of small talk he had been forced to make the past few days. Ser Allyn had insisted on bringing him along as he offered the king's hospitality to each liege-lord and lady. The horse and rider now cresting the first of the hills had to be on another mission.

Janto squinted, making out black feathers lining the rider's cloak and hat. *A Raven, then.* Ser Swalus, chief of the realm's spies, had arrived yesterday. Why would another of his men come to court?

Jory's voice pierced his thoughts. "My prince? Are you all right?"

"Janto." He pushed aside his worry to correct his friend. Janto's father, King Dever Albrecht, would deal with the Raven's mystery soon enough. "When you have been besting me since you were in swaddling clothes, you have earned the right to call me by my name." Janto reached for the hand he knew his sparring partner would offer. Lanserim always helped their enemies to their feet.

Janto retrieved his staff from the brush where it had fallen. "You know you have to suffer for that last hit."

Jory repositioned himself faster than a rufior could flap its wings. They circled each other for a time, attempting thrusts and cuts. Janto was hard-pressed to avoid Jory's blunt jabs. The tireless youth's tar-colored hair swung wildly with each parry. If Janto's companions at the Murat had anywhere near Jory's stamina, three weeks of agony awaited him, and Janto had had plenty of that already from Serra, his betrothed. He had chosen the year of their wedding to attend the annual competition, and she had made her complaints on that count well known before his father ordered their separation. King Albrecht thought women a distraction from the mental and physical preparations needed for the Murat, so Janto and Serra had not spoken in weeks, though they lived in the same castle.

"Whoa, now!" Jory looked over Janto's shoulder, lowering his staff.

The warning came too late. Something slammed into Janto with the heft of a spooked craval beast. Luckily, it wasn't one of those dim-witted creatures or Janto's back would have broken. Face down in the grass for the second time that morning, he saw Pic, a pockmarked serving boy of eight, tumble beside him. The lad had barreled straight into him while running down the hill.

Pic greeted his prince with eyes like a cat spotting a wolfhound. Janto laughed and patted the scared child on the back.

"Now tell me"—he stood and extended his hand to the boy—"what's so important you ran so fast your eyes could not keep up with your feet?"

Pic took a deep breath. "You are needed by the Lady"—he paused to take another big gulp of air—"the Lady Serra needs you, I mean. The king sent me to come find you and—"

"Wait a moment and think clearly." Janto could not imagine his father ordering any such thing. "Are you certain you remember correctly?" King Dever Albrecht did not bend his own rules.

Pic nodded, too busy panting to speak. Janto turned to Jory. "I'm afraid I'll have to forfeit." He added with a grin, "It's the only way you'd win, anyhow."

Jory laughed and poked Janto's chest with his staff. "Keep telling yourself that."

"I'm also afraid you'll have to carry two suits of armor back with you." Janto tossed an arm guard on the pile of outerwear he'd started shedding as soon as Pic's intent had become clear. Armor was too much of a hindrance if he needed to move fast. His father was willing to let him see Serra, so it had to be urgent. Not urgent enough to leave his sword behind, though—Ser Allyn would have his head for that.

"I think we can handle it, Pic, can we not?" Jory ruffled the hair of the serving boy, who stumbled under the weight of a pair of gauntlets. "Be off, my prince!"

"Janto!" He sprang into a run. One did not keep a king waiting, and this might be the only chance he'd get to see Serra before he left.

✳ ✳ ✳

Janto did not slow as he neared the castle gate—a shimmering curtain of thin rods of Wasylim timber, reinforced with platinum and gold threads strong enough to withstand an army's assault. None had ever come this close to the seat of Lansera, though Gavenstone Manor had nearly been overtaken by less traditional methods, and it lay but two day's ride to the southeast. By the time Janto reached the gate, the guards had already partway reeled the metal threads in, pulling the rods back enough for him to sprint through. He hurried past them, shouting thanks as he made his way to the stone well in the center of courtyard. Drenched in sweat was no condition in which to see the king. Janto splashed his arms and face with the lukewarm liquid, taking care not to spill any on his tunic. The plain shirt he wore beneath wicked up most of the sweat, so the tunic was clean enough. The handful of water he scooped into his mouth was barely enough to satiate, but he did not have time for a lengthy draught. King Albrecht waited.

Janto vaulted up the stairs to his father's chamber. His mother sat near the window, her skin the brownish-green of Ashran marshweeds in winter. The tight, copper-colored curls on her head contrasted with her skin. She wore bell sleeves to cover dimpled arms; few things made Queen Lexamy feel self-conscious, but her weight was one of them.

She moved from the window. "Come closer, Janto."

"Father called me."

"I know. He had to take care of arrangements for the council. Ser Allyn fetched him moments ago."

"Where did they go?" Janto kissed his mother's cheek but kept his eyes on the doorway, ready to resume his search for his father and Ser Allyn, the king's most trusted servant and unquestioned head of the castle's affairs.

"To the scroll room, but you needn't go after him. He told me why he called for you." She paused. "Serra needs you."

Janto swallowed. "Is she unwell?"

"No." His mother took his hand and rubbed a thumb over his knuckles. "Agler is dead."

Suddenly, the Raven's appearance made sense. Serra's brother, Agler, had joined the band of spies last summer, determined to prove his loyalty to the king. Agler had been sent on this mission, his first, at the onset of winter, and the hanging balac vines had only now begun to bloom. But something more than a failed mission must have happened; Meduans did not kill the spies they caught. Rather, Lanserim scouts found them in the mountain woods, their minds addled by the wizards' torture, or they disappeared completely. It took months or years before the Ravens declared one of their own gone with finality. "How do they know he's dead?"

His mother handed him an unrolled parchment bearing the broken seal of a raven in flight. The words were written in the thrushberry's violet ink:

Your Highness, King Dever Albrecht, ruler of the meritorious people of Lansera and keeper of the needful peace with the inconstant villains of Medua,

I have received unfortunate news for your charge, the Lady Serrafina of Gavenstone. It is grievous to me that I must send lamentable tidings to one who has already borne such sorrow, but as our leader has already departed for your council, this duty falls to me.

This morn, we found a strange box with a viper burned into its lid. The attached letter bore the words, "This bird sang too sweetly." The box's contents were harder to fathom than the container that held them. There was naught but a fine dust inside, which I took to be ashes, though they sparkled with a silver glint when placed in the light. I sifted through the ash and pulled out a gold ring. On it, a cluster of grapes and the initials A. G. were inscribed. I believe Agler Gavenstone took this ring with him on his recent mission and hid it from sight beneath his clothes—a foolish thing to be certain, but he was newly winged. I surmise it was discovered and the young lord slain by the Meduan lord to whom he was sent to gather information.

The Ravens in the Perch reported seeing a man in forest green. His cloak also bore this viper sigil. The man did not dismount but flung the bound box from his seat and galloped away at a breakneck speed. I have sent men to search for him, but I doubt they will overtake him before he reaches the mountains.

Please make certain Ser Swalus is advised of this development. May Madel grant you the fortitude to tell the young princess-in-waiting.

Ser Quentynil Werbose

"Father said I could go to her?" Janto placed the parchment on the desk.

His mother nodded. "But Janto, you must be censured, even in this hour. Comfort her as you will but do not lose your restraint. This is a time of trial for Serra as well as you, and how you both weather it is of utmost importance to your futures." She kissed his forehead. "Now, go."

He hurried back into the courtyard. Several servants were preparing for tonight's council feast, but he did not slow to speak with them. Eddy, the head stableman with hair smooth and full enough to rival the manes of his horses, stepped forward in greeting, but Janto waved him off. His lungs still throbbed from the run, and he leaned against the marbled stone wall of the courtyard to catch his breath and his thoughts. *What can I say to her?* Janto had never lost anyone closer to him than an aging servant, and Serra had already lost so many people. No matter his lack of understanding, she would need him, and he would be there as long as his father allowed. Serra had been his best friend since he was twelve and had walked her to her new room, grasping her hand so she would not feel alone.

That room's entrance was through the southern end of the courtyard. Serra's maid Bini, a woman of thirty years, sat at the table beside it. She held a black cloth in one hand and used the other to rip it in strips about an inch wide, the sound like ice crushed underfoot.

"My prince!"

He had reached for Serra's door, startling Bini in the process.

"You cannot go in. Your Murat, it's so soon!" She put down the cloth to wave him away.

He shushed her. "Father sent me, Bini, I promise. You are not doing any wrong by letting me through. Is she inside?"

"Yes, yes, but you are certain the king has allowed it?" Her eyes conveyed suspicion. She was from the northernmost tip of Lansera, the port town of Elston, and her people did not usually travel so far abroad as Callyn.

"I am certain." He gingerly pushed open the door, cringing when it squeaked. A crack of light fell on Serra's writing desk, bare as the bench in front of her mirror where he next cast his glance. *Where is she?* The room was too dark. Serra never closed the thick, rouge curtains. She loved the light and warmth the sun brought to the cold, stone rooms of the castle.

As his eyes adjusted, her unshod, pale-peach feet appeared on the bed covers. He lingered by the door, her refusal to acknowledge a visitor redoubling his worry. Serrafina was always decorous, even in the face of tragedy. Comforting her would be a harder feat than any Murat endeavor.

CHAPTER 3
SERRA

"Serra? May I come in?" Janto's voice, not so high since adolescence, betrayed his apprehension. His bronze-colored tunic hung over black pants, and his sword dangled from his belt, unsheathed. He must have been at the field sparring when he'd heard about Agler. Words reminding him to wipe the blade came to her lips, but she let them fall away unspoken. The heavy door closed as he stepped fully into the room.

"Serra?"

She met his eyes but returned her head to the tear-dampened pillow. Her fingers folded a handkerchief into eighths over and over again.

"Oh, Serra." Janto leaned his sword against the marbled stone wall and placed a hand on each of her cheeks. Amber eyes focused on hers. "I am so sorry." He traced a finger beneath her bottom lashes, wiping stray tears. "Please, what I can do to help?"

She said nothing, her fingers folding the cloth—Agler's handkerchief. She had not pulled it out of her dresser in close to a year.

Janto swept her hair behind her ear. "What can I do?"

She considered how to answer. Propriety told her to make him leave right away. He shouldn't be there, shouldn't be concerned with her right now when preparing for the Murat. She should tell him to go back to the field and train, that she needed some time alone to come to terms with what had happened, that she'd be better in a little while. What did it say of her that she would not?

"Kiss me. Kiss me and hold me close."

He withdrew his hands, shocked, though his eyes conveyed a desire to obey. "I cannot."

"Yes, you can. Forget your honor for a moment and comfort me." Her own boldness surprised her, but still, she hoped he would.

"I cannot. You know that."

"I don't know anything right now." She put the handkerchief down. "No, that's not true. I know my brother is dead and my betrothed is here, and I need him to comfort me." She took Janto's hands and pulled him down beside her. "No one could rebuke you for holding me a while. Not today. Please."

"You know I cannot." He whispered the words through strained lips. "It's not that they wouldn't understand—Father granted me leave to see you—but I must be pure of heart for the Murat to keep my mind clear. I cannot be so like this." He placed a hand on the small of her back. "All I breathe is you when you are anywhere near me."

A sob built in her chest and she did not try to subdue it. Janto dried the new wave of her tears before they could fall. His resolve fading, his arms clasped tighter around her trembling frame. "I would forget it all to stop your grief for a moment." Lips brushed over hers. "I am so sorry."

She buried her head into his chest and cried. "It's so wrong. It's all so terribly wrong." Her fingers clenched and unclenched on his thigh. "I would never have let him go if I knew this would happen. I would have demanded he stay with me. He was all the family I had left—his place was with me!"

"Shh, love." He soothed her, running fingers through her ochre hair. "There was nothing you could do, you know that. Agler was making amends for his trespasses. Joining the Ravens was the only way he felt he could gain my father's trust again." His arms clasped around her tightly. "He was restoring his honor—*your* honor. He asked for the mission himself, you know. Father had to grant Ser Swalus permission to send him out so soon."

"He did not ask to die!" Grief overcame her rage. "It was only supposed to be a short mission. He was supposed to come back." Hiccups swallowed her words, and she buried her face in her hands.

"Shh, stop talking. Be calm for a moment." Janto rubbed her back, and she relaxed into the steady movement of his fingers. "I'm here. I will always be here for you."

A creaking door announced King Albrecht's arrival.

"Son." His steady voice resounded through the bedchamber. Janto pulled his arms back to his side in an instant. Serra did not. Her brother was dead; Janto was there. Holding onto him could not be so wrong.

King Dever Albrecht stood taller than Janto by half a foot, his features starker. Thick eyebrows made his brow always furrowed, and his long hair was the gray of ashwood. He had kept it so since his studies with the Order, the Lanserim priesthood, when he was Janto's age.

The king's blue velvet cloak hung over his shoulders, swans embroidered on the black trim with rhodium threads. Their goddess, Madel, brought forth a three-headed bird to win the Battle of the Gods in ancient days, or so the myths went. Many lieges honored Her by taking birds as their sigils.

The king spoke to Janto. "I need you in the council room. There will be time for this"—he gestured toward Serra with his characteristic briskness some described as cold—"later."

"Yes, Father, right away." Janto went to kiss her goodbye, but she knew he thought better of it when his arms wrapped around her in a parting hug instead. Some pink fluff clung to his tunic from the feathers laced into her gown. He tried to brush them aside before exiting the room.

The king placed his gloved hand on Serra's shoulder. She shivered at the cold touch of its metal studs.

"Lady Serrafina." His voice was not unkind.

She returned his gaze but did not wipe her tears. *Let him see them.* "Yes, my king?"

"I want you to know my son is not the only member of the royal family who feels your loss." He regarded her thoughtfully. "Lord Agler Gavenstone will be remembered as he wished, as a brave and loyal man who served Lansera and its king." His eyes were warm, the same shade as Janto's. "All has been forgiven. It was forgiven years ago, though he could not accept that mercy."

She nodded and tried to contain her grief so she could show the gratitude she should at this kindness. Only an hour ago, such attention from her fiancé's father, the closest she'd had to one of her own since coming to Castle Callyn, would have thoroughly pleased her.

"I know he was the last of your family, and I cannot imagine how you must feel, but I want you to know you have family here." He squeezed her shoulders and made certain she looked him in the eye. "You will be a strong queen, Serrafina, a woman I will be proud to have bear my grandchildren. The wait is only another month."

He slipped back into his customary manner, his voice raised and firm. "I will let this moment of indulgence go unnoted—I should have expected your restraint to be relaxed when I sent for him—but Janto's focus must be unadulterated for the Murat so Madel can best influence him there. Do not seek him out again."

"I understand. I was weak with grief." The ache in her bones did not make it easy, but she stood beside the bed, clasped her hands together and raised her elbows toward him, holding them up a moment longer than customary in deference. "I will not let it happen again." She hoped she spoke the truth—she'd never dealt with emotions so choking before.

"I know you love him well. Think of this separation as a final hurdle that will strengthen your marriage. Even when absent, your love should be his strength." A moment later, he added, "I am truly sorry, daughter."

He released her shoulders and left the room with no further words.

"Let my love be Janto's strength as seeking your forgiveness was my brother's? That did not end so well for him." The angry words escaping her lips made her gasp. Her cheeks colored, and she whispered a prayer of thanks to Madel that the door had closed before she uttered them. The royal family had never been anything but honorable to her. They'd accepted her into their home, called her daughter, praised her worth as a suitable mate for Janto even after Agler had—

She had to steel herself through this grief. It made her rash. Agler died to redress his mistakes. She must be careful not to make any of her own.

CHAPTER 4
JANTO

He hesitated, hand on the iron handle of the council room door for the second time that evening. Ser Allyn had barely laid eyes on him before scowling and waving him back to change his grass-stained pants and tunic, which was plagued with feathers despite attempts to brush it. *One more glance will not hurt.* Janto hurried to the mirror hung on a column near the western archway. Luckily, he was alone, the servants in the kitchen or throne room preparing for tonight's feast. Janto did not wish to appear vain.

Comforting Serra had done nothing to calm the flush on his face from running. Otherwise, he was passable. Regal even, with his mother's chain hanging around his neck. She would be pleased, but Janto suspected she already knew the gold-flecked stone brought out the color in his eyes when she gave it to him two weeks ago, in case she did not make it home before the Murat. Queen Lexamy had been at Lady Xantas's annual raccoon festival, an event Janto had been excused from ever since throwing up the seventh course all over the banquet table at six years old. The queen knew better than to offend Lady Xantas by declining herself, even if it meant missing her son's farewell. He would return home in a few weeks; Gella Xantas's grudge-holding endured for decades.

"Son, it is time to go in." King Albrecht waited at the council room door, his voice startling Janto away from his reflection.

"Of course, Father."

Inside, a chorus of "Long live Albrecht!" greeted them. The king stifled it with a raised hand. The room was barely large enough to fit the heavy table made from the green-veined kratomwood of the Ertion Mountains. Ten chairs in all for the five provinces' lieges, the Ravens' chief, the army commander, the king and his servant, and a guest. There were no windows, only stifling air that held the smell of stale liquor from meals and councils past. Prying ears were not likely to find satisfaction here.

Two chairs at the table sat unclaimed. Serra's aunt, the Lady Marji who served as Meditlan's liege in Serra's absence, should have filled one. A king's messenger had probably stopped her on the road with news of Agler's death, turning her back to prepare her people for it. Lord Rufalyn was also absent—Elston was far, and making the trip twice in a little more than a month was a sacrifice. He and his wife would be at the wedding.

"Gentlemen and Lady Farami," his father began. "I've invited my son to attend our council as he will soon leave for the Murat."

"Here, here!" All the councilors shouted, except for Lady Gransyl Farami, liege of Neville, who clapped her hands instead. "Good for you, Prince!"

"Janto will return to us an accomplished man, and thus, a taste of his future duties as king is appropriate." His father took his seat.

Lord Xantas stood, buried in the brown, black, and yellow skins that augmented his considerable girth. "Pardon me, King Albrecht"—he raised his elbows and nearly toppled his wine goblet with his stomach—"but you don't mean to scare the young man away from the throne, do you? The kingdom's business is a rather dry topic for someone Janto's age—well, for someone of any age!" He winked at Janto, an ever-present smile on his lips.

"I suppose you would have me fill his head with nonsense of a king's life?" The king drummed his fingers on the table. "Perhaps tell him his duties will be mingling with beautiful women all day, of whom he will have his pick when he rules?"

"He can have my woman—anything to get her off my hands!" Lord Xantas bellowed, and the group laughed. Lady Gella was no one's idea of the perfect woman, though Janto knew Lord Xantas would be inconsolable to lose her, no matter his protests.

Captain Wolxas, the army commander, raised his glass. "No one would dream of taking your"—he coughed—"beautiful"—he coughed again—"wife from you, Lord Cino. Not even if you paid us in bear skins!"

"Especially not if you paid us in bear skins." Quiet Lord Sydley of

Wasyla shocked the group with the ending joke, and the laughter rang louder. He was older than the rest of the men, and a cane of burnished almond wood leaned against his chair.

"Fair enough." Xantas wiped tears of mirth from his eyes. "I shall be forced to keep her for now. But if she wants to throw a festival of the grouse next year, I cannot be held responsible for my actions."

Janto laughed with the others but stopped when his father directed him to take the seat on his left. Then the king opened the council by placing a dark wooden box on the table, its narrow, pinkish-red streaks exposing it as rosewood. He opened its lid to reveal a mass of white-gray ashes. "Lord Agler Gavenstone is dead. This is all that remains of him."

The air in the room thickened with tension as though a giant squeezed its walls together. Janto found himself fascinated by the sigil carved into the box's lid: a snake, hood flared and teeth bared.

His father continued, "I would like him to be buried at the Mount."

A few of the councilors gasped at the announcement, as did Janto. He had not thought his father would grant Agler such consideration. In truth, he did not think he should.

Ser Allyn dropped his quill. "Pardon, my king, but you have entrusted me to advise you on all matters as I see fit. It is my place to disagree." The spice from his hot licorice tea tickled Janto's nose hairs from two seats down. "Lord Agler was a traitor to the throne. A traitor to you."

Ser Allyn frowned, dark eyebrows making a "V" on his forehead. Janto could remember him laughing only once, when his daughter, Porcia, had convinced him to let her dance before the queen. She had been five then, dressed in a turquoise frock and holding a ribbon studded with gray feathers high above her head as she twirled. Janto had watched the haphazard lines it formed in the air until the ribbon fell straight down—following a dizzy Porcia who collapsed on her rear end, legs straight up in the air. Ser Allyn had chuckled along with the rest of the court, but his cheeks reddened. It happened nearly a decade ago, and Janto had never seen Porcia at the castle again.

"He cannot be buried with honor." Ser Allyn took a sip. "To do so would set a dangerous precedent for others who might seek their fortunes against you. They should expect nothing but retribution for such an act, not a burial among kings and nobles. The people will not accept it."

Captain Wolxas nodded, and Lord Xantas raised his goblet in agreement.

"Listen well to me, councilors and friends." King Albrecht's voice was firm. "Lord Gavenstone was a traitor once but no longer. He renounced his acts and made penance with the Order once he realized the gravity of his betrayal and the limits of his ego. He joined the Ravensmen to protect Lansera, the opposite desire of his former acts."

King Albrecht turned to the Ravens' head, seated a few places down. "Is that not true, Tirlon?"

"It is, my king." Ser Tirlon Swalus wore a black tunic nearly the same color as the swarthy brown hair gracing his shoulders. A cape lined with black feathers rested over his chair's back. The Ravens watched Medua from the Perch, their headquarters in the Ertion Mountains. The two realms had maintained an uneasy truce for most of Janto's life except for a few "scuffles" every year. Scuffles that now brought wooden boxes filled with human ashes rather than addled minds.

Ser Swalus's voice was gravelly but even. "Agler joined our clan willingly. If anything, he was too determined to make up for his crimes. In hindsight, I should not have let him leave the nest so soon."

The group balked at that assumption, and Wolxas made to disagree. King Albrecht's fist slammed on the table. "Silence! This is not a discussion. Agler *will* be buried at the Mount three days hence and will receive the funeral procession that is his due as a liege of Lansera. Ser Allyn, you will see the announcement is made throughout the realm and messengers are sent to Gavenstone immediately to ask Lady Marji to return."

"Yes, my king." He kept his eyes downcast.

"Good." The king gave his attention to the Raven. "Ser Swalus, please send word to Ser Werbose right away, by whatever means are your fastest. The funeral will be held as soon as the rest of Adler's effects are returned from the Perch."

"Certainly." He exited the room.

"I expect the rest of you to attend the funeral, all who do not have pressing duties at home." The king's tone softened minutely. "As king of Lansera, it is my duty to ensure any man who has paid for his crimes is forgiven and his rights restored. What sort of message would it send to our people to do anything less? Or to have their future queen be remembered as the sister of a traitor?" He placed a hand on Janto's shoulder, the focus of his words reminding Janto of what was most important in all this. Not justice, not revenge, but Serra. It would always be Serra to him.

"The Lanserim forgive their debtors," his father finished. "It is the Meduans who punish them."

The council room was quiet but for Xantas's nails clicking against his goblet. King Albrecht reached for the box, but the candlelight caught on something within it, and Janto remembered the ring mentioned in the letter.

"May I?"

His father assented. "It is Serra's now."

Grapevines formed a crest around the ring's large peridot stone. Janto wiped the powdery, greasy residue from it with his napkin.

King Albrecht leaned back against his seat. "Now gentlemen and gentlewoman, let me hear your news. Xantas, please begin."

Lord Xantas grumbled but refilled his goblet and recounted the numbers of furs, crates of salted bear meat, and other goods produced in Ertion in the last year. Ser Allyn wrote furiously, struggling to keep pace with the figures as he dipped his quill in the thrushberry ink again and again. Lord Sydley went next, relating the record crop brought in from Wasyla's fruit trees. Janto found his thoughts drifting from persimmon yields to Serra faster than Lord Xantas could reach for another glass.

He did not have the first idea how to help her cope with Agler's death. She was devastated, her manner changed. The Serra he knew was always composed, and today she had seemed . . . rash. After her parents died, she had been the perfect lady, greeting each mourner with lifted elbows and a "May Madel's hand guide you." She had been only eight then, but even now, when they were alone together, Serra maintained a semblance of propriety. "My prince," she would tease, "you wouldn't disgrace your princess, would you?" Then she'd peck his cheek and firmly hold his hands in hers, keeping them from straying. He had stolen a kiss or two or many in the garden and safe from servants' eyes, but she would never let him get carried away. If only he could carry her away from her sorrow.

Lady Farami, a slender woman nearly as dark of skin as his mother from many hours spent in the fields, went next. She insisted on visiting every farm or herd in Neville at least once a year and helping with the work, an extraordinary undertaking that her people appreciated for the kinship it fostered. She reported that a few farms near the Rasselerian border had lost their vegetable crops due to mold and yellowing from the heavy rains. Janto wondered how the Gavenstone grapevines had weathered the season. He hoped Lady Marji did not have to deal with a bad crop in addition to informing her people of Agler's death. Janto did not envy her position. Most Meditlans had remained loyal to the throne during Agler's rebellion and did not bear his living relatives great love afterward, though Serra, Marji, and her husband, Jehos, had been cleared of all wrongdoing. The Gavenstone ruling line was not as secure as it used to be, something Janto knew the king hoped would be strengthened by his marriage to Serra. King Dever Albrecht believed nobility were held in their places by Madel's hand. Only She should remove them, not the doubts of Her people.

"—twenty new recruits from the marshlands, my liege." Captain Wolxas's voice interrupted Janto's thoughts. Twenty from Rasseleria? That was a lot. The marshfolk had always been loyal to the throne, but they kept to themselves in their villages, groupings of huts on dry patches in the wetlands of Lake Ashra. They made their livings growing rice or sifting through the mucky water for antiquities, mostly pieces of colored glass rumored to be relics from the Battle of the Gods, if one believed that sort of thing. Janto had never had reason to.

Someone knocked on the door, surprising them all—the yearly council was never to be disturbed. Janto could not imagine what would warrant an interruption. The councilors fell silent as his father opened the door. Marta, one of the throne room stewards, lifted her skirts as she stepped over the doorframe. She had a head of sleek coal hair.

"Pardon, my lords." She clasped her hands and raised her elbows.

The king did not hide his irritation. "What is the news, Marta? Is the castle on fire? Have Meduans crossed the mountains?"

"No, of course not." Her cheeks colored. "I did not wish to disturb you, but the queen said you would want to know right away that a Brother had arrived."

"To see you off, no doubt, Janto." Lord Sydley's broad smile revealed his dimples. "Perhaps you'll catch a glimpse of the stag! The blessing of the Brothers would be a great sign of fortune for your Murat." It would, Janto knew, but the Brother could not have come here for that. They were the highest ranked members of the Order, above the ryn and rynnas who led activities at each town's temple. The Brothers were Madel's hand made flesh—one coming to advise the king had to be important. No, the Brother could not be here for him.

The king addressed Marta with gentleness. "Forgive my tone. I did not expect such a guest. Let him know I will meet with him as soon I have finished here. It will not be much longer."

Marta nodded. A hum of speculation arose as she closed the door.

"Do you think he could be here for me, truly?" Janto whispered to his father when he sat down.

The king did not answer but raised a hand for silence. "My lords and lady, it seems we must cut this council short. Any other news or concerns can be shared with me in private over the next few days."

Ser Allyn had already reached for an extra sheet of parchment. "Let me know if you need the king's time, and I will arrange a meeting."

"This council is dismissed." King Albrecht gestured to Janto, and they left the room together, leaving those inside to their thoughts about the Brother . . . and Agler's funeral.

Janto spoke after a few paces. "Father?"

"Yes, son?" The king did not stop walking.

Burying Agler at the Mount may not have been the best decision, but Janto thought he knew why his father had made it. "Thank you. Thank you for doing that for Serra."

The king did stop then. "I did not do it for Serra." He met Janto's gaze. "I did it for Lansera. If you don't see that, then I fear you have much left to learn."

The king continued down the hall alone. Janto watched him go, dumbstruck, until his father's gray head disappeared through a northerly entrance to the courtyard.

CHAPTER 5
VESPERI

"Bring me my tornian!" Uzziel threw the toy mace against the wall
with more force than Vesperi knew he possessed. For once, he
had the strength of his eleven years.

"I don't know which one the tornian *is*." She said it through gritted
teeth, watching her brother kick the wooden sides of his encased bed.
They'd built walls for it when his seizures had started at one year of age.
The family's useless, hoary old adver had tried to bleed him to remove
the infirmity with no success. Vesperi had known it wouldn't work.
Uzziel was sick from deficiencies of spirit, not any physical illness that
could be cured. No one could cure a cretin. Yet her father insisted on
naming Uzziel his heir.

She hated tending him. Lord Sellwyn had cared enough to smirk,
at least, when inflicting the duty on her again after her return from the
convent. Feigning interest in her suitors was loathsome, but that had
the potential for amusement and flight if she found anyone worth her
while. But there had been no one new since Ser Agler . . . disappeared.
And little excuse to leave Uzziel's bedside.

How she wished she'd been born with the pasty, misshapen lump
Uzziel called a cock between her own legs. If she had been, a trail of
bodies would already be left in her wake. The count would rival the
number of bones tied into the Guj's robe, chief priest of their advers and
thus the one with the most conquests to display. Forget Sellwyn Manor;
Vesperi might have risen in Meduan society as high as she liked on fear

of her talent alone, her father's holdings no more significant to her than a single stitch on a tapestry. But as a woman . . . as a woman she'd be dead faster than she could raise her hand toward Esye's essence when they realized she couldn't control it. What good was an arrow to the hunter if the bow was frayed? If she could learn to command respect with a flick of her finger, maybe then the magic would be enough to free her from this bedside. Maybe then she would be enough for Father.

"I want my tornian!" The whelp yelled again, his grating voice begging to be silenced. The raucous ogling of advers at the convent had been a more soothing sound. At least Vesperi had felt like someone there, the other girls too stupid to realize they'd been banished from their manors. They honestly thought being the whores of priests was a boon. She would have waved her finger and blighted them all from existence if she could do it safely. With her luck, she'd hit a levere shield and reflect the power right back at herself.

"I cannot bring it to you until you tell me what it is, dear brother." She glared at Uzziel openly—they were alone. Only a mounted replica of the family sigil kept them company, a welded, six-foot-long viper so old the blackened metal was visible beneath the green paint. Its garnet eyes gleamed with more life than there'd ever been in her brother's muddied ones.

Uzziel pointed at a peculiar object lying against the southern wall, a white club with a thin, metal circle projecting from its top. Light from the window glinted off its rim.

She handed it over to him.

"It's sharp, you know." He waved it, and Vesperi jumped to avoid the slim fillet of metal. "It's not a toy at all. Father let me have it." Another swing. "It's for beheading people. First you club them." He demonstrated the motion with vigor. "Then you slide the loop over their head and pull. Lorne told me all the lords' sons have one at court."

Doubtless, he had. Lorne was the eldest son of one of her suitors, Lord Cavallen Granich. Lord Granich had left the sixteen-year-old at Sellwyn to give credence to his offer for her hand. "A daughter for a son," he'd said, as though it were no more important than trading an old feather pillow for a new one. Yet the arrangement had made her feel valued until he'd spoken again. "Surely, you cannot say I would get the better deal now." Lord Granich had left Lorne as a ward and returned to Qiltyn to await Lord Sellwyn's decision. Vesperi had thought Lord

Granich a simpleton, but his son was cleverer than she liked. With his constant preening at Uzziel's side, she doubted she was the prize Lord Granich sought. Lorne's pluck, attempting to take Sellwyn Manor right from under her father's nose, was admirable.

Uzziel waved the club so lustily that he drooled. He paid no mind to the spit; he never did. Why should he, when Vesperi spent her days hiding such weaknesses for him? She pulled the rag off her belt and wiped his face more roughly than probably was wise.

With no warning, the blade of the tornian bit into her skin like a jocal fly, burning. She clutched her sliced forearm where it had grazed her, leaving an audaciously red, itching scratch. She cursed and pressed the rag against it.

Uzziel laughed. She spat at him. The ingrate looked like he'd pissed himself in shock, but then he took a deep breath and screamed. "Guards!"

Her hand lifted toward the window before she could think, the desire to retaliate strong. Her anger pushed her to channel Esye's power, but it would be madness to attack Uzziel. Her father would never forgive her, probably have her beheaded or worse—sent to Thokketh. She had to stop herself from using it *and fast*.

She forced her back to the window and faced the wall. Deep breaths tempered her rage as footfalls raced down the hall. By the time a pair of her father's newer guards shuffled into the room, clad in the dark green tunics of their House, the fury had ceased coursing through her blood. Perfunctorily, she shrank against the wall, made herself appear more diminutive than she was. It was best to be docile with new men until she determined how best to handle—or play—with them. She had avoided beatings since her return home, and she planned to keep it that way.

But the giddiness she felt at having stopped the flow of her talent into her body made it difficult. Esye's pull had always been too much to resist once she had reached for it. But now—now she might be able to if needed. She hid a smile against the wall, watching the room with one eye.

"Is there a problem here, my lord?" The guard on the left ignored her. His hair was graying blond, and his shoulders hunched. Too old to make bedding him fun but not man enough to beat her badly.

Uzziel looked to where she wilted against the wall and back to the guards. She dared to imagine placing her hands around his neck and wringing it. A rush of the familiar energy surged at the thought, but she suppressed it swiftly and held it within her, right beneath her skin. Harnessing it without releasing it—the sensation was amazing.

"No, you may leave." Her brother dismissed the guards. Vesperi waited until she heard the door grate shut to move.

"You should be thanking me"—he held his head up defiantly, not realizing his refusal to have her punished was another sign of his weakness—"crying with gratitude on the floor where you belong."

She could give him this minor thing—she had better things to explore than the strength of her will against his. The wound on her arm no longer bled, and she tied the rag onto her belt.

"I'm sorry." Her contempt was difficult to conceal, but she managed. "What can I do to repay you?" What he asked for did not matter; she felt weightless, the seeds of a drapian tree floating on a breeze before infesting the tilled soil with their sticky spires.

"I want you to go into town for me. I need something Father must not find out about."

How droll. Keeping things from Father was her oldest pastime . . . but it wasn't Uzziel's. Perhaps Lorne had influenced him more than she'd suspected.

"I need an herb called fallowent. It's black, and it's supposed to taste like honey."

"What do you need it for?"

He jabbed the tornian in her direction and sneered. "That is not your concern, wench." Just as fast, his features softened. The abrupt change made him again appear younger than his years. "You will do it, will you not? Get the herb?"

She gave him a brilliant smile. "Of course." With raised elbows, she made for the door.

"Don't forget—Father cannot know."

She pulled on the handle, reassuring him with dulcet tones. "I will not tell." *Unless it suits me.*

Lorne sat in the smoky hallway where incense always burned, his lean legs stretched out far in front of him. The boy drank from a cup made from some sort of white metal Vesperi had never seen before. Using his own cup was smart; poisoning him would be that much harder. Never mind his father, perhaps Lorne would grow up to be an intriguing prospect. Perhaps he already was one.

"Headed to town?" He took another lazy sip.

So he *was* behind the fallowent errand. Her mind thrilled at the possibilities. Did he plan to poison Uzziel by filling his head with some tale of strengthened limbs? She wished him luck, if so, but there was no need to reveal that yet.

"Why, I have not been since I returned home." She feigned enthusiasm. "Going to town sounds like an excellent idea. Did you have need of something, my lord?"

"I have many needs, but none involve you going to town." His stare was pointed.

She had never thought younger men her style, but he was a smooth talker. Yet she had more important things to do than a bold, handsome courtier with an alluring jawline. More important things than getting the herb, too, though she would have to do that soon if she wanted to avoid Uzziel's anger. Her father's wrath never followed far behind.

"I hope you are able to satisfy your needs." She allowed herself a hint of a seduction. "But I need to be on my way." Elbows raised, Vesperi waited for his dismissal.

He granted it with a wave of his hand, and she hurried to her room, not wanting to give Lorne time to change his mind and demand she stay. She had more pressing matters to attend to than pondering what advantage untying his breeches might bring. A flurry of energy still pulsed in her palm.

CHAPTER 6
SERRA

Musicians played softly at the far end of the hall, blowing flutes and plucking lyres and mandolins for the subdued feast guests. The villagers that had accompanied the procession to the Mount had gone back to their homes in Callyn, each with a tale to tell of an honorable funeral given to a traitor, or so Serra assumed as she stared at the roasted redbird and field greens on her plate. Her aunt sobbed intermittently, and her uncle smacked his gums as he finished cleaning a thigh to the bone, making Serra's appetite less than it already was. They were left mostly alone, perhaps out of respect for their grief. Serra thought it more likely the nobility in attendance did not want to associate with the Gavenstones and their stained reputation.

The thought was ungenerous, as hers were prone to be these days, and she chastised herself. Why Agler's death brought forth such resentment was a mystery. They had not been close, not when they were young and less so after she came to the castle. Her parents had willed in their final bequests that Serra live with the Albrechts. She had thrown a tantrum loud enough to wake the whole manor when told of the arrangement. But the royal family had accepted her without hesitation, and when she went back home for official family business, she found her brother had become nothing more than a surly youth surrounded by a cloud of advisors. All men, they'd stared with open lust once she had blossomed. She had not known they were Meduan priests and doubted Agler did at first, but it made sense when the truth came out. He let them poison his mind with old rivalries and thoughts of stealing power from the king. When the assassin he sent was discovered in Callyn with a vial of hemlock in one hand and a sharpened feather quill in the other, Serra went sick with shame. Only Janto's insistence on fresh air and food had succeeded in bringing her out of her room and her misery. Agler had done more than embarrass her. He'd made her feel out of place in the Albrechts' company, a molting rufior with trembling wings in a pool of svelte swans.

But now she clutched at Agler's handkerchief as though he had meant the world to her. He had left it with her the night before he joined the Ravens. Agler had been a broken man then. His face had always worn a smirk and a well-fed flush, but that day it was hollow and sunken. Still, his eyes lit up when she walked into her bedroom. He must have been waiting for hours in secret, knowing she would never agree to see him. She had closed the door fast, worried they would be seen together.

"Serra." He had tried to grab her hands, but she would not let him. "You must understand how sorry I am."

When children, he'd chased her around their manor's hall with spiders trapped in his hands. Apologies never passed from his lips unless threatened with spending a day curing wine barrels with their father—peasants' work, Agler had called it. The sight of him begging forgiveness that day had been impossible to fathom.

"You are ashamed of me." He fell into a chair, defeated. "You should be."

"You cannot be here," she hissed. "You have no idea what your presence could do to me."

"But I do, sweet sister." He did not say the endearment with the irony he once had given it. "Believe me, I do. Please, listen to me for a moment?" His voice quavered, tears in his eyes. "I'm leaving for the Ravens tonight. I wanted to see you first to make amends, if I could."

Queen Lexamy had told her of Agler's intent to join the Ravens after receiving his pardon from the king. She'd claimed he was genuinely remorseful. Serra had not believed her. Bewilderment was all she'd felt when the king did not sentence him to prison but forgave him instead. Yet there Agler sat, more sincere than she could have imagined. Did he mean to play her for a fool?

They had not lived together in years, but he read her thoughts fast enough. "I'm changed, truly, I swear." He pushed his chin-length, curling hair behind his ears. "The king, he came to me at Gavenstone. I was imprisoned in our study and allowed no visitor until he arrived. I knew I had been found out, of course. I knew it the moment my advisors—that pool of sheven—deserted the manor. They had received a message from our contact in Callyn. They did not tell me we had been discovered. They just ran, leaving me alone in my ignorance and pride as Captain Wolxas rode up with a battalion behind him. If I were smart, I would have run, too."

He paused, his eyes filled with disgust. "No, if I were smart, I never would have rebelled in the first place. Try to kill the king and take his place with a Meduan army I had never seen? By Madel's hand, I was stupid."

"You are an idiot." Serra did not hide the anger she felt. "A selfish, arrogant boy who thinks only of himself. Why did you do it, Agler? What possessed you?" His failed plot stunk of Meduans, and she could not stomach listening to it. How could her brother have taken part in such vile deeds? She was to become queen! What higher place than brother to the crown could he have wanted?

"I was an idiot," he responded calmly. "But I have changed. Serra, the king forgave me. He did not force me to kneel but sat in the chair beside me in silence for agonizing minutes. When he spoke, he described his Murat dream. It was about Lansera, about the peace he had maintained and the future he hoped would come to pass. He spoke passionately of us, of all Lanserim, and how we could become an ever nobler people if we but tried. He foresaw a time when the Meduans would reunite with us, no longer intent on working evil on others, inspired by our compassion, our deeds. He believes this time will come sooner than anyone can imagine. As he spoke, I realized I had no idea what valor was, what it truly meant for someone to live his or her life with a meaning and purpose. But the king is valorous, and when he shows it—by Madel's hand, Serra, he glows."

The passion in Agler's words had raised her gooseflesh. But she could not imagine such a meeting taking place. King Dever Albrecht fulfilled his duties efficiently and with wisdom, but she had never heard him express anything resembling zeal, much less seen his countenance consumed with it. Yet her brother sat directly across from her, nearly alight with some sort of fervor of his own.

"I asked for his forgiveness right then and there, and he gave it," Agler continued. "There are many who think King Dever Albrecht is a hard man. I once thought him a weak one, but I was wrong, horribly wrong. He is king because Madel wants him to be, not because he was the only Albrecht left after the war." Tears fell, and he made no move to wipe them. She reached across the table and took her brother's hands in hers for the first time she could remember.

"But why are you telling me this, Agler? Why have you come to me?" When he met her eyes, she could have sworn her father looked back, eyes green as young grape leaves. It made her yearn for a time and place she had forgotten. Did he see the same reflection when he watched her?

"I wanted you to know it was true—the plot, the poison, all of it. I wanted you to know it from me. And to know I am sorry. I wanted you to see I am changed, not to just hear about it and scoff as I knew you would." He unclasped the leather pouch on his weapon belt and pulled out the same handkerchief she held now, a sallow gray cloth stitched with the grapes of Gavenstone in pressed-gold thread. "But I'm here for more than that, Serra. I am here because I'm weak. A Raven's life is not a safe one. I need to know someone might miss me and wish me well. You are my only family, sweet sister." He smiled at her, eyes soft. "Would you try to remember me while I'm gone? Think of me fondly once in a while? Pretend if you must, but take this from me so I know someone has something of me."

Taking the cloth, she nodded, stunned at both the depth of her brother's remorse and his affection. "It would be a lie for me to say I forgive you. But I will not forget you. That much I can promise." She wiped his tears with it then placed it in her dresser drawer, where it had lain until three days ago, when she'd received the Ravens' message.

That afternoon, when she had kissed her brother farewell, the last member of her family had walked out her door forever.

✳ ✳ ✳

Dessert was warmed bread baked with bananas from south of Elston and topped with fresh cream and ground peanuts from the bushes in Callyn. It was Serra's favorite—Mar Pina, the chef, let no person go uncomforted if she could help it. Serra tried to eat but gave up, her stomach in disagreement. Janto caught her eye from the far end of the table. He tilted his head toward the door and mouthed the word, "Garden?" She nodded. She needed to get out of this room, and maybe their paired absence would not be noticed tonight. Serra was not certain she cared.

Janto rose first, excusing himself from the company of Lord Xantas and Lady Gella, who was balanced on her husband's lap despite the occasion. Ten minutes passed, and Serra bid her aunt and uncle good night, telling them she would meet them tomorrow at their chamber so they could see Janto off together. As she walked toward the southern door to the courtyard, she ignored the condolences from the servants and hoped they would forgive her the lack of a courteous response. Being a proper lady had never felt like such work before.

A wall of humidity greeted her in the courtyard despite it being early spring. She took the gravel path by the well and followed it to the grove of Wasylim orange trees on the western side of the castle. The tree branches were bare this far to the east, but Serra could not see through the many skinny trunks crowded together to form the hedge that marked the entrance to the garden. No one else would see her walk through them either.

Yet she felt eyes on her nonetheless. Serra spun on her heel but glimpsed nothing more than a dark robe's hem whisking past the alcove that led back inside. An out-of-town noble getting a little lost on the return from the lavatory, no doubt. Serra shook her nerves away and slipped through the trees.

Beyond them stood trellised arches arranged in an inward spiral that ended at a statue cast in silver. Braided balac vines had been laced through the latticework to form a covered path. She knew green leaf buds dotted them, but she could not see them in the dark. Rather, she let the pale light that shone from Oro, the golden moon, and Tansic, the copper moon, guide her. Esye was clouded, and Onsic never gave off light except for its nebulous cobalt halo. The soft gold and copper rays glinted off the statue and reflected from the metal exposed through the balac vines. She was careful not to step on any of the herb patches planted at the bases of the trellises—Mar Pina would call for heads if so much as a minty libtyl leaf was trampled.

The reflection off the statue gave Janto's strawberry-blond hair an ethereal cast. The sculpture was of Ginla Xantas, an ancient heroine of Lansera from the time before an Albrecht sat on the throne. Janto reclined beneath it, watching Serra approach, which made her blush. The sensation felt good, normal for a change. She knew how to do this, how to meet Janto alone in the garden. It was their sanctuary, the place they escaped prying eyes in the castle with the orange grove to hide them. She wondered at how it had never bothered her before, this occasional bending of propriety so they could just be themselves. Perhaps the new rashness she felt had been manifesting longer than she'd realized.

Janto drew her into his arms as she neared. She relaxed into them, feeling some of the tension in her body drain away. His familiar smell— eucalyptus and brine—comforted her, and she smiled for the first time all day.

"How are you?" He kissed her forehead.

"I've been better." It was an understatement. She had no words to describe the emotions she felt.

"You are amazing. And you'll get through this. You know that, right?"

"I know." She sighed. "Thank you for suggesting this. I almost suffocated in there. If I had to listen to Uncle Jehos chew any longer, I would have screamed. How do you always know what I need?"

Janto beamed at the compliment. "Knowing you is my life's work." The hint of a tease only reinforced his words. "Come here." He led her around Ginla's boots to the other side of the statue. On a nearby bench lay a cylinder, about two feet long. It sparkled in the dimness, which meant it could only be made of one thing: quartz.

"A seeing glass!" She gasped and swung her arms around his neck. Janto had given her a bantam one when she first came to Callyn. He had told her how to point it at Gavenstone. "Whenever you feel homesick," he had instructed, "just look through it." It had been blurry, and no bigger than a speck of dirt, but seeing the spire jutting from the top of her family's entrance hall had given her endless comfort after the move and her parents' deaths.

"Mer Groven had some new wares when I went to pick up my tunics for Braven. This caught my eye—how could it not?—and I had to buy it. It is heftier than your last one, and you will not be able to see as far as Braven, but I thought you might appreciate it anyhow."

"I love it." She kissed him. "I can imagine Braven in the distance, even if the sea I sight is only the brown waves of lamta herds. If I can point it toward my family"—she caressed his cheek to make her point—"then it is good enough for me. Thank you." She kissed him again and let her lips linger. In the morning he, too, would leave her. But for now, Janto was hers and she his, and that was enough to stem her sorrow and remind her of what was important. Not tears, nor anger, but love and hope for the future she had been destined for since she had first seen him at Gavenstone Manor, commanding Agler to give her back her drindem doll. "I miss you already."

He nodded, pulling her back into his arms. They watched the lesser moons of Lansera shine more intensely than ever before, trading the glass between them.

CHAPTER 7
JANTO

The touch of his mother's hand on his cheek woke Janto the next morning. He blinked, adjusting to the soft light drifting in from his window like ribbons of brushed gold. The queen wore a green gown with an overlay of speckled woranbird feathers, and a crown of golden brambles nestled above her red tresses. She did not wear the crown often, but seeing her son off for his Murat called for some ceremony.

"Good morning." Her face was cheerful as she stroked his cheek again.

Janto stretched and yawned. "I don't think you've woken me since I was twelve. You are lucky I don't keep a dagger beneath my pillow."

She *tsked* at the jest. "I did not raise my son to fear his own walls." Then she kissed his forehead. "Is it so wrong to want to see you this morning?"

He rolled his eyes. "Of course not. I will miss you, too, you know."

"You coat your words with sugar to humor me." She protested them with another kiss. "But I accept them nonetheless."

"You will be fine, Mother. I'll be gone less than a month, and then you can harass me about learning my part of the wedding ritual. You will find it thrilling."

"I think Ser Allyn is better suited for that task." Her laugh reminded him of sitting on her knee when he was very young, as she traded stories with her siblings come to visit from Mova.

"Did you want me to rise or not?"

"I want one more morning with my child before he comes back to me a new man." She was teasing, but he could hear worry in her voice.

"I'll be fine."

"You will. But you will not be the same Janto who leaves here today—you cannot begrudge your mother for feeling nostalgic."

"I begrudge you nothing. But I do need to rise, and you need to leave the room so I can dress. I may not yet be this new man you speak of, but I am not a child anymore, you know."

"I do." She pinched his cheeks anyway. "But you will always be my baby. I will go—your father waits in the council room for us to break our fasts with him." She gave him one last peck. "We must not keep him waiting or you know what will happen."

"'The people need me.'" Janto approximated his father's booming bass of a voice. "'I must not leave them waiting any longer.'" Sometimes, he could not imagine that his father had nearly become a priest. Dever Albrecht was born for kingship. Janto wondered if he would ever measure up.

"Your father found his motivation for the kingship at his Murat, you know. Perhaps you will find your strength there as well."

"Yes, yes. Now let me dress, please."

She closed the wooden door behind her. Janto dressed then picked up the crown lying on top of the desk, polished and gleaming, the same circlet of brambles his parents donned. It signified the victory of the Lanserim over the Meduans at the Plains of Orelyn. His was a thinner bough, and silver unlike their white gold crowns. He always wondered at the difference, but the answer had only ever been "Because the king decreed it so," whether he asked his parents, Ser Allyn, or the chief metallurgist herself, Mar Kurandyl.

With the pins laid out for him, Janto secured the crown. Riding with it on would be bothersome, but the occasion called for it, at least until well into the Nevillim plains. At Jost, he planned to send it back home with Eddy. Pic waited outside his door, and Janto instructed him to bring his traveling bag to his horse. The caravan would depart after breakfast. Then he crossed the courtyard to reach the council room.

Something caught his eye near the archway by the throne room. A gray-hooded Brother stood within it.

"Good morning, Brother," Janto called out.

The man's sleeves rose in greeting, but he did not move forward. In the early morning light, he appeared parchment thin as though a shadow.

That was precisely the role the Brother had played the past few days, silent and on the fringes of the funeral procession and day-to-day activities of the castle. Janto could not recall him at the funeral feast at all.

The thought of food made his stomach grumble, and the image of Mar Pina's flaky sweet rolls leapt to mind along with ghostly wisps of the warmed apricot preserves that would be dripping over them. Janto walked faster toward breakfast.

As Janto slid through the council room door, his father spoke. "My son deigns to bless us with his presence." Janto took his seat and one of the rolls from a heaping platter. He wondered how many he could eat before the caravan set out.

"Well?" The king stared, but Janto paid him no mind, closing his eyes in appreciation of the apricot, cinnamon, and yeasty dough melding in his mouth. "Are you ready for your Murat?"

"Of course he is," Queen Lexamy chided. "You know full well he has run himself ragged with preparations." Their disagreements always amused Janto. His mother may get cross, but she had never asked for her own quarters in their thirty-seven years of marriage. His parents' union was one of love . . . and banter. Constant banter.

"Stabbing at dummies stuffed with wheat and saying a daily chant can hardly be viewed as preparation for the Murat." His father reached for the pot of tachery brew kept warm over a fire in a clay ramekin. The smell of roasted seeds wafted over. Janto flipped his mug over for his father to fill.

"Is there tachery on Braven?" A sudden panic took Janto and he gulped the liquid, then had to force his lips closed to avoid spitting it right back out again—it was hot!

His father laughed so loud the cups and platters shook. "You see what I mean?" He appealed to his wife. "He asks if there's tachery on Braven." Another laugh followed by a wink, and then he regarded Janto with soft, if pitying, eyes. "There's naught on Braven of tachery or any other nourishment you are used to. You will be fed, but you best acquire a taste for jerked craval beast and the flat cakes Mar Pina has packed in your bag."

Janto felt like a dunce for not thinking of food before. His mother suppressed laughter, likely at his expense, but he could not share in the merriment. What sort of man would he prove to be if he did not consider his basic needs before an extended journey? What else had he overlooked?

He glowered and took another roll from the platter. "Father, the Brother . . . he is not here about me, is he?"

The king settled back into his chair, raising an eyebrow as he stopped to consider his words. That alone increased Janto's unease. Was the question that hard to answer?

"No, he is not here for you."

"Then why? Brothers don't usually come for a funeral."

"No, they do not."

"Then what is his purpose here?" Silence was the response, so Janto tried another way. "I mean, I should know how to receive a Brother when I am king, but they come so rarely, I have no idea what to do and there might not be another for many years."

The queen regarded him quizzically as she reached for a sweet cake covered in sticky almond frosting. "Do you foresee your father's death, Janto? I did not know you had such a gift."

His cheeks colored. "No, of course not. I merely wish to know why he is here, so I can learn from it."

"Luckily, his business does not concern you or it would be another obstacle to your concentration in the days ahead." His father waved away the subject. "You have had enough trouble recently. Ser Allyn tells me you did not include a rag for wiping your blade among your provisions."

His mother exhaled loudly. "Can you blame him for such a little oversight? He has been a bit concerned with Serra."

"As have we all." The king stabbed a piece of smoked tartine with his fork and brought it to his plate. The fish's yellow flesh was marbled with a greenish-blue hue where the bones had been removed. "Do you think these past few days have interfered with your readiness, son?"

Janto considered his answer. His body ached from the repetition of thrusts and parries, having sparred with no less than twenty of the noble children who had been holed up in the castle for days awaiting the funeral. Janto had made use of their different skills and sizes. An afternoon recitation and a run through the hillside had cleared his mind daily. But he had been tense, unable to talk with Serra or spend time with her. The separation had wrapped tighter around his chest every day like a rope, even before news of Agler's death had been received.

Or rather, it had felt that way until last night. Holding her, breathing in the smell of clove from her grandmother's necklace that she always wore, had made Janto more relaxed than he could remember. Focusing on being pure of body, mind, and heart had done less to prepare him for the Murat than that hour of stolen time.

"I am ready, Father, and these past few days have only made it clearer to me why this is so important. I want to be the man my country, and my lady, need. If the Murat will make that so, then I am ready for it."

"Well said, Janto." The king placed a hand on his shoulder. "You will be missed, you know."

"I know. I will miss you, too." Then he reached for another sweet roll.

✳ ✳ ✳

Doubts about the rashness of meeting with Serra last night did not return until Janto mounted his horse and took his pack from Pic's proffered hand. The pleasing tang of Mar Pina's sweet rolls had already disappeared from memory, but he could feel the specter of Serra's lips on his own. As he galloped through Callyn, waving farewell to the townspeople who lined the streets, his thoughts were not of battle tactics but Serra's soft tangles of hair and protestations of love made beneath the mingled lights of Oro and Tansic. He could imagine no worse—or better—companion on the road ahead.

CHAPTER 8
SERRA

King Dever Albrecht leaned forward on the throne. From the back of the cavernous room, his station was nondescript, yet walking toward it was a breathtaking experience. With each step forward, the throne gleamed with more luster, the sun reflecting off its seemingly smooth surface from the glass ceiling above it. A few paces closer and the illusion fell away as hundreds of copper cords, interwoven to give the impression of a bramble bush, became evident. Queen Scrulla Albrecht, the first of the Albrecht line, had the throne designed to resemble the chaparral covering the Plain of Orelyn, where she had spent her early life. She had not known then that her grandson three times removed—King Turyn, Janto's grandfather—would fight his final battle with the Meduans there. Nor were they called Meduans in Scrulla's time, or even in Turyn's. Before the war, they'd been an outgrowth of Lanserim, countrymen who no longer wanted to live in a country that prized valor more than greed. A truce created the dual kingdoms and the Meduan people.

Janto considered it a failure that his forebears had not crushed the Meduans outright. But Serra respected the wisdom of Turyn's Peace, recognizing no good could come from forcing darkness to mix with light. The Meduans would have plotted against their civil society no matter the cost—was not her brother proof of that? The rebels' deeds and words corrupted good people. Separating them out to wreak havoc only on themselves was the better plan. King Turyn gave up a quarter of his kingdom but saved his true subjects with that peace.

"Serra, thank you for coming," King Albrecht greeted her once she was close enough to hear. Gold leaves peeked out from between the metal branches of the throne. A few steps closer and rounded onyx thorns would be visible as well.

The king smiled today, no doubt proud of how radiant Janto had been in his crown, thanking each liege and commoner alike who came to see him off with raised elbows. As he fell in line with the caravan of stable hands, Janto had dared a wink at Serra from the back of his parsnip-colored mare. It was enough; she'd had her goodbyes last night.

Ser Allyn stood by the king with another man, whose shrouded head and dark gray robe, like a sword needing polishing, revealed him to be a Brother. No one else in Lansera wore that gloomy shade. Serra had heard of the Brother's arrival the same day she had learned of Agler's death. But she had not spoken with him, preferring the solace of her room, which did not demand decorum and duty. Her grief grew more difficult to curb with each stitch she dropped and "May Madel's hand guide you" she uttered.

Serra raised her elbows to the king. "For what purpose am I called, my liege?"

"Our Brother came to ask about you," King Albrecht answered, a dark brown eyebrow raised. It had yet to turn gray like the hair on his head.

Serra had only seen a Brother once before, two weeks before her parents died. A pair had come to pay their respects to her family. They stayed a few days, dining with the Gavenstones but mostly speaking in soft voices with her parents and never directly to her. She had paid them no attention, finding her newly carved drindem dolls with their tattooed faces and spindly, jointed appendages much more intriguing.

She raised her elbows to the man. "I thank you for your concern, Brother." He did not answer. *Am I to guess why I've been called?* Only one reason came to mind. "I am grieved by my brother's death, but I am well."

The billowy cloth of his hood hid his reaction. Was he displeased? He could not expect her mourning would be over already. Serra's training to not leave a silence unfilled kicked in. "Was there something else you wanted?"

King Albrecht answered. "The Brotherhood would like you to study with the Order for a time."

"But what could the Brotherhood want with me?"

Ser Allyn spoke tartly. "It is not unusual for royalty to spend time with the Order in their youth. Why, King Albrecht did himself."

Her cheeks colored. She must be careful not to offend the king on the subject. After all, he would be a ryn today had his brother, Gelus, not died from a poisoned wound a decade after Turyn's Peace. "I meant no disrespect. But I am unsure how my presence would benefit the Order. What is asked of me?"

The king answered again. "Our Brother wants you to study Madel's precepts more closely than you can here. It is a rare opportunity, Serra, not usually given to those not taking an initiate's pledge."

"But it takes a month to learn the rituals, does it not?" She tried to keep her voice level. "The wedding, it would have to be postponed." She would not agree to that—it did not matter if Madel reached Her fiery hand down in the flesh. Thoughts of the wedding and joining fully with Janto were all that brought her joy.

The king's face flushed. "You do not decline a Brother's invitation for a wedding, Serra."

The Brother spoke, gesturing with the sleeves of his robe. They dropped back to his side before she heard his quavering voice. "It must be her decision."

The king's flush deepened. "Of course, I apologize. I forgot my place for a moment in my respect for your Order."

That was curious. Serra had thought no man could overrule the king. "I apologize as well, Brother, but I know no one besides the king and our Rynna Hullvy who has been trained in the ways of Madel. Why have you chosen me for such an honor?" Perhaps she could learn a thing or two about how to govern a ruler if she studied with the Order. Not that she didn't trust Janto to make wise decisions, but she knew from experience that honest men could be led astray by false advisors. Agler's ashes buried within the Mount were proof of that.

"Serrafina Gavenstone," the Brother uttered her name leisurely, as though examining each syllable for meaning, "we tell you only that we want you to come. You need not stay beyond the initiation, if that is what you choose. But Janto Albrecht will not return in four weeks. He will be delayed." The words floated toward her as his arms fell to his sides.

She gasped at his proclamation. Was that a prophecy? How could Janto be waylaid? The king's eyes belied a shared reaction, but he said nothing to question the Brother, only drummed his fingers on the throne, waiting for her response. Serra suppressed the foreboding she felt—she was not thinking clearly, had not been for days. Madel would not allow more tragedy to befall her. She refused to consider it. Any number of things could delay his return. Tornadoes on the Nevillim plains. Janto attempting a special Feat after the Murat concluded. Every town on the journey home might insist on celebrating his newfound renown—he was sure to be entered into several of the Order's lists.

Reassured, Serra considered the Brother's invitation. A few more weeks might be beneficial for the wedding plans; Bini had mentioned a delay for the Elstonian lace and the seamstresses already complained of the modifications needed for the queen's wedding gown. And Serra had been so suffocated since Agler's death. Her garments and layers felt constricting. She wearied of the servants' chatter. Why *should* Janto be the only one off on his own before they married? She mourned Agler, to be certain, but that would follow wherever she went. Maybe a quiet place to finish grieving so she could be content again in these halls was just what she needed.

"I will go."

The Brother's voice wrapped around her. "You will leave in the morning."

Tomorrow? Tomorrow she was to see her aunt and uncle off and spend the afternoon quilting tapestries with the queen and the other noblewomen who remained at Callyn. The task appealed, suddenly, for its normalcy. Was her decision hasty?

"I will send a trunk to your room," Ser Allyn said. "And set your servants to pack it at once."

"Yes, please." She would need help to be ready so fast.

Ser Allyn hustled through the side door, and King Albrecht's smile returned. "My time with the Order was not easy, Serra. It was a different sort of training than the Murat, one for the soul rather than the body and mind. I have never felt such fulfillment as I did then, but it takes more work and strength of will than you might believe."

The king rarely talked so freely about his past. She realized they were alone.

"Where did the Brother go?"

"He must have left with Allyn." King Albrecht looked as perplexed as she felt, but his reminiscing soon took over. "I did not wish to rule, you know, but the world called me back and I had to sacrifice for that world. We all do." He stared off, lost in his thoughts of times past while she waited impatiently in the present, wishing he would find his point.

The past had brought her only pain, and now the future was not as well laid out as she had thought. *Why did I say yes?*

"You will come back to us a richer Lanserim." The king finished his speech at last. "For all are who touch Madel. I am pleased for you. Not many have been given this opportunity."

Serra forced herself to smile in return, but she had no words to speak. She had made a choice, but whether she would regret it, only time would reveal. Her family was not known for making wise decisions.

CHAPTER 9
JANTO

The canoes glided onto the black sand of Braven.

"Finally!" Jerusho, the portly Ertion whom Janto had been paired with during the row across the channel, lunged out of the canoe. It tipped over, rolling them both onto the beach and splashing them with the freezing water of the Northern Sound. Janto lifted a handful of the sand, letting the grains—fine as his mother's healing barrow root powder—spill through his fingers. The soft sand was surprisingly warm, the dark color retaining heat. Lying on the beach felt like a dip in one of Elston's many hot springs.

"Apologies, my compatriot." Jerusho raised his elbows in regret, his pallor green. "'The sweet lapping of waves,' as my ryn described it, is not as soothing as advertised."

Janto laughed and flipped over to let his drenched clothes soak up the warmth.

Jerusho regained some coloring as he spoke. "'You will be a legend,' my ryn told me. 'All the boys in Mova will dream of you and your Murat fame.' Let me tell you, my new and hopefully more trustworthy friends." Jerusho raised his voice so the other men pulling in their canoes could hear, "I'm the one dreaming. I am dreaming of my rug by the fireplace and sipping my nana's hot-brewed tachery."

A compact lad, no more than five and a quarter feet tall, came up behind the Ertion. His voice was heavy with the drowsy accent of

Wasyla. "We just arrived. I am certain we will not spend the whole time dripping wet." He gave Jerusho a reassuring pat then extended his hand. "My name's Napeler."

The Ertion shook it heartily, his seasickness apparently abated. "May Madel's hand guide you, Nap." The Wasylim made to object at the nickname, but Jerusho kept on talking. "I'm Jerusho, and I still wish I had a fire."

Conversations struck up around him, and Janto listened while enjoying the warmth. He had not introduced himself to anyone yet. A rynna had been the only person to greet him at the docks at Jost. Janto had bid his farewell to Eddy and the rest of the stable hands outside the small town. A pair of Meditlans had been there first, so alike in appearance they had to be twins. Janto had whispered his name to the rynna, who winked and crossed it off her list. He wanted to complete the Murat on his own merits, not those given him by name and birth. There were few enough times when he could walk unknown, without expectations for his behavior.

It wasn't that he disliked being prince, not at all, but the rules to abide by—or at least to bend only as far as his father and Ser Allyn would allow—could be stifling. For as long as possible, Janto wanted to see these men as peers rather than civilians posturing before royalty. With any luck, he could convince Sielban to keep his identity quiet, once their legendary trainer made his appearance.

Sielban loomed large in the minds of all Muraters, including those who had completed the challenges decades ago. He lived in complete isolation on Braven, except for the yearly group of Lanserim men whom he taught and pushed as he saw fit. Rumor had it Sielban had been banished to Braven, but many years later, the Order appointed him as mentor to the Muraters, a post he'd held for at least two generations. The man was longer lived than any other alive.

Janto's new companions moved from the shore, not knowing what to do next. He watched them from afar, unwilling to leave the sandy warmth yet. They were a small group at seven. There were never more than the number the Brothers proclaimed and no qualifications other than a firm belief Madel meant for each young man to go. The Brothers had accepted ten this year but some applicants must have decided not to come, likely due to the flooding in the marshlands and the western

Nevillim plains. Doubtless, the men had made the hard choice to take care of their farms and holdings instead. He prayed Madel repaid them for their sacrifice—they were proving their worth by other means.

Janto had always known he would enter the Murat. All Albrecht men had. As this year's competition drew near, he had felt more and more confident it was the right time. His failure to understand his father's reasons for burying Agler at the Mount merely made his need to become a better man that much clearer. What sort of king would he make if forced to take the crown next month or next year? One not worthy of it, that much he knew.

Near the tree line, thirty yards or so away, the Meditlan twins, of average height and build, talked in low voices before offering Jerusho a towel from knapsacks embroidered with the vines of Gavenstone. Janto wondered how they'd inevitably bring honor to their country, lands, and family—Murated men always did, yet surprisingly few Lanserim felt the call to come. Perhaps most did not want to claim such a fate for themselves. Glory and the promise of power allured, but his people did not thirst for such things as lustily as the Meduans, and he had faith anyone with purely selfish motives would be refused application by the Brothers. There was also money to consider. For Janto, affording the travel and time away from home was a simple matter, but for others, it could exact a great toll. Yet if a man was truly called to come, his community recognized it and they made the sacrifice together—it sounded as though that had been Jerusho's path.

The Wasylim called Nap stood with what looked to be one of his countrymen. They had the same hair, fine and pale yellow as an eaglet's down. None had Janto's mother's skin, dark as an Elstonian stout, which confirmed the missing men were Rasselerians or from the villages beyond the marshlands where his mother had grown up. He hoped their regret would be slight when news from the Murat was proclaimed. Criers went forth and spread word to the villages when a Feat of special valor was achieved. A record performance on the archery course would qualify or climbing Mount Frelom, the snow-covered peak in the far west of the island. Perhaps one of the island's mythical creatures would be killed this year: the jurgen's spiky tail was said to lash at its prey as it galloped through the woods, and the granfaylon was longer than a sheven, thinner than parchment, and invisible to most eyes. And the silver stag, well, it could leap through the forest in a flash. Many Muraters had been exhausted by the hunt for the elusive creature, and if the old adage were true, the good favor promised to any who caught it:

When the silver stag runs free, blessed will he who binds it be.
Rise up, ye treasured bird of three. Wing him what boons ye foresee.

Of course, the men might also see visions in the dreams they had toward the end of the Murat. Not everyone had them, but those who did used them as a compass to guide their future endeavors. His father had had such a dream, and whatever it revealed convinced him to take up the throne upon his brother Gelus's death. An easy choice to be king rather than a solitary priest, many would say, but Janto knew his father better than that despite how justly Dever Albrecht ruled Lansera. Only when the king's eyes closed during a meditation did he ever truly relax. Only then—and after his first bite of Mar Pina's sweet rolls, a fixation Janto had inherited. He groaned, recalling he had eaten the last one he had smuggled into his pack that morning.

The only Nevillim besides Janto was a solid man already gray of hair who had paddled his own canoe. He knelt over that boat now, cursing under his breath. Janto sighed and let the sand warm him for a second longer before rising.

"Have you lost something?" Janto bent down to examine the dark, quartz-flecked sand under a discarded oar.

"Yes, my cursed sister's seeds! She tied them to my belt so I could plant a few on Braven." The man shook his head, exasperated. "She's afflicted with some notion of spreading her latest cultivation over the whole country like feathers fluttering in the wind."

"Is she an herbalist?" Janto ran his hand between the supporting planks of the canoe.

"She thinks she is, but she hasn't been to Leba for training."

Leba, the Wasylim capital, was home to the society of herbalists. Janto's mother had spent considerable time there before she married the king—it was where they had met, in fact. He had come to purchase a satchel of libtyl leaves to take back to Callyn, being fond of their pungent taste. He left with a bride as well.

"What are the seeds for? My mother has some experience with herbs."

"I don't know." A fond smile for his sister overcame the man's grimace. "A ward against jocal flies or something ridiculous like that.

I told her I would bring them, being a good older brother, but I am afraid our rough voyage over that freezing water has made me a liar." He kicked the side of the canoe. "Like Braven needs help protecting itself from bugs. I haven't seen a single insect here yet." He paused, then clasped hands and raised his elbows. "My name is Hamsyn, by the way. What's yours?"

Janto ducked the question. "May Madel's hand guide you, Hamsyn. What color are the seeds?" He felt around the back of the vessel.

"Black."

Janto looked at the sand beneath his feet and back at Hamsyn incredulously. Then he bent over laughing.

The Nevillim threw his hands up and guffawed. "Well, I had to *try* to find them. My sister is formidable. She will strangle me when I return."

"How old is she?"

"Twelve."

Janto socked Hamsyn's arm good-naturedly.

"Come see her for yourself before you judge me!" The Nevillim's hands went up in surrender. "I promise you will give her the honorific of 'Most Frightening Woman in the Land' despite her age."

"I am afraid Lady Gella of Ertion already has that honor."

"You've met Lady Gella?"

He was saved from answering when one of the Meditlan twins ran toward them, waving his arms. "There's something in the trees throwing rocks. Come quick!" The man reversed sharply and ran back.

Janto and Hamsyn exchanged excited glances. It was probably a rhini, a fur-covered creature no larger than the twins' knapsacks. They lived in the trees on the northern shores and attacked any humans that came close with twigs, rocks, or whatever their three-fingered hands could grasp. It *could* be a cantalere or a jurgen or even the silver stag, but those beasts did not throw things. A rhini was much more likely—it existed. And they were dangerous.

Janto clutched the dagger on his belt. They reached the tree line in time to watch Nap climb the nearest pine.

"Wait," Janto called. "You don't know if it's safe!"

As if to answer him, a strange call like a raspy lute came from further in the woods, making his arm hair rise.

"That does not sound like a rhini." Jerusho looked treeward with a nervous tremble.

"No, it doesn't." Either way, Janto would not let Nap head toward it alone. He jumped at the nearest tree and climbed. Something whizzed past his cheek as he ascended. The call came again, and he grabbed a branch from a neighboring tree, glad the ancient growths were at least as thick around as he was.

Up ahead, Nap shifted direction.

"Do you see anything?" Janto called.

"Yes." He pointed further into the tree cover. "It blends in with the needles, but you can see it when it jumps." He grabbed the next limb and yelled back, "Definitely not a rhini!"

Janto heard shuffling below him as the others began to climb. He considered waving them off—there was no sense in everyone putting themselves in danger—but decided against it. They did not know what lay ahead, but he and his companions weren't afraid. Blood pulsed through him in a heady rush, and he barely felt his weight as he moved from tree to tree, following Nap's lead. The calls continued intermittently, and the group soon worked their way far enough into the woods that the shimmer of black sand and the rough waves that had brought them here disappeared.

Jerusho must have volunteered to take the Meditlans' bags. He huffed and cursed from below while trying to keep pace with the rest of them. Janto could barely make out the Ertion's knot of black hair through the tree cover. A dozen or so swings later, his collarbone began to ache from the constant strain to his arms. He rested on a branch, breathing in the crisp, evergreen air. A redbird hopped from one bough to another, twigs in its beak, but Janto did not stay long enough to watch it reach its nest. The other Muraters drew close, and he vowed to be the first to reach the creature, whatever it was. When another whoop sounded, he grabbed the next offshoot.

Soon, it became impossible to see farther than three or four trees away. On the ground with Jerusho, it was probably dark as twilight. Janto caught up with Nap at last, who lifted his finger to his lips. Obliging, Janto pulled himself close and scanned the vegetation. There were plenty of distracting noises: the rustling of leaves as flying squirrels leapt with more grace than he would ever manage, the clicking of beetle ants as they dug further into tree trunks, Jerusho's loud and clear panting. But the strange calls had ceased altogether, and no rocks had been thrown for quite a while.

One of the Meditlans swung up beneath him and tugged on his
boot. In a girlish voice, the man said, "Did he catch it?"

Janto shook his head. Then he noticed a shift in the brown and
green foliage of a tree to his right. He squinted and swore he could
see the outline of a man against the wood. But how could anyone or
anything blend in that well? Before he could ponder any longer, the
creature shifted again.

"There!" Janto yelled. He swung toward it, and the camouflaged
being opened its eyes. Lips shaped into an "O," and it let loose a high-
pitched hoot, the same call they had been following. Then the thing—the
human—swung away fast.

"I saw him, too," Nap confirmed, and the two of them led the rest
in the direction the man had gone. Janto could see him easily now;
either he knew what to watch for or the person no longer tried to hide.

They swung so fast from branch to branch, Jerusho's gasps and
pants disappeared entirely. One of the twins called out every so often
to confirm their direction. Janto's bones ached. With each new grab, a
pain spiked from his underarm to his elbow. They wouldn't be able to
keep up this speed. Nap's breathing was ragged, and he had appeared
to be the fittest man in the group. Yet the mysterious person leading
them had no problem setting the pace. He even grinned back at them
between calls. In the middle of one such stare, he dropped straight
down and out of sight.

"Stop!" Janto called. "He's on the ground!" He thanked Madel he
need not reach for another limb before hugging the trunk and working
his way down. His grip had weakened since they'd gone up, and his
hands were bloodied from the tree bark. The sting of scratches had gone
unnoticed in the thrill of the chase.

Once the ground was close enough, Janto jumped down to it with
legs of custard that made him fall to his knees. How long had they been
up in the canopy? The closest Meditlan hit the ground next but kept his
footing and drew close to their curious prey. "What are you?"

The human's garment fit tightly over his body, the same clothes the
marshfolk wore when they came to court. But this suit was different,
more vivid, more alive. Janto could not guess the material. Two bands
of color overlapped each other in a swirling pattern all over it, the exact
shades of the needles and tree trunks. Through a trick of the eye, they
shifted back and forth. Though he was only as tall as Janto's chest, the

man's arm and leg muscles strained against the cloth. No matter his height, he would be no easy foe in a duel. Unfortunately, Janto realized he would be challenging him soon . . . or at least taking his lessons.

Too tired to raise his elbows, Janto hoped respect came through in his voice. "I take it you are our teacher, Ser Sielban?"

"That is my name," the man answered. "You hunt identities as well as you do men, princeling. Welcome to Braven."

The others gasped. Janto wondered if the revelation of Sielban's identity or his own surprised them most.

"You? You are Sielban?" The Meditlan who had reached him first managed to raise his elbows, casting a cursory glance toward Janto as he did. "It is an honor."

The rest of the men repeated the deference, but Sielban bid their arms lowered. "It is not my honor you seek here but your own." His tongue flicked out of his mouth as though a snake tasting the air. Sielban was more reptilian than any Rasselerian Janto had seen.

An endless volley of curses grew louder and louder, preceding Jerusho who burst through a bramble bush. He stumbled to where the others gathered on the forest floor, and held the packs out to the Meditlans.

"Here, I'm here," was all Jerusho could manage, scarcely noting their new companion.

Sielban registered the last arrival with a cocked head, and Janto swore their teacher's nose wiggled. "Good. All the little children are here."

Then the man sprang over the same bush Jerusho had trampled and disappeared.

Janto leapt through only half a second behind him.

CHAPTER 10
VESPERI

She woke to a shift of weight in her goose-down bed. The faces of Lord Sellwyn's guards flipped through her mind, and she hoped for gentle Bellick rather than rancid Lokas declaring her period of resistance over. It required a delicate balance, making the men believe she respected their dominance while instilling a vague fear of what would happen if they pushed her too far. Sometimes, the pendulum swung the other way. At least this man did not smell bad.

"You know, you almost resemble the other women when you sleep. There's something vacuous about your frown . . ."

Lorne's was not the worst body she could wake up to. But it was dark out. She hated sex in the dark, too dim to gauge reactions to her touches properly, crucial information to amass. Maybe she could talk her way out of it. She *was* his potential mother-to-be, if his father made good on that offer of marriage.

Vesperi rolled over. Hair that fell to her bedspread covered all of his face but his pale blue eyes. He lay on his side, one arm trapped beneath him. She stroked his other one.

"Now, now." His hand rested over hers. "We would not wish to appear inappropriate. My father would be so chagrined."

Her response was pure instinct. "Your father would not have to know." *Wait—is he refusing me?* She sat up while pulling down her sleeping raiment to cover her legs better. If he did not want a show, he would not get one.

"It's as though you think I do not share all my activities with my father. You wound me, woman, with your lack of faith in my loyalty." He clutched his hand to his chest. "I am not here for your ample goods, tempting though they may be." That was punctuated with a bottom-to-top inspection and a smirk. "I'm here because Uzziel has yet to procure fallowent."

"Why do you want him to have it so much? It's just a weed." Lorne was a playful one—it was safe to try and tease out the real answer . . . and entertaining.

"Just a weed? Tell that to your brother when he gains three inches."

"Three inches? Uzziel has not grown since he was five. Has an adver blessed those seeds? I am sorry to tell you, but I scared our last one away."

Lorne laughed. "No doubt you did. Fallowent needs no blessing to work. And Uzziel is so excited to try it. Every day, he mentions how you haven't brought it yet. Come to think of it, where *have* you been? I so enjoy throwing you out before my afternoon visits."

"I have been predisposed. Father wanted me to inspect the servants." A lie. As often as possible, Vesperi practiced her talent in isolated corners of the manor grounds. It was useless. The progress she had made had stalled. Whole bushes caught flame when her goal was only a branch. She'd tried to burn the image of a snake into the wooden walls of a family cabin and had ended up singeing the entire structure. Luckily, no one lived in the cabins anymore. Families were not allowed in Medua, except for the noble ones. After the revolution, the liege-lords made their best men guards who kept watch over the common ones. *Those* men worked whatever trades the lords demanded—in Sellwyn, mainly field work and timbering the rosewood groves, though those had grown scraggly in these years of drought. The men lived in barracks, and women and children lived in the towns. No intermingling was allowed except if the men felt an urge—the women's cabins had no locks. Lord Sellwyn did not allow his men to form attachments to their progeny, either. He hung the child if it was suspected. "Their loyalty should only be to me," he'd explained to Vesperi once.

"If you are so concerned with my brother's growth, then why don't you go into town?"

"I do not have leave to purchase from your merchants." Father permitted only the Sellwyns and their guards to buy goods directly. Guards granted supplication if the commoners needed provisions beyond their rations. Apparently, wards came under the same restrictions. Her father was smart to demand it. Lorne Granich should be watched.

"It has always struck me as strange you have permission to go to town." His words were lazy. "One might think your father favored you over other women."

"I am not *other women*. I am his daughter."

"And yet, I have not met the daughters of any other lord. Once, I recognized my sister when she brought me breakfast because we share the same features. I have not seen her since." He sucked in air through his teeth. "Can you blame Uzziel for wanting to grow up faster when he has a sister like you?"

She could blame Uzziel for a lot of things. But it flattered her that Lorne thought her father respected her. Lord Sellwyn *did* treat her differently than the other women, she had always thought so. He would recognize how invaluable she could be when she revealed her talent someday.

Her smile fell when Lorne's voice hardened. "Enough of this play. You will purchase the herbs and soon. I command it."

She could not protest, and she did not mind complying. A break from her recent failures would be welcome. "I will go today. Uzziel will have his fallowent by your afternoon visit."

"Good girl." She grimaced when he kissed her head, but considering why she thought he had come, it was not so bad. She almost kissed him back for the delightful insight he had shared about her father's feelings. If only she could piece together his reasons for giving it.

✳ ✳ ✳

The hood of her charcoal-gray traveling robe obscured her face. Her father had been very clear about that rule when she'd run into the manor one morning, her head uncovered. The scars on her upper arms bore witness to that lesson ten years later. "My daughter *will not* be recognized on the street—do you not know how grateful you should be that I let you leave the house?" She did know—as Lorne said, her father favored her. Yet every time Vesperi lifted the hood over her head and tightened the rope that bound it, her anxiety rose. Anonymity did not suit her machinations.

The air was heavy with moisture that refused to fall as she stepped onto the walkway between the manor and its walls. The walkway had been built centuries before the war, before an Albrecht sat the Lanserim throne. Heat lingered in the gray-grained marble. Vesperi often took a breath of incense-free air on it before her father ordered her to Uzziel's side. Too much time spent indoors dulled her senses, and she needed to keep her wits about her. When they weren't, her tongue loosened and a beating followed.

She traced her finger around the elaborate carvings on its railing, scenes of knights-in-training and crowds cheering them on from bleachers. Most looked terribly boring, but one drew her in, a group of men in loose-fitting robes standing around a three-headed bird. She had no idea what the creature or ritual was, but she liked brushing her hand over it.

It had been years since she'd been to Sellwyn's tiny village, but her feet set out on the shortest path of their own accord. No one paid her any mind; she could have been any woman who worked at the manor, and the guards would not stop her unless they needed something, whether an urge quenched or a chamber pot emptied. Women were not known for conversation, too tired to utter more than a "Yes, my lord" or "Right away" while frantically raising their elbows in compliance.

Cabins rose up after only ten minutes of walking. "Keep your people close," Lord Sellwyn had once said, "or they will not be your people for long." Most holdings had changed hands after the war, but not Sellwyn Manor. Her father's steel grip was the likely reason why. What sort of man was dunce enough to let his villagers move freely from one town to another or admit unapproved guests past his city's walls? Not Jahnas Sellwyn.

Children's wails echoed through the empty, narrow street. The cracked windows were too caked with red dust and silt from Saeth's altars for anyone to see through, which suited Vesperi. A few men lived in town, those unsuited for physical labor. They became merchants or learned other trades the Sellwyns had need of. The herbalist had his own cabin, a luxury. A haze of incense smoke billowed into the street when she entered it. The man sat in a padded chair, another extravagance, by a table holding rows of miniature red-clay pots. His bloated legs gleamed purple from the veins straining against his skin. When she lowered her hood, he clapped his hands together.

"Vesperi Sellwyn! It has been ages since I saw you last. You have been too busy with those fancy lordlings to come visit old Graw." His voice scratched like the black scruff on his chin. "Though I have noticed fewer coteries riding through of late." He cocked his head. "Did those suitors find the merchandise too used?"

She glared. "None of them were suited to my needs."

"Oh, I am certain I have something that would suit your needs." He grabbed at the sagging bulge beneath his belt.

She ignored him. "You do, actually. I have need of fallowent. Do you know of it?"

"Fallowent, aye, I may have some of that, though it's scarce these days. The plants grow best by the river, and they disappear as fast as the Sell's waters. But I may have some in the back." His face lit up as he spoke, confirming what Vesperi had pieced together years ago—this man loved his craft more than his pleasures. He was harmless, as far as men went.

"What is it used for?" She hoped he didn't realize she should already know.

He didn't. "A few of the older boys swear it makes them taller. Some of the older folks used to call it 'weapon's helper' and ground it into a paste each night, smearing it over their mouths and noses. They said it would save them from the coming scourge." He shrugged. "It never made sense to me, but they died off, and we've not been scourged that I know of, unless you count this drought."

"Lanserim dreamers, clinging to some infantile ideal. Saeth smote them to end their misery." She gestured toward the back room. "I will take what you have, and be quick. Father does not permit me to be gone for long." He would not notice her absence for hours, but Graw need not know that.

Each hobbled step he took drew forth a curse. After some shuffling and banging, he returned with a pot in hand. Cloying scents of honey and musk rose up as he lifted the lid. She dipped a finger and it came out coated in black, sticky seeds no bigger than a flea.

"I will need more of it." She had no idea how long it would last. "So you had best figure out how to get some or my father will hear of it."

His face paled. "I will. There is no need to tell your father. I will have the guards take me foraging tomorrow."

"Good. I will return for more next week."

He raised his elbows as she made to leave but stopped her at the door. "You were right—"

She narrowed her eyes.

"—about those men, your suitors? To reject them."

Vesperi had little patience for stammering, but this was an unexpected compliment.

"I know you are a woman, and Saeth teaches that women are prized only for their cunts and the kitchens, but fallowent won't do anything to make that brother of yours a man. He would let us all fall into the hands of Durn, or Saeth forbid, the cow lords of Yarowen."

Graw shuddered, and Vesperi gave him a brilliant smile, encouraging him to continue. "I would—I would rather you take over than him someday, and you can't do that if you get married. I am very attached to my store, you see"—he petted the padded arm of his chair—"and I would prefer things stay this way."

"If we are lucky, my father will live many more years."

"Of course," he said hurriedly. "I did not mean to suggest—"

"You didn't," she assured him. "And Saeth may yet give my mother another son Lord Sellwyn can be proud of. We must pray for that."

He nodded, eyes downcast. But his head lifted when she placed an extra pile of souzers on the table.

"Your loyalty is noted by House Sellwyn." It was all she could say safely. She exited without another word, but the hood did not feel quite as binding when she pulled it over her head.

CHAPTER II
JANTO

After Sielban disappeared and reappeared multiple times over the next few hours. After they swam a stream with aching arms that made it feel as wide as the River Call. After they hiked through dense forest for half a day. After all that, Janto finally caught his breath. The cool, stone surface he leaned against was a marvelous balm on his back. His clothes would have been drenched with sweat in the dense mainland air. Had he lain on the sand to warm himself only a few hours ago? Janto closed his eyes, praying their teacher had no future lessons in mind that day.

Sielban had been nearly silent the whole sojourn, indicating what the men needed to do with gestures, looks, and the occasional muttering of "little children." He showed no signs of weariness. Janto half-expected a horn to sprout from his forehead like a cantalere's.

Napeler and the other Wasylim had kept pace with him and Janto for most of the journey. They collapsed on the ground beside the hillside now. One by one the others caught up, and loud gasps for air gave way to mild wheezing as they cast as many curious glances at Janto as at their leader. He sighed. *Everything I do is now the feat of a prince, not just a man.*

Jerusho rejoined the group last, but he came supporting one of the Meditlan twins.

"Little child, are you injured already?" Sielban's voice was reedy, and he moved swiftly to the limping man.

"I do not know what happened." The Meditlan grimaced through his pain. "I tripped over something and my ankle is swollen." Purple and pink bruising covered the area where skin stretched taut over the engorged ankle.

"This is nothing." Sielban *tsked*, waving the injury away as though a foul smell. "Tell me, what is your name?"

"Tonim of Urs, ser."

"Tonim of Urs, your leg will be healed come morning." The young man huffed, and all eyes inspected his ankle, expecting to see the swelling lessen. It did not. Sheepish glances came next.

Sielban's tongue tasted the air. "And you will call me *ser* no longer. None of you will. I am your teacher. You will call me only that."

"Teacher"—Nap rose to his full height, no easy task after so little rest—"if you can choose your name, can we choose not to be called children? We are men grown, and some of us have wives and children of our own."

"I call you only what you are." Sielban's face revealed no hint of a jest. "You can choose to become something else, but it will not happen in a day."

Nap appeared either sullen or crestfallen at those words. It was hard to read the Wasylim's mood. Jerusho's was much easier to decipher, his face flushed and a hand on his stomach. "Ser—no, mer—no! Teacher—sorry—Teacher Sielban?" He took a prolonged look at the nearby clearing. "Excuse me, Teacher, but I don't see any food. It is getting dark, and shouldn't we—I mean—hadn't we better get some dinner?"

"You are wiser than you think, little child." Sielban's eyes glimmered with a hint of something that might have been humor. "Food is just around the bend."

"The bend?" Nap peered into the distance. "But this meadow makes a circle. It is one unending bend."

Hamsyn examined the meadow's borders with his shepherd's eyes. "No, there's not a single bend, but there's a path a few yards that way." He pointed, and leaves rustled. The branches shuffled together to make an archway, and a path of brushed dirt appeared clear as day beneath them.

They gaped, but only the twin with the high voice spoke. "That was not there. We would have seen it."

"Perhaps you did not look hard enough then, but you know to look harder now?" Sielban walked through the center of the group and started down the path. He made a sharp turn to the left, beyond where they could see, and disappeared again. They hurried to follow, running around a couple of bends. Janto's stomach growled as they reached a more sub-stantive clearing than the first. It held a wooden table, a fire pit, and an uncovered well. The table was laden with food, more than enough for this group of eight. A few steps closer and the smell of squeezed lemons and charred fowl greeted him.

Jerusho could keep his appetite in check no longer. The Ertion ran as fast as he could, making it halfway by the time the others joined the mad rush. Janto may have spent half his days in fencing drills and archery training for the past few months, but those activities had only worked up a smidgen of the appetite this one day on Braven had. Even Tonim hobbled over as fast as he could, no longer needing the support of someone else's arm. That made Janto pause his rush—had Sielban done something to heal him after all?

Once everyone had taken a seat at the table, Sielban moved to address them. Jerusho put down an apple he had already bitten into.

"This is your meal," Sielban said. "Your first together, but not your last. You will come here every night for rest and nourishment, but you must always find the path. It will always be just around the bend."

Were riddles a central part of Murat training? Perhaps Janto should have spent more time with a bard than his sword.

"Teacher?" The Wasylim whose name Janto hadn't learned raised his hand. "Will we be sleeping out here in the open?"

"No. I will show you where you rest soon. But for now, get to know each other. Here, you are all you have, and out there—" he pointed at the sky and then around them "—you are all you need. I will be back before your fire runs out." He disappeared in a flash of green and brown.

"Whoa." The uninjured twin spoke everyone's thoughts. "Where did he go?"

Janto did not care to guess. Sielban was the biggest riddle on this island, and he could handle no more contemplation tonight.

"I bet he's still here." Tonim tipped his head toward the trees. "He's probably going to watch us all night, see how we act without him around. Sounds like something we would be tested on, doesn't it? How we act without him?"

The others mulled the thought over, casting nervous glances and expecting to hear an eerie whoop at any time.

"If we are being judged at the dinner table, then I, for one, do not want to be seen as wasteful. Making use of our resources is a virtue, is it not?" Jerusho picked his apple back up. "We must seize what Madel has seen fit to lay before us."

The laughter that followed eased the tension they had felt since the first rock flew from the trees that morning. Janto speared a leg of roast fowl and poured warm lemon sauce on top. No meal had ever smelled so good before—something he would be certain *not* to tell Mar Pina when he returned to Callyn. He was not prepared to give up his sweet rolls.

As he pulled the meat from the bone, he wondered where the provisions came from. Sielban could not have prepared it all himself; he'd spent the day leading a group of grumbling young men through the forest. Did cooks from Jost come daily to prepare such feasts? Janto shrugged, reaching for the platter of steaming Oostian greens. They tasted fresher and crisper than they would have from Lord Sydley's own table.

"So"—Hamsyn raised his voice so they could hear him over the din of smacking gums and clattering plates—"I think we ought to introduce ourselves to each other." The color promptly drained from his face as he remembered who remained at the table now Sielban was gone. "I mean, if you think that would be a good idea, my prince?"

Fantastic. Janto had to stop that behavior right away or it would only get worse. He gritted his teeth then rose. "That's a great idea. I will go first. My name is Janto Albrecht, and yes, I am your prince." He spoke faster and with more nervousness than he had hoped would show. "But here, I am no more than your compatriot, and I ask you please treat me as such. If we are children, as our leader believes, then consider me your sibling, the one who wants to get your favorite toy before you do."

He winked at them, hoping they would think of the Feats awaiting them in the coming weeks rather than of him. His father had once explained, after an especially grueling disagreement with Lord Xantas, that the best way to gain the loyalty of some men was to beat them. "The toy I will take is the peak of Mount Frelom, and I dare any of you to try and climb it first." Janto had no experience climbing but knew many of these men probably dreamed of being the first to ascend the famed peak that year.

The unnamed Wasylim stood. "I will beat you there with my arms tied behind my back." His legs appeared thick enough he could jump from ridge to ridge, ignoring the climb entirely.

"I would love to see you try," replied Janto. "But before we rush off into the dark of Braven, claiming victory, what is your name?"

"I am Rall, Your Highness—sorry—Janto." He raised his elbows. "May Madel's hand guide you."

"And you also. It is a pleasure to meet you." Janto took up a teasing tone again. "I cannot wait to see who will come closest, but fail, to beat me in the archery logs." He had more experience in that discipline, though he could never rival his father's aim.

"I will best you!" The uninjured twin made the declaration. "I've been picking crows out of the skies since I could hold a bow. No man's arrow flies straighter."

"That's a lie." Tonim's voice was deep though raised in jest. "If your line is straight, then mine is a beam of sunlight. There is no way you will defeat me at the targets, Flivio."

"I could shoot an arrow better than you with my eyes closed."

The group laughed at the sibling rivalry, obviously a well-practiced exchange.

"It seems we can expect an epic battle between our Meditlan brothers, Flivio and Tonim." Janto committed their names to memory.

"You could," Flivio broke in, "if Tonim were not the laziest arm this side of the mountains."

Tonim mimed shooting an arrow straight at his brother. Before the fake duel could continue, Rall prodded the Ertion to join in. "Jerusho, tell us what you hope to achieve."

"Certainly." Jerusho put down his fork full of fowl. "I plan to find and catch a granfaylon."

A couple of the men gasped, but Flivio laughed so hard, he nearly choked. "You are going to spear a mythical creature? Not only is it imaginary"—the sarcasm in his voice was strong—"but it is invisible. How will you tell you have the fish if you cannot see it?"

Jerusho's cheeks flushed, but his voice did not waver. "So I should save no slice for you when I skin and cook it, then?"

Flivio laughed harder, but Hamsyn spoke next. "I will take some when you catch it. Just don't forget to remove the bones when you filet it, please. They are hard enough to pick out when you can see them."

"And what is your name and Feat?" Janto asked.

"I am Hamsyn of Neville, and while Jerusho's hunting fish, I will be hunting the beasts of the forest. I know no one ever has, but I hope to snare the silver stag."

Flivio let out a sharp whistle. "The head of our council claimed he shot it at his Murat over forty years ago. But no one has proven a kill, have they? Has it even been seen since the war?"

"I don't think so, but I mean to try."

"*When the silver stag runs free, blessed will he who binds it be,*" Jerusho recited reverently.

"The way I figure, I may as well be the one to earn those blessings." Hamsyn folded his hands. "I could use a couple more heads of lamtas for our meadows."

"Finding that deer will be as easy as crossing the Giant's Pathway." Rall sliced off another hunk of meat. "Good luck to you, but cresting Mount Frelom will be a breeze compared to catching a creature like that."

Janto cleared his throat. "Who is left?"

Tonim rose, no twinge of pain evident from his ankle. "As I said before, I'm Tonim. My twin may be rumored to have beaten me once or twice while racing down Urs's main road—"

"You mean every time!" Flivio corrected.

"—once or twice, but I will show him who the true runner is by beating him across this island while I have the chance."

"So we have people for climbing, fishing, archery, hunting, and footracing," Janto recounted. "What else is there?"

"Combat." Nap spoke confidently, despite his height. "I will take any challengers at sword, axe, or mace, though I have not been bested since my hands were big enough to grip a weapon. I won the duels at Elston last fall."

Their accomplishments and ambitions impressed Janto. Greatness lay in their futures, notoriety they would earn rather than have bestowed on them by nature of their births. He hoped he could say the same someday. After the meal, Hamsyn and Jerusho worked together to start a fire, and the men spent the night around it, warming their hands in the brisk air and learning more about each other. Rall and Tonim were the only married men among them, though Flivio claimed he had his eye on a particular beauty who worked his father's vines. Janto had a hard time picturing any woman who would take a man who flung as many barbs as Flivio. If he was nearly as good a shot with an arrow as with his words, Janto had no doubt he would break the archery records.

When the flame burned itself down to a red jewel, Sielban appeared beside it, holding a dark pouch. A few nodding heads jerked back to wakefulness.

"Where did—how did—" Jerusho spoke for them all.

"Where and how are not nearly as important as did, little child."

Nap's features were sullen. "Are you here to take us to our beds?"

Sielban nodded, his eyes glimmering, then poured a handful of black sand from the pouch and raised it over the last embers. As it trickled through his fingers, a burst of blue swallowed the red, and darkness enveloped them.

"Are we to follow you into the dark, Teacher?" The baritone voice may have been Hamsyn's.

"For a time, but you will find the light wants to be found. If you cannot manage this hike, I fear you will not manage the Murat at all." With the quietest of rustles, he moved from the fire and toward the farthest side of the clearing.

Seconds later, Janto could neither hear nor see him. "Can anyone hear him?"

"I can." A Wasylim spoke, but Janto was unsure whether it was Nap or Rall—they both had the accent. The man hurried after Sielban, or at least Janto hoped he did. The rest of them walked forward as a group, listening for his calls of "this way" or "over here" every few feet.

As they stepped into the wood, the forest morphed into a canopy of crisscrossing branches. Bushes shifted in and out of focus, revealing another brushed dirt path. It shimmered in the moonslight with quartz flecks. They trudged on until the blinding glare of a torch greeted them. Sielban laughed as they stumbled over each other, not realizing their teacher was so close. When his eyes adjusted, Janto saw the mouth of a deep cave with more torches lit inside it.

Sielban beckoned them from past the lip. "The little children always think their beds are far away when they are just around the bend. Come in. You will find your packs inside."

They shuffled into the cave, which was tall enough to stand in. Each man wandered around until he found his pack. Janto's survived the journey over intact—Sielban either had the means to make them disappear and reappear like himself or his helpers paddled better than the Muraters.

Hard-packed dirt and pine needles comprised the cave floor. Many needles were clumped together in human-sized piles that Janto hoped weren't their beds. Rall dropped onto the closest one and closed his eyes instantly, confirming Janto's fears. Janto took the pile beside him, trying not to flinch as beetle ants darted from beneath it.

"Little children," Sielban spoke once all the spots were claimed, "this is your home. When you wake tomorrow, you will find it is not where you remember it to be. But it is always reachable, if you try. You will find this to be true of most things on Braven."

"Do we start tomorrow?" Nap unfolded a blanket from his pack. "Will the Murat begin in earnest then?" He appeared willing to start that moment, despite the day's events.

"Your Murat began the moment you stepped into your canoes," Sielban explained. "Tomorrow will be an exercise of skill and strategy, one many of you have enjoyed for years but forgotten."

Janto wondered what he could mean—surely the others had also been in Murat training for months. What could surprise or overwhelm them? The answer came faster than any had that day.

"You will play Lash the Feather."

Nervous chuckles echoed in the cave. Lash the Feather was a game for young children. Older children or adults strung feathers on sticks and dangled them over younger ones' heads. The children would leap and giggle, trying to catch the constantly twirling feathers. The sticks appeared from everywhere, especially during festivals when people lined up to watch the prince have at it.

"You are young, so we start with children's games." Sielban went silent.

"He's gone," Hamsyn announced from the front of the cave where he had claimed his bed.

"Naturally." Flivio turned over on his pile of needles, falling instantly to sleep. The others followed suit after pulling snacks from their bags or bunching clothes together to make a pillow.

Janto sat up, listening as his companions' breathing slowed and a few light snores began. Well, mostly light. Rall sounded like a bear in hibernation. In a few more weeks, it would be Serra's breathing Janto heard, nestled up beside her as husband to wife. He missed her, the way the corners of her eyes turned up when she smiled, the blush on her cheeks like sprinkled red quartz dust. By Madel's hand, he wanted to come out of the Murat a better man for her, a man who knew how to ease her grief and bring joy into her life again. She needed him, and he would never need someone else more. Of that, he was certain.

CHAPTER 12
SERRA

Bini cried when the rynna said no, she couldn't stay. They had arrived at Enjoin after three days riding in the carriage. Her normally tidy braid frayed, Bini clasped Serra's hand. The servant's skin felt smooth and cool as always, but her composure was the opposite. The pollen that drifted inside whenever Serra drew the curtains for fresh air had already reddened Bini's eyes, and her dress had wrinkled on the journey, but both worsened at this farewell.

Serra must have looked much the same. As they hugged, she felt the black mourning ribbons Bini wore and was touched by her handmaid's loyalty. The same black shreds of ribbon were tied around Serra's arms. Sometimes, she wondered if they wrapped around her mind.

"I will be fine." Though if honest, being left here with no one familiar frightened Serra. Alone was all she had craved for over a week, but with Bini leaving too, Serra found the idea less appealing than it had sounded in the throne room when the Brother invited her to come. Perspectives could change so swiftly. Had Agler thought the same as he burned?

"Oh, Lady Serra, don't let them make me leave you, not so soon after your brother's death. You need me!"

Serra breathed in the scent of Bini's salve, libtyl oil and the milky nectar of soothpricklers that made her skin so cool and inviting. She put on her fixed smile and poise that had been given much practice of late and pulled away from her handmaid. "It will be fine, I promise. The ryns and rynnas will look after me here. Besides, who else but Madel could give me peace?"

Bini gave another loud sob, but she withdrew. "Goodbye, Lady Serra." She sniffled. "I will relay all the plans we discussed for the wedding to the queen. We will make it perfect for you." Bini raised her elbows in farewell. Serra returned the courtesy then took Ser Allyn's hand and allowed him to help her down from the carriage. He was in charge of the small group that had brought her here: Bini, the carriage driver, and a pair of mounted guards who had hauled her trunk and their provisions on a cart.

"Where should we put her belongings?" Ser Allyn asked the rynna who greeted them, a slight woman with the strawberry-blonde hair that people from the Western regions sometimes had—hair like Janto's. Her garb was simple, a thin, ivory-colored garment. Serra envied her; in this thick air, her traveling gown made her feel twenty pounds heavier. If she had traveled more often, she might have known it would be far too confining for this weather.

"You may take them back with you. We will provide all the Lady needs."

Ser Allyn made to insist, or at least that's what she thought the quick reddening of his face meant. His cordiality stopped him as it nearly always did.

"It's fine," Serra said for the third time in two minutes. "My clothes would do me no good here. I did not think to ask advice on packing, and besides"—she leaned up on her tiptoes to whisper in his ear—"I would not want the other initiates thinking me pretentious. The princess should not put on airs, correct?"

He regarded her thoughtfully. "The trunk will go back with us." Sers Irven and Rullo, who sat on their horses heroically in the heat, tunics soaked with sweat, dismounted to place it back on the cart.

"You are welcome to refresh yourselves here," the rynna offered.

Ser Allyn waved the thought away. "This trip was unplanned—I cannot stay away from the king for long. But if you would replenish our water pouches . . ."

"I will send someone to you with fresh water." The rynna raised her elbows to him and then to Serra. "Follow me, Lady Gavenstone."

Serra followed the rynna down the short path toward the Temple of Enjoin, the central sanctuary of Lansera. It was the same shape as all the others she had seen, though perhaps twice as immense. The glass dome roof was capped by a model of Madel's hand reaching skyward. In the towns, temple walls were painted with vibrant, colorful murals done by artisans. These were plain white with a sheen of yellow from the pollen of Lake Ashra's flowering bushes.

Serra's arm itched as she walked. When she reached to scratch it, the mourning ribbons dragged against her hand, and the sensation shocked her like a bee sting. She whirled around, heart pounding, and ran as fast as she could to the cart that held her trunk. *How could I forget, even for a moment?* She lifted her skirt and jumped to where the trunk rested, tripping over all the fabric.

"The key," she demanded of Sers Irven and Rullo on their horses. "Where is the key?" Their astonishment at her impetuous behavior showed only in their eyes. Ser Irven fumbled in his saddlebag and pulled out a key covered with engravings of Gavenstone's vines. Serra grabbed it, her hand shaking as she turned the lock. *Where did I put it?* She had been in such a hurry to pack; Ser Allyn would faint from the sight of so many pricey gowns tossed in disarray. Luckily, he had gone into the carriage with Bini.

Her fingers grazed the pebbled exterior of Janto's seeing glass, and she hesitated, wishing for it, too, but it wasn't what her heart wanted right then. *There.* Agler's handkerchief peeked out from beneath a set of her undergarments. She snatched it and held it close to her chest, closing her eyes in relief. When she opened them, she found all her companions staring at her with concern. Bini's eyes filled once again with tears.

"I am sorry." Serra clutched the cloth in her hand. His ring she had left for safekeeping in her room, but this she could not part with. "I forgot something I needed, that's all. I did not mean to worry you."

Ser Allyn disapproved, but the others nodded with understanding. She supposed a near-princess who had lost a brother was allowed a few moments of gracelessness. Serra took Ser Irven's hand to disembark then gave Bini another hug. "Thank you, again." She raised her elbows to them. "Have a safe journey home. Tell the queen I will miss her greatly."

She hurried to where the rynna waited not ten feet from the sanctuary's door. In the distance, mud sucked under the departing horses' hooves and the wheels of the carriage and cart. Serra stepped past the threshold. The rounded walls inside were darker than those of Callyn's temple, covered in a layer of dusky green material. Serra pressed her hand against the nearest panel: reeds, immature, pressed reeds. In Callyn, it was the pale yellow of dried Nevillim grasses. At Gavenstone, preserved grapevines with berries that held a faint purple hue.

Thin cushions of varying shades lined the stone floors rather than rows of wooden chairs like in the other temples she'd entered. Serra hoped they were more comfortable than they appeared. Learning about the Order would likely require spending a lot of time on them. The few people inside stared at Serra, unused to seeing someone wearing such fine garb, though her gown was practically soaked through with sweat and splattered mud.

"Is this her, Gemni?" A ryn—perhaps fifty years of age, paltry in stature and with a mop of waist-length brown hair the color of caramelized boar's skin—came up behind her.

Rynna Gemni—Serra colored when she realized she had not bothered to ask her name—nodded. "Lady Serrafina of Gavenstone, betrothed to Prince Janto of Albrecht, future ruler of the realm." Gemni introduced her with raised elbows, but she let them fall quickly. "But in Madel's service, she is an initiate."

Taking on that title had been the main source of Serra's doubts about this trip. It implied she might have something to do with the Order after her initiation was complete. On the journey, Ser Allyn had spoken at lengths about the honor of going through the training. Most initiates never took the next step of becoming novices to the Order. Nevertheless, it made Serra uncomfortable.

The ryn raised his elbows to her, and they shook with his obvious excitement. "I am Ryn Gylles, also of Meditlan, my lady. And I have the pleasure of being your guide here at Enjoin." He stretched out his hand to her, and she took it as he led her back outside. Several well-marked trails of packed rocks emanated from the temple, and he walked the closest one at a brisk pace.

"Ryn Gylles." A few strides in the heat made her breathless after her earlier exertion. "You will need to walk more slowly if you wish me to make it wherever you are taking me."

He stopped immediately. "I am sorry, Lady Serra. How inconsiderate of me. I am always horrible at noticing what people wear. It's one of the reasons I pledged myself to Enjoin—everyone wears these sheaths!"

Her head swam with his fast conversation, but his laughter held genuine warmth. "We could keep a gentler pace if we talked as we went," she offered. "If you would not mind."

"Of course." He took her hand in his again, patting it. "Is there anything you want to know about the initiation, perhaps?"

"I know nothing of it, in truth. I did not plan to come, but a Brother came to Callyn—oh, you must know that already." Her guide would surely know her business, probably better than she did. "He asked me to come, so I said yes, but he did not provide any details."

"You may want to keep that invitation to yourself as you get to know the other initiates." Ryn Gylles frowned. "Most of them weren't asked to come, you know, but are here because it's what they want to do. You don't want to dredge up animosity."

Serra had not considered that. She expected rancor from those who scorned the Gavenstones, but she had not thought the invitation itself would be a problem, though she should have. The initiates came here as part of their chosen life paths rather than on a whim as she did. Her path was marrying Janto and becoming the queen someday. It had been as far back as she could remember. She had never pondered a different future the way they must.

"The initiation phase," Gylles continued, "is designed for those who believe they have a calling to serve Madel and her people. It is a trial to determine whether that calling is genuine. You will learn much of what we know of Madel, the role of ryns and rynnas in Her service and the Brothers also, though their duty is not something one can be called to pursue."

"But I am not interested in joining the Order."

Gylles looked at her pointedly. "That is something else you may not wish to mention to the others. I have an inkling of what the Brothers' purposes are for you here, but I do not pretend to know all. Nor will I explain it to you so easily. You are on a journey, and you will learn what you will learn as you continue it."

She liked Ryn Gylles's easy demeanor but being kept in the dark did not sound appealing. Serra needed something to focus on, something to distract herself from the gloom that had descended on her since Agler's death. She needed the light of clarity, not vague whisperings. What had she gotten herself into?

They stopped at a hut made of thatch and covered with more pressed reeds. Gylles opened the door, which arched like the temple's, and led her inside. One woman her age and one rather older were snuggled on their cots.

"Ladies," Gylles greeted them, "your third bedmate is here, Serra of Meditlan. Would you be so kind as to take her with you to supper when it's time?"

"Of course, Ryn Gylles." The younger, voluptuous woman with a messy, black tornado of hair spoke. "We are here to serve."

Gylles laughed. "Lourda, I think Enjoin suits you, or perhaps you suit Enjoin. Thank you, and I will see you all for class tomorrow afternoon." He beckoned Serra to join him outside then whispered, "We are going to spend a lot of time together, but not until you get settled in. Remember, you are an initiate whether that was your intent or not. Open your mind to Madel, and let Her minister to you. One of the ways She does that is through Her people. And they are to be your people also, yes? Do not forget that."

Serra nodded, and he took his leave. Back inside, two pairs of curious eyes trained on her. Lourda spoke first. "You must be Serrafina, the princess! You are, aren't you?"

Serra was pleased to be recognized so easily. "I am, though I am not technically the princess as yet."

"This is so exciting!" The older woman had blonde hair and fawn-colored skin. "I have never seen royalty before, and now, I'm rooming with a princess."

"It's not fair you know my name," Serra said, "and I do not know yours. Please, introduce yourselves."

"Lourda of Ertion." Lourda's hair tumbled over her shoulders, unrestrained. "May Madel's hand guide you, Princess."

"And you also, thank you." Serra turned toward the older woman. "And you?"

"Poline of Wasyla." She clasped her hands together. "This is too much!"

"Don't be silly. Now, is that my bed?" She gestured to the empty cot. A bundle of the loose material everyone wore lay on top, cheap fabric that had never been so desirable before. "Excuse me while I put this on."

Serra undressed in front of other women all the time. The intricacies of a gown—rows and rows of buttons, laces, and threaded ribbons and feathers—demanded it. But usually Bini or another servant swooped in as soon as she made to change. This would be difficult on her own. She managed to undo the first two buttons on her back, but the third was out of reach. Pulling at the hem of the gown proved useless.

"Would you like some help?" Lourda had already half-risen from her cot.

How strange, she thought. *I will be queen someday, but I cannot undress on my own.* It was not fitting to treat these women like servants, but she nodded nonetheless. "If you are willing, I would welcome it."

Both Lourda and Poline assisted, their able fingers making quick work of the buttons. Serra was soon ensconced in the sheath. The rough fabric felt as soothing as silk against her hot skin.

Poline giggled when they were done. "Imagine! I am going to a ritual with the princess."

"A ritual right now? How many are there in a day?"

Lourda spread the fingers of one hand and touched each in turn with her pointer finger. "There is the dawn ritual, which starts before the sun rises, and the midday one, after we pick our lunch in the garden and do our chores. The evening ritual comes after our studies and before dinner, and then it's the nighttime ritual, which we complete beside our cots. Four in all."

"That's a lot of time spent on our knees. Does it get boring?"

Poline gave her a queer look. "We are initiates and here to decide if we have a place within Madel's service. Is that much prayer not to be expected?"

Serra reddened. Of course, it was. "My guide did not specify the number of daily rituals on our walk here, is all. Four makes perfect sense, one for each of our moons."

"Your guide?" Lourda giggled. "Do you mean Ryn Gylles? Because he took you to our hut?"

"No, I mean he's my guide for the initia—" She realized her mistake too late. The others must not have guides of their own, or Lourda would not have asked. "I must have misunderstood his intent, I think. Is it time for the evening ritual?" She hoped so, to spare herself from further stumblings. It would be much easier to keep her role secret once she knew why she needed to and what it was.

"The kneeling does get tiring," Lourda confided as they made their way to the temple, "but I have a salve made with the lake's mud to help with the tingling."

She wasn't Bini, but Serra was pretty certain she liked this woman.

CHAPTER 13
JANTO

Janto woke to a flurry of voices, one shrill, some deep and tired, most with more than a hint of exasperation to them. It was similar to the sounds around the castle when Ser Allyn announced an inspection of the staff. But these were no servants gathered around the mouth of the cave . . . or maybe they were. Janto had not asked their occupations around the dinner table last night. The Murat was not limited to nobility, though many Muraters became such later in life.

"Perhaps it's a challenge—we must prove our abilities to search out food and catch what we need to break our fast." Nap paced near the opening, itching to conquer this apparent breakfast quest.

Flivio rolled his eyes a few packs over. "Of course it's a challenge. Everything we do here is a challenge. Imagine the novelty if our *teacher* gave us the rules."

"I do not care about rules." Farther inside the cave, Jerusho pulled on his pants. "I just want eggs and a rasher of craval sausages."

Janto cleared the phlegm from his throat. "Searching for our breakfast, are we?" He rubbed his eyes.

Tonim nodded from where he leaned with Nap against the cave wall. The room smelled of wet rock and a handful of men who needed a bath.

"How is your leg?" Janto shivered. He hated waking up cold in the mornings.

"Great!" Tonim turned on his heel to demonstrate. "As though I never hurt it."

Nap's face fell. "I did not think to ask about your recovery. My apologies—I was too wrapped up with today's opportunities to prove ourselves."

"That's all right. I am glad it wasn't easy to notice!"

Deciding to examine the ankle for himself, Janto stretched while he rose. "You are healed?"

Tonim wiggled his feet with a pleased smile.

Janto yawned. "This island and Sielban are full of surprises. At least we will not be harmed, it appears. How does that work?"

"Madel." Jerusho spoke with confidence. "The Murat is part of Her plan for us so She ensures our health. What good is a training of men if half are sent home injured?"

"I doubt that," Nap said. "What glory is there in conquering without risk?"

"I agree with him." Tonim grinned. "And I have a head start on all of you, because I've already conquered my ankle."

The others groaned. Recognizing a bad joke when he heard one meant Janto was fully awake. Tonim's ankle appeared normal, no bruises or lumps. Janto pressed his fingers around it gently to check for pain. Eddy had shown him how to evaluate lameness in a horse, and he figured it would work on humans as well. "How did it feel when Sielban touched you?"

"I don't know. I am not certain I felt anything physical at all. But I did feel differently in spirit, lighter, like I had completed a ritual. I am certain you understand. You must go to services all the time, being Dever Albrecht's son, the king who was almost a ryn."

Janto released the ankle when Tonim's stomach growled loud enough to wake Hamsyn, the last to rise. Rall stood over the barrel of water in the back of the cave, brushing his teeth with a foamy, black paste made of anise.

"Shall we go, then?" Nap chomped at the bit. "Find this breakfast table and then Sielban?"

"By all means. But we must find our next path first." Janto walked onto a ledge and into white-gold, blinding sunlight. Once his eyes adjusted, he gasped. They were not in the same place they had been last night. He was certain of it. It had been dark and the end of a weary day, but he could not have been so tired he failed to notice they had ended up here.

The forest canopy lay below him, a rug of pine needles. The shore was hidden, but past the forest's edge rose a huge rock face surrounded by a sea of salmon-colored grass. It had to be Mount Frelom. Dark gray clouds obscured its peak, but he was amazed he had not seen it towering in the distance from the docks at Jost. It was immense.

"Isn't it brilliant?" Rall came up behind him, eyes shining. "I cannot wait to climb it." He relieved himself over the edge of the cliff. Rall's enthusiasm was rousing, but the thought of climbing a mountain unsettled Janto's stomach despite last night's boasts. Too many memories of raccoon stew, raccoon roast, and raccoon pie at Lady Gella's festival in Varma flooded his mind. He did not trust his stomach at that elevation.

"Can anyone see a path?" Janto could see nothing but the thin shrubs that peppered the ledge.

"I see it!" Nap leaned over the edge, bare earth giving way beneath him. There it was, a narrow path hugging the rock face. They could not have climbed it at night.

Nap tested his footing then snaked around the trail and disappeared from sight. Tonim followed on his heels. Janto pulled on a new tunic and pair of pants. He laced up his boots in record time, blood racing. Then he ran as fast as he could down the path, Rall and Hamsyn close behind. The breeze felt perfect as it hit his cheeks, a little cool but dry and refreshing compared to the unusual springtime mainland humidity. Once the path became solid ground, Janto heard chattering ahead and the clanging of plates and utensils—the clearing could not be far. With food so close, he quickened his pace.

Until a flash of silver halted him mid-stride. Something grunted, and a branch whooshed near his leg as though it had snapped back and released. Janto could see something in the forest, hiding about ten trees back. A ray of sunlight broke through the canopy and glinted off it, but he could not tell what it was.

"Watch out!" yelled Rall, running around the last bend. Janto jumped to his left but not fast enough. Rall and Hamsyn barreled into him one right after the other.

"What were you doing, just standing there! We did not see you." Hamsyn was breathless. "Do you want to test Sielban's healing powers again?"

"I saw something." Janto turned to show them, but it was gone. "I'm sorry. I thought it might be important."

"How grand—a prince who sees things in the woods!" Flivio and his wit had obviously caught up. Jerusho reached them a few seconds later.

Janto sighed. Whatever it was had disappeared, and breakfast waited.

✳ ✳ ✳

Hamsyn located another path after the meal. It did not have a bend they could see, and Sielban had not made an appearance to guide them. With a little lively debate, everyone agreed to take it together. They yearned to explore now they'd had a taste of the island. That meadow Janto had glimpsed from the cave was especially alluring. He had seen neither grain nor weed that shade of pink before.

The noise of flying squirrels and birds had been louder in the canopy yesterday, but on the forest floor, frogs bellowed and chorna moths whirred. At least he thought they were chornas; the ebony insects wouldn't stop flying long enough for him to get a good glimpse. Chornas had an opalescent sheen on their wings, and all Janto could swear to was the occasional glint of rainbow. In this forest, the moths' many colors were hardly worth noting. Elongated purple, turquoise, and yellow ovals fluttered beneath tree limbs. Janto thought he must be seeing things, like the silver flash earlier. But the farther they journeyed, the more frequently the objects appeared, until one was close enough Janto called for the others to stop.

"Feathers. They're feathers! Look at the trees." He spoke fast with excitement. "They're everywhere."

Rall gaped. "I did not notice them at all."

"Wonderful." Flivio cracked his knuckles. "So we have found the feathers to lash, but who holds the ends of their sticks? Sielban cannot be in that many places at once."

"He cannot," Janto agreed. "But he must be nearby, or what would be the point of the game?" They peered into the woods, but no sign of their teacher appeared. Janto made out more feathers, some so far back as to be nothing more than lines drawn against the sky in more shades of ink than thrushberries could provide.

"Perhaps he means us to decide what to do on our own," Nap surmised. "As adults, we cannot wait for others to tell us what to do. I think we should make our own game."

"Or we need to be a bit more patient," countered Rall. "We should not behave like my son, ready to jump in a pond on a sweltering day without considering the leeches."

"You have a son?" Janto smiled at the man who beamed with the ardent pride many young fathers bore. "How old is he?"

"Three years. I have a daughter, too—Marla. You should see her, pri—uh, Janto. She's only been with us six months, but her hair is already a tangle of sun-kissed curls like her mother's."

Flivio cut in, a wicked look on his face. "You married young. What happened? Did you stick a child in her first?"

Rall laughed and shook his head. "No, our son was born just before our first anniversary. We fell in love young. And we have stayed that way. Sometimes, knowing the right one is easy. I could never love someone else as I love my wife."

"It must be hard for you, being away from them." Janto rubbed a finger over the embroidery on his belt pouch, a gift from Serra. He could not imagine enduring this separation if they had a child.

"Oh, yes, but I could not pass up the chance to come to the Murat! I do not know how I ended up here, truth be told." Rall was sheepish, and Janto admired his humility. He had known all his life he would be accepted for the Murat. What must it be like to have the experience thrust on you?

"You must have been thrilled when you felt called to come."

Rall nodded vigorously. "Besides the birth of my children, there is nothing that can compare. It was an honor when the council nominated me to go."

To earn respect like that was something Janto hoped to do. Perhaps he could learn how from Rall and the rest of these men.

Tonim pushed off from a speckled tree trunk. "Are we done standing around, pondering our options? We can stay here parsing out Sielban's intentions, or we can have some fun. I vote for fun—and I'm claiming the purple ones, easiest to see against the sky. Try and catch me, you nambies." He leapt into the woods and yanked at the nearest purple feather, pulling his knife out to slice the rope from which it dangled.

"Yellow!" Nap ran into the woods, not the type to let others gain an advantage.

When only he and Janto remained on the path, the rest of the men having claimed their colors, Jerusho sighed. "It is going to be this way every day, isn't it?" His tone was mournful. "What colors are left?"

Janto had kept a tally. "Silver and blue. Silver's mine!" He gave Jerusho a hearty pat on the back then raced after the others.

❊ ❊ ❊

An hour later, Janto had enough feathers tied to his belt to make him wonder if he could fly. His arms ached from climbing to reach the ones hung from high branches, making the pain from yesterday sharper. The men had stayed close together at first, but as the feathers thinned out, they'd spread farther apart. Janto had worked his way back to the line of trees where he had caught a glimpse of that creature earlier. Silver feathers hung here and there, so it must have been one of them. So much for the hunting prowess Sielban had complimented him on.

Tonim swung from branch to branch a few dozen yards away, lashing both blue and copper feathers. He and Jerusho had developed a partnership. The Ertion retrieved any feathers he could reach from the forest floor while Tonim claimed the higher prizes. An interesting strategy, but Janto did not want to share the glory of victory, even if that victory was holding a belt of peculiarly colored feathers.

Janto crossed the trail when he spied a feather dangling from a low branch and a couple tied a few feet up the next tree. He grabbed the knot that bound the nearest one then pulled its rope taught, wincing as the motion deepened a sore where the rope rubbed against his forefinger. Then he drew his knife through the rope. As he reached for another, high enough he had to stand on tiptoe, a hundred temple bells rang out. A more puzzling noise joined the clanging—Sielban's voice, as clear as if he stood beside him saying, "The game is complete. Follow the bells and find me."

Janto gripped the knot that bound his final feather, but he knew better than to add it to his collection. The game was over.

"Shall we find him together?" Tonim hung right above his head.

"So you heard him, too, then?"

"Like a bear storming through my head, rooting around for his pot of jam." Jerusho caught up to them in three strides. "I hope he does not do that often. That clanging is loud enough to wake a jurgen."

"You know those don't exist, right?" Janto teased.

"What is it with my *honorable* fellow Muraters and their prejudice against things unseen?" Jerusho displayed a disdain Janto would not have thought him capable of. "Next, you will be telling me Madel isn't real."

"Of course She is," Tonim scoffed as he lowered his feet to the ground. "She reaches out to us all the time, bestowing us with Her blessing and protection."

"But have you witnessed Her hand of blue flame reaching toward you?"

It was one thing to believe in Madel and another thing entirely to believe creatures of legend were real, or so Janto thought. Yet Sielban had spoken into all of their minds at once, and Janto had accepted it without qualms. Why not a jurgen? Or the silver stag for that matter?

Tonim shrugged. "Should be much simpler to find him this time. I don't think we could get lost following that noise." He started off in the direction of the bells' ringing.

"What do you make of Sielban doing that? It is not normal, being able to talk to us that way."

"I have heard rumors Rasselerians possess such magic." Jerusho pulled dry leaves from the branches as they walked, crumbling them beneath his fingers. "And of course, several times in our history, Madel blessed people with powers when the need was great enough."

Didio Albrecht's Silver Guard. Might it truly have existed? Janto had considered magic a convenient explanation for events for which they had few records. But with what he had witnessed here . . .

"Do you believe in magic, truly?"

Jerusho did not hesitate. "Certainly. If you spend enough time in the study of Madel, you will learn all the ways She uses Her power to make our lives better. Magical gifts are but one of many."

"That's daft." Tonim wiggled his ankle while they walked. "Why didn't she give us magic before Turyn's Peace? It would have come in handy fighting the Meduans."

Jerusho shrugged. "Who can say? Maybe she considered it a battle we brought on ourselves."

In the next clearing, they found Sielban wearing the same suit as yesterday, its patterns shifting with the sunlight to create an effective illusion, appearing an arm's length away or as many as ten yards. He waited to speak until they all gathered, feather-laden belts dragging behind them. "Good morning, little children. I hope you have enjoyed your game. Tell me, what are its results? Who has won Lash the Feather?"

Janto assessed their fortunes, most having done about as well as him, fizzling any hopes of victory. Nap had an impressive array of yellow feathers lashed to his belt, including a few larger than any bird had the right to lay claim to. Jerusho and Tonim's partnership yielded the most voluminous pile. Both men had more feathers individually than the others had managed, and together, it was an impressive sight. They were covered in them, blue and copper hues as intermingled as the layers of Sielban's camouflage. They stood proudly as the others eyed their haul, yet Nap stepped forward first.

"I think I have the most, Teacher." Nap held up his belt for inspection. "Jerusho and Tonim have more, but they worked together. Is that not cheating?"

Sielban flicked his tongue across his teeth. "Do the rest of you agree? Did those with the most gain them unfairly?"

By the expressions on their faces, Jerusho and Tonim did not consider themselves cheaters. The thought had not crossed Janto's mind . . . but surely no man could have claimed that many feathers on his own.

"I agree with Nap," Rall supported his fellow Wasylim. "They did not play by the rules, so Nap should have the win."

"They did not play by the rules." Flivio mocked the statement with a smirk Janto now considered his usual expression. "Are we five years of age? I thought we were men. You sound like they pinched your money in a game of Sheven Teeth, not Lash the Feathers."

"So you would award the win to the pair," Sielban mused, "but your reason would be to deny the children their candy, not to give the winners their due."

"Well, yes." Flivio raised his elbows to their teacher, taking no offense at the charge. "It's a lot more fun that way."

"We have two votes in favor of Napeler. And three in favor of those with the most feathers, assuming our partners would vote for themselves. Will others weigh in? There are two voices yet to be heard."

"But you gave us the answer." Hamsyn laid his belt at Jerusho's feet. "They have the most feathers, and so they win, despite the methods."

Flivio nodded in agreement. "And who's to say the methods were wrong? We were quite happy to start without any rules. I would say they did better than the rest of us at coming up with a way to win, not a way to cheat."

To his credit, Nap blushed at the reprimand. Janto did, too, gladdened he had not proclaimed in Nap's favor so fast. *I almost did, though.*

By Madel's hand, he had much to learn from these men. Nap may have been wrong, but his drive to excel was amazing. When had Janto needed to excel at anything?

The joy on Jerusho's and Tonim's faces as Sielban dubbed them the winners was reason enough for Janto to abandon any lingering doubts of their worthiness. But he had plenty about his own.

CHAPTER 14
SERRA

"We are only partway through your initiation, but it is never too early to say it—some of you will be leaving us." Ryn Gylles sat on a raised stool in the middle of the Trilling Hut. The teaching hut would be a more appropriate name, but the initiates had rechristened it in honor of the speed and flow of Gylles's speech. "Some of you will find the Order is not your calling after all."

The room quieted. Several initiates shook their heads in denial, but others stared at their feet.

"I am here to tell you that's all right." The ryn's face brightened so greatly, Serra thought Madel's hand reached down to him for a moment. She gasped, drawing curious gazes from the initiates seated close by. She was used to that by now. It had been a week and a half, but she had not found a place among them, though Lourda had been wonderful, accepting her instantly with a warmth that reminded Serra of Lord Xantas's bone-crushing hugs. The woman had even allowed Serra to brush her wild hair, though she yelled at every tangle pull, causing Poline to laugh.

"All of you will remember this month for the rest of your lives. But only a few will continue with it. And that is all right." Ryn Gylles sipped from a quartz-studded chalice. "Those who stay will become novices and continue with Madel's training. Those who go will live their lives more fully than they could here. It is not a failing to go, but a recognition this life is not for you."

Serra wondered which of the thirty or so men and women would stay. How strange these few weeks might be the ones to determine the courses of their lives. Serra was still unsure why she was there. Maybe the Brothers considered a spiritual queen a greater ally. Or they thought of her grief and gave her the space to deal with it. Calming her tempers *was* easier away from the day-to-day activities of Callyn.

Gylles spoke again. "Not to change the subject—okay, I mean to change the subject now that two-thirds of you are as pale as a granfaylon's underside." That elicited laughter and smiles all around. "Let us turn our thoughts back to the designing of rituals. What is the purpose of the bells?"

Asten, a wisp of a man she imagined had ended up at Enjoin while chasing drapian seeds on the breeze, shot his hand up. "My rynna said the bells are struck to tune our minds to Madel's resonance."

"Your rynna was correct, and if you continue, Asten, I hope you will give the same answer to others who seek it in the future."

Colini spoke next, a middle-aged man from Neville. "Ryn Gylles, I have never heard anyone talk about resonance in relation to the rituals. That answer sounds meant to shut up a questioning child, not teach her about the Order."

"Oh, but it's not!" Gylles's voice pitched higher in his excitement. "Madel reaches to us from another space, a different *resonance*, you might say. She is here, all around us, but a goddess does not live in the world as we do. She has always been and will always be. Such an entity cannot be part of our world. She is outside of our existence but connects Herself to us. The bell, when struck, reminds us to open ourselves to that."

Serra found that a rather beautiful thought, one she would have never considered before coming here. She could see why Dever Albrecht had been drawn to a life full of such remarkable images and ideas.

Ryn Gylles struck the bell that stood in the middle of the room then dismissed them. He caught Serra's eye as she made to leave, and she whispered to Lourda that she would meet her back at the cabin. She had grown quite fond of Ryn Gylles, especially these occasional afternoon chats together. He was as easy to talk with as Queen Lexamy.

"Are we to have a walk today?"

He shook his head. "No, I have a little extra teaching for you, something the others will soon learn, but I wanted you to keep in mind for now." He sounded graver than normal; the joy she had glimpsed a moment ago drained out of his countenance so thoroughly he resembled a granfaylon himself.

"But why tell me?" She laughed and played with her clove necklace. "I am not an initiate."

He ignored the question. "There are other things out there, Serra, truths besides Madel we shut our senses to. The war between the gods did not eliminate all darkness from our lives."

"Surely the existence of Medua is proof enough of that?"

Again, he did not answer. She left the room with a foreboding she had not felt since Ser Allyn had brought her the Ravens' letter.

* * *

Lourda stood under the lip of their hut, lacing up her knee-high sandals, and Poline walked out of the doorway as Serra approached. She raised her elbows in greeting. "Do you want to come for a walk by the lake with us?"

The invitation took Serra by surprise. "I would love to." It would help her forget how Ryn Gylles had turned her blood to ice with a few words. Serra laced the golden ribbons of her sturdier sandals around her legs. Her fingers moved quickly—it would take nearly half an hour to reach the lake, and they would barely have time to skip stones on it before having to return for the evening ritual. Plus, she was proud of the speed of her lacing, a significant improvement from being unable to unclasp a single button by herself. She imagined Bini turning her other servants away at her bedroom door. *Lady Serra will dress herself today.* Serra giggled then joined Poline and Lourda on the path.

* * *

The afternoon light was dimming when they reached Lake Ashra, its surface gleaming as the sun's rays broke over the water. Regardless of the picturesque surroundings, Serra wished Madel or the Brothers would dispel the jocal flies. The pests were thicker than the spider webbing that covered grapevines at harvest time.

"Does Callyn have anything this beautiful?" Poline's eyes glittered. Serra shook her head but recalled the city's bridge over the falls and smiled.

"Oh, yes, it does. But only our bridge can compare to this. You should see it, Poline, a thousand stones of sparkling quartz. People claim you can go blind from staring at it."

"That sounds wonderful."

"It is wonderful." Serra considered the woman before her, swatting at flies. Poline was in her sixties, but she'd seen so little outside of her Wasylim town. Not that Serra had seen much more than Callyn and Gavenstone. "You should come sometime, after your studies here. You can visit me at the castle."

"Do you know you will return? Will you not continue as a novice?"

The question took Serra by surprise. Of course she would return to Callyn and everyone she loved. Janto, Queen Lexamy—by Madel's hand, she missed Bini's prattle. She had needed time away, but the castle was her home. Had she talked so little of it the others would think she did not want to go back?

No. She had been reserved here, but that was not why Poline asked. The other initiates did not know she was here at the Brothers' request, and royalty sometimes studied under the Order. Some continued up until the moment they'd pledge their troth to Madel—the king certainly had. Lying by omission to these women felt shameful, but Ryn Gylles had asked her to—that had to make it right. *Right?*

"Lady Serra! Poline! Come right away!" Lourda called from the shore. A plume of black and red smoke hovered above her head, but it dissipated too quickly for it to have been real. Serra blinked her eyes, then Poline grabbed her hand and they ran.

What they found made Serra lose the remnants of her lunch in the nearest bush. Poline merely screamed. Serra wiped her lips with leaves once she'd stopped heaving, leaving a sharp, metallic taste in her mouth. Then she faced the sight again.

Two green-tinged skins lay on the ground, sacks as thin as scrolls. One was smaller than the other, and they both looked concave, like something had been sucked right out of them. Through the holes puncturing them, she could see a crimson liquid inside. It oozed like congealed blood, but it couldn't be blood. There was so much of it and nothing else inside the sacks. They could not be bodies, at least not human ones. *They cannot.*

"Are they animals left to rot?"

Lourda shook her head with pronounced sadness. "These are people." Her voice was steady, though she had tears in her eyes. "Look here."

She lifted an edge of one skin with a stick, revealing a tiny drindem doll beneath it, almost identical to the one Serra had had as a girl. The thickened liquid had leaked all over it.

"A child." Poline clutched her chest.

"And here." Lourda prodded the other skin, exposing a string of hooked fish beneath it.

"The fish do not smell." Poline's voice trembled. "This is fresh. They have died recently. But that is not possible." Fear besieged her visage as Poline continued, "I had heard there had been deaths, but I did not believe it."

"Did not believe what?" Poline's words confused Serra. "What sort of deaths have you heard about?"

"Rumors, I thought, people spreading rumors of a killer in Rasseleria that sucked the blood out of its victims. Some of my daughters thought it was a *Meduan*"—Poline uttered the word with contempt—"come back to torment us again, but I figured it was a pack of wolves at worst. I did not think it could be real."

Serra gawked at the skins. "But that cannot be right. These people are drained of everything but blood. What sort of animal could do that?"

"I do not know. It is too dreadful to be real."

"What do you think we should do?" Lourda deferred to Serra, a responsibility she did not want right then. The thought of bringing the skins—the people—back with them to Enjoin made her queasy, but they could not be left to rot. Lanserim did not leave their dead to the elements, especially not ones who had suffered like this. They deserved more.

"We must bury them, and then we will tell the priests. They will know what to do. They have to."

The lake had darkened, now ominous instead of beautiful, something only a vast body of water could do. She was cursed to relearn, again and again, how fast perspectives could shift.

"Here." She pulled a greenish shard of glass out of the sand, perhaps a relic of ages past. "We can use these."

Serra was grateful the thickness of flies lessened near the bodies. They dug shallow graves, anxious to leave, and used bunched leaves to shift the skins into the holes. The skins were heavier than they looked, and Serra cringed as blood dripped onto her sheath. *They were people,* she reminded herself, *my people. I can wear their blood.*

A fly bit her as they took their first few steps away from the graves. She cursed, and Lourda and Poline moved away in fear.

"I'm sorry. It was a fly—I'm fine. Let's keep going."

No one said they should keep a fast pace, but they fell into one all the same. They knew they had reached the temple when they could hear the evening ritual chants. As they neared, the bell rang, and it felt like a premonition. A few initiates she had yet to meet walked out first. The peaceful expressions on their faces were quickly replaced by ones of disgust. Serra had never been observed with such eyes before.

"What happened?" They moved aside for the others coming out. "There is blood all over your clothes!"

"There were . . . there were bodies at the lake." Serra cursed the tears welling in her eyes. She should be stronger than this, should be able to react with calm to such events. "We buried them."

"It was horrible." Lourda made no attempt at composure, her tears an engorged mountain stream overflowing the banks of her creamy skin. "A child and maybe a man—something happened to their insides, dissolved them."

One of the initiates recoiled. "From the inside? What do you mean? That's impossible."

"No. It is very possible." Serra closed her eyes. "I wish you were right."

Rynna Gemni stepped through the doorway next. Her face clouded when she saw them and the blood on their clothes. "Serrafina, Poline, Lourda,"—she took all three of their hands and clasped them between her own—"what happened?"

Rynna Gemni bore no resemblance to Lady Gavenstone, but the feel of her hand's warmth reminded Serra of when her mother would clasp her hand to comfort her. She filled with longing for a woman she would never see again, and then for Agler and Callyn and a time when she did not encounter something wretched and wrong around every corner. Then she sank to the ground and wept. Lourda knelt, wrapping Serra in sturdy arms and rocking gently. Serra did not stir as Poline told the rest of their tale of blood-stained drindem dolls and things that should not be.

Time passed, and Poline placed a hand on her back. "Serra, Rynna Gemni wants us to come with her to see Ryn Cladio." Cladio was head of Enjoin, the chief priest of the Order. "Will you—can you come?"

Serra extricated herself from Lourda's arms. The rest of the initiates and several priests had gathered around them now, wearing a mix of confused and horrified expressions. And why shouldn't they? The almost-princess of Lansera had broken down in front of her people. *It will not happen again.* Serra wiped her tears with filthy hands.

Gemni led them to one of the huts nearest the temple, where the priests made their dwellings. Inside sat a desk made of Wasylim wood, covered with stacks of bound paper, inkwells, and quill pens topped with tan, silky threads of marshweed. The man at the desk had an appearance so odd, she wondered if he was a Brother uncloaked. He wore the same sheath they all did, but his Rasselarian-dark skin wrinkled finely and completely, a beach shore lapped at by waves. His eyes were lavender and so radiant, she was unable to look away once he greeted them. That marked him as a descendant of Deduins, one of the oldest peoples in the world, though they'd rarely been seen outside of Medua since the division.

"Ryn Cladio," Rynna Gemni raised her elbows in deference, "I am sorry to interrupt you, but we have had more strange deaths."

More?

Ryn Cladio's face fell at the news, but his eyes shone brightly. "I take it these women found them?" His voice was warm. "I am sorry you had to see such a thing. What are your names?"

"I am Lourda of Ertion, Ryn. We are initiates here." She said it proudly.

"Of course you are, Lourda. And who are you?" He gestured to Poline.

"Poline of Wasyla."

"And you?"

Serra raised her elbows. She had introduced herself to the other initiates as a citizen of Callyn, following Ryn Gylles's advice, although the truth of who she was had spread fast enough. But saying that felt like a lie here. "Serrafina of Gavenstone, Ryn."

The purple of his eyes deepened, enchanting her.

"Lourda found the bodies," Serra continued. "We did not think them people but something that had decayed a long time ago. But then Lourda found belongings beneath the . . . the sacks of flesh, the corpses, I mean."

"And what did you do with your discovery?"

"We buried them," Poline answered. "Is this what has been happening throughout the marshes? We had word of it down south. Does the Order know the cause?"

"We have suspicions, but we know nothing for certain. That it is evil, there is no doubt. We pray Madel brings us the tools we need to combat it before it spreads."

He took the news so calmly. How had Serra never heard of this before if it was well known to him? "Someone should tell the king. He will send people to hunt down whomever committed such crimes."

Lourda murmured her agreement, but Serra's jaw dropped at Ryn Cladio's next words.

"The king knows what is happening."

Such horrible deaths would surely have been all Callyn talked about. If King Dever already knew, then why hadn't Serra heard news of them?

"Thank you for sharing this with me, initiates. I will see to it the kitchen has fresh food for you, once you have had the chance to bathe and replace your clothes. You may go."

Rynna Gemni exited first, the others shuffling behind her. As Serra reached the threshold, Ryn Cladio called out, "Serrafina of Gavenstone, would you stay for a moment, please?"

"I will find you both later," Serra said. Lourda nodded as she ducked through the doorway.

Once they had left, she raised her elbows again. "How can I be of service?"

"Serrafina of Gavenstone? That's a strange choice of home for a woman who's lived so long in Callyn and is nearly the princess of the realm." A hint of amusement showed in the corners of his luminous eyes.

She was confused. There were many names she could be called, but Gavenstone was always the first she reached for, outside of Enjoin. "I apologize. I did not mean to hide myself from you."

Ryn Cladio laughed. "You could not do that, Lady Serra. It struck me as an odd choice, is all. I would encourage you, however, to consider yourself Serrafina of Lansera. You will soon be indispensable to us all."

Words said in kindness, but they made Serra feel as cold as Ryn Gylles's words had done before. She shivered despite the humidity of Enjoin. "I do not want to be rude, but did you wish to speak to me about something else? I would like to wash myself of today's events."

"And you shall in but a moment. I want you to know you are not alone here, Serra. You have made few friends—yes, I have been watching you. Times of mourning are troubling ones, and you need all the support you can get. Reach out to your companions. Show them more of who Serrafina of Lansera is."

He was right. She had thought her grief abating, yet her collapse in front of the temple indicated that her sorrow had only been mollified. "I will try to take your words to heart. Thank you."

His lavender gaze followed her out of the hut.

CHAPTER 15
GARADIN

G aradin followed the swinging, clanking mass of brown velvet robes and bones, making sure not to trip over his own in his haste to keep up. The ache in his hip killed him, but it would be far more fatal not to eavesdrop on the walk to Mandat Hall. The heads of his two closest fellow priests locked together as though a pair of swans in love. Squawks of excitement occasionally punctuated the steady drone of their conversation, but they were well-trained plotters, and Garadin could not make out their words. One head twisted around, hunting for curious ears, and Garadin rubbed his hip and groaned with augmented pain.

"Adver Garadin." the schemer inspected him with the indigo eyes of the Deduins. They took on that inhuman color from the flesh of the sheven that swam the moat of Thokketh. "Why do you walk alone?"

Garadin always imagined being pricked by a sheven's thousand sharp teeth when a Deduin looked his way. "I did not want to interrupt, Adver Votan. You seemed quite intent on your conversation."

"Never too busy for you." Votan wrapped an arm around him, causing a rattle as a row of sharpened bones sewn onto his sleeve rubbed against the ones on Garadin's shoulder. "Besides, it does not matter what you hear, old man. You are no threat to me."

"And why should I be?" Garadin's shoulders tensed, the movement undetectable beneath the layers of his robe. "I have no desire to become the Guj."

"Who said anything about the Guj? We were not talking about the Guj, were we, Yan?" Votan did not break his gaze while addressing the second priest.

"No, no," the milky Yarowen replied raspily. "We merely wondered what ghastly things the cook would declare 'food' this year."

"Saeth's fist!" Garadin pounced on the excuse to reach into his wealth of stories. "Do you remember the murky pool of entrails he called 'Feast of Flavor?' That was the worst soup to ever pass my lips or anyone else's. I will never understand why the Guj didn't lop off his head right then and there!"

The three of them laughed high and hollow, a chorus of teakettles, and went on to the dinner feast. Garadin's maturity made him suppress a sigh of relief at how the interaction went. He rarely came under suspicion, and that was precisely how he liked it. It had taken many years of work to be so pitied by his peers. This crop of priests were young, inexperienced twits—they hadn't even realized he rarely ate at Mandat Hall. None had been alive during the Revolution and only he and Romer, the Guj, had survived the fifty-odd years since—Romer because he was too powerful to touch, and Garadin because no one paid him attention. Garadin's memories of the Revolution were often clearer than recalling whether or not he had locked the door to his chamber at whatever manor he was assigned to that year. He accepted it as part of aging, but he also knew loss of memory was not the same as loss of lucidity—a mistake his comrades often made.

They entered the dining hall, pausing to kiss the feet of the Guj's statue, which had been completed soon after he and his wizards had incinerated King Laz Suma, putting an end to the brief monarchy in Medua, a failed idea of some of the "nobler" rebels. This was all done openly in front of Laz's second son, now King Ralion Suma. Ralion understood to whom he owed his crown, and ruling through a figurehead was easier than dealing with hundreds of lords trying to claim the throne. The priesthood knew where the real power lay, and each one of them plotted to take control of it themselves.

At least seventy men filled Mandat Hall, named for the idiot who had tried insisting a religion was not the way to rule a country after King Turyn Albrecht ceded them the land. They came here to gather and shovel mush together whenever the Guj sent a command to do so. Advers did not tend to spend time together otherwise, usually stationed at court or at separate manors, ones where rumors of a lordling gaining favor with his people had been reported. Romer sent out priests to stir things up by shouting in the town square, only the shouting was really whispers behind closed doors. Garadin took pride in such work. He would tell villagers of a scream he heard from the manor house the same day a little boy went conveniently missing or some other ploy. But he would only foment enough discontent to keep the people wavering between disloyalty and revolt. That balance was how they maintained control, and it was brilliant. Romer had seen beyond seeking embarrassments like trade pacts and understood the need for the complete isolation of Meduan lands.

Garadin took a seat at one of the far tables to avoid falling under the Guj's gaze. He had stayed alive by playing the imbecile and keeping his distance. A guard on the stage pounded the urum drum, an immense ceramic vessel placed over a hole in the floor. When struck, it emitted a hollow sound that resonated so the ground would rumble. Garadin had heard some of the young priests claim it magic, but he knew better. The Guj's three wizards held the only real magic here. They entered first, each draped in a thin, lengthy veil of pounded levere. The Guj entered the room next, hale despite his seventy-some years, though Garadin thought he spied a miniscule limp as he walked in. Otherwise, the Meduan leader appeared well. *More's the pity.*

Silverware clattered against tabletops as those eating stopped mid-bite. The wizards stood at the corners of the stage, waving their hands in semicircles in a protection spell they would continue until the Guj finished speaking.

"Advers." Romer's voice was balmy and soothing. "Thank you for coming at my behest." He clasped his hands together and raised his elbows in greeting. "Some of you need new missions, and I will take care of that. But first, there is a more important matter at hand."

A twitter made its way through the crowd. More important matters weren't in the script. The Guj had a group of advisors he kept close, the only people he consorted with beyond the giving of commands.

"It appears King Ralion is getting a bit anxious these days. He has planted his seed in every whorehouse this side of Lansera."

A few priests nervously chuckled, but Garadin doubted the claim. King Ralion Suma preferred whores of the hairier persuasion, even kept one at court, though he was smart enough to pretend the man was just a councilor. Romer was scheming.

"We do not want a hundred illegitimate sons of Suma challenging our claim to rule in twenty years, do we?"

Yells of "No, my Guj!" and "Cut off his member!" came from the crowd. Romer smiled, exposing a mismatched line of teeth. "I don't plan to kill yet another Suma after we have spent so much time building up their loyalty. Instead, we will give Ralion what he needs, a woman for him to use at his leisure, one who would never deny him anything—a wife. One of our own choosing, of course. Now, I have called you here to gather the names of the women in your manors that may be suitable for the title Queen of Medua."

Consulting his priests in the? Maybe Garadin was not the only one growing senile in this room. This move would be seen as a weakness by the younger advers. They stared unseeing as they shuffled through memories of the young women in their precincts. Garadin thought it a risky business to offer up a name. Choosing the right woman could bring great distinction, but avoiding such attention was how he stayed alive. And if he picked the wrong one? Well, his head would not stay on his shoulders, either way. No, he would stay silent. Garadin wanted to die in his sleep, a bottle of mead tucked under one arm and a woman in the other, not with his skin burned off in a haze of wizard's smoke.

"Advers, this will be a written, secret vote." The Guj bared his teeth again in a smile, and the tension relaxed noticeably. "I do not want blood spilt over this task—not that any of you would think of revenge if your woman wasn't chosen, of course. If you will write a name on your slip of paper"—guards passed them out at the tables—"then we will collect them. I will choose a group of you to decide between the nominees, a group I can trust to be quiet about the proceedings. Please consider your names carefully."

Garadin could not risk being ratted out for not submitting a name with all the other advers crouched over, considering the task. He wondered which women might be ideal from Yarowen, where he ministered presently. There were few of noble birth to choose from; most had been killed in the last battle over lordship of Sunkin Manor. Perhaps little Elvia Sunkin would do. He had never heard her speak a word—Lord Sunkin kept her locked away except for manor dinners. Garadin could not imagine she would be anything but grateful for the new surroundings. Yet such gratitude might release her tempers; women were so hard to peg down. Maybe a married woman would be best, having had any rebellious tendencies beaten out of her years ago. Lady Guntha was a safe bet for temperament. Her sunken eyes never sparkled at any feasts he had attended. He wrote *Simor Guntha* with the supplied feather pen.

Most of the priests had already laid their quills down, nitwits so eager to submit the right name they left their own safety out of the thought process. Some would learn with time. Others would die for their naivety.

The guards gathered the slips, and the Guj spoke again once the baskets were brought back to the stage. "I will now call the names of those who will help me choose the woman: Adver Cormal, Adver Hin, Adver Raino, and Adver Garadin."

Garadin gasped, horrified. *This is bad.* Or perhaps not. Perhaps Romer chose him for his prowess at keeping secrets—he concealed his presence well enough most of the time. *Not this time.* His thoughts raced, searching for an excuse to avoid such a close audience with Romer, but he could think of no way to refuse.

"The rest of you may adjourn for the evening. We will meet again for the morning meal, and I will give assignments to those of you who will be changing them. I will also announce the name of the chosen woman for our dear king. Named men, meet me here."

Garadin fought the urge to slip in with the exiting advers and approached the front of the room.

"Garadin, my old friend," the Guj greeted him. "It has been too many years!"

"Indeed, my Guj." He raised his elbows in deference. "I am honored to be in your presence."

"As you should be."

Advers Cormal and Raino made their ways forward as well, but Garadin was shocked to find Hin missing. Romer spoke calmly to one of his guards. "Find Adver Hin and kill him."

The guard sprinted out of the room, holding his spear before him.

"Come." The Guj walked through a doorway behind the stage. Garadin clambered after him, cursing his hip under his breath. The other priests and the wizards trailed behind them. No one mentioned Hin and Garadin would not mourn his death. He had always come across as a sniveling child, though he had been an adver for at least half as many years as Garadin, part of the first generation of true Meduans.

The Guj opened the door at the end of the passage, then they walked into a dark hallway empty of servants. A grand door covered in levere shields stood at its end, a security measure anyone would assume the Guj needed. But Romer stopped at a tapestry that depicted him wielding his hammer on the plains of Orelyn instead. One of the wizards stepped forward and lifted a finger. The tapestry rolled to the side, and a plain door swung open from behind it. Romer stepped through it into a room less sizable than Garadin's manor quarters at Sunkin. The members of his council already sat at a round table in the corner of the room, laughing uproariously as they read through the collected slips of paper. Romer took the last seat at the table.

One of his counselors, Adver Nouin, a rotund man from the tar sands of Kallon, took a slip and held it to the pillar candle on the table. "Useless. A shame to see all this paper wasted."

The Guj nodded. "But necessary. We don't want the chattel thinking we planned for her to be placed on the throne."

The woman is already chosen. Garadin knew Romer would never leave a thing such as this to chance. It was far too risky. But whom did he have in mind? Had the king taken a liking to one of his Qiltyn consorts?

"Vesperi will be brought here under the guise of banishment. Her father has written three times asking for permission to send her to Thokketh," Adver Tolliv said.

Vesperi? Garadin knew only one woman by that name in Medua, and she was no candidate for royalty. "My master,"—he kept his eyes down as he addressed the Guj—"you cannot mean Vesperi Sellwyn, Lord Jahnas's daughter?"

"I see you have learned why you were brought here, Garadin. Good. I thought perhaps you might have trouble remembering." He smirked. "Yes, Vesperi Sellwyn is the woman I intend to marry Ralion. Do you have an objection to that?"

Romer plays with me. He could not consider that creature worthy of Ralion, even if Ralion was no more important than the dirt on his shoe. Garadin had to think fast. "If you mean it sincerely, then I must admit to some misgivings." Romer gestured for him to continue. "Vesperi Sellwyn would be a grave mistake. She refuses to be tamed, and Saeth knows Lord Jahnas has tried to from the moment of her birth. He had not succeeded by the time I left Sellwyn. She has a mind of her own and ambitions, none of which suit a queen of Medua."

"You speak truth, which pleases me. Perhaps you have some intelligence left in that addled brain of yours. Adver Cormal, please inform our friend why I have chosen Vesperi for this honor."

Cormal, descended from of a pair of Rasselerian thieves, had skin always shriveled as though a fish out of water and webbed feet, though his hands bore only extra flaps of skin. He spread his fingers apart as he spoke. "She may be the silver weapon."

Both Garadin and Raino choked on air, but only Raino lacked the forbearance to restrain his shock after. "But that must be a lie!"

"A lie?" Romer sounded thoughtful. "What would any of us gain from a lie like that? You know what the prophecy foretells when the weapon appears. *With it, all will again be one.*"

Garadin was at a loss. "But she never—I never saw anything." He had lived at Sellwyn Manor for a decade, had presided over her brother's birth. She had shown no signs of possessing magic.

"The first report of her . . . skill was not received until she was sent to the convent, well after you had left Sellwyn." Nouin supplied the details as he burned the sheets by candle flame, filling the room with the smell of smoke and ashes, but thankfully no incense. The advers did not keep altars at Mandat Hall. "We did not think much of it then. A nun died, and the Sellwyn girl saw her last. But Cormal reported a shift in the field that same day."

"A Rasselerian feels a breeze the same day a nun goes missing and this is considered proof of the weapon?" Garadin was surprised Romer could be taken in so easily.

"That is not all, old man." Nouin did not hide his disdain. "Cormal came to us again three weeks ago reporting the same sensation he had had then. A fortnight later, we received word from Lord Sellwyn that a suitor of Vesperi's had gone missing. He was certain his daughter had something to do with it and asked, again, for her banishment."

Panic's fingers grasped at Garadin's throat. *This will not turn out well, not with that girl involved.* He pleaded with Romer. "But if she is the weapon foretold, then why have you not killed her? Why would you bring her here instead? The prophecy implies she will destroy us!"

Romer picked up an apple from a bowl near his bed. He pulled a sharpened bone from his robe and sliced into the fruit, making a multitude of fast, precise incisions. "To keep her close, of course. I am not yet convinced she poses a threat. None have seen her wield the gift. And if she does have it, well"—he retied the makeshift blade to his robe then tossed the apple in the air, and it fell, splitting into dozens of strips, each one twisting as it sank to the floor—"I will deal with her. As of now, with or without magic, she may prove useful to us. Rather, she may be the perfect weapon for our needs. A woman with a mind of her own filled with a thirst for power? It will not take more than offering her the queenhood to sway her to our purposes."

Garadin knew better than to disagree. Romer had plans—foolhardy plans—but the timbre of his voice brokered no argument. If Vesperi was the weapon, then the prophecy was true and the Guj could do nothing to stop it. The silver weapon would be the end of their rule, the end of Medua. Garadin needed a plan to survive if the empire fell, a plan that involved getting as far away from civilization as possible.

"You will bring her here."

For a moment, Garadin let himself imagine the Guj's brown eyes were not on him.

"Sellwyn will welcome you, will he not?"

Garadin nodded. There was no use denying it. He and Jahnas had bonded right away, like men with a keen eye for self-preservation. "Yes, my master."

"First thing in the morning, you will leave for Sellwyn. Bring this letter with you." Romer snapped his fingers, and Adver Nouin handed over a piece of parchment sealed with an imprinted fist, the mark of Saeth. "Entreat Sellwyn to give her up. She will come cheaply, I suspect."

Garadin raised his elbows. "As you wish."

CHAPTER 16
JANTO

Free time was not to come until after the climb, and that would not come until tomorrow evening, or so Sielban said over their breakfast table two weeks into the Murat. The slim man leapt from one edge of the table to another, balancing on his toes. His excitement was probably the most mysterious thing Janto had seen since the Murat began, but it made everyone else nervous. The plates and glasses shook with each footfall, yet Sielban made no sound as he landed.

"How many attempt to climb the mount?"

As each man raised his hand, Janto counted: Nap, Rall, Tonim, Flivio, and Hamsyn, who surprised Janto. Neville was not known for its rough terrain, and Hamsyn was a hunter who kept his bow, called the Old Girl, always nearby. It was a treasure, strung with silver thread and carved by his grandfather out of cherrywood that had been preserved in Rasseleria's swamps since ancient times.

"Excellent!" Sielban clasped his webbed hands together. "The rest of us will camp at the base, ready to assist if anyone has need. You will begin in an hour. Meet us at the edge of the grasses." Then he disappeared, causing Rall's cup to clatter to the table.

"I wish he would stop doing that."

The others laughed as Flivio teased, "You must work on your wishes, friend, because I see no hope of that man staying where he can be found." Flivio dipped his spoon back into his bowl of steaming oats.

Rall brandished his sausage toward Janto. "I thought you were to be my competition!"

Janto cringed. "I may have been speaking above my skill level that night," he offered by way of explanation. "And if you've paid any attention to my scrambling down the steeper bends, you'd know I speak truer now than I did then."

The other men laughed, but Nap clapped his shoulder. "A wise man knows his boundaries," he considered.

"And we'll have the pleasure of being waited on by a prince for the only time in our lives," Flivio finished with a sly grin.

Nap finished his thornberry tea, placing his mug back on the table. "I best be off to ready my pack for this Feat." The Wasylim raised his elbows and went in search of the path.

"He is right." Hamsyn laid down a half-eaten salmon pie. "I'm also off to pack."

Hamsyn rose to leave, but Janto waved him over, selecting a few items from the table that would keep: dried slivers of dark, peppered craval meat and thin wafers flecked with anise and rye seeds. He slipped them inside his pouch and handed it all over to Hamysn. "Take this. I'm certain Sielban has ways of knowing if any of you fare badly, but this climb will be tough, and you should keep nourishment nearby."

Hamsyn gave his thanks, stringing the pouch over his neck.

Rall laughed from the other end of the table. "I would hope my fellow climbers knew to bring food! I would hope it went without saying, but if not, all the better for me." The seasoned climber made his way with Hamsyn in the direction Nap had disappeared. Tonim and Flivio looked sheepish as they, too, gathered food from the table. Jerusho and Janto exchanged glances and tried not to laugh, sharing the same thought: *Thank Madel, I'm not climbing that peak.*

✳ ✳ ✳

Janto's boots hit the ground, and the release of his muscles felt so good, he fell to the ground and kissed it. The climb had started in the dusky pink grasses on the south face of Mount Frelom, their sticky seed pods dotting his pants, but black sand dominated here. He had delivered a fresh canteen to Rall on the northern face through a series of moving platforms that ascended it, powered by a force Janto could not name. It was his and Jerusho's job to go up them when one of the climbers called for aid. They used ropes to rappel down after. Apparently, Janto had taken a wrong turn—or several of them. He had hoped to make it back before the climbers did, but the starting line could not be seen, meaning this was the western side of the mountain. The sea between Braven and northern Rasseleria was a thin line of white above the dark sand.

They complained, but he forced his legs to start walking and fast, following the base of the mountain. The chill air felt like a steam bath compared to where he had just been. Climbing was definitely not for him. He wanted to lie down on the sand for hours and let it warm his skin. He hoped his fellow man of the plains fared better.

As he walked, a brown speck appeared on the horizon over the water. It grew closer with each step he took. Janto felt foreboding, remembering the last time he had seen something curious approach from afar, a horse and its feather-cloaked rider. Why would someone come to Braven and interrupt the Murat? It was unheard of. He murmured a prayer to Madel that Serra and his parents were safe.

By the time his legs had stopped aching, the speck had morphed into a canoe, and he could make out a few dark-haired heads within it. They reached the shore as Janto reached the edge of the beach where the grasses took over in earnest. To the east, he could make out Jerusho's form standing near their small camp.

Sielban walked briskly in Janto's direction. *He must have seen the paddlers.* His teacher's suit blended in effortlessly with the line of trees in the distance. There was no concern on Sielban's face when he reached him.

"There is a boat." Janto gestured toward it.

Sielban peered at him, his head cocked to one side. "Do boats always cause you such concern, princeling? We are on an island."

Janto sputtered. "I did not realize you knew them, Teacher. I thought it might be trouble."

Sielban flicked his tongue. "They come every day from the shore with our provisions and to prepare our meals." His sparkling eyes conveyed his amusement. "You must be a Lanserim first, Janto Albrecht, before you can be anything else. And Lanserim do not jump to conclusions so fast. Not everything is a mystery." His tongue lingered in the air for a moment. "And now you will excuse me. I must be fast before my next task."

Janto knew he should offer to help unload, but he was flabbergasted.

He leaned back against the mountain's slope and watched as the three men and Sielban piled a cart he had failed to notice with frozen bundles of meat, sacks of grain, and jugs of teas and ale. Laughter mixed with short gasps of pain drew his attention elsewhere. Near the base camp, Janto could make out two climbers coming down the mountain's path, carrying something between them.

"And now, my next task," came Sielban's voice by his ear, making Janto jump. How had he crossed the distance so fast? Sielban grinned then hurried over to the camp. Janto trailed behind him.

Jerusho reached the climbers first. Janto heard him bellow, "What happened? Did you reach the crest then impale yourself on it?"

Hamsyn and Tonim, shirtless, carried a contraption of ripped tunics strung across tree branches. A form answered from within the pallet. "If only. The women at home might forgive my voice if I had managed the Feat." Flivio's sharp timbre was unmistakable. "I lost a foothold and slid many yards until my leg got stuck inside a crevice. These two heard my *manly* cries of pain and reached me thirty minutes later—"

Hamsyn cut in. "Ten minutes later. You were not so far ahead of us as that!"

Flivio laughed, though pain furrowed his brow. "Can I save no pride? I am a man in pain here!"

Sielban shook his head at that. "A *child* with pains from broken bones. You are lucky to be on Braven. And to have such good friends to aid you." He waved his hand over an unnatural lump below Flivio's left knee, the size of Mar Pina's enormous meatballs. Janto grimaced, imagining how it must feel.

Sielban held his hand out flat then curled it into a fist and released it. Flivio bolted upright, his head covered in sweat but his face relaxed with relief.

"Teacher"—his tone was nearly worshipful—"thank you."

Sielban raised his elbows. "You are welcome. And before you ask it, no, you may not return to your climb. You are not healed yet. I can only set things right so time can do the rest. You must remain off your leg and stay down here with us, and you must drink plenty of water."

Flivio nodded in obedience, the quietest Janto had ever seen him. Hamsyn and Tonim lifted him up by the armpits, each man under one shoulder. The wounded man *umphed* at the effort. He wiggled his hurt leg as they deposited him on a bale of pink grasses.

"Men," Sielban addressed the rescuers, "you may return to your climbs, if you wish."

Janto stood agape at Sielban's choice of words, but the others did not seem to notice. Another utterance to ponder later.

Tonim laughed, his dark blond hair shifting as he shook it. "There is no hope of catching up. Flivio was on Nap's tail up the southern face, but no one has seen Rall for hours. Better to stay here and celebrate victory with them. Besides, I should keep an eye on my brother."

"Agreed," said Hamsyn, "and I have learned climbing is not my Feat."

Janto scooped up each man's canteen and took them to the water bucket, returning full ones to a round of thank yous. Hamsyn took his in silence, lost in thought before addressing Sielban. "Teacher, I am uncertain what my Feat should be. I had thought it hunting, but my skills are nearly useless in the cover of Braven's woods and climbing is not my strength. I'm adequate at archery but hopeless at racing far distances—the burning in my lungs rises far too fast. What should I pursue here? I am afraid my Murat will know no victories."

Sielban cocked his head. "How many men have you known who have been to the Murat?"

"Not many. Two of my village's council. The man who runs Carafin's markets mentioned he had gone when news got out that my application was accepted. There is the king—" he glanced briefly at Janto "—and his man, Ser Gomalyn, who comes to inspect our holdings once a year."

"Have any of these men told you what titles they claimed at the Murat?"

"Well, no, though the king, of course, won the archery Feat in his year." Janto had heard the honor brought up many times by servants and members of the council, but it struck him now that his father had never boasted of hitting thirty bull's-eyes in only fifty minutes of competition.

"Did you wonder what the others had won, after you met them?"

Hamsyn stared toward the woods as he considered the question. "Well, no, I was too impressed by them. Each man struck me as someone to admire, and I enjoyed being with them, talking with them. I don't even know what my councilmen achieved."

Sielban flicked his tongue over his teeth. "I have lived here many years, training men for Lansera and its good fortune. They have all been champions when they left, though there are never more than a few with a title to their names. For most, those come with time." He cocked his head to the other side. "You have learned limits, Nevillim, which is more than most men can say. Do not worry about a title. You are already succeeding here."

Hamsyn's lips curved up. "Thank you, Teacher."

Sielban raised his elbows but quickly dropped them, cupping a hand to his left ear as though the wind spoke to him. His lips moved wordlessly for a moment, then he declared, "This Feat is nearing its end. The rest of you should see to water and food for our last few climbers. The victor will soon win his acclaim." He winked at Hamsyn. "Not all Muraters win fame for Feats, but the celebrations do provide a nice change for one as long on Braven as I."

Sielban leapt toward the woods, disappearing faster than Janto could blink.

✳ ✳ ✳

They had dealt a second round of Sloshed Ryn when Rall came around the mountain's curve. He was exhausted, stumbling forward. Janto grabbed a filled canteen as he rushed over to greet him.

"Did you reach the peak?" He tilted the water into Rall's opened mouth. "Were you the first?"

Water dribbled down his tired face, but there was no mistaking his satisfaction. Janto hugged him. "He did it!" he called out to the others who were soon upon them. "He defeated Mount Frelom!"

Hamsyn hopped from foot to foot, while Tonim clapped Rall's back. Jerusho remained at the supplies with Flivio resting his leg. "Congratulations, Rall! First name for the record books!"

Rall wiped a dribble of water from his chin. "Thank you, all of you. And I aim to gloat, but I may collapse first." To Janto, he said, "More water, please," and then, "Nap is not far behind."

Janto was relieved to hear it. He knew Braven was safe, and yet with Flivio's fall, he had been anxious. He went to fetch more water, thinking of the feast the sailors were preparing.

"It is almost ready," Sielban whispered into his ear, making him jump. "But first, you must listen to their tales. A good king always gives his men their glory."

What did I do to merit that piece of advice? Their reappeared teacher offered Rall his congratulations, and Janto went back to wait at the path.

He did not have to wait long. Nap's short, stocky shadow rounded the bend in no more than ten minutes.

"Second." He looked disappointed but mostly exhausted as Janto gave him water. "But what a place to be the first loser! The view from the peak before the angels came"—Janto's brow arched and Nap reconsidered—"well, not angels, maybe, but little creatures that floated on wisps of air and spoke my name." Nap clasped his hands. "I swear I'm not crazy. That's what I saw. And the view! It was amazing. You would think the clouds would obscure it, but I swear I might have seen your city's sparkling bridge from there."

Janto had never heard Nap speak so much. Perhaps the air had been too thin at the peak. Something had to explain his hallucination, but did it matter what, when the effects were so joyous? "That sounds amazing. Now you must come and rest awhile. You are the second to finish but the last down."

"How so?"

"The others were disqualified," Janto said, and Nap's jaw dropped. Janto assured him, "For good reasons. Flivio hurt his leg sliding down one of the faces, and the others carried him. They returned over an hour ago."

"How disheartening it would be to not only lose but be unable to finish and see those sights!" Nap wondered.

"I would not say the same to them," Janto considered. "It would be sticking a leech into a fresh wound."

Nap agreed, though he appeared more saddened over their inability to finish than his second-place ranking.

✶ ✶ ✶

The feast that night was memorable, mainly because Sielban stayed with them through the whole meal. There was, of course, much backslapping for the two men who finished the Feat, but Hamsyn, Flivio, and Tonim hardly complained. Sielban, right after pouring the first round of ale, lit on the edge of the table and announced, "Tonight, we have our first champion."

The cheers erupted immediately but did not last. Everyone was completely worn out, even Jerusho and Janto, who had spent most of their time on the ground. The intense sun over the meadows had affected them, too, as did all that hopping between platforms.

"The name of Rall Basilo will go forth on the lips of our provisioners tonight and be recorded forever in the records of the Murat." Sielban had been watching Tansic and Oro, the two moons so close they appeared in the shape of an eight rather than a pair of circles. But he lowered his gaze to scan the faces of each man at the table. "Do you know what it means to be recorded in history, for Lanserim to know your names?"

Rall shook his head, a buttered clover roll in hand. None of them ventured a guess. They had not grown up with constant reminders of family legacies, Janto realized. It was an easy answer for him, having spent his life surrounded by tapestries depicting the founding of his kingdom by a woman pulling a cart and the splitting of it in a briar patch.

Janto stood. "It means you are now bonded to those who know your name. You have achieved glory, and they will expect glorious things from you."

"Very good." Sielban raised his elbows in recognition. As he did, a powerful silver light flashed far away, visible just above Sielban's right shoulder. It was gone fast, though Janto thought he saw a residual haze left in its wake. He raised his hand to point it out but remembered the day they had chased feathers and Rall and Hamsyn had laughed away his creature in the woods. His hand went back down.

Sielban did not note his averted gaze. "Rall Basilo will always now be known as a great climber, a man who can accomplish great things. Now, child"—he gestured to Rall—"what sort of things will you do with that standing?"

"I—I do not know. But if it makes my wife and children proud, then I will do whatever I need to."

Sielban raised his elbows in acknowledgment and addressed the group. "Think of this, as you continue your Murat. You have spent months in physical training, but you must also be men with actions that speak a different language than fists and weapons. The Murat is not about Feats but about preparing you to be the men Lansera needs, the men Madel knows will best serve Her purposes."

Janto nodded along with the others, pushing silver flashes out of mind as he reached for a clover roll.

Jerusho rose from his chair, a wooden mug in hand. "To Rall, our first champion, and to becoming who Madel wants us to be."

"Here! Here!" They agreed in rounds about the table. The ale differed from the thick brew they had had on other evenings. This one was blond and went down tasting of apricots.

Sielban did not disappear as usual but leapt from the corner of the table to the ground and wedged himself between Jerusho and Nap. The men hid their amazement at dining with Sielban in their midst and dug in heartily.

CHAPTER 17
VESPERI

The horse huffed as the cherry-sized ball of silver energy buzzed through its mane like a jocal fly. Vesperi focused on channeling the talent in her palm into the faint stream connected to that ball. It was so indistinct no one would notice it but her, and her control over it was thrilling. Besides, if her concentration faltered, no one would blame a dead horse on her. Vesperi rarely deigned to enter the stables—the servants cared for the animals, and she would never let herself be considered one of them.

Smells of tobacco, sour ale, and sweat alerted her she was not alone. She lowered her hand, and the ball of energy dissipated. The guard Lokas, the least appealing of the lot, wore a faded green tunic embroidered with House Sellwyn's viper, though the garment's tattered threads obscured its raised head. *Father ought to dress his men better.*

The guard cleared his throat, yellow spit hitting the ground. "Your father wants to see you, Vespy."

"Don't call me that." She had always hated the nickname. It had not suited a four-year-old child, much less a woman of nineteen. But Lokas was one of her father's personal guards, the only ones who dared chastise her when her father or Uzziel were out of sight. The others had learned not to trifle with her.

"I will call you what I want, whore." His voice was gruffer than usual, and his breath reeked of the stale brew the guards kept in their quarters. The barrels sat in direct sunlight most of the day, making the ale hot and rancid. Lord Sellwyn probably had to pull Lokas out of one to come get her. She nearly giggled at the image of her slender father struggling with an ogre of a man like him, dripping with ale.

"I have never been your whore, Lokas." She said his name with disdain. "Is that what has you in such a displeasing mood?" She had bedded most of the guards by the time she left for the convent—it was the easiest way to control them and sometimes fun. Lokas, however, repulsed her with his constant drunkenness.

Lokas spat at her. "I wouldn't take you if you lay down in front of me, legs spread wide. The smell of your used-up cunt makes me ill."

She wiped the spit from her face with the loose velvet at the end of her sleeve. Then she made to soothe him with warm tones, making sure to brush up against him. "Oh, Lokas. There is no need for such venom. I refused you out of love—I did not want your ego bruised when you couldn't perform. Liquor can have that effect, you know."

"Shut your mouth, harlot." He prodded her side with a dagger always kept in hand. He was not fast enough to pull it from his belt if attacked, so he held it instead. "Let's go."

She complied. He did not have enough wits left to make this game of insults a challenge. They walked on the cobblestone path back toward the manor house and over the bridge that crossed the dry riverbed of the Sell. It had not rained in western Medua for as long as Vesperi had been at the convent, though the air had felt heavy of late. They reached the main door, and it creaked opened as three guards pushed it from inside. She was tempted to see if her talent could push it faster. Perhaps it wouldn't sear if she let it out as a wave rather than focusing it into a stream. If it worked, the guards would be spared a lot of effort, but what reason did she have to make their lives easier? Her father often said tired guards were loyal guards. Maybe someday she could burn through a wooden door without destroying what lay beyond it. She had already lit a couple of incense sticks when practicing and nothing else had flamed.

And of course, she had done the same to two people. The burning was completely unexpected that first time, when she charred Sister Vandely to a crisp. The woman had ordered Vesperi to stay behind after a training session. She had rambled on about submission and duty, and Vesperi was not in the mood to listen. The moon Esye had been especially clear that night, and Vesperi stared at it through the window as the woman had droned on. As her anger built, Vesperi had fixated more on the moon, noting how the others formed a ring around it. Sister Vandely rapped her with a stick to get her attention, and Vesperi had raised a hand to slap the old crone. But she did not hit flesh. Instead, a blazing silver shaft nearly blinded her, and her palm sliced through a sheet of falling black ashes. The smell had made her gag, the same as when her father burned runaways outside the gates of Sellwyn. Vesperi hoped to do the burning for her father someday without using wood at all. When she mastered her talent, he would see how invaluable she was to him. Better a wizard as an asset than an enemy.

"Lokas, you can leave me now. I will be safe inside." She did not wait for his reply but went through the doorway and up the stone steps to the open-air walkway, happy not to hear his plodding gait follow. She did not stop to touch the carving but kept on toward the manor—Father was waiting. As she walked down the hall, servants with brooms in hand darted away. One weaver was too slow getting back to his loom. She noted his balding head of black hair in case he should dare look her way again. If she had to endure the guards' fists and lashes, then so did everyone else. That her father allowed her that power was dignifying. Perhaps she'd have the weaver's cloak trampled. But destroying a good cloak with the guards so shabbily dressed would be a waste. She would have to mention their lack of repair to Father.

Bellick, another of his guards, stood in front of the door to Lord Sellwyn's chamber. She gave her hips a bit of a swish and tugged down her chemise enough to reveal the white trim of her bodice. He gave her a complete top-to-bottom inspection. He had been one of her first lovers, the comeliest man in the manor with those dimples and sage-green eyes. She would not mind another tussle if she got him alone.

Placing her hand on his chest and tracing her fingers downward but not too far, she greeted him. He shuddered with pleasure but hastily straightened up. "Your father is waiting inside."

"I know that. He can wait a little longer," she whispered in his ear, giving full breath to each syllable.

Bellick pushed her away reluctantly. "He's in a foul mood. I would not try him if I was you."

"I know how to handle my father."

Bellick laughed in her face as he pushed open the door. Lord Sellwyn hunched over his desk, scribbling with his favorite pen made from the hide and taxidermied head of a forest viper, complete with fangs. Its venom could kill, should her father decide to pierce someone's skin with it rather than merely lace it into his words.

She took a deep breath and walked in, closing the door behind her. Lord Sellwyn did not acknowledge her.

"Father? Lokas said you wanted to see me?"

He did not shift as he spoke. "I searched for you in Uzziel's room. Then I went to the kitchen, to see if you had joined the other women, but you were not there—again."

"You know I hate the kitchen."

"What you hate does not affect me. It is your place to be there whenever your brother does not need you." He barely spoke above a whisper. "Since you are so content to stay at Sellwyn Manor, then you need to learn to stay where you belong."

"So that's why you called for me." She had thought it might be about the suitors. It was always about the suitors. There had been one more this past week, Lord Dusen Rolang, a man so old his feather-thin frame had to be supported by two of his servants. She should have put him out of his misery, but instead she refused to see him at all. Lord Sellwyn's daughter would not wed a decrepit old man. Her father should realize it would portray him as weak.

"I called you here because I do not know what to do with you." Jahnas Sellwyn laid down his pen. His green-eyed gaze licked its way toward where she leaned against the wall, not having been asked to sit. "You reject every man I allow here." He strained his lips into a thin line. "Scare them away or insult them until they demand I have you beat for insolence. Saeth only knows what happened to Lord Agler."

"Agler was an idiot. An affront. I thought you meant him as a joke."

"A joke? Do you not know how desperate I am to be rid of you? I don't care if a slime-sucking frogman offered to take you away. If one hopped here with a bag full of souzers clutched in his webbed feet, I would throw you at him. I want your dowry, *darling daughter*. And I want you out of my hands." He held her in a narrowed gaze for a moment then returned to his parchments. "What happened to Agler?"

The lie leapt to her lips easily—she told it to anyone who asked. *Why, I asked Agler for time to consider his offer,* she would say, *one more night. Agler left the room, and I watched as he exited the manor through the door to the walkway, watched the light brighten the dark hallway for a moment then dim again as the door closed. Then I never saw him again, and what could I do about that? I cannot force a man to wait for me.* Such a simple tale, and her reputation was such that everyone believed she had scared him off. Everyone but her father. He knew her better, knew she would not meekly agree to consider a suitor's offer. She was her father's daughter, and by Saeth's fist, no one else would ever know her as well.

Her heart pounded, and she felt as though a child again, peeking at him from the kitchen doorway, hoping he would ask her to join him at the table one night, if she could prove how worthy she was. This was that moment, time to show him, show him everything. She had not singed one horse's hair.

"I killed him."

He was at her side faster than she had ever seen him move before and yanked her by the shoulders. She did not flinch.

"You killed him? Is that what you said?" His voice was a hiss.

Vesperi stood firm. "Yes. He was a spy, Father, a spy from Lansera. One of those bloody Ravens." She did not blink. Now was not the time for submission. He must hear her.

"You are telling me I let a spy into my household and only you noticed it?"

Oh no. Vesperi had not considered him taking it as an insult, a grave misstep. His pride was too quick to bruise.

"You could not have known," she placated him. "Only when we were alone did he make mistakes. He called me *Lady* several times." She spoke fast, trying to pacify him before he really grew angry. "I killed him for you, Father, to protect the Sellwyns."

He loosened his grip a little, and her heart leapt. She strengthened her plea. "Don't you see how much use I can be to you? I can get closer to your enemies than your spies because I am a woman. They will not suspect me. And that's not all I can do." She raised her pointer finger toward the high window and willed the energy to come slowly so as not to alarm him.

"When are you going to give this up." He groaned and pulled away from her to pace the rug on the floor, sending cockroaches scurrying like servants. "You are a woman, Vesperi, a woman. Uzziel will inherit Sellwyn Manor, not you. He is my son."

"He is a blight on us!" The yell escaped her. It *always* came back to Uzziel, that pathetic whelp. Her talent churned rapidly, caution forgotten, and she did not care, did not want to control it. She forged on.

"Uzziel has been in his sick bed for all of his eleven worthless years. He should have been put to death at birth like the offal he is. The advers proclaimed it so."

"Do not speak of your betters, Vesperi. You are the mistake."

"Fine." She spat out the word. "Fine. I'm a mistake. I'm an embarrassment. Uzziel is your heir, the light of your life. But what happens when he dies? Do you think he is going to outlive you? Truly?"

He stopped pacing and bent over at the waist, chortling at her words. Vesperi shrank against the wall. *This is not good.* She had never heard him laugh before—never. Her father was a serious man intent on amassing and maintaining his power. That left no time for laughter.

The talent ceased within her instantly, and its absence left her cold. Thank Saeth it had not built up enough for her to demonstrate it. She thought he would be proud of it, thrilled he could use her to further his reach, but she could not know how he would react now. Not when he was laughing.

When he caught his breath, Lord Sellwyn said, "What will I do? *What will I do?* If Uzziel does not live, I will disown you and your mother and take a new wife."

"What?" She could barely speak. It wasn't supposed to go this way. "You, you would do that?" Disowned females were outlaws, tainted, untouchable. Only one option remained for them, one place they could find shelter, if it could be called that. "You would send me to Thokketh?" Saying the name gave her chills. It was a place of exile, a fortress built of ice on the edge of the desolate Giants' Pathway. Females unclaimed by liege or nobleman ended their lives there in bitter cold and banishment. No one came back from Thokketh. The sheven in the moat waters and their always-opened mouths tore them to shreds if they tried to escape.

He could not mean it. He wouldn't send her away. She was a Sellwyn, she was his. Jahnas Sellwyn did not give up his property. He burned his deserters rather than let them escape, destroyed what betrayed him. He did not *abandon* it. This was—this was not right.

"My doors would be locked to you faster than Uzziel's blood ran cold." The laughter again, mocking her. She wanted to cry, to wail, to beg, but only her instinct worked and it screamed to run, to leave his presence before he could shame her anymore.

She flung open the door, slamming it into Bellick. His curses mixed in with more of her father's horrible cackling amusement. It sounded louder than it should have, echoing through the hall and her head. She ran toward her room at the far end of the manor. *As far from Father's room as possible*, she realized as she flew. How could she have been so stupid to believe he would ever give her what she wanted, that she meant anything to him? She was more afraid than she could ever remember.

The kitchen doorway loomed up ahead. She stopped running, thinking to warn her mother, too. The room had no door; the heat from the kitchen's five stone-encased ovens warmed the corridors, and the women would sweat to death if enclosed within it. It reeked of bloodworms roasting in the central oven, their putrid scent akin to the fumes that rose from Durn's swamps. With the river dried up, no game came to graze outside Sellwyn manor, and everyone had to make do with insects. Plenty of those crept around in dark corners.

The kitchen's walls were smeared black from someone's vain attempt to clean the smoke stains. Nearly all of the manor's women were there, stirring one of the stew pots, poking at the hot coals in the oven, or huddled together beneath the sole window cracked open about as wide as Vesperi's pinkie.

Lady Sellwyn was at the closest oven, her back to Vesperi. She wore her usual mud-colored skirt with threads of pressed copper sewn into it so it would sparkle in the light, if she ever saw the light and the copper had not turned a dull green. A green apron covered her ruffled chemise, and her dark hair was pulled back in a snood of the same shade, the color of Sellwyn's viper. She was a slight woman. Vesperi could not imagine the agony it must have caused her to give birth the many times she had. Only she and Uzziel had lived past their first birthdays.

Her mother pushed a pot into the oven and rested a giant wooden spoon on the counter. She spun around, perhaps sensing Vesperi's gaze. Her face dripped with sweat. Rust-colored liquid from the pot stained the apron. For a moment, all she did was stare, shocked to see her daughter in the kitchen, much less the manor. She probably had not known Vesperi had returned to Sellwyn. Vesperi had not sought her.

When Lady Sellwyn reached out an arm, beckoning her forward, Vesperi bolted. She ran back into the hallway and lunged past the last few doors to her room. Hot tears poured down her face, and she cursed them as she grabbed at her bedcover. No, it would never do as a sack. It was covered with Sellwyn's crest, the snake stitched into every patch.

She would be found out before she made it to the next town. *Next town?* There was nowhere she could go in Medua. She pulled off the sheet instead, its edges frayed. It would not last, but she did not have time to search for something else to use. She had to move fast to get to the mountains. She had to run.

✳ ✳ ✳

The riverbed of the Sell cracked from thirst, a massive piece of lacework stretching ever westward. Vesperi's feet struck the dry clay with a louder stomp than she had hoped, though no one should be seeking her yet, at least not here. Her father would not think she had the nerve to run, and when others tried to escape, they went for the cover of the swamps to the northeast or to the eastern road to Qiltyn, hoping to outrace both her father's mounts and the liegeless men living in the wilderness surrounding it. All hanged from Lord Sellwyn's rosewood tree in the end, but they never ran west. No one ran to Lansera. They'd already been rejected there.

He would decipher her course eventually but not for a while. She hoped—nay, depended—on his underestimation of her. His inattention, that lack of the regard she had craved only half an hour ago, might be what saved her. She gripped her improvised pack more tightly.

A dark form loomed around the first bend, and her heart fell. It couldn't be him, not *this* fast—

"I am not your father, Vesperi." A dulcet voice she could not immediately place called out to her. But she did recognize his lengthy legs that dangled from where he sat on the riverbed's bank.

"Lorne? What are you—how did you—why are you here?" She could not begin to guess how he knew she had gone, much less where to find her. The voice in her head shouting *Run! Run!* grew louder, but she resisted it. He might simply think she was out for a walk . . . a woman, walking alone at twilight. It was ludicrous, but she had to try.

When she drew close enough to read the boredom on his face, he spoke, "I am not going to tell him. You are making my task easier, actually. Uzziel will be much calmer without you stirring him up."

She could not bring herself to bat an eyelash at him, no room left in her thoughts with the pounding in her head and the panic in her chest.

"Take this." He handed her a petite sack.

"What am I to do with it?" She undid the tie. The heavy scent of honey and musk made her gag. *Fallowent.*

"You will need it."

"I think I'm tall enough already."

He laughed at that, sniffed the air, and reached behind him, producing two sturdy sticks of rosewood and a square of fabric coated in some sort of resin. "You will need this too. It's going to rain."

She took it from him, eyes round. He fixed his azure ones on them. "Good luck, Vesperi Sellwyn." Sadness crept into his playful tone. "You will need it. And so will the rest of us."

He disappeared into the brush on higher ground. Vesperi did not stop to process how bizarre his behavior had been or why he would let her go. She needed to run. It was all she could think to do.

As she took the next step forward, a drop of rain hit her head. More fell on the parched ground as she went, strikes on the stretched skin of an urum drum.

CHAPTER 18
JANTO

Janto's vision blurred as he walked along the path, trees and bushes indistinct, as though spied through an inverted reading glass. He had spent the morning at the archery Feat, shooting flying-squirrel-shaped target after flying-squirrel-shaped target to no avail. After dashing through the woods for an hour, wasting not an arrow as he picked off each target he could find, Sielban's voice had rang in his ear. Tonim broke the king's record: all thirty targets hit in forty minutes. After the announcement, Janto had yelled in frustration, but only the birds stirred. By the time he had reached the others, he meant the congratulations he gave Tonim with a backslap. He also commiserated with Hamsyn over how neither hunter had won before heading out on his own to make peace with the defeat.

The air was crisp, as though a breeze had swept up from the Giants' Pathway. Around the next bend, he sighted Jerusho by a stream, holding his fishing pole. The Ertion stood tall, no sign of weariness in his body—he had not attempted the archery Feat. His head bobbed with the current, eyes fixed on the water. As Janto drew close, Jerusho raised his fingers to his lips to hush him. He pointed to the water where water bugs skimmed the murky surface, leaving little pools no grander than a cent-piece in their wake. Jerusho's brow was smooth, excitement evident only in the shaking of his free hand as though a tambourine were in his grasp. Janto's eyes crossed from both confusion and missed targets cycling through his mind.

As another bout of weariness came, something sparkled in the water. Something thin as a scroll.

"Is that the gran—"

Jerusho clapped his hand over Janto's mouth. "Silence!"

Janto watched the fish wiggle, a saw of brushed steel in motion. The humongous creature was nearly four feet long. How could he not have seen it before? Yet each time he blinked, it disappeared until he focused on it with crossed eyes.

The line jerked. Jerusho used two hands to hold it. He raised his arms high in the air and lifted the line out, stepping backward as he did.

"The net!" Jerusho yelled as the granfaylon rose out of the water, exposing its flat snout. "Behind the tree!"

Janto spotted and grabbed it in one movement then held it beneath the struggling creature. It was completely out of the water, but he could only catch glimpses every few seconds. He eased the net forward blindly, adjusting his aim as Jerusho called, "Left! Right! Higher!" Then the Ertion unhooked the creature's fat lip, the thickest part of it Janto could see. The fish fell into the net, and Janto nearly dropped it. It weighed far more than he would have guessed, heavy as the fattest trout he had fished out of the River Call.

"You did it! You caught the granfaylon!"

Jerusho laughed raggedly. "I did, didn't I?" He leaned against a nearby pine and wiped the sweat from his head. The fish struggled fiercely in the net, and Jerusho pulled out his knife, a simple blade with a handle of beige rock from the Ertion quarries. He shook the fish out a few yards from the banks. One hand on the wiggling body was not enough to settle it, so Janto knelt down, trapping its bottom half. Jerusho took the knife and sliced into the shimmering flesh above its eye. It thrashed more violently, and he cut a deep "X" into its head. The fish flexed once more and went limp. As it did, the full body formed on the ground, no longer flickering. Its flat, iridescent backside only made it appear paper thin. The fish was about three inches thick, and it would make quite the feast for the men.

Now that the killing of the fish was complete, Jerusho flushed red with excitement. He clapped Janto on the shoulder with a *whomph*. "You must be a good luck charm. I have been tracking this fish for days, but it never stayed so well in sight until you joined me around that tree."

"Give me no credit, Jerusho! This victory is all yours. I did not think it existed until I saw its scales shimmering in the water. *You* came to the Murat knowing you would leave with a purse full of those scales."

"Hmm, I like that idea. Would your father accept a new fish-scale currency? I will be the only one with it, but that seems a fine idea to me."

Janto laughed, but his thoughts zoomed. Right in front of him was proof the granfaylon existed. If it did, what else was possible? What if the creature in the woods that first morning had been—

"Don't keep staring off like a craval beast that's forgotten where the grass is, help me move it. I have been wanting to rub this catch in Flivio's face for weeks."

"Of course." Janto lifted its tail. "Lead the way."

✳ ✳ ✳

The fish sizzled over a fire not long after, its fat sparking as it dripped down the spit. The others had been amazed to see it, and Jerusho enjoyed their attention, especially Flivio's fake faint as he and Janto came around the bend. Janto thrummed with the excitement of it and with the certitude that another creature hid in those woods for him. He scanned the tree line constantly, hoping for something bright and shiny.

"You must go find it, Janto. There is not much time left in our Murat." Hamsyn's hand fell to his shoulder and squeezed. "And you must take the Old Girl. She's the best weapon here." He held out his treasured bow.

"I could not." The hunt felt preordained, but Janto would not risk marring the beautiful weapon during it. He had no idea what lay before him.

"If you don't, I will spread rumors of a prince refusing a gift from his fellow Murater." Hamsyn smiled as he made the threat, but it had the desired effect. Janto raised his elbows in defeat. He brushed his fingers over the Old Girl's polished curve. It felt smooth as Serra's skin.

Just as he cocked his finger to test the string, a bedazzling, silver flash shone in the woods. Janto jumped to his feet, bow clenched in hand.

"If only I could see what you see now," Hamsyn said, pushing him forward. "Go, my prince. Go."

CHAPTER 19
SERRA

"A re you all right?" Poline leaned toward Serra at the breakfast table full of stewed oats and dried fruits. "You are pale."

Serra nodded to her blonde-haired friend who never failed to treat the younger initiates as her grandchildren. "I'm fine, I promise. I waited too long to break my fast this morning." She had taken on the same ghastly pallor as the initiates, but for a much different reason. They would be leaving in three days and were not allowed to discuss their decisions on whether or not to continue as novices. Ryn Cladio gave them the instructions himself, after their morning rituals two days ago.

She . . . well, she had felt especially relaxed and clear-minded that same morning, maybe for the first time since finding the bodies. Her good mood had lasted up to the moment when Ryn Simsi, a Rasselerian, struck the ritual bell and Serra opened her eyes. It was then she saw a Brother near the western wall of the temple, his gray hood contrasting with the green, pressed reeds. His presence made sense—the appearance of one of Madel's closest servants might deepen the initiates' meditations, taking them to a place of greater tranquility—but Serra had tensed. If destined for this life, maybe the Brother's presence would have brought her comfort and peace, but in her experience, Brothers did nothing but spout confusing prophecies and refuse to give her straight answers.

After acknowledging the Brother, Ryn Cladio had instructed the initiates to confide their decisions in a priest when ready. They were not to share them with each other to avoid rumors spreading as to why anyone made the choice they did. When some of them returned as novices in two weeks, they would know what those choices were. Lourda had pulled Ryn Simsi aside that very afternoon, and her face lit up as she confided in the little marshman, the joy of her decision easily read in the happy wrinkles around her eyes. Serra had laughed, imagining Lourda's someday parishioners hesitating to confide in a woman who wore her emotions so easily.

She had watched as Poline did the same the next day with Ryn Gylles, though Serra could not discern what decision Poline had come to. Her older roommate always smiled. What she did see, though, above Poline's head, had been an effervescent, blue orb suspended in the air like a raindrop that forgot to fall. Quickly, the orb vanished, and Serra knew she was seeing things.

But she wasn't. Each time an initiate gave his or her decision, a lambent orb had appeared above their heads before flaring and vanishing. After two days of watching it, Serra was jumpy enough to shriek whenever a butterfly flitted by.

With Poline's eyes on her, Serra scooped out a generous helping of the gloopy oats. She had little appetite, in truth, but the earthy steam lifted her spirits a tad, regardless. Poline was satisfied with the overture and turned her attention to the others at the table. "Vironyl, you should eat some more, too. You look near to fainting."

Vironyl, a middle-aged Meditlan, reached for the ladle. His hand shook as Serra passed it to him. The strange orbs playing Lash the Feather with her frayed nerves were one thing, but she was glad to be spared the choice the initiates were making. She couldn't imagine deciding her life's course on a few weeks of lessons and rituals, but she knew what it would be, if she had to make it. *Flee*. Blue orbs, human skins, and proximity to the Brothers were not things she would ever choose. The unexplainable was undeniably alive in Lansera, and she did not want to be near it any longer.

Yet her time here *would* make her a better queen for Janto. She had learned much about her people, about Madel, and about how life shut up in Callyn made ignorance of both easy. If she was to be the Serra of Lansera that Ryn Cladio had named her, she would do well not to accept the walls of the castle as her world in the future.

Another initiate walked into the kitchen cabin, Rynna Gemni right behind her. The priestess's beautiful hair was bound in a braid, but

Serra first noticed the orbs over their heads. She focused on her oats, imprinting her mind with their cardamom tans and pearly creams, colors that were meant to be there. When she raised her head, Serra nearly screamed.

A Brother stood outside the window, staring at her with no eyes she could see and surrounded in a coruscating blue haze. His voice reached out to her through the glass with a frosty bite. "It is time. Come."

No one else stirred. Serra trembled and examined her bowl again. Poline put a hand on her shoulder. "You do seem ill, Lady Serra." She called out, "Rynna Gemni, please come here. We need you."

Serra tried to wave away the help and saw that the Brother was gone. Rynna Gemni soon filled her gaze instead. The rynna tucked her braid inside her sheath and leaned over Serra.

"What's wrong?" Her voice was sweet as the syrup Mar Pina served with creamed cheese dumplings.

"I am fine." Serra's voice shook so no one believed her.

The rynna felt her wrist, closed her eyes, counted, and opened them again. Serra had never seen Queen Lexamy do *that* when a servant fell ill. "You have no fever, though your blood flows faster than it should. Did something upset you?"

"Yes, there was a—" Could she tell them? If the others had seen him, they surely would have mentioned it. Even in Enjoin, a Brother's appearance did not go unnoted. And how would she explain the dread that had come over her? They would think her mad for being afraid of Madel's servants. She could not say they were wrong.

She gulped. "It was nothing. Perhaps all the tension in the air is getting to me." She took Poline's hand reassuringly in her own. "You know 'Grandmother' here. She would have us in our huts, resting all day, if she could."

Poline pursed her lips but the others laughed.

"That's the truth." Colini picked up his spoon again. "She would call you over if one of us stubbed a toe."

Poline's consternation quickly resolved. "Well, someone needs to look after the likes of you—I cannot imagine a rattier group taking care of Lansera's people."

"All the same," Rynna Gemni took Serra's arm, "I'm taking Serra to my hut until I'm certain this is a passing mood."

Serra let herself be led from the common area, no excuse leaping to mind. "Thank you, Rynna. It's probably not necessary, but I would not mind some rest."

The rynna's braid fell against her tanned skin as they walked toward the semicircle of priests' huts surrounding the temple's rear. Ryn Gylles leaned against his doorway as they neared. Serra raised her elbows to him, but rather than return the gesture, he stepped into their path. "Gemni, how did you know I was in need of our initiate here? Did Madel whisper it in your ear?"

"No, I did not know. She took ill in the common room."

"That's not true." Serra was unwilling to lie to her guide. "At least, not completely."

"What do you mean? Either you felt unwell or you did not. If you fetched our healer, then something was wrong. Correct me, but drawing attention to yourself here has never been your goal."

"I did not mean to. Poline thought I looked pale, and she called Rynna Gemni over. I *am* fine."

Rynna Gemni nodded. "You are. Your blood was racing, but there is more color now in your cheeks. If you want to go with Gylles, I see no reason to force you in my hut."

"Thank you. I would like to speak with Ryn Gylles." She trusted him, and she needed someone to confide in. There was too much pounding in her brain to keep it all hidden. She raised her elbows to Rynna Gemni in dismissal, remembering too late she had no right to do so here. *Habits are hard to break.*

"Time for one of our walks, then?" Ryn Gylles took her arm. "I want to know what the princess thinks of insect migration—"

She interrupted him with a hug.

"Wha–what?"

She released her hold. "I will miss you. I have grown accustomed to our walks."

"As have I." He was frozen with disbelief. "But are you certain you're all right? You have never done something like that before."

"I do have an ulterior motive," she admitted as Gylles led her past the huts and toward a path they had not taken before. "I have questions, and I need answers. Part of me wants to go back to Callyn and pretend that much I have seen here never happened. And part of me cannot help but wonder, though it makes me fear to learn the truth. Answer my questions, Ryn Gylles? Please?" She used the voice that had always succeeded in convincing Janto to stay with her rather than attend to his duties.

Ryn Gylles quieted. "I am not permitted to answer them all, but I can sense that making you wait any longer would not be right. The Brothers may be Madel's hands, but She speaks to us in our bones. Ask your questions, Serra. I will answer what I'm allowed to."

It was a small one, but the best window she'd been given this whole time. She jumped through it. "Why am I here?"

"You accepted an invitation."

She rolled her eyes.

He chuckled at her obvious consternation. "Of course, what you want to know is why you were invited. Asking the right questions is of utmost importance." He patted her shoulder, and some of her annoyance drained away. She wanted to be angry with him, but she wanted to be done with this emotional tug of war more.

"What you wanted to know is that you have a role to play in the future of Lansera, if you choose to play it. And no," he responded to the befuddlement on her face, "it is not that of future princess and someday queen. Serra of Lansera is more important."

More riddles. "I was brought here to learn I will not marry Janto?" Simply thinking it made her temple thud. It could never be true. "That's ridiculous! He loves me. He cannot have found another woman on Braven."

"I did not say that, Serra. But I cannot tell you more, not yet. And why you were brought here is not why you needed Rynna Gemni's attention earlier. Tell me what happened."

"Why should I? You will not tell me a thing. Why should I confide in you?" She crossed her arms and made to walk in front and lead, but she did not know where the path went, and the mangrove roots thickened with each step.

"The mist and orbs you see are signs of Madel's presence. Not spiritual ones, like the peacefulness after a ritual, but physical ones."

She stopped short at his words, and a jocal fly landed on her arm. The short, sharp pinprick of its needle was enough to doom it. She smote it then rubbed the remains on a nearby tree trunk. By then, she felt she could speak. "You have seen them, too?"

"No. Only you can see them, Serra."

Impossible. Yes, no one else had mentioned seeing the same marvels she had. *But you have not asked anyone either.* The thought filled her with dread. The strange occurrences made her nervous and afraid, yet she had not bothered another soul to see if they—the very people attuned to Madel's spirit or at least trying to be—had also seen it. Maybe it was the answer to this question she feared.

"Why would only I see such a thing? I was not supposed to be here in the first place."

"You have some interesting ideas about fate. It's as though you believe events just happen to you, and you have no role in making them so. You were invited to come here, but an invitation does not require a yes."

"But I couldn't say no. It would have embarrassed King Albrecht if I declined a Brother's invitation. I could not risk that. My place, well, surely you know with my family . . . my brother . . . I am not in the habit of denying the king what he expects."

"I thought you had learned that things are not always what they seem. That sometimes a disloyal brother can be a man reformed? Or a king perhaps not as stalwart as you imagined? Do you always let others' expectations guide you so easily?"

Rarely had Gylles's conversations been so pointed. Yes, she had wanted to avoid the king's disapproval, but she had said yes to get away . . . and to learn more of the Brothers. The thought did not sit well with her.

"Do you still say you had no choice?"

She shook her head. The humidity was relentless as they walked, a wool blanket drenched in hot water.

"Ryn Gylles, where are we going?" She did not want to head so far into the woods, and she had learned to dread not knowing what might be up ahead. The fog was so dense, it was impossible to see more than a foot through it.

"You have a choice to make, Serra, not the one the initiates are making. That is important for their lives, but your choice affects us all."

"Then what *is* the choice? I am so tired of being led like a child with a blindfold over my eyes, grasping at feathers I cannot see."

To her surprise, Gylles smiled at her tone of voice. "Well, Lady Gavenstone, let us get you your answers."

He leaned against something—perhaps a boulder? It was so hard to see—and then he disappeared. She took a few steps toward where he had stood. Then she gasped as the muddy ground gave way beneath her.

CHAPTER 20
JANTO

Something shimmered in the corner of his eye, and Janto did not dare to breathe. There it was, every bit as shiny as granfaylon scales. Its eyes locked with his, as though teasing him closer. Then it flitted into the woods. This might be destined, but that did not mean it would be easy.

He ran after the stag, eyeing the low bushes that covered the ground between pine trees. There were a few cracked branches in the direction the stag had retreated, an almost glaringly obvious trail for an impossible creature to leave. Janto did not give it much thought, though he suspected seeing a granfaylon in the flesh may have boosted his confidence. After watching that fish waver between a physical presence here and . . . elsewhere . . . he had no doubt the stag was real. The dung that assaulted his nostrils confirmed it.

Janto found it ten yards ahead, nearly obscured by thick branches in this darker stretch of forest. Its distinctive silver coat shone through the gaps. A few light steps closer, and Janto could make it out entirely. The stag was slighter than he'd thought it would be—the lustrous halo from its coat made it appear a few inches wider around than it was. It kept its head down and eyes unblinking as it ate weeds at the base of a tree, but it would not be caught off guard.

Janto eased a bolt out of his quiver and lined it up against the taut thread of the Old Girl. It slid into the groove on his index finger with a wince of pain—he had taken aim so many times the past few weeks,

Chapter 21
Serra

Serra fell—no slid—about ten feet down into a cave. Surprisingly, it was not dark. Yet the blue light infusing the room did not give her comfort.

Ryn Gylles knelt beside her, his profile highlighted by the glow. "Are you all right?"

She stood and brushed the cool, dry dirt of the cave floor from her sheath. Strange it would be dry in here when it was so moist outside. Stranger still that she and Gylles were not alone. The light emanated from three Brothers near the back of the dirt room.

And they were floating. The Brothers were floating.

She could see solid ground beneath them, nothing but a foot of air between it and the bolder blue that rimmed the hems of their robes. Nothing at all. The fear she had been forcing away came back with a vengeance. Instinct guided her to edge away and seek an exit. But the chute she had fallen through was too steep, and there had been nothing to use as handholds on the way down.

A tendril of blue energy resolutely sought her out from the hood of one of the Brothers, whirling about like snow dust on a breeze. She heard the voice before it reached her. "You do not need to escape, Serrafina Gavenstone. We will not harm you."

"What are you?" It was hard not to gape at the . . . the . . . specters in front of her. "You cannot be real."

"We are as you have been taught. We are Madel's hand. That is no mere figurative speech. We exist through the power She gives us and are here to do Her work."

Madel would not allow such inhuman wraiths to exist. It was not possible. Madel was the protector of all, She who had triumphed over the other gods and brought the Lanserim forth. She would not bring such horrors to the world.

"I don't believe you." Her voice quavered. "You shouldn't exist."

"Again, your words are true. We had our time, but we squandered it. Madel gave us second chances to atone for our misdeeds while living."

Ryn Gylles placed a reassuring hand on her shoulder, but she jumped at the touch. Concern etched his raised brow. "Serra, I would not guide you to harm. Surely you know that? All the time we have spent together, you must know that."

There was a blue mist about him, dim in comparison to the Brothers' glow, like a moon's reflection in a muddy pool. The rays encircling them were vibrant, brilliant, and terrifying. How could she never have known the Brothers were this? It was plain before her eyes.

"What are you?" She repeated the question again to the Brothers. Serra did trust Ryn Gylles, but as her fear lessened, an equal amount of trepidation replaced it. What could such beings want of her?

"We are as you have realized. We are the dead."

They spoke the truth, she felt it, but she did not want to believe it. She closed her eyes and murmured, "No, no, no."

"Serra, you must keep your eyes open," Gylles spoke urgently. "The Brothers have more to show you."

"If they are dead, then what in Lansera do they want with me?" She gritted her teeth. "I do not want to see it. I refuse to hear any more of this lunacy."

The Brothers' words slipped beneath her skin, a needle into silk. "Then you doom us all, princess."

She opened her eyes. They scrutinized her though they possessed no eyes of their own. Only blackness and the blue energy that filled their hoods. "What do you mean? What would Lansera's doom have to do with me? I am only—"

"Only what?" It sounded like a taunt. "Lansera's princess? Is that not the place you seek? Someday queen is no petty dream."

They were right. By Madel's hand, they were right. She could not claim to be—to want to be—a nobody. She had shrunk back from the attention of the court, certainly, but not because she lacked ambition—because of the shame of Agler's betrayal. Shame of what he had done and how it might hurt her standing, if she were honest. She might have acted one for years, but she was no drapian blossom, floating where the currents took her.

"What is my role then, Brothers?" She invested the last word with as much distaste as her ingrained graces would allow. "And what is yours?" These were not leaders of her faith. They deserved no true courtesy.

"*When evil spawns and overruns, from silver the weapon comes. Without her sight, mankind is done. With it, all will again be one.*"

The Brothers chanted with one voice that was many. It sounded like a rushing through a caffir horn, amplified by the narrow space.

"When evil spawns and overruns, from silver the weapon comes. Without her sight, mankind is done. With it, all will again be one."

A great dread built within her chest. What could they mean by the chanting? Why didn't they make their intentions clear?

"*. . . Without her sight, mankind is done. With it, all will again be one.*"

"What do you want of me?!" She struggled to hold onto courage in the face of their eerie recitation and rushed forward, wanting to pound at them, but she could not reach them. They had risen higher off the ground with each chant and now floated almost at the top of the cave.

She deflated. "Please, please, tell me."

"You must stay until you can see for yourself, Serra. That is what they want of you. It is what all of Lansera would ask of you, if they could. We need you to weather this storm, to sacrifice to hold our world together." Gylles pulled her back toward him.

"But I cannot do that." His words confounded her. The only storm she knew was the one in her head, eddying thoughts of the dead living, the unexplainable existing. What sacrifice could she give to make sense of that? What did she have to sacrifice at all?

Discernment froze the blood in her veins as she remembered what she'd said to Gylles outside the cave. *They cannot ask* that *of me—they can't!*

"I am to be wed to Janto by month's end." It came out as a whisper, a plea.

"That is not your fate." Gylles's voice soothed, but his words never would. Not those words, not a future apart from Janto. "He will soon slay the silver stag, Serra, and be bonded to the weapon. It's the first part of the prophecy. A great evil has risen, as its words foretell and you have seen—"

The bodies at the lake. She shuddered.

"—and you and he are of utmost importance in fighting it, but your tasks are different."

"But I am to be the queen-in-waiting, the wife of the king! What better position would there be for me to offer aid to my people? I don't understand, Ryn Gylles."

"Your role is not to be wife to Janto Albrecht. You must leave that behind so he can focus on the weapon. He must temper it, and he cannot do that if you are his priority."

"You cannot ask me to give up Janto!" She felt no shame at spilling tears this time. What did her comportment matter with a chamber of ghosts as her audience? Janto had been everything to her since she was old enough to cherish more than the doll she held and the brother who tormented her. Yes, she wanted to be queen, but she wanted to be *his* queen. There was no other future she could imagine.

"... *from silver the weapon comes. Without her sight, mankind is done. With it, all will again be one.*"

"Make them stop, Ryn Gylles. I will not stay here, I will not!"

"Serra, please, you must consider this carefully. You must choose between staying here and becoming what Lansera needs, or going back to Callyn to marry our prince and imperil our world more than it already is. It is not a fair choice, but still, you must make it. You must choose what feels right to you—you must follow your heart."

Her heart belonged to a man with short-cropped, strawberry-blond hair, who brought her wreaths of balac vines every year when they bloomed by Lady Ginla's statue.

"... *Without her sight, mankind is done . . .*"

"I have made my choice. I am going to Callyn. I am going home."

The blue light and the cave vanished with a flash that darkened the Brothers' outlines before they too were gone. It faded into mist, and she found herself clutching a handful of dirt and moss, jocal flies pricking her skin. Ryn Gylles was there, regarding her, crestfallen.

"I'm sorry," she said, hugging her knees. "I cannot leave Janto. He's my life."

He helped her up. "Your life is your own, child. And so are your choices. I will not try to sway you otherwise. You were brought here

its mistake. Janto went faster, adjusting his aim in concert with the movement. A rush of air sped past his ear with the release. The arrow hit broadside, about a hand's length from the stag's shoulder and right into the lung. He quickly loosed another into its other side. The stag ran in a frenzy around the cabin, but it fell fast, no reserves left for a death dance.

Janto whooped once, but he quieted as he approached the shuddering animal. Its gray fur was slick with sweat. Blood poured from its wounds. Janto placed one hand over its snout, stroking the scratchy fur between its eyes to give it some peace as its breathing calmed. This close, the antlers were breathtaking in their intricacy, covered in scales that shimmered with a light of their own as the granfaylon's had. The antlers had more tines than he could count, some as fine as a writing quill and others as thick as his wrist. They all pointed forward, like seed heads of a dandelion directing Janto's gaze. He traced their aim, and a strong lightning bolt hit the wall to the left of the cabin's door. Beneath his hand, the stag took its last breath and grew still.

Sudden grief surprised Janto. A feeling of accomplishment came as well, but the loss was stronger. He leaned the stag's stiffening body against a sizeable, sturdy bush so the blood would drain from the wound. He wondered, briefly, if his grandfather Turyn had felt a similar sadness when he signed the peace accords with the Meduans. Turyn's Peace had never been a victory, but Janto had imagined his grandfather taking some satisfaction from sparing his people further violence. Did defeating a foe feel more like this?

He needed to circle around the cabin to find signs of a path back. But his legs did not move to the woods. Instead, he shuffled to where the lightning had struck. There was barely any light—all four moons shrouded—so Janto pressed his hand against the wood where he thought it had hit. The resin was sticky. It smelled of tar, must, and damp soil. He felt a dip in the wood that could not be the space between logs and traced the shape—one, two, three ovals with triangular notches off the sides of each. The ovals were connected to a sizable circle with two much grander triangles coming from its sides. A greasy substance smeared on his finger, and he raised it to his tongue. *Ash.* This was not a carving. It had been burnt into the wood.

Another bolt of lightning lit up the sky, revealing the image in front of him for a split second: Madel's three-headed bird, wings outstretched and ready to take flight. The depiction of their earliest myth sent a charge through him and focused his mind from the grief he had felt at the stag's slaying. As he walked back toward the animal, a familiar rustling sounded and a gap in the bushes took shape. Two rows of trees shifted into focus, their branches lacing together and a trail of brushed dirt running beneath them. Spreading his cloak on the ground, Janto heaved the stag onto it with a shout of exertion and secured it with the feather-studded rope at his belt. With his quiver and the Old Girl slung over his shoulders, Janto gave the rope a tug, glad the path back would not be a lengthy one.

As he dragged the stag behind him, a snatch of song skimmed through his head, a melody from his old religious lessons he could not quite place. Every bone in his body ached. His legs trembled as he lifted them, as though weighted down by bags of sand. Hearing the far echoes of voices surprised him; it had to be well after midnight. The thought that his friends had waited for him to return, had faith that he would, buoyed Janto forward.

It took him a few minutes to reach the others in their lamp-lighted glen. Each second felt excruciating—until they quieted and eight pairs of eyes locked onto him and the prize he dragged. The Muraters erupted in cheers. His back was slapped repeatedly, his body hugged, and they laughed in amazement at what the cloak held.

"When the silver stag runs free, blessed will he who binds it be.
Rise up, ye treasured bird of three. Wing him what boons ye foresee."

Jerusho's deep bass sang the common maxim, and Janto's jaw dropped. The melody! He knew, of course, that the stag he hunted was the one in the verse, but there was more to the song than those two lines, if only he could remember them. The first stanza had been repeated so many times over the centuries, an encouragement to chase after the impossible and seek the reward, that it may as well have been cleaved from the rest of the ritual chant. If his head would just stop swimming . . .

His stomach lurched. Janto hadn't eaten since before the archery Feat. He put all thoughts of songs and sayings aside as he realized how faint he felt. Peeling his stiff fingers from the rope took effort, but he clasped Jerusho's hand. "You don't have any of that granfaylon flesh left, do you?"

Jerusho laughed, shaking his head. "We stuffed ourselves on it."

"It was delicious!" said Hamsyn. "The cheek meat—I will be dreaming of that the rest of my days. But steak of silver stag might rival it. Should we dress it? If we begin roasting it now, it should be ready in time for tomorrow's dinner."

"I—I suppose." Janto stumbled into a chair.

Napeler handed him a sliced roll stuffed with meat and a tanker of potent cider. Janto grabbed them both with the speed of hunger, though the fast movement made his head hurt more. He bit in, salivating over the cold craval meat and the congealed cheese sauce spooned over it. He hoped the thanks in his eyes was clear enough for Nap to read, unwilling to speak again until he had inhaled every last morsel and sucked his fingers of crumbs.

So engrossed in the sandwich, Janto did not notice the hush fall over the group. Not until Rall spoke, his normally jovial voice laced with shock, did he stir.

"What's happening to it?"

Sielban moved to the stag's body, and so did Janto, swallowing his last bite. He ignored the instant rush in his head as he stumbled toward the beast. A fog with a silver sheen hung over the stag and cloak. Through it, the body flickered as the granfaylon's had before Jerusho killed it. The stag's eyes remained closed, its body lifeless, but the air around it was different, charged with . . . Janto had no word for the energy, but the lightning by the cabin had brought the same sensation. He went to his knees, clutching at the clumped fur to assure himself the stag was there.

It was and it wasn't. One moment, bristly hairs rubbed against his fingers, and the next, only air was clasped between them. The creature flickered in again, and Janto felt relief that was replaced with panic when it disappeared for a third time.

"It's not right." Frustration finally overtook him. "I slayed it. It cannot escape me now."

Sielban grasped his hands in his own, moving them away from the stag. "Do you need the spoils to know you have succeeded? This creature served its purpose. It goes to its rest in Madel's realm."

His words rang true, though they gave Janto little comfort. Hamsyn stood behind him, and Janto leaned back against his legs, watching as the stag wavered a few more times between here and wherever there was. When its form did not return, the fog evaporated, spilling droplets of silver fluid all over the abandoned cloak. They pooled together in a wrinkle of the fabric and seeped through it into the ground below.

None of them knew what they had just witnessed. But that did not stop Flivio from declaring, "Bloody shame. I just recovered my appetite from all that granfaylon flesh."

The others laughed, including Sielban. "An interesting group of men you are," their teacher said. "And with the catches of today, I think you have learned a thing or two of children's tales. There is nothing more for you on Braven. Congratulations, you have completed your Murat."

"You mean we're done, like that?" The disbelief in Nap's voice echoed in Janto's overwhelmed brain.

Sielban made a noise of assent. "You will find your trainings have been worthwhile soon enough. In the meantime, men of Lansera, sweet dreaming." With that characteristic twinkle in his eye, Sielban blinked out of sight.

And they were done. They had finished the Murat. Some of them had conquered mountains, caught unimaginable beasts, or simply made it through the weeks without family or friends in sight. Pride and satisfaction sunk in, then Nap and Tonim flanked Janto, pulling him up between them. They walked together to seek the path to the cave and whatever lay farther afield.

CHAPTER 23
VESPERI

V esperi cursed her short-sightedness at not having grabbed so much as a mallet from the arms room before she ran. Four days had passed since she left Sellwyn Manor, and she had eaten the last of the hard Yarowen cheese that morning. Knowing such an immense round had cost her father at least three hundred souzers was little comfort for her hunger. The previous night, she killed a hare with a rock and ate it barely cooked. All attempts at fires fizzled at a few sparse licks of flame, which was ironic considering what she could do. But she was afraid her talent would leave a trail wizards could track, and she was unsure she could control it beyond rifling through a horse's mane. Her stomach would have to be content with rodents and bugs for now.

She spit on a nest of barools, earthen-colored worms covered with thin spikes she'd stepped on at least five times already. Her boots had good soles, but nothing resisted their pricks. Except for the relief of knowing each stride took her farther from the threat of Thokketh, Vesperi headed west with no real direction. She hoped the Lanserim were all as pathetic as Agler, too busy tending sheep or wooing women with poetry to sell a Meduan back to her manor. Maybe she could seduce one of their men and take over his land, prey on their notions of manners and chivalry. As long as she gave a good tumble, he would never realize she was in charge. Men were so easy to control.

At that thought, her father's laughter echoed in her mind. She kicked a pile of thatch, groaning with frustration. Why did he not recognize a woman with her ambition was worth twenty of her sniveling brother?

A branch broke behind her, and Vesperi jumped off the deer path. The culprit was a flying squirrel hustling up a tree. She restrained from obliterating it with a finger point. Her talent was such brutal temptation. Other than the occasional brush with unwanted beasts, however, she did not mind the forest. Her legs minded the constant uphill climbing since yesterday morn, when she had reached a steeper elevation in earnest, but she did have the foresight to bring an extra set of boots, so the going was not as rough as it might have been. The woods gave her respite from her constant alertness. The motives of chattering snavelin as they hunted with their elongated snouts and sticky paws required little consideration.

She made her way through an overgrown patch of thistle that snagged the draping sleeves of her gown. A rock overhang appeared in the distance, a patch of darkness looming beneath it. A few steps closer, and Vesperi recognized the vast mouth of a cave . . . a cave with a man stepping out of it, struggling to lace his breeches while shielding his eyes from the sun's glare. She ducked behind a bush and peeked through its leaves. The man peered in her direction and took a few steps.

She could expose herself, perhaps flirt until Esye poked out from beneath the cloud cover. The man was attractive, darker skinned than she with a head of pale, reddish hair, though he was skinnier than she usually liked. Maybe a mountain man with no idea what lord and his daughter lived nearby. Even so, going to him would be a grave mistake— she was a woman alone. He would take her for his own or tie her up until he could sell her at market in Durn.

The clouds did not break, but she had to risk her talent, had to try to pull out the energy somehow lest she be discovered. She raised her finger and nearly squealed when she felt the talent gather in her palm. It swirled in a slow, steady trickle rather than cresting in a tidal wave, but it was there.

The man came closer, examining broken twigs near another deer path, his back to her. He started down it, inspecting shrubs as he went and stopping to wipe his boots on the underbrush.

Now. She pointed and released a ball of silver no bigger than the ones she had teased the horses with. But her aim was off and it flew past him.

His eyes widened as it flashed and disappeared down the path. He ran off after it, and she released a second to keep him running.

He had made her escape from Sellwyn a million times more difficult, but at least he was searching the other path now. She would avoid it and all deer trails she had been taking.

Another branch broke, and fear that the man had thought better of chasing after silver sparks ran through her. She shifted toward the sound, but what caught her eye shocked her more than his return would have. There was no cave mouth where it had stood moments ago. The overhang met a sheer wall of rock, not an opening. Was he a wizard? Had he cast a façade over the exposure?

The enormity of such a trick moved her legs forward to investigate despite the risk. She ran her hand over the rock, cool to the touch, its coloring a mix of pinks and whites. She scrutinized it, watching for cracks or a chisel mark but it was solid. There were no signs someone had made camp, either. Dainty blossoms covered the ground beside the rock face, not a petal trod.

The rabbit last night addled my mind. Or maybe the barools had a touch of poison on their spikes. It was possible, more likely than a wizard taking the time to play with her when her father would want her caged in a return caravan.

She slung her pack over her shoulder and picked up a considerable rock. Carrying it would slow her down, but she had a feeling she might need it. The delusion was easily explained away, but she still felt as though something had its eye on her. If there was, the cold of a higher altitude might scare it off. Vesperi set off determined to reach the highlands by evening.

CHAPTER 24
JANTO

Janto is exhausted by the time he makes it back to his inviting pile of pine needles and cobwebs. He cannot muster the energy to curse Rall's snoring, merely tumbles to the ground. Something crunches beneath him, a bug that failed to scurry away fast enough. That he slayed the silver stag—a creature of legend!—is still so unreal. His eyelids roll closed, but starlight wavers inside of them. He wills his head to stop swimming. The cider Nap gave him must have been potent, or his tolerance was weakened after such a tiring day of running and adrenaline rushing. The ache of his bow arm and feet demand sleep, but hours after he pulled the stag through the path on his cloak, Janto is too amazed to rest.

He cannot wait to tell Serra. She will laugh at his excitement then pull him in for a kiss, her green eyes sparkling like the waters of the River Call. He misses her, so much does he miss her. He can picture her now, wearing the purple dress from his last birthday, the one with green lace where the neckline plunges low. There are purple feathers sewn into it. Her hair tumbles over her shoulders, glinting almost gold as it blows in the breeze like the sun peeking between its strands. She wears the same necklace she always does, a gift from her mother before the accident. Its ribbon is the yellow of an overripe lemon and dotted with brown specks of clove buds her grandmother threaded through it decades ago. Serra told him it signified the spice trade and how it had brought Gavenstone back from the brink of famine when their vines failed for a decade. To Janto, it calls to mind only her scent and the warmth of her skin.

He dozes off, certain he can smell the sharp bite of cloves in the cave.

Daylight wakes him, and he shields his eyes. Has he slept through to morning already? There is no doubt now—that cider addled his senses. With a yawn, Janto pulls himself up and sweeps his pile of needles together. It must be late—even Rall, always last to rise, is gone. Janto is surprised no one woke him. Perhaps a man who slays a silver stag is granted an extra hour of sleep before training. He runs his fingers through his unruly locks, grown past his ears without his mother insisting they be cut. He plucks a few needles from his hair then walks to the cave mouth, his boots slopping up mud. It must have rained overnight, which is odd because it rarely rains here in the spring if Janto's tutors can be trusted. But the rains have been relentless in western Lansera this year, and who is he to scoff? He did not believe the silver stag existed before yesterday.

Janto breathes in the fresh air, sweet like a cracked open honeymelon. He relieves himself in a nearby bush. Next, he must find the others, which will not be an easy task. The cider erased his memory of where they planned to meet. He notices broken twigs at the base of another bush and takes off at a trot down the path that opens before him. He pauses to wipe mud off his boots. Ser Allyn would scoff at the prince of Lansera not taking time to clean them.

Ahead, a slight dip rises up and Janto sees a glimmer of silver disappear past its crest. He stops moving. Can there be another stag? Maybe the one he killed had a mate, and this is the doe. Only one way to find out! He strains to see ahead. Another metallic glint jumps further down the path. Janto pulls out an arrow and grips it in his hand, though he does not remember taking his quiver or the Old Girl. He follows the silver into a wooded glen and shivers at how much colder it is out of the sun's path. Darker, too. The deer, and he's sure it is one now, stays out of arrow's reach, enticing him onward. Janto's body tenses, but his blood throbs with the thrill of another chase. He never enjoyed hunting this much when out with his father, half the court trailing behind them. No, this is how it is supposed to be: silent, chilly, and unknown.

He steps into a clearing. Barely ten feet away, the doe stops and turns to face him. Its coat of sweaty, gleaming fur pales in comparison to the light emanating from its eyes. They are uniformly silver; no pupils interfere with the sparkling pools. Yesterday's stag was nothing compared with this creature. Its whole body pulsates as it stares, not blinking or making a sound. Janto instinctively threads his arrow and pulls back the bowstring. He doesn't *hear the twang of release until the deer collapses onto the grass, the arrow protruding from its ribcage. Something pours from the wound, but it is not blood. It cannot be blood. It is quicksilver, pumping out into a growing pool by its stomach. Janto, transfixed on this spreading radiance, is not sure if time passes or everything surrounding them is simply dimmer by contrast. The deer's eyes drain of color as the liquid slows to a trickle. The rising of its flank ceases as its heart stops. It is utterly dark, except for wisps of gray fog rising from the puddle of quicksilver. Soon, Janto cannot see the doe at all, only those lingering life threads shifting and swaying like rays catching the edge of dark, luxurious curls.*

Not like *curls—they are curls. There is no deer at his feet but a woman twisted beneath him, naked. Her eyes blaze open and he gasps. They are the deer's eyes but more brilliant, the color of stars at their birth, at the very moment the world was conceived. Janto is drawn to her, to her eyes and the hair writhing around her head. He reaches to touch her, but she dissolves in a flash and his fist strikes a boulder. He yells, not because of the pain but because he has lost her.*

The glen is lightening—grass stalks and tree branches reflect the bourgeoning sunlight. It is too glaring, too gaudy compared to the graceful silver he has grown used to. He hears voices, loud but hidden, and he turns on his heel, hoping to see her again. Instead, there is another doe, or the same one, up ahead. It holds his gaze, its eyes flowing silver, then flits into the woods, leaving Janto alone and shivering in the golden light of day.

✳ ✳ ✳

But he was not alone. Voices surrounded him. And boots. Many pairs of boots. Janto jolted upright, the scratchy threads of his blanket rubbing against his arms. He felt out of breath and very thirsty. A familiar voice called his name. He rubbed the sleep from his eyes, willing his vision to focus.

"There he is!" His father laughed as he clapped his son's shoulder, leaning over him. The king had dressed down, wearing simple jade pants with a sand-colored tunic, though the crowned swan at his neck dispelled any question of who he was. The way he spoke and the smile on his face, grander than Janto had ever seen before, conveyed the pride he felt. The king never needed to speak loudly, but he did so now, addressing him.

"My son, the sleepy slayer of the stag."

His father was only one of many strange sights. Lord Cino Xantas raised his elbows to a stunned Jerusho. Eddy and Captain Wolxas beamed with nearly as much pride as the king. Wolxas's raised bushy brows reminded Janto of the barools in the eastern mountains.

Despite the new sights greeting him, the silver deer and woman covered in curls lingered in Janto's mind. It must have been his Murat vision. That had to be why it felt so real and why his chest ached in a way he could not explain. He yearned for the woman, and that emotion turned to shame. It did not matter that she was imagined; Serra was all he should desire.

Janto shook his head to dispel the images and greeted his father. "I did slay it, but you could not have come to congratulate me this fast."

"We were already coming," his father explained. "That you have done such a deed only sweetens your Murat completion. I would not have missed coming to you on the day of your vision, regardless." His face held a knowing expression, though having a Murat dream was never certain.

"Do you know of the woman, then? Of the—"

The deep resonance of Lord Xantas's laugh echoed through the cave. "Ah, you dreamed of a woman, too!"

The still-sleeping men around them stirred at the sound, their faces reflecting the same mixture of confusion and understanding Janto had felt moments ago. But none of them appeared pained at waking, except for lack of sleep.

"I dreamed of my Gella back then and getting lost in her many— well—her many curves." Lord Xantas's face turned wistful. "It was before I realized she was the wife for me, you see. I knew her only as Ertion's newest axe-woman who smelled of tree sap. She had been on a logging trip in the mountains for months. But there she was in my dream, more desirable than any woman I had taken notice of before." He sighed, his expression besotted. "We were married in Varma before the next year ended." He winked at Janto. "I imagine your Serra played quite the role in your dream?"

Janto's heart fell. Did it mean something that Serra had been no more than a passing thought in it? It could not—Serra *was* his dream. He did not need a vision to tell him that.

"Not all Murat dreams are of women, Xantas." His father chided his friend, and Janto was grateful he could defer his answer. "Mine was not."

"So you say, my king," Lord Xantas teased. "But you have refused to talk about yours all these years. I have only become more convinced a woman is exactly what you dreamed of!"

Janto's fellow Muraters were quiet as the burial Mount in Callyn. The mornings these last three weeks had been filled with Flivio and Tonim teaming up to tease Nap into smiling—a task they had yet to achieve—and Jerusho regaling Rall with stories of Lady Gella's many attempts to beautify Varma's bleak stone walls and buildings. Rall appeared starstruck now. Sometimes, Janto forgot the presence of the king and his noblemen was a notable event.

"Hey—" he nudged his friend "—did you dream?"

Rall blushed, shooting a glance toward the king, but Janto prodded him to continue. He wanted his fellow Muraters to know their futures were important to him. And he was compelled to remind them of their friendship, especially with his father there. Losing it, after all they'd shared, would be a shame.

Rall gathered his courage, squeezing the stuffed koparin cub he slept with, a farewell gift from his daughter. "I saw my son. He was older, mayhaps twelve or thirteen, and he held a delicate figurine carved of Wasylim wood. It was decorated with copper threads that mimicked my wife's sigil, an opened thrushberry blossom. It was skilled work, and I complimented him on it with tears in my eyes." Rall smiled broadly. "I did not see my wife, though, or Katya. I would have loved to know how they will look then."

Flivio had also dreamed, and he described a thundercloud over a manor he did not recognize but felt certain was his and a woman's from his dream who wore a gown of a thousand feathers. He was recounting all of the gown's colors as the king gestured for Janto to join him outside the cave.

He slipped away. "What is it, Father?" Janto dreaded having to recount his dream after all.

"You've changed. You manage those men without them noticing your fingers pulling their strings. That is a good skill to have, son. But is there a reason you don't want to talk about your dream?"

Janto opened his mouth to speak, but nothing came out.

His father nodded. "I have only told your mother and one other person about mine, not even Ryn Cladio when I withdrew from the Order after the war, though he pleaded with me to change my mind. I think you would benefit from hearing it now, Janto. Would you like to?"

"I would." It would put off telling his own for a little while more, and Janto had always been curious about it.

"I was on a hill above Callyn. The colors were soft, as though an artist had painted it in pastels, but the bridge shone as brightly as it ever does. Past it, the perspective shifted. It seemed I could see the whole of Lansera at once, honing in on different towns and cities as though in a kaleidoscope turned at my eye. And it was not just Lansera I saw—or rather, it was true Lansera, not this divided land we've accepted. My eyes followed the Giants' Pathway, the tents of the Deduins thick beneath Thokketh's ice walls. Across the waters, the spires of Qiltyn beckoned, sun-faded reds and turquoises I had not seen since a child. Great herds of cattle roamed beyond them in Yarowen, a sight I had never seen and I knew could not be—drought had whittled away their numbers for decades. That was when I knew this was no vision of the present but of the future, and a better one."

The memory of it enveloped the king. With each word spoken, years of stress and responsibility eased, and he appeared younger, as though that twenty-two-year-old again. "I was excited to see the Meduan lands in a better state than before the war, and I had to know what caused it. I don't know how, but I went down from that hill and my foot landed on the Yarowen grasses, the sour smell of their seed pods' milk in the air. I found a herder, his brown hair matching the dark spots on his palomino mount.

"'Excuse me, mer,' I said, noting he did not recognize me despite my royal garb. 'When did you get so many cattle? Has the rain returned?'

"The man regarded me with consternation. 'We have grown our herds for decades as the king past the mountains decrees. The drought has not troubled us in years.'

"'You trade with Lansera?' I beamed at the thought of relations being restored. The war had been brutal. To think it might not have been in vain was a relief, truly.

"The man narrowed his eyes. 'We *are* Lansera. Have been ever since the king saved us from the plagues of man and Madel. Where are you from, wanderer, that you do not know in what country you travel?'

"'And who,' curiosity got the best of me, 'who is this king? Is he an Albrecht?'

"'Is he an Albrecht? You are addled, surely. Have we ever had a king who was not an Albrecht?'

"'Is it Gelus?' I was thrilled at the thought of my brother bringing this great change about—I had admired him greatly as a little brother is apt to do. 'Is Gelus Albrecht on the throne?'

"'Never heard of him.' The man's expression softened, concerned at my mental state. 'A distant cousin, perhaps? No, Gelus Albrecht is not the man who sits the throne.' He dismounted and extended a leather-gloved hand to me. 'Come home with me, traveler, and let us break our fasts together. My wife will have a fresh pot of tachery steeping over the fire by now. We can talk all you want of thrones and droughts then.'

"As I reached my hand toward his, I had the sensation of rushing through water, a river's current forcing me down a rapids. I closed my eyes against the pressure, and when I opened them, I awoke here in this cave, and nothing had changed."

The same loss Janto had felt that morning reflected from his father's face, though the subjects could not have differed more. Then it was gone, replaced again by pride as their eyes met.

"So that's why you left the Order when your father and brother died?" Both deaths had been unexpected. Turyn Albrecht fell prey to a bear's attack when hunting with Cino Xantas's father during a snowy, blustery day in the northern mountains. Not a fortnight later, Janto's uncle, Gelus, succumbed to a sudden infection of his flesh where his arm had been shorn off at the Plain of Orelyn. It had remained painful but unchanged for a decade before festering. Janto continued, "There could be no peace between Medua and Lansera if no Albrecht ruler existed to bring it, as the man said in your dream."

His father nodded, pleased but quiet, waiting for Janto to connect the rest of the dots.

That's ridiculous. It cannot be—it cannot.

"You think—" Janto's voice caught, "—you think I am going to restore Lansera?"

As his father answered, the weight of his words landed straight on Janto's shoulders. "You are the slayer of the silver stag, my son. Do you doubt what else you can do?"

Janto knew nothing this morning, not after a dream that had shaken his core. His father's had been full of hope and possibility. Janto's brought dread he prayed would leave him once Serra was back in his arms.

But that was not to be soon. His father continued, joy evident in all his features. "Tomorrow, after our celebrations are done, you will depart with Lord Xantas. He is leading a survey group from the southern Ertion mountains down toward the first Meditlan vineyards. We have heard of strange plants in that region, and I thought you might wish to take stock of them. They are likely to be a new resource for Gavenstone, and you and Serra should be familiar with them. Plus, your mother could use some specimens for her collection."

"But what about the wedding?" Serra had been furious when he announced his intention to attend the Murat so close to the ceremony. There would be no appeasing her if it had to be postponed, no matter the reason.

"It will only take a week. Serra knows of your delay. She has accepted it."

"Then yes, of course I will go." He wanted to refuse. The only thing that appealed to him was losing himself in Serra's lips and honey hair. But duties to the realm came first. Serra knew that.

CHAPTER 25
GARADIN

Garadin peeked through the carriage's levere curtain. The stone walls of Sellwyn drew close, and the hanging tree Lord Jahnas was so enamored with loomed near its gate, a rosewood transplanted from the town's nearby groves, the streaks on its trunk of no natural origin. Jahnas was fond of lashing his recaptured deserters while they jerked. The ground beneath the hanging tree's sturdiest limb had the reddish tint.

Sellwyn had been Garadin's lengthiest and easiest assignment. The advers had spent fifty years carefully building a hierarchy of dominance through brutality and fear mongering, but nevertheless, few people were quite as cruel as Jahnas. He was, in essence, the ideal Meduan, so concerned with protecting his power he had no appetite for fighting his neighbors or aspiring to a greater rule. If all lords were like Jahnas Sellwyn, Medua would be a peaceful land.

At the gate, his driver, a sallow fellow who knew better than to meet Garadin's eyes, presented Garadin's papers to the guards. The man's boots hit the ground with a squish, a curious sound. *Is the ground wet?* The region had been in drought for at least half as many years as Yarowen, almost two decades. Rain clouds loathed crossing the mountain divide. Sellwyn's water was shipped in from eastern Lorvia, lugged once a week by the workers Lord Carnif housed. Carnif had offered to make the trip every few days in exchange for the first pick of Sellwyn's timber, but Jahnas had said no on Garadin's advice. Thirst made his men compliant.

It was difficult for the half-parched to complain, and they were given just enough to fulfill their needs. When they knew nothing else, people accepted anything as normal.

They proceeded into town, and Garadin relaxed his grip on the Guj's letter. Few would attack a traveler rich enough for a levere curtain for fear he kept a wizard as well, but travel was perilous. If Garadin lost the letter . . . it did not matter now. This would be a simple task. Jahnas would not refuse the offer of marriage—it was unimaginable. Rather, he would kiss Garadin for offering such a pleasing solution to his trouble with the girl. Yet Garadin's chest cinched and his hip ached more sharply than it had in Qiltyn. The humid weather made his thoughts fuzzy. He had been shaken by the Guj's sudden attention and had not formed a plan yet for slinking back into the shadows after completing the errand. Hopefully, the Guj would grant him leave to return to Yarowen, to his warm room in the manor where one of Lord Clardill's daughters would wait in his bed to welcome him home. It did not matter which one. All five had that soft, milky skin that reminded him of his sister's friend back in Ertion before the war. It was her fault he had joined the rebellion. Oh, she had been delicious to take, but the whore reported him to the town council. Garadin had slipped away from Lord Xantas's guards and joined the uprising, never understanding how tasting something so sweet could be wrong.

Clardill's daughters were good women, unlike that tramp had been. They knew their place, even when it meant bedding a wrinkled old man like Garadin. Vesperi Sellwyn had never learned hers. At her mother's teat, she'd been thirsty for more, sucking Lady Sellwyn dry. In time, when it became clear Lady Sellwyn's womb had shriveled, Jahnas considered making Vesperi his heir. He admired her pluck. Garadin had valiantly dissuaded him. *A female heir will bring contesters to her claim,* he had whispered in Jahnas's ear. Then that miserable wife of his bore a son after all, a sickly whelp who was no miracle. If Uzziel had died, as Garadin had thought certain, Jahnas may have tried again to position Vesperi as his heir. Garadin arranged for a transfer then—he did not want to be present when that failure of the social order attracted the Guj's attention.

Yet Uzziel had lived. And somehow, the brat Vesperi had wrangled herself a position far better than that of Jahnas Sellwyn's heir. She would become Ralion's queen, an empty post but one that should sate her ambition. *Bah.* She was too smart, that girl. She would see through the farce of royalty and work her way into the Guj's bed. Romer would think he controlled her, but nobody controlled Vesperi Sellwyn. If she *was* the weapon, it would be their doom. Better to smite women like her as soon as they showed a spark.

The carriage lurched to a stop, and the driver offered Garadin a hand, a courtesy Garadin let stand uncorrected because of his hip. Manners should not be allowed to propagate, but if Garadin jumped down with no help, there would be groaning, exposing his weakness. He landed with a splash. There *were* puddles. *Curious, though it could be the damned humidity.* It had been so much drier in Qiltyn.

The driver dragged Garadin's trunk up the stairs. Garadin sounded the knocker, a bronze-cast viper coiled in sleep, and the entry door creaked open.

"Who goes there?"

Garadin recognized the proud, clear voice instantly. "Bellick!" He instilled his own with a disarming merriment. "It is I, Adver Garadin, and I need a drink!"

The guard laughed and swung the door open. Normally, an adver would be greeted with deference, downcast eyes and elbows raised higher than their greeter's head, but Garadin did not insist on tradition. To be loved, even in Medua, was a powerful tool.

"What brings you here? I thought we had rid ourselves of your ilk years ago!"

That is a bit too far. Garadin considered correcting the joke, but it was late. Instead, he instructed the driver that two days hence they would return to Qiltyn, a passenger in tow. The Guj had almost sent a battery of fighters to collect Vesperi, but Garadin persuaded him not to. Better to have her within the walls of the palace before her identity was known, and soldiers were prone to violent quarrels. "No harm should come to her before the presentation to Ralion," he had advised. In truth, Garadin had not wanted to deal with the entourage, but he did not hint at *that*.

"Lord Sellwyn is in his bedroom." Bellick led the way, stopping to yank a servant by the tie of her robe and demand a torch be lit. "You must give me a moment to prepare him."

Garadin dipped his elbows in acquiescence. A few seconds later, he heard shouting—the familiar sound of Jahnas's anger—and Bellick came back out with a wink.

"Lord Sellwyn will see you now."

Garadin walked through the door and stifled a gasp. Clothing was

of the few Lanserim who lived within it. Most had moved farther into the valleys, wanting to put as much space as possible between them and the Meduans. Who could blame them? Many people had not believed it would be that bad when the orders came to evacuate or try their fates with the rebels, but emigrants from the new Meduan lands had come over the mountains in droves once the reality sank in. With them came tales of constant raids and brutal overthrows, knocking down new lineages as fast as they could be claimed. The later ones brought accounts of a false god called Saeth and said his priests, the advers, took tribute from the execution of anyone who resisted the Suma family's might. Qiltyn's old ruling family had always held illusions of grandeur, and living among the rebels had only strengthened them.

The foraging party made their way through the countryside as the early morning passed, stopping every few miles for the surveyors to take measurements and the herbalists to search for plants they did not recognize. It had been the same every day since parting ways with the other Muraters at Jost. Rall and Flivio had teased Janto mercilessly about the feasting they would partake in on his behalf. Festivals had been arranged in villages on the ways to each of their hometowns. Nap had expressed how much he respected Janto's decision to leave with Lord Xantas and his team instead, choosing responsibility over celebration. The slight upward curve of the Wasylim's mouth conveyed his pride, which delighted Janto. It was another lesson learned: the respect of his people was the reward of leadership. Now if he could earn Ser Allyn's someday . . .

Not today.

"Stop staring, Your Horse-assed Highness, and come investigate this with us." Marabil, the only woman in the group, called to him with her typical vulgarity. Everyone had gathered at the edge of a pine-covered foothill, and Janto had apparently let the steady panting of his horse soothe him too much as he'd leaned against him after dismounting.

They gestured excitedly toward patches of valley below when Janto caught up to the group. Dozens of rows of a plant with many thick-fingered, jade leaves grew within them. A burst of shocking violet was at each of their centers, as though the plants were giant flower buds and not some form of bush.

"What are they?" He had never seen such vibrant flora before.

"No one knows." Lord Xantas gestured toward the herbalists who were hugging each other in their excitement. "And you know how they get when they don't know."

Janto laughed with Lord Xantas. "I guess we are going down."

✳ ✳ ✳

The farmer—a slender, older man—invited them in after Janto, Lord Xantas, and the surveyors had spent an hour watching the herbalists work. Two plants even odder than the bushes grew on either side of the man's thatched hut. They had thin stems the color of ground mustard and multitudes of tiny black seeds hanging from the sprouted tendrils at their tops.

"What are those plants outside?" Janto asked as he entered, remembering Hamsyn's sister's seeds that first morning on Braven.

"I thought your herbalists were determining that." The farmer offered them mugs filled with lukewarm tea. This royal visit and the interest in his plants obviously thrilled him.

"Not those, but the ones outside your door with the black seeds. I have a friend who may be interested in them." They had to be the same plant as Hamsyn's sister's. Perhaps he could send her word about their origins.

"Oh, you mean the fallowent!" The man waved a hand away. "Presents from our neighbors—if you can call a half day's ride neighbors—when we settled here. All the houses in this valley have a pair of them at their entries."

His wife laid a platter on the table holding crackers and some sort of paste made from the soft, round discs that grew beneath the thistly purple blooms of the bushes. "They say the fallowent wards off pests, at least according to the locals. Honestly, I don't know what good they do. We've had many flies after these rains. It's as though a bell was rung, calling them to dinner." Her frizzy brown hair shifted as she shook her head.

"Lord Xantas," Velak, one of the surveyors, interrupted after trying out the food with a grimace, "may we have your leave to take measurements near the hillside? The light is perfect right now, and I don't think the herbalists will be finished anytime soon."

Xantas laughed and took another cracker. "Not likely indeed. Just wait until they try this paste! Go ahead."

The surveyors raised their elbows in exit, and Lord Xantas and Janto were left alone with their hosts.

"So you are the prince, an Albrecht?" The farmer's tone and the way he kept clasping and unclasping his hands conveyed his delight. "A prince in my house! Who would have ever thought it when we came over the mountains."

Over the mountains? Janto straightened up. They were not old enough to have moved right after the war. So they had been Meduans, this affable man and his charming wife. *How is that possible?*

"When was that?" Janto hoped his shock was not too obvious.

"Oh, twenty years ago now," the wife answered. "Seems like yesterday. We were both so young . . . we had never known other ways to live. My stepfather shunted me and my mam off to the new women's house in town when I was—oh, I think I was ten or so then. We had thoughts of escaping, but the other women who tried . . . well, they weren't quite the same when they came back. So it was darkness but for the kitchen fires and cutting and boiling parsnips for years until *this* man came in and swept me away." She kissed the farmer's cheek then ruffled his remaining patch of white hair.

The farmer did not pause before continuing his wife's story, one they must have told often. "I wanted a wife. Taking one was discouraged for the working men, but I wanted one anyhow. I had dug ore out of the mines for at least a decade by then. The others swore I'd gone blind when I brought Lileh here home to our cabins, but well, it weren't right sleeping with so many women as they had done. They teased me for my Lanserim streak but gave me my own hut all the same—I was very good at finding a new lode, you see. But I could never force Lileh to stay inside like I should have, not once I got to know her. She never strayed far, but she kept a garden and hung our laundry to dry outside. The men in their cups never let me hear the end of it. But Lileh was worth it."

Janto struggled to suppress the outrage he felt at what these people had considered normal, but a stern look from Xantas quieted him. This was obviously nothing new to the Ertion liege's ears. To Janto, it stirred the embers of a fire he hadn't felt blazing for a while, distracted by the Murat from Agler's murder and all the Meduans had done.

The farmer stared at his wife with adoration. She rested against his chair, wiping her hands on a towel nestled in her apron.

"It had become too much, the other men's taunts, so we ran. You understand." He winked knowingly at Janto. "You're a man in love, too. Aren't you newly married?"

If only. Then maybe his dreams of that woman sprawled on the forest floor would stop. He wondered how easy it would be to take that innate attraction between a man and woman and twist it into the oppression and subjugation these people had experienced. A pain throbbed at his temple.

"I need some air." He made for the door.

The herbalists did not halt their note-taking when he stepped out-side. Nothing could distract them from their work. He watched as they broke off a few tightly rolled leaves that protected the soft flesh beneath the plant's buds. The herbalists swabbed their broken edges with cloth. Then they held the cloth up to the sunlight to inspect it.

Something on the breeze drew Janto's attention. *Yelling. Someone's yelling.* The herbalists heard it too. One jumped up, reaching for his sword. The surveyors were alone in the woods.

"I'll go." Janto did not want them to abandon their work. "It is probably nothing, maybe a barool's nest."

The man nodded, relieved, and Janto mounted his horse, taking off in the direction of the sounds. He braced his knees against the animal. "Heeya!" The horse reached a gallop in a few strides. Janto's head throbbed, but he had to find the surveyors, and fast. It could be a bear or a koparin, and the surveyors were not equipped with bows. They would be forced into foot combat with a wild animal.

The rows of violet-topped plants disappeared fast as Janto reached the forest line. He pointed the horse in the direction the last yells had come from, hoping the wind played no tricks today. They could not be far, in any case, or he would not have heard them at all.

"Janto!" Velak spotted him, sounding relieved, though he only turned his head from whatever the surveyors had flanked, backs exposed to him and not it. "We are glad to see you. None of us know the protocol for this."

"Is it a gorgon? I heard yells and came as fast as I could."

Marabil laughed. "No, no gorgon. We know what to do with one of those. This here throws rocks, not claws."

"And it'll be a mite more trouble than a gorgon, I suspect," Velak said. "Come see."

Janto dismounted and looped his reins around a pine. The surveyors parted to let him see. But he closed his eyes, willing the sight away as soon as he had looked. Silver stars danced beneath his eyelids while he counted to ten, calming his breathing though no exercise could calm the increased pain in his temple.

He opened his eyes on a pulled net of drapian rope held in place by arrowheads embedded into the tree trunk. A human-sized trap, likely the farmer's design. Twenty years in Lansera had not cured him of Meduan distrust.

But it was not the net that had Janto feeling panic and a compelling fascination. It was the woman held within it, her black curls caught in its fibers. They writhed as she struggled to escape, tossing out angry grunts as she thrashed. Her eyes were brown when they glanced on Janto's, and for a moment, he felt relief. But as she raised her hand as high as she could within the net, her irises became twin pools of molten silver.

CHAPTER 27
VESPERI

A constant sensation moved under the skin of her hands, but not in the way she wanted. No surge of energy, no rushing electricity—only pins and needles. Her fingers were bound so securely, she could not wiggle them. And it was all the fault of the red-haired one. She hated him, hated them all, but him most because he knew about her talent. Some way, somehow, he knew, and the first thing he did was restrain her, just like a man.

The moment she raised her pointer finger, he was on her, trapping her hands beneath him. "Rope! We need to bind her hands!" The others had quickly complied. Vesperi fought violently, trying to get out from underneath him and the net, straining to reach for Esye. It had been no use.

So she waited. They asked questions but did nothing else to her. At some farmer's house, the burly one introduced himself as Lord Cino Xantas then asked her name, but she was not so stupid as to give it. Who knew what they did to Meduans in Lansera? If she could not get away, then it was in her best interests to be quiet and listen, to observe as she had as a child, learning which of her father's guards grew meaner after milk wine and which went to the kitchens to leave with a woman following meekly behind. But these people were strange. No one leered or grabbed at her. Maybe they waited until their work was done for the day. Yet the women they kept were far too energetic to have spent all night on their backs. And they smiled. They smiled all the time.

After the midday heat passed, the riders left the farmer's hut. Vesperi struggled as they secured her to the back of the gigantic man's equally gigantic white horse, but she could gain no leverage. That he, Xantas, was the group's leader became obvious throughout the afternoon's journeying. The others showed him deference, asking for permission to chart a tree line, examine a plant, taste the wind, or something equally inane. Only one man had not approached Xantas in that manner, the one who had bound her. She could feel his eyes drift toward her every two miles or so. Each time she met them, his scowl deepened.

At a particularly uninteresting patch of sallow moss, Xantas turned to her. He held up a water horn. "Are you thirsty?"

She was, but she did not trust what these people had to offer.

He lowered the horn to his chest. "Is there anything else I can get you?"

"Would you?" She raised her arms. "My fingers, they are so numb." It was worth a try.

The redhead shouted, "No!" He drew close nearly as fast as he spoke. Vesperi suppressed a sigh then considered the young man. His face was freckled despite his deep olive skin, and he bore himself like an adver who had earned his first bone.

Xantas regarded him with cautious eyes. "And why are we keeping her hands bound? It is not becoming to leave a woman in such discomfort."

The man's shoulders slumped, and Vesperi's spirits soared. *He does not know*, she thought. But he had to, had to at least have felt something or why—

"I just do not trust them." His voice wavered, the same way Uzziel's did when he tried to lie. A man this age should be more practiced; it was almost endearing.

"After Agler's death, I mean," he said. "With how wildly she fought, it is obvious she's one of them, the Meduans. They sent him back to us in ashes."

Agler? The spy she'd killed? But how could this man know about that? True, the rosewood box had born Sellwyn's mark, but she was careful to bring nothing displaying the viper with her.

"I won't trust any of them," the man continued, "not with Serra on my mind. This woman will answer for her crimes with my father, and I am not anxious for her to commit more on the way."

Xantas nodded in assent, and the redhead returned to his mount.

His father? She should have realized he was in charge earlier. The rest of the men had been too nice, helping her up when she fell, speaking in gentle tones, addressing her with courtesy. This man had done none of those things, sparing her no regard beyond the scowls and the insistence her hands be tied. He was the real leader here, the one who treated her like what she was, like an afterthought.

But he handled the other woman—Marabil—differently. Marabil had introduced herself when she helped Vesperi break water earlier. The woman had yammered on about how she had never been this far south and how they would reach the central road soon, and wouldn't that be a sight, reaching the jeweled bridge and attending the wedding? Vesperi had paid her no mind, but when night fell and they made camp, Marabil unleashed a torrent of playful insults directed at the redhead. He chuckled but refused to banter back. His behavior reminded Vesperi of Bellick's, acting as though he enjoyed the woman's company, not just imagining her undressed. After dinner had been cooked and Vesperi had refused a bowl—it could be poisoned—she realized none of the men had gone near Marabil except to crack jokes or bring a new candle as she hunched over maps in the darkness. She had not stirred their stewpot once.

At the evening campfire, the puniest man among them, his head bald and orange like a pumpkin, spoke. "Are you ready?"

"It is only a few days more," said the one she thought was named Velak, "and you will be a married man."

They addressed the redhead, who fell into surliness, apparently not fond of the conversation turn. Who could blame him? Her father had always resented her mother. But having only bastards was anarchy for a man who wanted to preserve his fortune.

"Best rest up, all of you." Xantas rose, brushing off a few ashes. "Lady Gavenstone will have our heads if we return the prince late for his wedding after it has already been delayed."

Vesperi sputtered. "The prince?" This group of weak-willed men concerned with will o'wisps and drapian seeds was a royal sortie? They were not soldiers, that was clear, and what prince was fool enough to travel without a guard? King Ralion kept a dozen nearby at all times, and the Guj had his wizards.

"She speaks." Xantas lifted an eyebrow. "Aye, this is our prince, Janto Albrecht. I suspect he is not yours, however."

She quieted immediately, her throat aching with the effort of speech. Tomorrow, she would have to take water. Avoiding poison was no benefit if she died of thirst. But the shock of falling into the prince's hands might kill her regardless. Could her father have sent word over the mountains about her escape and they had meant to capture her? She shook her head. Lord Sellwyn would never go to the trouble. That she had been captured by a Lanserim prince who had known how to restrain her talent was a bizarre coincidence. Perhaps he was merely lucky and she was not.

Vesperi was so tired, had struggled so much first in the net and then with understanding these people and their ways. She knew Lanserim were different, but she had never considered how much. *Foreign* did not begin to describe it. All she had accomplished was learning Lansera's prince could not tell a lie to save his life. Yet while her hands stayed bound, he succeeded at saving his and his men's. Perhaps he was smarter than he appeared. Vesperi would figure him out, figure them all out . . . come morning.

CHAPTER 28

JANTO

Rope grating against wood and a passing whiff of smoke from the breakfast fire woke him. Janto lurched from his bed roll and blinked several times as the image of a woman with silver eyes and illuminated hair was replaced by the same woman with brown eyes and black hair struggling against her ties with increasing desperation.

"You will never undo those," he called out. "The Ertions tie knots tighter than a boggart's embrace."

She struggled more fiercely. *And will break a bone with this insolence.* He sighed as he brushed off ants that had crawled beneath his blanket in the night. Then he went to her.

"You are giving yourself welts with this madness."

Her skin was inflamed where the rope bound her to the tree. She glared but stopped her thrashing. "Your servants have abandoned you."

She was right, not about them being servants but about being alone. All of the group's things remained minus the horses and a few packs. The fire had been recently extinguished and beside it lay two bread rolls stuffed with lukewarm eggs and strips of beef. Beside them, a message was scribbled in the dirt in Marabil's graceful hand.

Left for town. Will be back by nightfall. Watch the captive, your royal horse's arseness.

So he had been elected to captive duty. Maybe it was Madel's way of forcing him to sort out this mess. Yesterday, he had hoped it a waking dream, but the woman was still there, too real and angry to be one.

"We appear to be alone for a time at least." He raised one of the stuffed rolls to her mouth to help her eat. *Her hands must stay bound, but she need not starve.* Why he had restricted the movement of her hands the moment he laid eyes on her was a mystery to him, but he had felt as sure of that impulse as he had running into the Braven woods, following a silver flash.

She spat at the offering. "I don't want your Lanserim filth."

Janto tensed but remained calm. Days of restless sleep had frayed his temper and being confronted with her—her existence—had only made it worse. Yesterday, he had acted unkindly, treating her with less respect than was her due as a captive, no matter her citizenry. But with the new day came new perspective. Braven had proven Janto could accomplish the unthinkable. He only wished he knew what was asked of him with her. Maybe she could help him piece it together.

He wiped her spit from the roll and took a bite. Then he held his own to her mouth, confusing her more than handing Jerusho a battle axe would do.

"Why are you eating that? Are the Lanserim mad?"

"Perhaps, if I am imagining your voice. I was uncertain you possessed one after yesterday's silence."

"I am not prone to talking with people who keep me in chains." She took a bite and chewed loudly, her mouth hanging open between bites.

"Tell me why I should take you out of them. What is your business in the mountains?"

She narrowed her eyes, contempt running through them. "You think you can break me, while your servants could not? You aren't half the size of your fur-covered friend, and he could get nothing from me. Unless they have left you so we could have some privacy? Is that it? I will not be much use without fingers for stroking." Another bite, and she rolled her tongue around it with faked pleasure. "I have never pleased a prince before."

You are not pleasing this one. "You did not recognize me?"

She looked at him, forehead cinched in confusion. He covered his tracks quickly. "Of course, it has been many years since my family was in Medua. My great-grandfather spent every winter in Qiltyn, to make certain the people of your region could be heard without the burden of far travel."

She laughed. "What sort of ruler comes to his people rather than the other way around?"

"A caring one. I hope to be the same someday."

"Would a caring leader keep his people restrained thusly?" Her voice sweetened, though a scornful edge remained.

He plopped the last bite of roll into her mouth. "He would when he did not know what danger she posed to his people." Crumbs had fallen in the tangles of her hair, and he brushed them out. That it was only hair almost startled him—rougher than Serra's, but hair just the same. No unearthly shimmers of silver tinged the curls. "I will not unleash a Meduan among us. We let you have your own land to avoid that danger."

Janto took his dagger from his belt and lifted it to the rope her right arm's skin puckered around. She was rendered speechless as he sliced through it . . . for a moment.

"*Let* us have our land? I am surprised we did not decimate your people. Only a few of your servants carry weapons."

"They are not my servants. If anything, I am their servant on this trip. We have been cataloguing the plants of this region and their layout for the maps. I am here to assist and learn."

Her mouth hung open as he cut through the ties on her legs. It might be risky, but keeping her hands secured and feet bound should do. If she escaped, she would not get far, and the ropes had worked her skin to bleeding in a few spots. The flesh was puffy, and irritated pink bumps lined the white rings on her skin where the rope had been snuggest. The worst wounds were scabbing already, but trickles of blood seeped out from beneath them.

From his own pack, Janto retrieved a vial filled with an orange powder and tipped some of it into his hand. A quick search led him to a rubar leaf the size of his opened hand. He poured the powder onto it, added a few drops of water, and mixed it into a paste.

The woman watched skeptically as he advanced. She looked at the ointment with disdain. "What is this?"

"Salve for your cuts."

She sniffed it and wrinkled her nose. "It smells like an adver stumbling out of a milk wine barrel at the convent."

Janto knew her false priests called themselves advers, but he did not know they had such a reputation. "You might want to keep that description of its smell to yourself," he cautioned. "My mother takes pride in her medicines."

"Your queen made this refuse?"

Her skin was incredibly dry, and he rubbed it onto her forearms, hips, and calves, wondering if she'd ever had the luxury of a mineral soak, something Queen Lexamy insisted on at the beginning and end of every winter. "Are you a slave?" He softened his voice.

"A slave? You take me for a slave?" She laughed and the sound rose from the depths of her throat, genuine for the first time. "The last week must have treated me worse than I suspected."

So she had been traveling for a week. Enough time to make it over the mountains, certainly, but she must be from a close province. A Durnishwoman, perhaps, like the farmer and his wife? Work in mines could explain the chaffed skin. "Not a slave, then. I apologize for any disrespect I gave you."

"Do you speak that way all the time?"

"What way?" The rope burns paled in hue. They would heal in a day or two.

"Like you are glued to your mother's teat and begging for a taste."

It was too much. Marabil could come up with more inventive insults than any of Eddy's stable hands, but they were in jest. This woman's words inflicted pain, not humor. "You should not be so quick to besmirch the queen as my captive." He pulled his dagger out to sharpen it against a stone, intending the implicit threat of his action.

"Now that's more like it!" She hopped over to him. "Do you want me to extend my neck? Or do you prefer a slice at my wrists? Be careful—you might loose them."

He should have kept her tied to the tree and gagged as well. This Meduan would tell him nothing, nor did he want to learn what his connection to her might be, did not want there to be a connection. How could he have one with any of the people who had killed Serra's brother? If Madel had sent a message in the form of this woman, it would remain unread.

"More like you might lose your bargaining chip." His dagger hovered over her hands, and his cheeks flamed red, knowing he was letting her goad him.

She jerked her hands up, flinging the dagger high in the air before it fell to the stony ground with a tinkle. "If I knew the Lanserim were the idiots my father claimed, I would have run away months, nay, years ago!"

Run away? He could not imagine anything scaring *her* enough to send her over the mountains by choice. Madel's hand, he hoped the others returned soon.

✳ ✳ ✳

They did not. It was well into evening before hooves plodded into camp. Janto vacillated between anger at the woman and anger at himself for his behavior all day, more sullen than Nap when ordered to play Lash the Feathers. As afternoon fell, he busied himself making dinner, ignoring her except for frequent checks that she had not wandered off. The food was cold by the time the others arrived, but they feasted on rabbit legs and boiled potatoes without complaint while Janto started their evening fire. Questions at finding the Meduan untied went unasked.

Lord Xantas sat down next to him near the flame, not bothering to smooth out a place in the dirt. He leaned toward the fire, holding his hands out. There was a crack on his right hand between thumb and forefinger that had to be painful. From his furs, Xantas pulled a flask that flashed orange and red in the firelight.

"Want a sip?" He took a protracted swill.

Janto shook his head, alcohol not a good idea after that day. "I have some of the queen's salve in my saddlebags."

The older man regarded him quizzically.

"For your hand." Janto gestured at the cracked skin.

Lord Xantas laughed. "If I patched every wound on my body, I'd be slathered in the stuff. You could smell me coming from a mile away."

"You already can." Janto wrinkled his nose. "Might be an improvement."

Xantas gave no defense, taking another swig. "True enough, prince." His salt-and-pepper hair appeared wilder than normal, practically forming its own bramble bush.

"Where have you been? Fall in a briar patch?"

Xantas chuckled. "No, not quite. We went to Urs, a town half a day's ride from here."

"I know of it. Two of my fellow Muraters are from there. I would have liked to have seen them. What good is a ride through my countryside if I must stay out of sight the whole while?" Janto sounded petulant even to himself. The day had been too long. "I apologize for my tone. Spending all day with a Meduan is not my idea of a good time." He eyed the flask. "I will take some of that after all, if you don't mind."

Lord Xantas handed it over. Janto's fingers rubbed across the etched metal. The liquid burned, tasting of sourmint and mushrooms. "Bombal draught?" The spirit was an Ertion specialty, said to make the man who could drink a whole wineskin tougher than a koparin, if not first struck dumb.

Xantas nodded, and Janto took another drink, holding his nose.

"Was she all that bad, prince?" Lord Xantas teased. "She must have won you over enough to untie her, and she is easy on the eyes."

"It's her mouth that's the problem. She does not speak often but when she does, her words are full of malice. She is a fiend straight from her false god's lair."

Xantas stroked his beard. "I know you have not met many Meduans, but the division between our people happened only two generations ago. Our farmer friends from yesterday were not so far removed from us, and neither is this woman."

"We are as different from her as Gavenstone wine is from this undrinkable swill." Janto took another draught. "They might mature in the same skins, but their base ingredients make the difference. Ripe grapes and scraggly, wind-tossed herbs do not yield the same water."

"That is an astute observation for a freshly Murated young man. What did Sielban teach you there, wine appreciation?" He gave Janto a good-natured poke.

"You call that slop wine?" Marabil came through the clearing, just as Janto reached for a stick to scratch an itch on his leg. She had bathed and brushed her auburn hair, which Janto was surprised to see fell to her hips. She usually kept it in a pinned braid.

Velak came up behind her, holding a wrapped parcel.

"What do you have there?" Janto pointed with the stick.

"My baby's third birthday present, a doll made by one of the Ursfolk. Dreadfully ugly, but the place was such a hovel, I could find nothing else. I thought Meditlan was supposed to be a paradise compared with dry, cold Ertion."

He handed Janto the package to hold while he pulled up a log. "Didn't want to leave it near *her*." He gestured back to the camp where the Meduan remained. "Besides, the fire is over here."

"Is it that cold?" Maybe Janto should offer the captive a blanket. He groaned at the impulse to protect, unable to shake her presence despite the return of the group. It was like she'd burrowed beneath his skin, and he could not escape her. *Think of Serra. Think of two more days until you are wed.*

"Nah, it is early summer. On the icy streets of Varma, you could sleep outside naked. Not that I would know." Velak winked. His wife was obviously holier than a Brother to put up with him.

Marabil braided her hair near the fire. "I don't know how you had time to find anything in that town. We were only there long enough to hire the messenger."

Ah, so that was the reason for the sudden trip. Lord Xantas had sent word of the woman to Janto's father.

"What did you say to the king?"

"What do you think?" Xantas's eyes drooped with sleep. "Caught a Meduan in the woods east of Urs. Female, angry, will not talk. Will bring her to Callyn. The prince fares well." He closed his eyes.

Janto wondered what his father would do with her. Perhaps trade her for an imprisoned Raven. Or more likely, bribe her family to take the intolerable woman back. She did not belong in Lansera, in his lands, no matter his Murat dream. It had not made sense when he first dreamed it and it made even less now. The sooner she was gone, the better. He would insist someone else guard her tomorrow rather than deal with her insolence for another day, pull rank if needed.

That's ridiculous. The admonition came in Serra's voice, and it was right. He made the picture of a spoiled brat, an infantile king-in-waiting. Serra would have words of wisdom about how it was a test, a way for him to understand the Meduans should he need to entreat with them in the future. She would remind him they were his people too, by right, and maybe someday they would be again. "Understand her," she would caution. "Get to know her." Or at least he thought she would. It had been too long since they'd spoken, and his spirits were the poorer for it. He ached for the touch of her lips on his neck and the warmth of her body next to his beneath the flowering vines of the queensgarden. The blooms would be browned by now, fallen in piles beneath the trellises. As though he had not missed Serra enough already, his longing for her had grown far worse since that cursed dream. Picturing her clearly was difficult sometimes, especially after waking, and her voice sounded wispy when he imagined it, not strong and full of life as he knew it to be. What an unwanted twist of fate to have his beloved more difficult to bring to mind than a woman who assaulted his pride with every flip of her hair and steely jape of her eyes.

The moonslight glimmered in the woman's hair now as she peered into the forest, her face in profile. She seemed scared for a moment, and it softened her features. But the emotion fled her face so fast he must have imagined it.

"What do you see when you watch her? You have been doing a lot of it." Xantas scrutinized him as best he could with liquor-drowsy eyes.

Janto did not hesitate in his answer. "An enemy."

"Are you so certain? What would Sielban have said?"

Janto need not reach back far to remember the lesson, and his face colored that he had set it aside so easily. "To look harder." Rynna Hullvy might have added that she was a child of Madel, too.

"So you did learn more than how to slay mythical beasts? I am glad to hear it. I was beginning to fear Sielban only told bedside fables around the campfire these days, planting paper creatures painted silver where a prince's ego would surely find them."

The admonishment burned from his throat to his cheeks, though he knew Lord Xantas only teased. But his point was clear. Janto had not gone to the Murat to kill the stag, nor to dream up a nightmare he did not understand. He had gone to become the man his people deserved.

"You must be a Lanserim first, Janto of Albrecht," he recalled Sielban saying as a pair of canoes had rowed onshore, "before you can be anything else. And Lanserim do not jump to conclusions so fast."

CHAPTER 29
SERRA

Ellari, a popular hair weaver from Wasyla whom the queen hired for the occasion, tucked another gold-dusted feather into Serra's hair, securing the last loop of locks to her head. One glance at the mirror, and Serra squealed. "It's perfect!" She was grateful to be back at home, back in a place where hired hands made her beautiful and she did not spend half the morning pulling tangles out of her hair or flaking dried mud off her sandals.

"Of course it is, my lady." Ellari's drawl was buttery. "I take pride in my work. Wouldn't want rumors of how I ruined the wedding, sending the bride off to meet her prince with hair fiercer than a sandstorm."

"There is certainly no danger of that. The bard will sing your praises in all Lansera, and Lord Sydley will throw you a celebration parade worthy of any Murat Feat. Now go take your seat before the throne room fills up!"

Serra pushed Ellari out the door then sat back at the mirror, alone for the last few minutes before the wedding ceremony began. Her hair was a masterpiece, dark blonde tresses tamed in rows of loose loops. Janto would beam with pride when he saw her. She could not wait. It was *their* day, *their* marriage, and she hoped it would feel that way despite the crowd. She wished they had reunited beforehand, but she'd had no more than a glimpse of him since his return home, when he was leading the Meduan captive through the eastern wall. She had inquired after him many times, but the response from Ser Allyn was always the same: "The king has greater need of him than you. And your wedding preparations have greater need of you than him. How many hand cloths are left to be embroidered?" It never failed to make her panic. Appearances were important, and this wedding must impress. She would have forever with Janto; there was only this one chance for their union to leave an indelible mark.

The door grated open against the stone floor, and Queen Lexamy slipped inside, gorgeous in a powder blue gown and an overlaid skirt of sapphire ribbons and sparkling feathers. An enameled jade comb swept her red hair up and made the green of her eyes more prominent. Ellari had obviously done her as well.

"Please, come in." Serra smiled at the woman who used to sneak her jelly cakes when her parents weren't looking. The queen returned the expression and settled behind her chair.

"Serrafina, you are beautiful."

Serra's cheeks colored. "Thank you." She beamed in the mirror at the queen's reflection and her own.

"You are welcome." Queen Lexamy placed her hands on Serra's bare shoulders. "The king and I are as overjoyed as you and Janto this morning. It is not every day we watch our only child take his bride. But do not think we have forgotten you are alone today, sweet one."

Serra's breath caught in her throat. There had been no time to think about her family since returning to Callyn. The rush of preparations had been such a welcome distraction. She'd hardly given a second thought to the Brotherhood, either, or her decision to come back.

"I am sorry your family cannot be here. Your father and Agler, but today especially, your mother." The queen paused. "I thought I might play mother of the bride for a bit if you will let me."

Serra nodded, and the queen called out the door, "My gift, please!"

A servant shuffled in from the hall holding a bottle filled with a peach, transparent liquid.

"Mystallan wine!" Serra exclaimed. She had never thought she would partake in the toast between a mother and daughter before a wedding. "How did you know?"

The queen tittered. "I was friends with your mother before you stirred in her womb. I know a few Gavenstone traditions."

Serra was stunned. "Thank you." Tears welled in her eyes while the queen poured the wine in two goblets by her dresser. Serra hugged her, repeating, "Thank you."

"Enough with this superfluous gratitude." She handed over the nearest goblet. "Drink up! It is time you married my son." Their goblets clinked together. "To good health, happiness abounding, and a myriad of children running within the castle walls."

"Here, here!" Serra took a sip. The Meditlan wine was high quality with no acidity and a dazzling cinnamon nose.

The queen finished her glass in one gulp. "And now, because I do not have a daughter of my own, I am subjecting you to a Brendel family tradition. A bit of advice for a new wife, if you will." She winked.

"I will."

"My mother repeated this to me on my wedding day and her mother before her and so on and so on for generations: 'Her patience weathers the storm. Sacrifice holds her world together.'"

A pit dropped into Serra's stomach. "What did you say?" Those words . . . Ryn Gylles had said them in the cave before she refused to stay.

The queen took no notice of the quaver in her voice. "It's an old Ertion saying. My mother explained it to me on my wedding day. It's advice on how to survive fights with your husband." The queen laughed. "Believe me, Serra, it has kept me from attacking the king on several occasions. Patience is a virtue, but it also keeps you from murdering your loved ones."

Serra nodded at the queen's words but her legs shook. She put a hand against the wall to steady herself.

"Are you all right?"

Serra gulped. "Yes, just my nerves, I suppose."

The queen gave her another embrace. "We all get those, dear. Finish that glass of wine and focus on Janto's bound-to-be ridiculous reaction the moment you step through the throne room doors."

"I will." She felt nauseous.

"Good." The queen pecked her on the cheek and left.

Serra let the chill of the stone wall sink into her skin. Those words could not be a coincidence, but she had made her choice. They said she *had* a choice.

A knock came at the door, followed by Ser Allyn's voice. "Lady Gavenstone, it is time."

She swallowed the rest of her wine. "I am coming! Go ahead and begin the opening chant." She waited until his footsteps receded then went back to the mirror, her pallor white as its alabaster frame. Then she opened the door.

The hallway leading toward the throne room was empty. Everyone was inside, waiting for her beyond its first set of closed doors, everyone she loved in this world. Janto would be there, willing her to come to him.

Her eyes filled with tears as she took the other path, the one that led away from all that. She spun around.

A Brother waited in the shadows behind her, a gray robe with no limbs to hold it up. How had she never noticed their lack of feet before? She clenched her jaw and stepped toward the wraith.

"You lied to me." She threw the words at it.

"We cannot lie." The Brother's voice raised the hair on the back of her neck.

Her eyes burned as tears rolled down her cheek. She did not wipe them. "I made my choice."

"Yes, you have." It took her hand, and the castle's stone walls dissolved around them. When the pressed reeds of Enjoin's temple replaced them, she took her first breath in the week since she had left.

CHAPTER 30
JANTO

Janto was distracted. The belt was not in the trunk. He had rummaged through it twice already. But as he felt under a cloak for the third time, the sharpened end of it pricked his finger. The belt was an heirloom, a piece of interlinked metalwork two centuries old, crafted by the head metallurgist for Queen Drustalla's husband. Janto should know his name. *What is it? Hersh . . . no, Mershen . . .* neither sounded right.

The belt's tip drew no blood, luckily. Janto did not want to present himself to Serra in a stained groom's tunic. He clasped the belt around his waist, careful to avoid the edges of the links. *Now, do the fur-lined boots from Ertion come next or the cloak the Rasselerian weavers sent?* He could not keep anything straight. The damned dreams continued unabated, though Vesperi was locked in the dungeons until his father decided her fate. All night, Janto had been with her in spirit, chasing her in human and deer form around decrepit buildings in an abandoned village he had never seen. It could have been in Medua, he supposed, but that did not seem likely. The village's temple had Madel's hand reaching from its dome, not the fist of Saeth. He should ask Vesperi if any temples remained undefiled in Medua.

I will not ask her anything. He would be married as soon as he finished with his preparations—it was bad enough he could not get her smell, of all things, out of his mind. A phantom musk invaded his senses each time he dreamed. Janto took an earthenware jar from his mantle and dipped two fingers inside, pulling up a glob of perfume. The scent of lemons and anise filled his nostrils, and he rubbed it over his chest and arms. The wedding guests would titter about the strong perfume on a prince, but Janto did not care. Crinkling her nose, Serra would hold her questions until after.

"An accident," he'd tell her and she would laugh, strings on a lyre being plucked. *And if I say that, I start my marriage with a lie.* His stomach clenched. *Damn it!* He hurled the perfume jar against the wall. The shatter was briefly satisfying.

"My prince, are you all right?" Ser Allyn queried from the hallway, waiting to escort him to the throne room.

"I am fine. But send in a servant with a wet cloth, please."

"Right away." Ser Allyn's faint tread disappeared down the hall.

Janto sunk his head onto the mantel. He lifted it a few moments later when Pic entered the room, followed by Ser Allyn.

"Thanks, runt." Janto ruffled Pic's hair and pointed at the dripping ooze. "Right over there."

Ser Allyn raised an eyebrow, his gaze landing on Janto, unimpressed. Doubtless, he noted how many pieces of ceremonial apparel were still missing. Janto's head hurt to think of it. His acquiescence was not easy.

"I could use your help. I may have some wedding jitters after all."

"Of course." Ser Allyn huffed as he went to the open chest. He took out the brown and green cloak embroidered with silhouettes of marshfolk scattered among cattails. "Rasseleria came before Ertion, so you will need to take off those ridiculous boots. And the belt, please. The Albrechts bind us all together so that comes last."

Janto lifted an arm or leg when asked and focused his thoughts on Serra. He imagined how she would appear in his mother's beaded wedding gown. A garnet, the jewel of Gavenstone, would adorn her crown. She would be luminous, and the shine in her eyes would draw him to her, would be all he needed to feel content. *That* was his destiny, joining with Serra and taking his place as the heir to his father's throne. The last couple days of breaking bread with the enemy, a woman who could not begin to understand the concept of affection for anyone but herself, was a foray into the wilderness. And over.

Ser Allyn slipped a pair of gray gloves onto Janto's hands, lettering embroidered over the palms in an ancient script, one he had not seen since his religious studies with Rynna Hullvy as a child.

"Who sent these?" Janto worked out the words. They sounded familiar, at least the part he could translate: *Without her sight, mankind is done.* Perhaps one of the ritual chants? He rarely paid attention to the words, usually hummed along.

"A Brother delivered them for you early this morning." Ser Allyn tugged them on. The dense, velvety material felt weightless as lace. "They must bless your union, though I do not remember them bringing your father a gift for his wedding. There, that's the last of it. You are ready."

From the chants, then. He would have to research the passage. "Do I look a fool with all these accoutrements?" The gifts worn together made a weighty outfit.

"You look like the prince of Lansera, proud to wear the goods his people provide. You smell like a fool, though." Ser Allyn straightened his surcoat. "On your order, my prince."

Janto took a deep breath and stepped into the hall. "Let us go on to the throne room, ser." He would not keep Serra waiting any longer.

Balac blossoms decorated each chair, and green grapevines from Gavenstone laced their way around the tall posts. A quick glance toward the front of the room revealed Serra's absence, which meant Janto would have to exchange pleasantries with their guests. He was surprised to arrive first with all the readjustments needed to his attire. "Ser Allyn, would you please check on my bride?"

"Of course." Ser Allyn raised his elbows and walked out the back entrance.

The room was packed with councilmen and lieges from all over the country. Janto greeted Lord Sydley, who was seated near the front of the room. Lady Gella had also arrived, never one to miss a celebration. She wore a fur-trimmed shawl and fanned herself relentlessly. *May as well get the worst over with.*

"Oh, Janto, my prince." She jammed him between her arms. "I am so happy for you both." Tears moistened his cheek. "Here I am crying and getting you all mussed up." She dabbed at him with a violet handkerchief. Lord Xantas walked up behind her and pulled her back from the embrace.

"Gella, are you trying to smother the groom?"

She stopped mid-shush of her husband when she saw Janto's boots. "Oh, how lovely. I had my best trappers hunting for the perfect fox for those boots, you know. They *are* perfect." She beamed and fanned herself again. "Just perfect."

"Come now, let the man greet his guests."

Janto mouthed a thank you over her head. He greeted Mer Refusa next, owner of the marketplace in Callyn. "I am delighted you could attend."

Mer Refusa wore a tunic studded with feathers, as did most of the guests in the room. "Much honor to you, my prince." He snapped his fingers, eliciting a chorus of howls from the piebald dogs at his feet. Janto gave each a pat on the head before moving on. He was grateful for the small talk, no thinking needed to go through the motions, and he could keep one eye on the door. A creak sounded as he shook hands with Mar Welset, owner of an inn, and her husband. He stopped mid-sentence and straightened up, but the doors remained closed.

"That was your mother in the front." Mer Welset's smile was knowing. Queen Lexamy had entered from the door closest to the throne. She wore a blue gown today with some sort of darker blue netting over the skirt.

Mar Welset coughed into her handkerchief. "You were talking about the cost of soap?"

"Don't be silly." Mer Welset refused to talk shop. "It is his wedding day! He can be distracted. And rumor has it you have not seen her since before your Murat. Your eyes must be thirsty!"

Janto chuckled. "They are in dire need of a drink."

He excused himself from the Welsets when Queen Lexamy waved him forward from where she talked with a pair of Rasselerians near the throne, dressed in suits of gray and white that blended well with the walls. As he reached them, he heard his mother ask, "The waters are rising?"

The marshfolk nodded in affirmation. The woman spoke. "It reaches to the floor of our lowest huts. Twelve families have moved in with others."

Her companion leaned into the queen, speaking low. "The waters bring darkness with them, the hidden swarms." His mother clutched a hand to her throat.

Janto frowned, the exchange confounding him. "Mother, what's wrong?"

"I am well. Fine, I promise." She patted his arm and returned to the Rasselerians. "I will talk to the king as soon as the ceremony is complete." She smiled weakly at them both. "Thank you for coming."

"Yes, thank you," Janto echoed. He didn't know what else to say, not understanding their conversation. "Where's Father?"

"I am not certain." Her voice belied no anxiety. "One of the

Brotherhood was here earlier, and"—she nodded toward the Rasseleri-ans—"they may have had pressing news."

"I think they were dropping off these gloves." Janto held his hands up.

She inspected them. "What a lovely material. I have not felt spec-tersveil since—"

A loud creak resounded from the back of the hall as the doors opened. It was time, finally, it was time. A figure stood at the end of the hall in the shadow of the frame. The crowd ceased their conversations, and Janto's heart leapt. It had to be Serra. She took a step forward, the beads of her dress sparkling as the sun streamed in from the ceiling. Her upswept hair, held by feathers, left her freckled shoulders exposed, and her necklace of cloves lay against her chest. He shouldn't see it all at this distance, but he did. She was crying tears of what had to be joy—they *had* to be. He teared up in response, and his legs trembled, a sign of their overwhelming love, he was certain.

A moment passed, then she took a step closer. Janto blinked and shook his head. A panicked groan came from his throat unbidden. It . . . it was not Serra, was not a woman at all who entered the room, but his father wearing his formal goldspun tunic. Had Serra stepped behind him? Janto's vision clouded with tears, and he did not know why. *Serra is there. She is right there*—

Only the brown-tinged darkness of the candlelit hall could be seen behind his father. King Dever Albrecht marched at a fast clip, and as his features came into focus, Janto recognized his glower, lips pulled taut. People whispered, their voices a sharp pain in his head.

"Janto." His father placed a firm hand on his shoulder, and Janto's breath fled at the touch. He clapped his hands over his ears too late to block the words out.

"She's gone."

Part Two

The Culling

When the silver stag runs free,
blessed will he who binds it be.
Rise up, ye treasured bird of three.
Wing him what boons ye foresee.

When evil spawns and overruns,
from silver the weapon comes.
Without her sight, mankind is done.
With it, all will again be one.

CHAPTER 31
GARADIN

G aradin braced himself for the sound of galloping hooves on the road to Kallon. Normally, their absence would give him cause to doubt the wizards' prowess, but Garadin was too scared to pay that potential weakness much mind. Instead, Romer's face in battle filled his head, a memory from when they'd fought King Turyn's army in the bramble that final day of the war. Swollen and dotted with blood from a thousand thorn pricks, anger had twisted Romer's face into a gargoyle's as he swung his axe madly, chopping their enemies in two. Garadin had rolled out of the way to avoid the blade himself.

Romer's rage had not lessened over the years. Garadin had seen it in action many times, usually when the Guj reprimanded advers who failed in an attempt to kill one of their peers. The assailant would be flayed during a meal at Mandat Hall, hung upside-down and left to shudder in death's throes on the stage. Once, decades ago, Garadin had been the target of a failed attack, and eating had been difficult during those conclaves ever since. The other adver had been a Durnish man— he never knew his name. The man had been jealous of Garadin's post as a whisperer in Qiltyn, which did have its benefits, including visits to the girls at the convent. His enemy was flayed not twenty feet from where Garadin sucked the marrow out of a duck bone. The young man twitched and swung in torment but kept his pain-filled eyes fixed on Garadin who refused to meet his gaze. Instead, he watched the copper medallion hanging from the man's neck—a thin, round disk with an opal at its center. The man jerked harder when the flayer moved from his arms to his chest, and the disc spun like a burning globe with a fiery white core at its center. When it finally came to rest, the man dead with half his ribs finished, Garadin had rushed to the privy. The duck did not stay in his stomach. He applied for reassignment from Qiltyn the next day, and the Guj had sent him to Sellwyn.

Facing Romer's justice was no option Garadin would take. If his hip were not lame, he would have ridden off alone on horseback to spend his last days covered in tar like the workers of Kallon, unrecognizable. But there was naught he could do about that, naught but put as much distance between him and his inevitable capture as possible. He had lived a full life, and who knew? Maybe Saeth, or Madel rather, would grant him another day of it.

✹✹✹

A Pigeon

The bird tired. Her wings, ringed with gray and brown stripes, beat barely fast enough to keep her in the air. Many insects flitted about the closer she drew to the city and the refuse where they bred. Flies and moths rushed past but also bugs she had never seen before. They flickered in the light like red and black glitter and stuck together in groups, which would make it easy to catch a few for a meal. But she could not stop to suck them in yet, not with a paper tied around her leg. The only way to get it off would be to arrive at her next perch and let the human there remove the annoyance.

The tall poles sticking out from the city's buildings were in sight. Only a few more strokes needed to reach the familiar ledge. And then, she would feast.

The pigeon landed on a ledge beneath the tallest structure, the one that shone red when the sun set. A layer of white, yellow, and brown droppings in various states of decay covered it. With the window's shutters closed, the bird hobbled about, pecking at the wood as she was trained to do. She waited. No one came. She poked around the shutters' edges but could not fit her beak between them, so she sat back down on the sill, curled her claws around its edge, and cooed. Still, no one came.

Something dark flew by her right. She twisted her head and spied a swarm of the strange flickering insects. She was hungry, so hungry after such a long flight. The pigeon hobbled over and jabbed her beak into their midst. It filled with many bugs, nearly choking her as she swallowed them down. They tasted like the shiny metal disks she always tried to pull from the raised pool of water in the middle of the city. The pigeon did not have to hobble over to the insects for a second helping. They came in force.

* * *

EYRTI

After the daily prayer to Saeth, Adver Eyrti flung open the window shutters to bring a fresh breeze into the tower room of the temple. The pigeons inside flapped their wings at the rush of air but could not take flight, their legs tied to the branches of their shellacked perch. Eyrti stared out over Qiltyn. It was a pretty sunset, the rooftops peach with touches of deeper red like honeymelon flesh. This time of day gave them borders, each building a framed painting hung on the same wall.

He did not notice the dead pigeon at first, mistaking it for a pile of molted feathers on the ledge. The bird's shape and girth were gone, leaving a grotesque sack of skin, claws, beak, and feathers. Eyrti lifted his handkerchief to his mouth as he made to flick it off the pane. At the last second, he noticed a minute scroll attached to what might have been a leg. Using a twig, he pushed the mass aside and cut the string with a dagger. A viper sigil sealed the letter.

House Sellwyn. Eyrti's blood quickened. Any word from that manor was to be brought to the Guj right away. The letter had taken longer to arrive than expected. Eyrti would give a million souzers to know what it contained, but he could not risk peeking at something so important. If it was as valuable as he'd been led to believe, the wizards would probably inspect it before opening and detect the magic Eyrti used to read words through rolled-up paper.

He tucked the scroll inside his robe and did not close the window in his haste. Nor did he notice when a pigeon on the perch collapsed in on itself, beak opened wide. Another quickly followed then another and another, masses of feathers swiveling upside-down and dangling from claws tied to branches.

✷ ✷ ✷

"The Guj is not taking visitors today." For the third time, the guard on the left refused Eyrti with obvious enjoyment. Eyrti refrained from waving a hand in front of the man's face and moving his pea-sized nose to his ear, where he would likely never find it. No need for these buffoons to know he possessed a little magic, though he really, really wanted to show them. They always gave him a hard time, because he stood a full foot shorter than the lot of them.

"You are not understanding me." Eyrti gritted his teeth. "I am under strict instruction to bring this message to our esteemed ruler immediately or I will lose my head, and both of you will, too, when he finds out you delayed me." Threats to their bodily safety were the only language these men understood.

"You cannot go inside without permission." The guard's smirk swallowed his tiny nose whole.

"Then go ask for my permission!" Eyrti hoped he yelled loud enough for someone behind the door to come investigate. But the next voice he heard was not a welcome one. It was Adver Votan's, that Deduin cretin, rounding the corner with two of the Guj's council trailing behind him, the fat Adver Nouin and the silver-haired Yarowen, Adver Tolliv. Half the bones Votan had sewn into his robe had to be fabricated by some sort of spell. He wasn't old enough to have killed so many men. And he spent far too much time whispering in the halls to make that great an accomplishment. Being near other magic users unnerved Eyrti despite the levere talisman he wore at all times. Maybe it worked to shield him, or maybe the Guj's wizards simply saw him as no threat. Votan would not be so kind.

"Having problems, my friend?" Votan raised his elbows in greeting. Eyrti returned the gesture begrudgingly. He did not want to mention the letter with Votan around but this . . . this could mean his head.

"I have a very important message for the Guj and these simpletons will not let me deliver it to him. I should report them for their insolence."

"Hmm." A simpering smile lingered on Votan's face. "Insolence against the bird keeper? That is a remarkable crime. Perhaps I could deliver this message for you?"

"*You*? They will not let you in, either. 'The Guj is not taking visitors today' or so I have been told a million times this—"

Eyrti gasped as the guards unlatched the door and swung it open without a word.

"Oh yes," Votan gloated, "the Guj did tell me he was not seeing visitors earlier. That *is* correct." He leaned down to meet Eyrti's eyes. "Now did you want my assistance with that message?"

This is . . . this is ridiculous, insufferable! Votan had access to the Guj's chambers? The man was barely out of swaddling clothes. Had he charmed the Guj somehow? Was his magic that strong? More importantly, should he give Votan the scroll? The purple-eyed sheven waited, pale hand palm up. He would undoubtedly take credit for whatever the message said. The guards would not provide witnesses in Eyrti's favor. Then again, the Guj might slaughter everyone in the room should the news be ill received. But if good tidings, well, Eyrti would not let that slimy Votan steal his reward.

"No. I must deliver it personally. If you would tell him I am here—"

"Enough!" Votan snatched the scroll from his hands, and Eyrti grunted in consternation. He stamped his feet, fuming, as the Deduin and the Guj's councilors went through the door.

What now? The minutes passed. But as he went to return to his birds, a sweet sound stopped him—Adver Votan screaming. The piercing yell was music to Eyrti's ears. Footfalls followed it to the door, which opened to reveal Adver Nouin out of breath and beckoning Eyrti inside.

He had not been in the Guj's chamber in ages, and truth be told, he had not wanted to return. Being in close proximity to their leader was not usually a pleasant experience, but Eyrti followed Nouin to the large levere-shielded chamber at the end of the hall where a pleasant sight greeted him, that of Adver Votan crouched in the far corner, whimpering. Votan's body jerked all over, and the man covered his head with his arms as though in the midst of a needlestorm back on the Deduin ice plains. Eyrti felt a passing pity for him, as their positions would be reversed if Eyrti had handed in the message. Sometimes being only the bird keeper was an advantage.

The Guj sat on a pile of pillows in a number of bold, jewel-toned colors: amethyst, jade, emerald. His voice resonated although the walls were covered with cloth.

"Adver Eyrti"—the Guj paused his speech as Eyrti raised his elbows in deference—"Votan tells me you gave him this scroll. Is that true?"

Votan's head lifted at his name, and eyes that normally glowed with a life of their own looked flat as a snuffed fire. Eyrti noticed, suddenly, the wizards in the room. They stood in an alcove behind the door, their hands joined while they chanted inaudibly. *Perhaps Votan's needlestorm is not imagined.*

"Yes, Your Greatness. I gave him the scroll from Sellwyn."

"Why did you not bring it yourself?" His voice was measured, calm. Could the news not have been that bad after all? Perhaps Votan's torment was for some other affair.

"I tried to, Your Greatness, I swear it. A . . ." How could he describe the disgusting mess on the window ledge? "A pigeon brought the scroll. I discovered it after the evening ritual, and when I saw the sigil it bore, I ran straightaway to your chamber door. The guards did not believe I had your leave to enter unbidden."

The Guj turned to Adver Nouin. "You will kill these guards." His manner was easy. Nouin left the room immediately. Everything was turning out better than Eyrti had hoped.

Votan's whimpering started up again. *Such a hideous noise.* Was the man trying to ruin his mood?

"Did you read the scroll, adver?" The Guj rolled it up and stood.

"Oh no, Your Greatness. Other than the viper on its seal, I have no idea what it contained."

"Good." He tossed the parchment into the fireplace. Its top edge caught fire instantly. "You would do well to keep it that way. Tell no one you received it."

"I would not dream of it."

"That's very wise. You are dismissed. See you keep your birds well fed. I may have need of them tonight."

"Of course." He wasted no time making his way back out through the narrow hallway and crashed into Adver Nouin in his hurry.

"Apologies, Adver, I did not mean—"

"No harm done, Eyrti. You best be careful as you leave. The exterior hall is a mess, and the servants have not been called yet." Nouin's face betrayed nothing.

"I will." Eyrti continued on his way, making sure to grab an extra bag of seeds from the kitchens.

✳ ✳ ✳

Nⴲuin

Adver Nouin clutched the guards' wet, sticky thumbs in his hand. Once inside Romer's false chamber, he bent his knee and offered them. "Yours, Your Greatness." It was a shame he could not keep them himself.

Romer threw them against the wall. They hit a tapestry, leaving a smattering of red blood on Saeth's hairy chest. When the Guj spoke, all pretense disappeared. "Run away? How could she have *run away?*"

Nouin watched Votan, who appeared to pay no attention to their conversation, his hands covering his ears as he whimpered, trapped in the wizards' spell. "Do you want to keep *him* here? While we discuss this?" Why the Deduin lived was a mystery. He had heard too much. Seen the sigil.

"What does it matter?" Romer spat at Votan, who did not flinch. "Without her, none of it matters. You know that."

I do. The Sellwyn whore was the key to everything. All these years they had sought to be ready, keeping the women controlled and under strict observation so they could use the silver weapon once found. Medua was a wasteland compared with the riches of Lansera, and they were too few strong men to raise a true threat against the Albrechts' army again. But the silver weapon destroyed threats to mankind. It could surely kill man just as well. Its power had been prophesied for millennia, and they had watched and waited, but somehow, their best chance of attacking the Lanserim had escaped them. It—she—had been their battle plan. The weapon needed someone to sight it, and they were determined to be the seer.

Votan slumped to the floor, his chest rising weakly. The wizards stopped chanting, waiting for instruction, but Romer stewed in his anger. The veins of his bald head pulsed.

"I will contact Ralion at court, make him ready—"

Romer's silence disheartened Nouin, but he tried again anyhow. "We should send a company after her."

"Yes." The Guj brightened at the suggestion. "I will find her no matter where she's gone. She cannot outrun me. And send one after Garadin—word cannot get out that he failed to contact me. Send a bird to Lansera as well, warn them against her. They will not want our discards."

Nouin complied swiftly; being far from Romer was wise during these moods. But he did sweep the guards' fingers into his robe before exiting. Such trophies should not be left to rot. The pigeons would peck the bones clean, finding the flesh tastier than anything Eyrti had gathered for them in the roost.

CHAPTER 32
VESPERI

"There is a prophecy."

The king leaned against the dungeon's stone wall. Its two barred windows filled the room with more light than anywhere Vesperi had resided before. His voice was more tired than the last time he had questioned her, before the wedding that was not to be.

"It has not often been uttered in these last two generations. In part, because time makes it easy to forget what our forebears heeded. In part, because my family did not want to face its implications. War makes intangible threats disappear."

Why he bothered to discuss a Lanserim prophecy with her, she could not guess. Why he made no advances toward her was even stranger. She did not fear being alone with him, but she did not know how to respond, either. The guards regarded her with curiosity, not conversation, which was easier to ignore.

"Have you heard these words, Lady Sellwyn? *When evil—*"

"Don't call me that." The titles they insisted on using were annoying. "I am no one's lady."

The king regarded her thoughtfully. "You gave me to understand you are from House Sellwyn. Do not the viper's fangs clasp your cloaks at home?"

"They did." The truth flowed freely around this man, her resistance worn down. She was tired of lying. She had been doing it her whole life. "But I am not a Sellwyn now. I doubt my father would welcome a parley party. He would rather you march me straight to Thokketh than ransom me. Any messengers you send will be hanged outside the manor walls."

His eyebrows raised. "I see. Few here, not even my son, are still taught the sigils from over the mountains, so it will not be hard to put that past behind you. We have not wanted to open old wounds—" he sighed, looking out the windows "—nor do I wish to afflict new ones. It may be best that you keep your family crest hidden."

She wondered what he thought of then, his voice resigned, sad, but he continued nonetheless. "Still, I must ask if you have ever heard these words, Vesperi with a house no longer."

She considered telling him not to worry his royal mind with religious recitations. She had heard none since the convent and doubted the followers of Saeth sang the same praises as the worshippers of Madel. If they did, their female god was a lot more interesting than she had thought.

"*When evil spawns and overruns, from silver the weapon comes. Without her sight, mankind is done. With it, all will again be one.*"

Energy caressed her fingertips as he spoke, and she gasped. Her hands were bound, Esye hid from view. *Then how?* The king stared at her, amber eyes relaxing only when she met them. It was then she realized he glowed, glowed like she might when her talent flamed, a mesmerizing vibrant blue ringing his body.

"I do not know those words." The truth spilled out of her again, her mind reeling from the display. "What are they?"

He smiled then, the first time she had witnessed it, and the blue shone more brilliantly. But there was no threat in the energy. Rather, she felt more at peace than she remembered ever feeling before. *It is a different talent.* The realization was a relief; he may not know all her secrets yet. Vesperi wanted, no needed, to keep hers close, and this dungeon was a comfortable place to rest. She needed time to develop an escape plan that would work.

"As I said, it is an old prophecy. I first committed it to memory while going through my novice training with the Order—our priesthood—as a teenager."

The aura around him faded as swiftly as it had come. Something ached within her to see it go, but Vesperi scoffed at his words. *A prince who wanted to be a priest of Madel, to serve a female god?* No, the king was lying to her, and he was as bad at it as his son, thus the smile.

"I am sorry. Please continue," she tried not to smirk as she added, "my king."

"It was recited at the beginning of every ritual before my father's war—I suppose I must have had it memorized as a child, too. What is it you call our great conflict?"

"A revolution."

"Of course." Grimness took the place of his smile. "The Brotherhood considered the prophecy of utmost importance to Lansera's future. All their messages touched on it, but after the war . . . well, we did not have the stomach for pondering what other evils our castoffs might create."

"Your castoffs? You mean, us, the Meduans?"

"Yes. Do you mind?" He gestured toward the sole chair in the room.

She shook her head at the absurdity of a king asking her permission. The alienness of his behavior made her second guess what she had seen and felt moments ago. The king had not acknowledged it. *A trick of the eyes. I am out of sorts.* And if the king insisted on acting baser than he was, granting her needless courtesy, then she could risk poking a little fun to see what she might learn from him. "That's quite an interesting term, *castoff.* The Sisters at the convent taught we had *won* our freedom in the war from the likes of you and your pretentious brethren."

"One man's freedom is another man's perversion. But tell me, Vesperi, my spies report that the women of your land are not exactly free. Is that not so? And I am most intrigued by the Sisters you mentioned. Were they in charge of your schooling?"

"Your spies—the Ravens, I assume you mean—are correct. And I learned nothing from my teachers at the convent school. Most women are useless." She shrugged. Telling him these things was harmless. They were known.

"And you, Vesperi, are you also useless?"

The proper answer at home would be to agree, but this was not her father asking nor did anyone stand ready to strike should she say otherwise. This man had traded more words with her in two meetings than Lord Sellwyn had spared her in years. So she deflected. "Tell me the prophecy again, my king. I may have recognized a word or two." If she pretended to, she could buy herself more time.

"Certainly. I will start with the beginning stanza. It is the most remembered among my people. *When the silver stag runs free, blessed will he who binds it be. Rise up, ye treasured bird of three. Wing him what boons ye foresee.* What do you think? Is any of that familiar?"

"Stags and wings? I do not know them." But the words *were* familiar. She felt it in her blood. Or maybe in the hair rising on her arms as the king was again bathed in blue. He made no note of it, just stared with curiosity. No doubt she appeared spellbound.

"Vesperi, are you all right?" He touched her, the aura dimming.

Have I gone mad at last? Father would be pleased. If she was sane, then that prophecy held some sort of power here. Perhaps she had heard the words as a child before the Lanserim sympathizers had been weeded out entirely, but she could not remember anyone singing chants in the manor, not ever, and she was never in town for long. "It's sung during rituals, did you say? I am sorry, but I do not think we have kept any of your hymns."

Did she utter the words *I am sorry* and mean them? These people infested her with their goodness. She would forget how to survive if she spent any more time with them. But she was not ready to leave. She wasn't. *And it has nothing to do with how serene that blue . . . whatever it was . . . made me feel.*

"That is a shame. I had hoped you might know something of it." He knocked on the cell door. "I apologize for all the questioning, but it's not often a Meduan comes to Callyn. My Ravens provide me with information, but they cannot fully understand what it is like over the mountains. They were not raised like you."

A guard opened the door while another walked inside to escort the king out. He raised his elbows in farewell, and as he turned, his cloak fell flat against his back. It bore a three-headed bird ready for flight with radiant plumage of silver, copper, and gold. Minus the colors, it was the exact double of the carving at Sellwyn Manor. No, Vesperi did not know the words of the prophecy, but she knew how they appeared in an old, forgotten language chiseled out of marble. "King Albrecht!"

"What is it, Vesperi?"

She stammered, unsure whether she should reveal the connection. It meant something to him but not to her, and sharing it would give him the advantage. "I . . . I am surprised at the emblem on your cloak. Janto did not have such a creature on his."

"The swan is the sigil of the Albrechts, but this is mine, chosen when I became king. I took it from one of our stories of creation. I don't wear it often, but it seemed appropriate today. Are you not familiar with the myths of Lansera?"

She shook her head, and he sighed again, sadness returned to his voice. "May Madel's hand guide you, Vesperi."

He left. More out of habit than desire, she checked that the door handle was stuck fast as best she could with tied hands then flounced onto the bed. The coincidence was uncanny—the carving had been the only thing that gave her comfort in Sellwyn, and the feeling the blue light had ushered in was much the same. *No, I need not be so hasty to escape from here.* Trusting the Albrechts to keep her safe wasn't as unsettling a notion as she thought it might be.

CHAPTER 33
SERRA

Footsteps trailed away from the hut, waking Serra. She grimaced as she opened her eyes to the dark. Serra hated waking in the dark. For the last five days, nothing had forced her from bed before her natural rising. No one knew what to do with her, so there were no demands to fill. *Funny how that works.* She had left her whole world behind to play whatever role the Brothers had foreseen for her, and none of the ryns and rynnas knew what it was. No Brother had shown its . . . hood . . . since her transportation from Callyn in a blink of whirring air that dissipated as soon as her feet materialized on the sloshy ground outside the temple. A novice had seen her first and screamed, but Ryn Gylles had shushed the woman with a shake and a whisper. Then he came to Serra, not asking why she had returned but accepting her presence with a wave of his hand and a hug. He then launched into a list of all the lessons he needed to prepare for the novices trickling in every day, and he was surprised to see so many, and did she want a room to put her things in?

Serra did not question the peace and quiet. The noise in her head was plenty, drowning out the initial relief she felt at making the choice to return. *What will they want of me?* was her most common refrain. *He will never forgive me* was the next. The worst, which grew louder each day she was left alone, was *they wanted Janto to marry someone worthier.* To her dismay, it never failed to make her cry. She had had enough of tears, enough of feeling as though her life were out of her control.

So she slept as she liked, waking when the first farrowbird raised its voice to complain with high-pitched trills about the heat of mid-morning. Then she started a fire for tea in the hearth and hoped none of the mice living beneath its stones nibbled at her toes. Food was left at her door each morning, and she drank her tea while she ate, imagining how much better the porridge would taste if Mar Pina had sprinkled her famous spice blend on it. Then a walk for fresh air and a short visit with Ryn Gylles. He shared the news of Lansera freely, though he never spoke of the prince. Serra was grateful. Once or twice, she had joined the novices in their training sessions instead of seeing Ryn Gylles. They'd learn a bit of every trade in Lansera, and the ones who had returned to Enjoin earliest got a head start.

Serra yawned in the dark and rolled off the bare cot. Perhaps a message arriving this early meant the novices planned an excursion into the woods. Learning more about the herbs used for healing might be sufficiently distracting. Serra had always been fascinated watching Queen Lexamy mix up a compound. On the dusty rug outside, she found a piece of slim, pressed birchwood with a message scrawled over it: "Meditation begins soon. A novice would be there." It had to be from Gylles. No one else knew how to challenge her here. But Serra had attended no rituals since her return. She was *here*. What greater display of faith could she make to Madel of her willingness? Everything—everyone—had been given up for it.

But another day of searching for cracks in the huts' walls sounded worse than holding on to that stubbornness. She pulled on her sheath, ran a brush through her moisture-thickened hair, and started up the path.

✳ ✳ ✳

The novices were already assembled on their prayer mats. About thirty initiates had returned to take the next step, meaning a quarter of their number had stayed home. By the doorway sat a welcome face. *Lourda.* Seeing her friend, wild hair pulled back and laced through with a marshweed-colored ribbon, made Serra happier than she had felt in a month. *Perhaps my calling is to be a hairdresser for wayward Ertions.* A genuine smile bloomed on her face.

"Lourda!"

Lourda clapped her hands with delight. "Serra, my princess!" She hugged her close. "I thought you had returned to Callyn to wed that prince!"

"So had I." Serra sunk into the hug. There were questions in Lourda's eyes, but a Brother swept in through the door and floated to the center of the temple, grabbing their attentions. Yet the novices looked awed, not disgusted at its presence. How could no one else see them for what they were? Still, Serra had come back knowing the truth, had let one of them whisk her through their spirit realm to get here. What did that make her? She rested her head on Lourda's shoulder while the Brother gave its instructions in an ethereal voice.

"Chosen few, you are here to learn how to breathe and to be. You have done this before, whenever you've attended a ritual. But a priest must endure more than an hour's worth of show. A priest must continue his or her meditation until Madel instructs them to stop or the last parishioners have received their fill of glory. Sometimes, that will take only a few moments but at other times, it may be hours. Those who experience true distress or true rapture lose track of time as we know it. They inhabit another space where Madel resonates within them. So today you learn to breathe, and through breathing, you learn to let Madel in."

The exercise would continue until the last of them reached their limits, unable to lie prostrate on the mat any longer. There would be breaks for meals, but no touching, no communication. Lourda withdrew from Serra and returned to her mat. Serra claimed one of her own, thinking it better to be lost in thought among others than alone again in her hut.

They began by counting to seven, the number of regions in Lansera before Turyn's War. They counted slower with each recitation, the words spoken between inhalation and exhalation of air. As they went, they lengthened their breaths, a technique taught in religious courses growing up. It naturalized the meditation process, purifying the mind of all thoughts but the vital task of breathing. This allowed one to feel Madel should She reach out Her hand.

One. Two. Three. Serra had never participated in the breathing rituals before, not really. Maintaining her composure was more important than practicing religion, according to her mother, who'd said, "Meditlan lieges must have their wits about them at all times, especially so close to the mountains and Meduans." Lady Gavenstone had shown Serra how to breathe shallowly rather than deeply so no one would think her meditation faked. When Ryn Raspier hit the ending chime of the ritual bell, Lady Gavenstone had always fluttered her fan to give the illusion of faintness.

Six. Seven. One. Agler had ignored their mother's training and was quite devout as a child, though not that great at meditation. The first time Serra saw his lips turn blue, she was four and determined to have blue lips, too. Fervor was something her brother had that she did not, and she had wanted it. Luckily, by the time he planned assassinations, his irresponsible actions no longer held any romance. She would never want to imitate *that* behavior.

Five. Six. Sev—was it One, now? She struggled to focus on the exercise. Sitting motionless was difficult, even with a lady's discipline. Her body ached above her ass, where the stretch was most pronounced. Her hands occasionally went numb, wrists pressed to the ground. Sometimes, she gave in to the temptation to open her eyes and inspected the room. The novices mostly murmured the counts by that point in the meditation, their breathing soft and bodies stilled. Once in a while, her eyes met the tired gaze of someone else's, and they exchanged grins before closing eyes again.

As the morning passed, Serra relaxed into the exercise. The mundanity of repeating numbers out loud comforted her. After an hour or so, she was so at peace, she hoped she would not fall asleep. She felt, rather than heard, the instruction to breathe slower as time went on. When midday arrived with the chime of a bell, a single breath took her nearly ten seconds to finish. She opened her eyes, blinking to rid her vision of reddish-black spots. A few dark specks lingered in the back of the room. She blinked again. *Gone.*

Are my lips blue? she wondered as she walked the short distance to a kitchen table laden with lentils and bread, food meant to sustain acolytes rather than supply pleasure. She sat next to Lourda, but they did not speak. No one did. The extended meditation had drained them of conversation. She recognized most their faces but had not learned all their names during the initiation. Tiny Asten and Gullo, a young grainsorter from Neville, were among them. Poline's absence surprised Serra. But she had learned that Madel rarely led people down paths they expected.

She took solace in their proximity. Feeling part of a group was nice, although the others were there with the clear purpose of working to become Madel's servants. Maybe she was, too, though her role was a different one.

✳ ✳ ✳

Soon after lunch, people began to collapse. Serra had easily slid back into meditation, but she heard them fall with muffled thuds on prayer mats. Some had probably fallen asleep, but others may have passed out, perhaps forgotten to take a breath somewhere between *five* and *seven*. The meditation continued through the afternoon and into the late hours of the night after another meal break. There was no official word about sleep. The Brother had left before dinner, and the ryns and rynnas keeping watch left pillows at each prayer mat. The novices curled up on them in their own time. When morning dawned, they returned to meditation after breaking their fast, half of the novices gone. Serra did not feel out of sorts rising so early for once; she was surprised to still be there at all. The meditation was not draining as she had expected. It made her skin tingle and her senses sharpened. She could hear beetle ants scurry around the temple's perimeter.

Lourda collapsed near the end of the second afternoon. Serra did not bid her farewell. She hardly noticed the movement, her mind a limitless void in all directions. When dinner came, she almost begged to stay in place. But she did not want to mislead anyone. Serra did not feel the presence of Madel, only a measure of serenity she had not known since the Raven had arrived with news of Agler's death.

In the night that followed, Serra dreamed of her father calling to her, but she could not see him. A river's roar muffled his voice, and she kept running toward it, trying to glimpse him through the thorn bushes along the bank. His voice grew fainter and fainter, and when gone entirely, she woke and immediately prostrated herself on her mat in the dark. Breathing deeply was more of a solace than dreams. She wondered how much longer the exercise might last and sneaked glances at the others who had endured. Four remained, the other three asleep on their mats. Serra prayed they also got what they wanted from the exercise, maybe improved stamina or experiencing Madel in a new way. For her, it was respite.

She breathed deeply and rhythmically, slowing her thoughts with the count. It was familiar now, this strange ability to feel every drop of blood flow, every pulse of her heart move them one miniscule unit farther on a circuit of her body. When a limb fell asleep, it was not an inconvenience but a new sensation she felt in her spirit.

"Open your eyes."

The whisper annoyed her, interrupting her concentration. It was not yet time for the breakfast meal. She clenched her eyelids down in protest.

The voice grew louder.

"Open your eyes."

"No," Serra whispered. "It's not time yet."

"Yes, it is, Serrafina. Open them and see."

Father? The rush of emotions defeated her previous resolve. She opened her eyes, hoping for a hallucination, that he would be here for a moment if only in a dream. Instead, she saw the temple in the partial dimness of daybreak. The other novices were awake and meditating, but only two remained. She hadn't heard the last one leave.

The atmosphere of the temple felt off, something that shouldn't be there mixing with the peacefulness. She lifted her head toward the glass dome. Smatterings of dusky redness hung in the air like comet tails. The eerie sight remained after blinking, speckled orbs of red and black grouped together and . . . fluttering? *I must not have woken.*

A mass of them churned toward the open temple door, leaving a trail of red dust in their wake. The mass rotated in on itself as it moved. It had to be made up of hundreds of . . . of . . . insects, maybe, like a swarm.

Menace emanated from them.

Sudden panic made Serra look up. One of them hovered above her head. It had red wings and pulsing red eyes, the dying embers of a flame. Silently, it swooped downward. She screamed, hand covering her nose and mouth, eyes closed.

Water—or what she hoped was water—splashed over her face. Rynna Robelly, a quiet woman barely taller than a ten-year-old with warm, golden eyes, stood above her, holding the pitcher. She stroked her cheek reassuringly as Serra stirred, realizing she had fainted and wondering if the others who had passed out earlier had shared the same hallucination. How had they held in their revulsion? It had been so real.

Gullo was one of the two remaining novices. "You gave us a scare!" He supported her with muscular, sinewy arms. He had also done carpentry back home in Jost.

"I am sorry . . . I . . . I screamed, didn't I?" She was flustered. No one else had screamed, Serra was certain of it. And seeing evil bugs? Surely, the goal of meditation was not to have a nightmare. The peacefulness she had built up was shattered. She missed her servants. And fresh clothes. And oh, how she missed Janto. He would not laugh at her for those last two complaints, only run his fingers through her hair until she stopped ranting.

Ryn Gylles hurried through the entryway, Rynna Gemni by his side. "Are you recovered?" Worry was apparent in his voice.

She leaned away from Gullo, feeling steady. "I think so. I am not sure what happened. I must have pushed myself too hard."

Ryn Gylles helped her to her feet. "You should return to your hut. Gullo, would you give her your arm on the walk?" Gullo nodded. "Good. I will have a meal sent to you, Serra. Rest and relax."

She raised her elbows in acquiescence though resting and relaxing had caused her to faint in the first place. Maybe food would ensure she saw nothing in her dreams this time.

CHAPTER 34

JANTO

Janto stumbled in the dark of the underground passage leading to the dungeons in the hillsides. They were disguised as barrows, their aboveground windows and roofs covered with grass. It was important prisoners be allowed sunlight no matter what they had done. No one deserved to live in the dark.

Serra, apparently, did not share that conviction. It had been a week since the wedding. Janto's initial panic subsided once his father received a bird from Enjoin. But knowing Serra was safe opened the floodgate of his anger. How could she do that to him? He was now the prince who had been jilted for Madel, and maybe that would be tolerable if true, but Serra had never been devout. There had to be another reason she left. Their love could not have simply changed—he would know, wouldn't he? But he had barely seen her in months and so much had happened. *No, Serra is not like that. There has to be a reason.* She would not give up on him without explanation, especially not now when he needed her more than ever. He had planned to tell her about the dreams after the wedding, tell her how killing the stag had been more of a curse than a boon. He needed someone to understand. He wanted it to be Serra, but now . . .

Disbelief warred with the hurt as he grasped at the rough edges of stone tiles used to reinforce the passage's walls. He had only been to the dungeons a few times before. They were rarely used after Turyn's War. Town councils settled most grievances. Only when the charge was more serious, like treason, did prisoners end up here. Vesperi qualified as a potential threat, not because she was Meduan, but because she had indicated no desire to defect. Indeed, she seemed to revel in the base selfishness of her people. Yet he made his way to her through the cold, damp passage, because he had nowhere else to go. "I dream of Vesperi constantly, and it is the only thing that feels familiar now Serra's gone," was not exactly dinner conversation for his parents.

The passage took on an olive-green hue as he neared the cells. Two guards outside Vesperi's straightened up as he approached.

"May Madel's hand guide you, Ser Firl, Sar Pella."

"Your Highness." Sar Pella raised her elbows as high as she could with a pointed halberd in hand. "You must be here for the Meduan? She has had no visitors since your father two mornings ago."

"Yes. I need to speak with her."

He breathed a sigh of relief when they asked no further questions. He had no explanation to give them. Unless "Serra is gone and I don't think she's coming back" would suffice.

Sar Pella opened the door while Ser Firl took position behind them, one hand on his halberd and the other shielding his eyes from the burst of light that filled the passage. Janto went in, and the door shut fast behind him.

A gasp, and then a peal of laughter. "Why are you here? Need someone to make you feel virile now your princess has absconded with your manhood?"

"Why do you do that?" This was precisely what he needed. All thoughts fled his mind but the irritation this woman made him feel, always fighting, always on guard. Knowing how she'd react, that she could not hurt him without true feelings motivating her attacks, was a relief.

"Do what?" She smirked. "Speak the truth?"

This time he laughed. She could have given him no better opening. "Speak the truth? If you are so fond of that, then why won't you tell us why you came to Lansera? You are not a defector—you revel in the repugnant habits of your people, take joy in flinging barbs and feel satisfaction when they sting. And you do not speak truth. If you did, you would admit that you know me. It would give your taunts more weight."

Confusion sprang over her face, but she recovered quickly. *Perhaps she does not share the dreams, but she has to know something.* Madel would not have thrown her across his path otherwise. It was too much of a coincidence. He had tried to make sense of it on his own but no longer. She had to help.

"Silver, Vesperi. Tell me about the silver that enshrouds you, follows you everywhere."

"I do not know what you mean."

"That is a lie. I know it is a lie. I have seen it too many times."

"Seen it? But how could you have—"

He whooped at her slip up, adrenaline flowing like water over a falls, and he would follow it wherever the depths took him. Serra was gone. How much farther down could he go? "I have followed you, chased you through many woods. You flit from hill to bush, from town to countryside, but always, always the silver is your calling card. It can be a brilliant flare, but usually it's a spark I chase, night or day. A spark that brings me from the cave and leads me around many, many bends."

"It was *you*." She circled him, trembling with shock. "That day in the mountains. I sent you away from my trail. Was that how you found me? Did you wait to track me later?"

Her words made him giddy. *I am not crazy.* "I dreamed that. I dream it every night." *It has all been real.* And just that fast, his reverie broke. He wished some things were not real at all. *Serra, why?*

"You are insane." She watched him, eyes wide. "You were there in the flesh. I saw you. I should have killed you when I had the chance."

He did it before he could stop and think. His dagger was very sharp—honing it against stone had been soothing these past few days. It sliced right through the three worn coils of rope binding her hands.

"Do it." He did not know what power she possessed but was more certain it existed than ever. "Go ahead and do it. Do you think I care right now if you try? I have lost her already. I have already lost my life."

Vesperi looked between him and her released hands with open shock. She rubbed them, moved each finger slowly to make sure she could. Then she jammed an arm toward the window, out at the open sky, and a moonbeam reached back. Its radiance made him turn away. When he recovered, she had lowered her arm and sat back down on her bed.

He did not know what he had expected, but it was not this, not Vesperi rocking back and forth, holding herself and shaking her head. He moved as fast as he had with the dagger to rest a hand on her neck. With another beneath her chin, he lifted her head.

"Why am I still here?" He didn't know if he was relieved or more upset than before.

She did not meet his gaze, just clasped and unclasped her hands. "I don't want to kill you. And I do not know why."

Her voice was so quiet, he barely heard the words. When she fell silent, he kissed her forehead and stood. "That is one of the sweetest things I have ever been told, coming from you."

At the door, he paused and she met his gaze. He *had* recognized her before, in that net. Her irises were molten chocolate now, not silver, but for the first time she was truly the woman in his dreams.

CHAPTER 35

SERRA

The humidity of midevening woke Serra from her nap. Her eyes opened to something flitting around the back corner of the hut. *A bird?* Serra blinked. Nothing but terra-cotta walls. It was twilight, the sun setting, no fire lit, and any flashes she saw probably a residual effect of the meditation. She had seen young Agler faint more than once after a ritual.

Serra laughed at the thought, a harsh one that reminded her that her throat was raw and not just with regret. She had emulated Agler in a way, had betrayed the Albrechts. Betrayed Janto. So much for avoiding the family disgrace she had spent years trying to atone for. All of it washed away because she agreed to follow a spirit in a gray hood. Agler had a den of evil councilors, but a Brother had been her tempter. If only Janto were here to laugh with her at the irony.

She poured a cup of water from the pitcher and was reassured to see her lips had not turned blue in the mirror. Dots of reddish-black shimmered within the glassy depths. She threw her cup at them. *It cannot be.* She had imagined those . . . things . . . in the temple, had been light-headed.

Turning around may have been the bravest action Serra had ever taken. She screamed.

They were there. Very, very there. They covered the backside of the hut, flying in circles as they dodged each other. The mass of them worked together to suspend themselves in constant motion. Single bugs broke away from the group like red sparks, scouting, and when they did, she could sense their malice, malice and hunger, the worst sensation she had ever felt, worse than leaving Janto at the altar, worse than reading Ser Werbose's letter.

She had to flee, and she had to do it fast before they scented her. Once they did, she knew deep within herself they would chase. She slipped through the door, eased it shut, and ran. Dozens of little pins pricked her skin—jocal flies, but she slapped her arms again and again just in case.

Thanks be to Madel, the Order scorned personal effects as Serra would never set foot in that hut again. The only thing of value Serra had at Enjoin was the necklace around her neck. *Had they been there the whole time?* No, that was impossible. It had to be impossible. They would have overtaken her, consumed her. The bodies at the lake had had no time to run.

Up ahead, some novices talked and laughed together. They appeared out of focus, as though caught in shimmering heat waves over sand, though moonslight had more power now. She grabbed the nearest man's hands.

"Where's Ryn Gylles?" She pleaded, her voice desperate. "I need to find him, please."

The rust-haired novice looked at her askew. "I don't know. I think Ryn Simsi said he left for Oost right after the noon meal."

Serra shook her head. "No, that's not right. That cannot be right." He was there. She could feel him too, same as she could feel the shadow of a thousand tiny eyes staring at her. The pulsing blood in her veins and the rushing pressure in her ears confirmed it.

"He is right." A novice behind her spoke up. "Ryn Gylles told us at supper he would be back in a fortnight. Rynna Robelly is giving his classes instead." She placed a concerned hand on Serra's arm. "You are shaking. You fainted this morning at the meditation, did you not? Can we help you?"

Her eyes burned as though salt had been poured on them. She had to keep going. *To the temple.* She would give this burden to whomever was there, a Brother if no friendlier faces were about. Someone in charge had to know and fast, before that swarm found its way out of her hut. She had built no fire. They would come through the chimney soon.

She whispered, "No, thank you," to the woman and raised her elbows to release the gathered novices from her audience. *Stupid. What a stupid thing to do.* Old habits. The temple's walls rose higher with each step. Bypassing the main entrance, she went to the kitchen where the priests convened after evening prayers. It was locked. She ran to a smallish door off the hall that connected the temple to the kitchen cabin and pounded on it. "Let me in! You have to let me in!"

No one came, but the handle swung open easily. The hallway appeared darker and lengthier than it should have been but no matter. Darker things lurked behind her. She placed a hand on the wall to guide herself as the hall sloped downhill steeply. It must lead under the temple rather than from it as it seemed from the outside. The passage was not humid. It was probably the only place in all of Rasseleria that was not.

"Breeding season," her mother had called this weather one late fall when it had been nearly this bad in Meditlan. Her emerald eyes had twinkled. "When all creatures have energy for naught but making new ones." Serra had refused to attend the harvest festival in the vineyards surrounding Gavenstone. She had claimed her new doll, a present sent from Aunt Marji, did not want to go outside either, and she couldn't leave her alone, could she? Serra had been five then. Her mother kissed her on the head, smelling of cloves as always and of the sweet wine she had sipped before fetching her misbehaving daughter from the manor. Twirling one of Serra's pigtails, Lady Gavenstone had taken her hand and held it tight on the walk to the main festival tent. Serra had wailed until the rows of indigo feathers dangling from the tent's overhang distracted her.

She doubted she would find anything so captivating at the end of this passage.

The hall curved and packed ground gave way to cool stone so flat and smooth she had to tiptoe to avoid losing her footing. An open door came into view, and a blue-tinged haze came from it. *Of course.* At least she feared the blue less than what was in her hut. Serra peeked inside.

She swiftly leapt back out. The room teemed with Brothers. By Madel's hand, she prayed they were an illusion as the waves of heat had been. But another look denied her plea. She steeled herself and slipped inside, slinking up against the wall. The room spanned the width of the temple and a force at its center lit it. The Brothers crowded around whatever gave off that light. Tendrils of it snaked into the hems of their robes and cuffs of their sleeves. They came back out through the hoods, worms poking their way through an apple.

"Serrafina Gavenstone," a whispery voice made its way into her ear, "why have you come?"

She found herself face to hood with a legion of eyeless Brothers, unless the streams of blue counted. "What . . . what is this place?"

"Madel's Reach." She could not tell which Brother spoke.

"Madel's Reach? But that's impossible! That's a fairy tale!" Her thoughts flew too fast to master. *Madel's Reach?* She had not heard of the place since learning the history of the Gods' War. It was a vortex that Madel had reached Her hand through to give orders to Her commanders. To think such a place actually existed—

"Are we not also fairy tales? Do you still not believe what your eyes have seen?"

They know. "What are they? Those creatures in my hut?"

The Brothers rustled, but she could not decipher words or intent. The glow flickered then burned stronger. Warmth emanated from it as one of the tendrils reached her way. It swept around her body, leaving a tingling trail in its wake as though hot syrup had been dripped on her flesh. The muscles of her face relaxed and she closed her eyes, relishing the sensation. When she opened them, her head felt clear again and she was drawn toward the focal point of the room.

A burning hand of pure silver flame shimmered in its midst. She blinked, and it disappeared.

"Did you see Her?" The blue lines flowing into the Brothers dimmed as they absorbed the energy, each Brother engulfing a galaxy of pale, twinkling stars.

"I—I saw something. A hand of silver at the heart of the glow. It is gone now."

"Then you have also seen *them*. What we have suspected is confirmed. You have the sight. You are the seer, and you are greatly needed."

Her feeling of peacefulness gave way to a sinking weight. "What do you mean, I am the seer? What is the sight?" Panic knit itself back together as she thought of sacks of skin and red-winged pestilence.

The blue pulsed through the Brothers' robes, growing dimmer with each passing second. The illumination at the center of the room was nearly extinguished, though she could feel the warmth of it on her skin. The Brothers parted in two, leaving a path between them. Someone walked toward her through it. Someone with mass and blood pulsing within his flesh.

Ryn Gylles smiled, his crooked teeth oddly comforting. "Serra, we have much to talk about." He took her arm and led her out of the room and back into the tunnel. Seeing him relieved her and her sense of peacefulness increased. This was right. She had done the right thing, and Gylles and the Brothers knew about the creatures. They would know what to do next. So she was the seer, whatever that meant, and she had seen those creatures. Perhaps her part in all this had been fulfilled, her destiny completed. Maybe she could return to Jan—

"You are of more importance now than ever before, Serra. Praise be to Madel we found you and you have found your sight. You have much work to do."

When would she learn to stop hoping for anything?

CHAPTER 36
JANTO

Vesperi wore a plain black tunic over a pair of brown leggings, eschewing the gowns stocked in the guest rooms. It was the third combination of shirts and pants she'd worn since being released from the dungeons the night before. His father had agreed to let her out rather easily.

"You are quite fond of pants." Janto pulled out her chair.

"Lansera might get a few things right." She offered no thanks for the courtesy, but her reply was reward enough. A week ago, he would never have wagered that Vesperi would say something nice of Lansera. That she would sup with him and his family in the council room, hands unbound, was one he would not have taken yesterday. A pair of guards trailed her, and an archer was posted in sight of her bedroom window, but she made no attempts to escape.

Today, Janto felt he could breathe again, though it hurt to do so when he remembered he should have been joined with Serra by now. Yet, Vesperi was meant to be in his life, too—yesterday had determined that.

Those pants suit her. They pulled tightly across her hips in an alluring manner. If she wanted, Vesperi could find a man who appreciated her particular charms. The poor bloke would probably end up with his head—one of them, at least—wacked off by first light. She'd wear an expression identical to the one she wore now, licking her lips after stripping rabbit meat off the bone with her teeth.

"Don't they have forks and knives on your side of the mountains?" He was glad to have someone he could taunt without remorse. Exchanging insults with Vesperi had worked wonders for his temperament over the past day. He would have punched the stone walls to pieces otherwise.

Her fierce gaze made him blush. "Why bother with such idiocy? It is meant to be consumed, not carved into a dainty piece of filigree to hang on the walls."

Queen Lexamy laughed. "True, Lady Sellwyn—"

"Don't call me that . . . please." Vesperi shifted in her chair.

Please? Janto mouthed the word to her over the table. She glared.

"As you wish, Vesperi." His mother's countenance held a hint of fondness. "But silverware does make a meal easier to sit through. Who wants to remain at the feasting table for hours with greasy hands and bits of cheese stuck under your nails?"

Vesperi bit into a crescent roll, getting flour on her face in the process. Ser Allyn stepped in from the doorway to offer a handkerchief, which she regarded with confusion. "We do not have feasts at Sellwyn."

"That's a shame." His mother took the cloth and folded it, placing it by Vesperi's plate.

"I disagree. Sitting at the same table as my family for a whole evening would be torture." Anger simmered within her eyes.

His mother began to ask another question but Janto shushed her. "It's no use. She will only try to counter everything you say. It's what she does." His expression was playful, but Vesperi returned it with malice.

"I only speak the truth, princeling. It is none of my concern that you find Meduan ways distasteful."

His father, silent until then, put down his goblet. "It *is* your concern, Vesperi, if you plan to remain in Lansera. The Guj himself gave us warning to watch for you. Do you want us to send word to Sellwyn of your capture? Your manner confuses me."

Was he teasing or being serious? The thought Vesperi might leave panicked Janto. She had his confidence now, which was not wise, but what other choice did he have? Madel had brought them together for some reason. Janto had enough faith to believe that after Vesperi had confirmed his dreams.

The color drained from Vesperi's face. "No, Your Majesty." She bowed her head low. Janto nearly choked on a rabbit bone. He had not thought Vesperi knew the words *your majesty*.

For dessert, Mar Pina brought in a tray of spice meringues and whispered something in Ser Allyn's ear. He left the room, and Janto wished for news that Serra had changed her mind and was returning. *Stop that. She is not coming back.* Rynna Hullvy had likely sent a boy from town to gather wine for the next day's rituals.

He was reaching for his third crescent roll when Ser Allyn gestured to him from the doorway. Janto grabbed the roll and bid good evening to his parents and Vesperi, pausing to consider whether he should leave her alone with them. But his father had trusted her enough to let her act as a guest here, not a prisoner, so he felt confident Vesperi would return that trust. She had not killed them yet, had she? She cut a bite of roasted turnip as he stared, further proof she was trying to adjust.

Ser Allyn tittered, so Janto followed him down the hall. Maybe Serra had sent word, a note to assure him of her safety. She had to know how worried he was. They could not be so far divided that she did not care.

Ser Allyn stopped in front of the throne room's opened door. "They asked for you, or I would have alerted your father. I probably should have."

"Who?" *Not Serra, then.* He was practiced at dashed hopes.

"Friends from your Murat, or at least they claim to be. They have ridden hard from Wasyla to get here according to the short one. The other did not speak at all. He appears ill." That last bit came out in a whisper.

Nap and Rall. Janto was touched. *They must have heard about the wedding.* He walked through the threshold with a smile of welcome on his face. It morphed into concern as soon as he saw his friends. "What's wrong?"

Nap was sweaty and smelled strongly of horse. He clasped Janto's arm wordlessly and led him to Rall, who stared forward vacantly from the benches.

"What has happened?"

Rall stirred at Janto's voice. More pain covered his face than being left at the altar a hundred times over could place there.

"They are dead." Tears spilled out of his bloodshot eyes. "My wife and my child . . . my little girl . . . they're dead."

Janto pulled him close.

"It was the claren." Nap uttered a word Janto had never heard before, yet it made his blood run cold. "They have returned."

Ser Allyn gasped from the doorway.

"Bring my father," Janto called to him. "Whatever he means, the king must know."

CHAPTER 37
VESPERI

Vesperi paced her room, impatient for . . . she did not know what. Certainly not a spoiled prince who had forgotten her once his friends came calling. Not an imbecile who had beguiled her into good behavior by cutting her ropes, who had claimed they had a shared destiny when no one had wanted a connection with her before, who had ignored her the rest of the night. If her wrists had not healed from the chaffing of rope, she would have thought herself dreaming in the dungeon.

Vesperi had pried the gossip out of a servant with an attractive braid of hair who never shut up. The woman sounded more concerned than intrigued by it, and soon after she started talking, Vesperi had wanted to clamp her mouth back shut with an iron claw. Bini, the woman was named. Knowing that made Vesperi ill. She had never bothered to learn a servant's name before. *Soon, I'll be offering to empty my own chamber pot.* Disgust shuddered through her.

A familiar knock sounded four times in quick succession. The prince was probably unaware he always knocked four times. *So oblivious.* Her excitement rose though Vesperi would deny it.

"Come in." She shouted permission because he would *wait* if she didn't. *Incredulous.*

"My lady." He was such a mess that she refrained from cackling at his formal greeting. A forest green tunic hung slovenly off his shoulders, and his hair was unbrushed or maybe mussed from running his hands

What made her do it she did not know, but she went to him, placed her arms around him and wondered at how she had never touched someone this way—softly, with no sexual intent. She wanted to provide him with . . . comfort.

The broken man cried against her chest, gripping the fabric of the tunic on her back. It was heartbreaking. But it did not last. No one should affect her that easily. No one had the right to. Familiar rage built within her. She spit out the word "coward" as she ran through the door.

A mess of people filled the hallway, groups of servants huddled together, comforting each other from whatever was happening in the kitchen. *Idiots.* They should be fleeing, saving their own hides, not waiting to see what happened. Her skin flushed, heat gathering beneath it that she welcomed. This—this felt familiar. And damned if she would stop it now.

She recognized Janto's voice from among the people yelling and headed toward it. *This is his fault.* She had never had these impulses before, impulses to help, to provide solace. He would pay for making her feel that way.

CHAPTER 38
SERRA

Ryn Gylles led Serra out of the passageway and temple and into Ryn Cladio's hut as the first light of dawn was breaking. The chief priest's head was bent over a book and his beard nearly swept the floor. "Gylles, the Rejuvenation is complete so soon?"

"Yes, but that is not what I have come to report." Ryn Gylles sounded giddy. "We were right, Cladio. She has the sight!"

At that, Ryn Cladio lifted his head. "Does she?" His purple eyes beckoned from across the hut. "Tell me, Lady Serrafina, what have you seen?"

"Ryn Gylles, I do not understand." Serra tugged on the arm of her mentor, impatient. "What is the sight?"

"Did you never hear the old chants from your rynna?" Ryn Cladio pinched the skin between his brows. "Madel's hand, I should have insisted on it being restored years ago." He rose from the table and took her measure with each step closer. "*Without her sight, mankind is done.*"

Those words followed her everywhere, it seemed.

"Serra, you are the one who can see where the darkness dwells so it can be destroyed and peace returned to us. You are our savior from the evil that breeds in Medua." Ryn Cladio clasped her shoulders firmly. "Now tell me, have you ever used magic?"

Magic? It had been plentiful once in Lansera, and some people claimed to have talents others did not, but she had never seen a true exhibition of it. Agler had performed little tricks, pulling rocks out of his tunic sleeve or making a goblet float, but she had always seen the strings. "Ryn, I do not know what magic is."

"Oh, don't you?" He laughed. "Just what do you think the Brotherhood is?"

Not men. They did not live, eat, nor speak with voices they could call their own. But they appeared perfectly normal to everyone else. Was that magic? And what of the blue mantle under the temple? Lessons she had been taught at temple and in her classes came to her lips. *The Brotherhood is Her hand working among us.*

"Ryn, is magic . . ." Finding the right word was difficult. "Is magic the hand of Madel?"

His face brightened. She was right, then, or close.

"And the Brothers. They are magical creations of Madel's. Suspended between life and naught by Her spirit?" She had never seen so clearly. "They were being infused . . . sustained . . . under the temple with Her magic."

"Yes." Cladio nodded excitedly. "You understand what power flows through this world. Only thusly can you grasp what power threatens it."

Serra sunk into a chair. "But what are they then? The vermin I saw? They are not the same as the Brothers. They cannot be creatures of Madel, can they?" The thought that those horrible things may have Madel's breath within them made her ill.

"Oh, they are certainly alive. Those vermin, as you called them, are not Madel's magic, but they are similar. They have been brought into being not by the hand of a loving God but by the filth of a fallen people. Serra, that mass you have seen is a manifestation of evil. It has come to be because we, those who call ourselves civilized, have allowed vile deeds to propagate right outside our doors. We thought ourselves untouched by the Meduan thirst for power and greed as long as we kept ourselves separate. But we were wrong. And now, we are being eaten alive by that mistake."

Serra closed her eyes. Ryn Cladio was telling her Turyn's Peace was wrong, that the kingdom she had always served and might have ruled with Janto was a sham and a selfish one at that. But the Meduans had chosen to be their own people, hadn't they? What responsibility did Lansera have for Meduan reprehensibility? *The same responsibility King Albrecht had to pardon a traitor whose vision had been clouded by lies.* "What am I supposed to do? Talk to the king? Beg him to invade Medua so they will stop hurting each other?"

Ryn Gylles went on his knees before her, pride and worry commingled on his face. "You are to destroy the claren with *your* magic. Your sight is what was prophesied."

That made no sense. Yes, she had seen those creatures, but she could not kill them. She hoped to never be in the same room with them again. And she could not believe she was the only person who had ever seen them. They were so vivid, so menacing. Anyone near them would have been forced to take notice. *I cannot be alone in this.* "I do not understand. Surely you have seen them too or how would you know what I saw?"

"We don't." Ryn Gylles explained. "Not entirely. We have made assumptions from the marsh village reports, including the one you, Lourda, and Poline brought. The first deaths from Wasyla were reported a few days ago. They are breeding fast and you are needed."

"What am I to do? Go to King Albrecht and tell him what I know, that I can see them?"

"Sharing this with the king will be necessary, but you have more to do than that, I'm afraid. Without your sight, we cannot kill them. So it falls to you to be the guide for us all."

She had chosen to serve her people, not to be their savior, and she had fought against it for weeks, held onto Janto as long as she could. She wasn't a hero. Was she?

"What did they look like?" Ryn Cladio reached for a bound scroll on the highest shelf of his hut. A copper imprint of a giant graced its front cover. A compendium of monsters, perhaps, or of fairy tales she could not depend upon to stay within the confines of a book.

"They were many. But they acted as one, a black mass with red wings churning in on itself. They sounded like a hive of bees muffled by a heavy cloth." She closed her eyes, trying to recall the creatures more fully. "I did not see any up close, but a few broke off to make wider circuits of the room."

Ryn Cladio handed the book to Ryn Gylles. "Tasters. They were expanding their search for things to consume." What would have happened had she stayed a moment longer? The memory of two deflated skins made bile rise in her throat. *Thanks be to Madel I did not.*

Gylles yelped when he turned the page. The writing it contained was too ancient for Serra to decipher, its ink dark green rather than violet. The opposite side held a charcoal illustration of a funnel with many eyes and teeth. It was colored in with red powder, and a caption above it held thick letters.

"What does this say?"

"The Claren Hoards," Ryn Gylles translated. "An ancient evil that straddles our world and Madel's realm. It has been a thousand years since last they bred. They enter through uncovered orifices—mouths, noses, ears—and breed in the bracken water of violence and hatred among men. Our complacency since Turyn's Peace has given them enough time to come to maturity through the Meduans."

Ryn Cladio's quill fell to the desk with a clatter. "Serra, you must begin your work. The weapon must strike. You must destroy them."

The Brothers had said that Janto needed to bond with the weapon—that was why she could not marry him. But if she was the sight, then was she also the weapon? *Could I still be his?* Her cheeks flushed with hope, yet she had no idea how to eradicate the claren. "Ryn Cladio, what is the whole of that prophecy?"

The older man stared out his window, considering each word as he spoke. "*When the silver stag runs free, blessed will he who binds it be. Rise up, ye treasured bird of three. Wing him what boons ye foresee. When evil spawns and overruns, from silver the weapon comes. Without her sight, mankind is done. With it, all will again be one.*"

The moon Tansic pulsed in the evening sky. Ryn Cladio focused his sharp eyes on her. "You are certain you have no other magic in you?"

"I am, Ryn. Other than this"—she waved her hand over her face—"this sight, I have not felt anything magical in me. But how is the silver stag related to this prophecy?"

"Of course!" Ryn Gylles clapped his hands together, voice fast again. "How silly of me not to remember what the Brothers said to you in that cave, Serra. I had been so worried about you that I . . . Cladio, they said the weapon was connected to the slayer. But they stressed that Serra could not interfere with that bond, insisted she would if she continued her betrothal."

The reminder deflated her, and Ryn Cladio paced behind the desk, a hand pressed against his forehead. "We had considered the stag's slaying a confirmation of the time in which we lived, another proof the world was in peril and the prophecy was coming true. But it would make sense that such a creature might leave a weapon made of its essence, or that he who slayed it might be the weapon." He stopped his movement, sighing. "We may need to ask you a greater favor than Madel already has, Serra. Would you meet with Janto, question him for us?"

If she could handle leaving him on her wedding day with nary a word of explanation, then she could handle that. She had made her choice in Callyn, and it appeared she would assist Janto with sorting out his own. If doing so helped him understand why she had so disgraced him, all the better. She would not seek his forgiveness for giving into her destiny, but she ached for it, nonetheless.

"I will go to him. But what am I asking?"

"Ask about the stag, if he noticed anything after the hunt. Ask if he has magic like yours but different, something that would complement your own. You can see the claren, but you need a weapon to guide. Perhaps Janto is the weapon and he does not know it yet. That would be the best solution. You must find out."

"Of course." She took two steps toward the door before remembering she had nowhere to go, no belongings to gather. "I am ready when Madel is."

She did not hesitate to grab the Brother's robe when it appeared.

CHAPTER 39
JANTO

The familiar apron mostly covered the corpse, and her stalwart wooden spoon had fallen to the ground only a foot away, but Janto could not admit it was really Mar Pina.

He was not the only one. Pic refused to leave with the smattering of kitchen staff when the king ordered them out. The boy's wide-eyed stare was stuck on shock. Janto braced Pic with his arm, ruffling his hair and turning his head from the body—the skin—that lay in front of the oven.

"I do not understand." Pic gripped Janto's arm as strongly as a boy of eight could. "There's nothing there. What could have—"

The king yelled to everyone in the room. "Cover your mouths and ears. Do it now."

Janto pulled out his handkerchief, tying it around Pic's face. He grabbed a cloth from a nearby counter, using it for himself. Nap and two of the guards made slow circles around the room on his father's instructions, waving their hands in front of them like parting waters.

"How will we know if we touch them?" Nap continued his search.

The king hesitated. Janto could tell by the way his left arm drooped and his right one rose to his forehead, pressing down for a moment. "I don't know."

It was the most terrifying thing Janto had ever heard. The most terrifying thing he had ever seen came next—a tidal wave of silver that rolled through the room. Crackling sounds like corn kernels popping and onions sizzling on a griddle erupted from nowhere as they ducked.

Near the fireplace, hundreds of red and black insects sparked into existence in the empty air then collapsed to the ground. Smoke rose from the wooden fixtures all around them. Even the brick of the fireplace radiated heat. Janto spun around, holding Pic with one arm. Hopefully, the sight of what caused that flame would be easier to take than Mar Pina's remains.

Vesperi stood inside the doorway, her hair lifted from her skull as though she'd been hit by lightning. A silver orb tipped each black strand, her head a candelabra of elongated, skinny tapers. A thicker strand of silver energy pulsed to her hand where it eddied in a swirling mass, alarming to behold. Janto felt her fury as she raised that hand again and again, one finger lifted higher than the rest. A brilliant bolt came from it each time, followed by a cloud of smoke wherever she struck. *I had good reason to bind those hands.*

The air crackled behind him but no more insects fell, and the servants screamed anew when Vesperi lashed out again. She was out of control, raising her hand two, three, five times in a minute, setting cloth aflame and striking most of the furniture and earthenware to pieces.

He shielded his eyes from the magic's glare as Vesperi raised her hand again. She needed to be stopped. Maybe he could do something to restrain her. Maybe this was why they were connected. Patting Pic's arm, he said, "Stay here," then tried to step forward. But he could not move. Something held him from behind—a soft, firm touch from supple fingers, fingers that had grazed his arm innumerable times over the past decade. He turned in shock.

Serra wore the Order's garb, and behind her stood a Brother, arms raised as though about to chime a ritual bell. Janto forgot how to breathe.

She rushed past him, more determined than he'd ever seen.

"Watch out!" Whether his warning was for her or Vesperi he did not know. Neither woman acknowledged it. Serra grabbed Vesperi's arm and pointed it toward a spot below the western window. "There. You must aim there."

Vesperi released another surge and shimmered in the haze of heat around her. The magic hit the wall—no, not the wall, but a dark and massive cloud of insects in front of it that lit up with a thousand different flames. The throng dropped to the ground, releasing more of the acrid smell that filled the room.

"Janto," Serra called to him. "You must talk to her, tell her she can stop." She sounded confident, assured. But she hesitated before continuing, "She looks strange to me—is she from outer Rasseleria maybe, like your mother?"

Typical Serra to be befuddled by lineages in the midst of all this. Janto almost laughed as he reached them. Instead, he placed a gentle hand on Vesperi's arm so as not to spook her. "That's enough." Then he rambled on with no idea what to do. "You got them, I promise. You can stop, Vesperi. Focus on drawing it back in. Would you try, please?"

Vesperi said nothing, but her silver glow dulled. She lowered her hand. Janto felt victorious. It took great restraint not to hug Serra, twirl her around, or kiss her. But another part of him was angry, very angry at the sight of her. Where had she been this past week? Why come now when he had needed her every second since then? His mind flooded with confusion, but the strongest emotion he felt was relief to see her at all.

So he answered her question once he could see brown mixed in with the silver of Vesperi's irises again. "She's a Meduan. The one we captured while on forage. Your Brothers did not tell you that?" It was ridiculous to feel jealous of them, but he did.

Her eyes narrowed, then she whispered, "Of course, she is," so low and bitter she may not have realized it. Then she shook her head. "The Brothers are not known for forthrightness. I have learned that many times over since you left for your Murat."

"What is going on here?" Vesperi's hair no longer flailed, though it was puffed up more than it should be, like her curls had thickened with sea air. The last few servants huddled together by Mar Pina's remains.

"Pic," Janto called to the child, "I think it is safe now. Can you lead the others to my mother and Ser Allyn, and please tell them what has happened?"

"What about Mar Pina?" The lad wiped away tears that had not ceased since the cook had fallen to the floor, a corn husk in the breeze.

Janto put his fingers under the boy's chin and lifted his head so their eyes met. "I will take care of her body. I am sorry I could not stop them on my own."

Pic nodded. His comportment reminded Janto of the child he had been so many years ago when Serra had needed someone to lean on and he decided it would be him. Sometimes, you had to be a man at eight years old without Sielban's training.

"Let's go." Pic stood tall with the pride of being given a duty. "We need to tell Queen Lexamy what happened as the prince asked." The servants rose together as one and shuffled toward the corridor.

"That was well done." His father stepped out from a shadowed corner of the room. Janto did not know which of them he addressed. The king greeted Serra with a kiss to the cheek, something Janto would not dare to do, not anymore. "Welcome. Your companion appears to have left, but I think I see—*you* see—why he has brought you back home."

"I am not sure I have a home anymore, my lord." Serra raised her elbows in deference to the king, but her eyes were only for Janto. "I wish it could be otherwise."

No words formed in his throat. Nap's hand clapped his shoulder. "Let's help Rall."

Rall. His friend who had lost so much had slipped into the room unannounced and spread a cloth beside Mar Pina. He worked silently, something resembling calm on his face. Janto knelt down and helped spread the corners straight, averting his gaze if it happened to fall over an inch of the skin. But Rall, Rall stretched the body and smoothed it flat. Nap found a sleeve and pulled it to the side until an arm was recognizable. Once again, the absurdity of being born a prince struck Janto when other men did work like this every day.

Not like *this*, though. Not work like this.

The cloth Rall used was one Mar Pina had taken pride in spreading over the main hall's feasting tables. They tucked the fabric around her, the skin barely leaving an impression of anything in the muted shroud. By coincidence, a representation of the hand of Madel reaching from the Enjoin temple in silver and gold threads rested where Mar Pina's head should be.

"Are you all right?" Janto placed a hand on Rall's shoulder. "This must be horrible for you."

He shook his head. "No, I need to do this. I did not think I could face it again when I heard the screams. But I realized it would be less of a shock for me than for anyone else here, so I came." He paused. "You have to stop this, my prince."

"But how can I? I'm not—"

"You are the slayer of the silver stag. You will find a way."

"We all will." Serra spoke, soft but sure. "That's why I've returned."

CHAPTER 40
SERRA

Not for the last time and many, many times removed from the first, Serra wished the Brothers had given her more information. She sat in the throne room, in a chair placed too far forward from the others to feel comfortable. She was under examination, but she could not blame any of them for the questions.

Her unruly gaze wandered toward Janto for the twentieth time. He wouldn't meet her eyes. The exhilaration she had felt when she arrived in the kitchen vanished as soon as she had learned she hadn't been fast enough to save Mar Pina.

Ser Allyn asked again, "You are certain there are no others here?"

She had spent the last two hours covering every inch of Castle Callyn, venturing into areas she had never been admitted before—the king and queen's chambers for one—and others she had never wanted to see such as the servants' quarters just south of the castle. Mar Pina's snug dwelling had overwhelmed her. The woman had always been such a homey presence in a cold castle. How could Serra have never visited her? Even that far from the kitchen, the air smelled of toasted flour. It confounded her that the claren had targeted a woman who would never have committed the acts of depravity they bred in. She reaped the evil others had created.

Once she had wiped her tears, Serra had searched, focusing on breathing deeply as though meditating with her eyes open. There had been no traces of the claren, no masses or trails of red suspended in the air.

"I'm certain."

"But how can you know?" She had never seen Ser Allyn so flustered, his mind unwilling to take the leap needed for Serra's presence to make sense. It had been so obvious to her when she saw Vesperi and the magic she yielded. Some things simply *were*. Like Serra's love of Janto and why she could not keep his any longer. His link to Vesperi had become so quickly evident when he talked her down, knowing just what to say.

"She is the seer, Allyn." The king's calm demeanor contrasted sharply with Ser Allyn's. "You do remember the chant? We have heard it many times since Janto killed the stag."

"But what does that have to do with this? The slayer's boon has no bearing on an invisible pestilence!"

"Repeat the chant," the king commanded. "Then see what you understand."

"*When the silver stag runs free, blessed will he who binds it be. Rise up, ye treasured bird of three. Wing him what boons ye foresee.*" Ser Allyn raised his hands, pushing his hair neatly behind his ears. "I do not understand, my king."

"Continue. What are the next lines?"

"Next lines? But we never say those anymore. We repeat the first three in rounds. The stag, the slayer, the bird, and treasure earned." He had no trouble recalling them, however, and his jaw dropped lower and lower as he recited the complete prophecy. "*When evil spawns and overruns, from silver the weapon comes. Without her sight, mankind is done. With it, all will again be one.*"

Serra felt possessive of the prophecy now. To her ear, the verses sounded better when united. They were all that still tied her to Janto. The slayer and the seer at least appeared in the same song.

"Father," Janto interrupted, "could you speak plainly? I know this has to do with Serra returning—she's the sight mentioned in the second verse as you said. And Vesperi must be the weapon spoken of, or she wouldn't be able to kill those creatures. Nothing else we tried before she appeared had any effect, and I would bet money Nap could fell anything killable by arms. But what does the stag have to do with this? It may be obvious to you and her," Serra could hear his frustration as he pointed her way, eyes trained on his father, "but there has been too much, far too much today with Mar Pina's death and . . . and I don't know what's being asked of Vesperi or me."

And me, Janto? Do you care anymore what is asked of me?

The king rose from his throne to give him the comfort Serra could not, that she would never be able to again. She wanted to cry, too, for the loss of that privilege and for Mar Pina, but not now. Not when she needed to nurse Lansera's wounds instead.

"I am sorry, son. I sometimes forget others haven't been preparing for this moment forever, least of all you whom it most concerns."

Janto pulled back. "What do you mean? How long have you known these claren were coming?"

The king returned to his chair. "Since I agreed to ascend the throne. I knew then this time would come. You remember my Murat dream, Janto?"

His son nodded, and the Meduan coughed, trying to hide how closely she listened behind raised hands. Serra's distaste for her grew by the second. Vesperi's nonchalance was so forced—a mask would appear more lifelike than her face.

"I never knew when it would come true, but I knew what to search for once the Brothers came to me after my brother died. It was the same night I had to make a choice I have never regretted yet always begrudged. I had to leave my life in Madel's Order and become king so you could bring Lansera an era of true peace."

The Meduan laughed out loud. "I don't understand what you think is so exciting about peace. Everyone living together, sharing, caring—people aren't made for that. It is fantasy."

Serra glared at her for interrupting, then a knock came at the far door.

"Enter," the king bellowed. The door creaked open to reveal two guests. In the streaks of sunlight coming through the ceiling, Serra recognized the form of Rynna Hullvy in blue and green raiment. Someone with a dark braid walked beside her.

"It *is* you!" Bini's excitement was loud, even at that distance. "Oh, Lady Serra, I did not believe the servants—how could you have appeared in the kitchen? But it's true!"

Serra smiled despite the tension in the room.

"Enough. There will be time for that later. Please escort Rynna Hullvy here." To his chief servant, the king said, "Retrieve the bell from my chambers. We must get started on this right away." Ser Allyn exited from the side door.

Serra smoothed the flyaway hairs of her own braid, and Bini and the rynna neared the group. She did not want to give Bini cause for concern, and maintaining her appearance had stopped being a priority around the time a horde of all-too-visible insects had taken up residence in her hut. She gave Bini a comforting squeeze as she passed by.

Her servant gave the announcement in a sure voice. "Rynna Hullvy is here."

The king welcomed the rynna with raised elbows and dismissed Bini. "Thank you. Now please prepare Lady Serra's room."

"I couldn't—" Serra started, and the king shot her a look that forced her silence.

"Yes, of course, Your Highness." Bini exited.

Rynna Hullvy was elegant, her tan head scarf covering all but the longest of her gray hairs. "What ritual do you request I perform?"

"The Calling. I would do it myself, but I need to talk with these young people more. They have many questions to be answered, and the Calling takes far more concentration than I can spare."

If the request surprised the rynna, she did not show it. Serra did, wrinkling her brow. The Calling was not covered in her childhood trainings nor in Ryn Gylles's classes. And the king performed rituals by himself?

"I sometimes forget you were almost a priest," Janto filled in, as though reading her mind. Sharing thoughts probably could not be helped after so many years together.

"Figures," Vesperi muttered. Serra questioned why the woman was there. A weapon need only be pointed.

The rynna removed herself from the group, choosing a space with concentrated sunlight near the back of the hall. She rolled out her prayer mat and waited for the bell.

The king spoke. "All three of you, come closer to me. I trust our rynna, but there are those who would listen in at our doors with intentions much worse than gossip. What we decide tonight—what each of you decide—must be kept secret at all costs. Some people would prefer the claren not be stopped."

"The Meduans, you mean." Serra stared accusingly at Vesperi.

The king responded with a bit of reproach in his voice. "Some of them, perhaps. But certainly not all. People who lust for power are often the same ones who would avoid death at all costs. The claren would only be welcomed by those who seek to use them as a tool or who are afraid of someone strong enough to defeat them."

"Afraid of me?" Doubt lined Vesperi's narrowed eyes. "You think there are Meduans afraid of me?"

"I know there are. Your decision to run away when you did was fortuitous, Vesperi. Some might call it Madel's hand intervening. A messenger was already on his way to Sellwyn to command you to marry King Ralion when you made your way over the mountains."

Her veneer dropped. She was utterly flabbergasted, showing a mixture of shock and pride. "But why me? Why would he have chosen me? We never spoke when I was at Qiltyn."

Janto was concentrating hard, looking as though he grasped feathers of information from the air and had bound them together into something that made sense. "For your magic, of course. That's why they wanted you." He smiled at Vesperi, pleased with his conclusion . . . and with her. "No one else has what you have."

She returned his gaze with only more evident confusion.

"Didn't you know that?" Janto was bemused.

She gave a nearly imperceptible shake of her head. "I knew of my talent, but I am not the only person who possesses magic. There are many wizards in Medua. I thought I could be useful to Father, but as a woman, I—"

"You killed a horde of claren. And you could have killed any of us at any time—I don't know why you haven't, actually." That was a deeper realization for Janto than figuring out Vesperi's role in the prophecies. Serra could tell by the softer tone he took. "You have no idea what you are, what you have that no one else does?" She hated the tenderness in his voice.

"But there are wizards—" Vesperi started.

"Their magic is not the same as yours," the king broke in. "No one has had the silver flame for hundreds of years. Not since the time of Didio Albrecht, my great-great grandfather. He and his Silver Guard eradicated the last of the cantaleres on Braven."

"Those were real?" Serra gasped. This room held the slayer of the stag, the possessor of the flame, and the wielder of the sight, yet she kept hearing more amazing things. *What has my life become?* Planning a wedding had been a lifetime, not a week ago.

The king did not acknowledge her outburst. "The letter I received from Mandat Hall warned me that Vesperi was dangerous as well, a curious way to describe someone they seemed so desperate to find again.

I will not be surprised if they have dispatched men over the mountains to capture her. Caution is of utmost importance." He stroked at the stubble on his chin. "Now, I was speaking of the night the Brothers told me my brother had died. They told me to watch for signs. A woman who possessed the silver flame reborn—" he beckoned Vesperi closer and she obliged him "—and the death of the legendary stag." Janto nodded at his acknowledgment.

"I have been on watch for those signs ever since. I suspected Vesperi's gift, but Serra's role in this was not clear to me until today. When they came for her the same day you left, Janto, I assumed it was because she was to wed you, and you would need her strength of spirit when the time came."

Janto, the man she would have called husband, regarded her finally. His fists were clenched, but the twitch of his chin and fast blinking of lashes revealed cracks in his visage. He wanted her to deepen them, for his father's words to be true. "Is this why you left me? Because of these prophecies?"

She was so glad no one else was in this room. Vesperi's presence was enough of an invasion of privacy. "Yes." Her voice quieted as her eyes grew watery. "There is no other reason I could ever leave you."

His fists relaxed a little.

Ser Allyn came back, huffing from the urgency of his errand. He positioned the bell and its stand beside Rynna Hullvy, who lay prostrate on her mat. She did not look up, but once he stepped away, she began chanting. From the other end of the room, it was only a murmur, a distant chorus of crickets in summer.

Vesperi had made use of the distraction to slip her mask back on. The woman's eyes and stance screamed of boredom.

"I know we are supposed to fight the claren," Serra addressed the king, "but how will we know where to find them? Are the Brothers to be our guides, sending us where the claren are through the means of travel they have used with me?"

"I hope to ask them soon. But I think what we need to do now is make sure the three of you are willing to do that, if asked. Will you work together to save us from the claren? Will you do whatever it takes?"

It was an easy answer for Serra by now, though she wondered how many times she would have to make the choice. "I have already committed my life to Madel's work in this. I will go wherever She needs me to."

claren until every last one of them is killed and our people have nothing left to fear. If the three of us are the only ones who can do it, then I must believe it so."

"Then it's settled. The claren will be defeated. Where you are headed is not yet known, but that you will be leaving soon is. I suggest you clear your heads, rest and pray for the remainder of this day, and we will meet in the morning, break our fast together, and figure out your next step."

The three of them nodded. Serra did not linger, refusing to meet anyone's eyes as she left. There would be plenty of time to talk things over with Janto on the road. She was in no hurry to rush that conversation, uncertain having it would make this easier on either of them. And if she delayed it, then maybe she could delay finding out how deep the bond between slayer and stag went.

Knowing Bini waited by her door was a greater comfort now than it had ever been before.

CHAPTER 41
JANTO

Serra's braid of spun-caramel hair flew up from the speed with which she fled the room. *She looks so much nicer without feathers or ribbons,* Janto thought. But she could wear a gown made of koparin tails, and he would find her beautiful. Yet the Serra he knew would never have left a room without a proper exit, greeting even Vesperi in turn. She would have hid her emotion until the two of them were alone. The hurried exit indicated a clear desire to avoid him, something else new about her like the cool confidence she had shown in the kitchen, a transparency he envied. He wished he could run out himself, demand to know how she could give them up for anything, including Madel. But he did not have that luxury, not with his father in the same room, and the rynna and Ser Allyn. Madel's hand, Vesperi would never let him hear the end of it. *Poor little princeling.*

"Until tomorrow then." He raised his elbows to the others. "I need to check in with my guests before the evening gets much older."

On warm nights such as this, the servants often had a bonfire in the courtyard, raising a glass together and watching the moons and stars. First person to catch a glimpse of Madel's hair, as the shooting stars were called, won a glass of sparkling ale. But the courtyard was empty after that day's events. Janto wished it were otherwise; a hello or two would lighten his mood.

He knocked on Rall and his son's guestroom door. It opened slowly, Rall greeting him with a finger lifted to his lips. "I don't want to wake Evon."

Janto moved aside so Rall could join him in the passageway. He looked weary, but his countenance had lightened some, as though the world he carried on his shoulders was a town or two less heavy. Janto had thought another claren attack would redouble Rall's grief, but it must have been different not being *his* family, *his* home.

That's it! Janto smacked his head with the palm of his hand. What sort of hunter missed such obvious tracks? "How many days ride to your town?"

"Four days, with healthy horses and no weather. Why do you ask, my pri—Janto?"

Janto smirked at the familiar slip up, and Rall smiled. It fell away quickly, too quickly, but Janto could not worry about that. He felt as though he'd hit all thirty of Sielban's targets in sixty seconds flat. "Because we are going to destroy the creatures that did this to your family, Rall. And I need to know how far so I can count down the seconds until we do."

Nap came out of his adjoining room and stalwartly pronounced, "I am coming with you. It would be my honor to serve with you on this quest."

"I was hoping you would say that." Janto raised his elbows in acceptance. "Now that that's settled, I need you to bring Serra and Vesperi here. Can we meet in your room? They need to be ready right away. This affects them more than anyone else."

"Of course."

Rall peeked back in on Evon, giving the boy's hair a caress while Janto watched from the hall. Then they took seats at the table built of Wasylim wood in Nap's room. Its metallic sheen came from gold flakes mixed in with the resin.

"You will ride out with us tonight." Janto spoke fast as he always did when excited. "We will ride straight to your home, and we will rid it of any of those vermin we find. It will be safe, cleansed. Then we will ride on to Lake Ashra, where Father said most reports of attacks had been made and Serra found other bodies—"

"That sounds fine." Rall fidgeted with the sleeve of his gray tunic, threadbare in the spot where his thumb rubbed. "But I am not coming with you."

"What do you mean? Imagine the excitement for Evon, riding with our party! Not that he can talk about it. Will he be able to keep the secret, do you think? We will need to leave tonight. We cannot let any more time pass."

"Is that an order?" Rall tapped his fingers against the wood. "I need to know if it is, please. Because if it isn't, we are not returning with you. I—I cannot live there anymore."

New tears formed in Rall's eyes. It had been cruel to ramble on like that. Rall sat across from him, too heartbroken to return to his home, and Janto had let the thrill of the chase cloud his vision. Again. He reached for Rall's hand.

"I am sorry. I assumed you would be returning. It is not an order."

Rall let out his breath. "Thank you."

"What are your plans?"

He shrugged. "I have not thought that far ahead. Evon and I need somewhere new, I think. It will help us . . . help us grieve and move on. Going back would be too much for me and that would be too much for him. I cannot do that to him."

Serra spoke from the doorway, "Of course you can't." She had changed from the simple garment she wore earlier and was his Serra again. That made it more difficult on some level. On another, he was overjoyed just to see her. The feather tufts on her white skirt looked like balac blossoms.

She caught him staring and blushed. "I could not resist putting it on. I love my gowns, but they're horrible to wear at Lake Ashra." Then she crossed the room and gave Rall a hug. "It was many years before I returned to Gavenstone after my parents' deaths. I couldn't bear it."

He returned the gesture. "Three months ago, I would never have dreamed I would be hugging a princess."

"You're not." Her reply was soft. Janto dropped his eyes to his feet.

A knock on the door saved them for the second time that day.

"May we come in?" Nap's voice sounded from the hall.

And I thought Ser Allyn's manners ridiculous. "It's your room, Nap. You do not have to knock."

The man did not disagree, which Janto considered progress. He shuffled inside after Vesperi.

"Why did this prawn pull me from my room when the king specifically ordered me to bed?" Vesperi's customary disdain grated. Nap and Rall frowned at it—at her—so out of place here. Janto wondered if that would ever change.

"I think we should go to Wasyla," he explained, "ride to where Rall's family was attacked. And then to Lake Ashra, where the claren have struck most often."

"And then kill them?" Vesperi smirked. "That sounds fun."

Serra agreed to the plan with a forlorn glance at her skirt.

"You will need more guards." Nap shifted his footing. "Rall and I will not be enough."

"Rall is not coming. And you're more right than you know, but we cannot take many." A sudden draft made him smack his head, imagining a chiding from Sielban as he went to close the door. His father said Vesperi was threatened, and he'd relayed his plan through an open door. "And—and we have to leave tonight. Nap, I need you to speak with Ser Allyn. Tell him to send word to Hamsyn in Carafin that he and the Old Girl should join us in three days at the Crossing. I'm certain he will come—he hates the meadows once they're browning, and all the rain has been in the east, not there. Send word to Flivio, also. He is to take that trip to Rasseleria he's always wanted. Tell him the priests will greet him at the temple of Enjoin in seven days."

"Flivio?" Rall laughed, some of the worry disappearing from his brow along with it. "Are you trying to get caught? He tries to impress with that 'wit' of his every time he meets someone new."

"Actually, I am trying to bring someone along who can keep up with our charming companion on my right."

Vesperi did not hide her interest. "He must be hung like a craval beast then."

The image of Vesperi with Flivio—with anyone—made Janto incredibly uncomfortable, but he refused to acknowledge it, especially with the plain horror on everyone else's faces. "He's the only man I know who has a faster tongue than you. Make of that what you will." *Now I'm exchanging lewd barbs with the woman.*

"You'll need fly masks, too, for the horses, special ones to cover their noses and mouths and ears. Do you have lace crafters in the castle? I can show them the ones we improvised back home." Helping made Rall's voice grow fuller, a heartening sound.

"Yes, do that. Also wake Ser Eddy in the stables when you go to retrieve them. He sleeps in a room at the end of the barn. Tell him we need four horses, fresh and fast ones. Serra, you will need to pack for us. We'll have to—"

"Travel light, I know," Serra finished. "I will take care of it, and I'll have Bini pack us food. I doubt there will be anyone in the kitchen tonight to question her about it."

Having her here, safe and dependable, was such a relief. Yet he was aiming her—them—straight at a prey more dangerous than a dozen angered rhini. He did not have time to ponder the irony of it. "I will go tell my parents. They'll want to see us off, and . . ."

And he needed someone to tell him he was making the right choice. He hurried out of the room, Rall and Nap at his heels.

CHAPTER 42
VESPERI

The woman—Mertina, *Sar* Mertina—tightened the ivory-maned horse's saddle, and Vesperi could not stop watching. It was not the act of saddling that fascinated her; Vesperi knew how to do that herself. At ten, she had begged her father to let her ride and won his permission only when she claimed that horse riding must be beneath her if he would not allow it. That did the trick. Lord Sellwyn always enjoyed teaching Vesperi her place.

What drew Vesperi's eye so steadfastly was the swordbelt slung over the woman's waist. She was slight, only an inch or so taller than Janto's short Wasylim friend, and had ebony hair twisted into a bun. Once everyone had gathered at the stables, Janto had explained that Sar Mertina would accompany them to Wasyla as another armed guard. Vesperi had laughed at first, thinking it a joke. But the laughter died as soon as she saw Mertina's sword and the assured way the woman kept her hand close to its pommel. It was spellbinding.

Vesperi barely noticed when the king arrived, his queen at his side. Her single-minded attention did not shift until he spoke, his voice hushed, as the others secured the bags Serra had packed over their horses and practiced fitting the lace masks over the animals' ears, latching them around their muzzles.

"Janto, you are certain you don't want to wait until tomorrow evening? It would give us more time to be confident in the preparations."

Janto shook his head. "It would give the claren more time to target our people. And any Meduan spies more time to get word back to Qiltyn that Vesperi travels with us."

Janto's mother, her hair wrapped in gold and copper threads that glinted in the moonlight, clasped her hands together. "That's smart, Janto, but your party is so small. We cannot help but worry." She took inventory of everyone gathered there. "At least you are taking Sar Mertina. That's smarter."

Janto grinned sheepishly. "She caught me walking across the yard toward the stable and would not let me go until I accepted her service. I will fill her in on the task at hand as we ride. I have also sent word to two of my Murat companions to join us along the way."

The king made a noise of approval while the queen moved to the guardswoman and raised her elbows to her. "Our thanks. You have served the realm for over thirty years, and we pray Madel keeps you with us for another thirty."

"As do I," Mertina answered, her stature proud. "Serving Lansera is all I have ever wanted to do."

The queen hugged her, paying no notice to the muddy ground her skirts rested on. She moved to Serra next, and Vesperi wondered at the warmth in her eyes. King Albrecht had remained aloof except for that one afternoon in the dungeon, but the queen was full of tenderness for every person she neared. She spoke in hushed tones, but the tears Serra loosed at her touch made it clear the girl appreciated her words greatly. It was all so . . . so . . . honest. Did they realize how exposed they made themselves? Were they comfortable . . . happy with that?

Do not do this. You cannot simply go where they want you. You cannot trust them. They let women be armed! It was beyond comprehension.

But so were hooded figures appearing from a bell and the idea that Vesperi—*she*—could save the world with her talent. She had known its value but had not thought beyond helping her father wrest Durn from that dullard Lord Riven. Vesperi had never considered it making her appealing to another man. But King Albrecht thought the engagement promise from Ralion was a threat, which meant the Guj had plans for her and whatever they were had been foiled. Vesperi had run from Medua. She would never be trusted to play her role properly there, yet she could not help but wonder what might have been.

A hand on her shoulder disturbed her thoughts. The queen trained her green eyes on Vesperi with curiosity and the same warmth she had shown the others. Those two eyes searched her, no words spoken. Then she smiled, the red of her hair luminous as she leaned in to whisper, "Stop running, silly girl. Live."

Vesperi sucked in her breath as though punched. The queen did not linger, moving back to join her husband. Vesperi hated that she had been read so plainly. Her body shook with the vulnerability of it. So she shifted toward her mare, focused on its smell of straw until she could collect herself again. Its rough, scratchy hair soothed until Vesperi remembered the last time she had paid such attention to a horse's mane, torturing one with bursts of her flame. This animal would have to bear her for a hard, fast ride, and Vesperi had tormented its cousin once, without a thought. *Is this regret?* She checked the knots that tied her pack to the animal, then stepped into the stirrup and launched herself onto the saddle.

The king spoke again, raising his hand toward a sky studded with stars and all four moons haloed. In a few more hours, that sky would turn royal purple as the sun began its upward journey.

"May Madel's hand guide you, keeping you safe as you do Her work. Lansera believes in you, as do I and the queen. May swift feet bear you and courage keep you on the path."

King Albrecht was not lit by the same light as he had been that afternoon in the dungeon, but she felt his words keenly. Janto spurred his horse to ride, followed by the Wasylim and then Serra. Not until Sar Mertina fell in line did Vesperi take reins in hand. As she pressed a firm kick into the mare's flank, she focused on the line the woman's leather sheath made against the white hair of her horse. The contrast was striking.

CHAPTER 43

JANTO

The sky darkened fast into a cerulean horizon with a deep green layer above it. It looked no different than any other evening spent watching the stars, but Janto felt foreboding. The weight on his chest was not from the sky, but from the man he'd left at Callyn cradling his son. Janto had given Pic strict instructions to show Evon around the castle. A new friend would do both of them good after what they had lived through.

Sar Mertina led their group, keeping them far enough from the main roads to avoid attention but not so far they might lose their way. They trod on hundreds of grasses, varieties that ranged from ivory tones to shades matching the darkening sky and the reeds of Rasseleria. The moist ground made Janto glad they had not delayed their departure. The farther west they traveled, the plainer their trail was to follow in the mud.

Vesperi rode straight in her saddle, her contemptuous expression earned, for once, by the rough travel. She glared when she felt him stare, and he smiled back. *No, I do not want her to be caught.* He had grown quite fond of her scornful expressions now he knew most of them were faked. Serra's mere presence still did not seem real. Janto did not know how to be with her without *being with* her, and he had never felt so unsettled.

A whistle, pitched nearly as high as an angered drasmo's shriek, cut through his thoughts: Sar Mertina's call of warning. Nap, second in the line, increased his pace at once, and the others followed suit. A pair of tall, thin monoliths loomed ahead, two figures silhouetted against them. The stones rested lengthwise against each other at a 90-degree angle. They rose twice as high as the people in front of them were tall. Mertina was one of those, still on horseback. The tension eased out of Janto's body as he recognized the second figure: Hamsyn kindling a torch. The Old Girl leaned beside him against the rock face.

"I hope you brought a horse." Janto climbed off his own to give his friend a hug.

Hamsyn scoffed. "You think I show up to a royal summons unprepared? You mock me. My horse is tied by that citrus grove to the south. The Wasylim tendency to plant trees wherever they roam comes in handy on occasion."

"Your horse will need this, and I hope you packed the extra handkerchiefs we asked you to." Janto drew an extra, newly cobbled together, lace mask out of his pack.

Hamsyn raised an eyebrow but asked no questions. "I did, Your Highness."

Too exhausted to correct Hamsyn's formal address to a friendlier one, Janto sighed. "I see you have met Sar Mertina. She is one of my father's most trusted guards."

Sar Mertina blushed. "The prince is a shameless flatterer, but I have been in Lansera's service for thirty of my years."

"That's amazing. And these others?" Hamsyn gestured toward the women behind Janto, their faces obscured but for the flickering of his torch. Nap extended a hand to Serra to help her dismount, and Janto felt shame he had not offered it but . . . but he was not ready for that contact. He moved to help Vesperi instead. She scorned his outstretched hand and eyed the ground on the other side of the horse. He went back to introductions.

"The lady on her mount, who prefers no assistance, is Vesperi Sellwyn of Medua."

The narrowing of Hamsyn's eyes indicated the need for more explanation, but the Nevillim held his tongue. They narrowed more acutely when Janto nodded toward Serra.

"The Lady Serrafina Gavenstone, my betrothed—" the word slipped out fast, a habit not easy to break. He coughed and tried not to sound bitter, "—my formerly betrothed. You may have heard?"

Hamsyn nodded in assent. "But I did not hear why. There were rumors of a Meduan plot"—he glanced toward Vesperi—"or that the Lady Gavenstone had lost her head."

"Oh, those are not so far off." Serra did not bother to tender her tone as Janto had. *She has changed so much.* "In truth, I am not certain *Lady* still applies."

"Don't be ridiculous." Janto was aghast. "We would—I—would never strip you of your title."

"If any of this was in our control, Janto, do you think we would be standing here at the Crossing, unwed, unhappy, and with a Meduan in our midst?"

He did not reply, examining the monoliths in the evening gloom instead. Imaginary lines extended out from where their crossing made three planes and marked the borders between Wasyla, Rasseleria, and Neville. The stones had stood longer than maps had been drawn, and the people of those regions never complained at their perimeters. Janto had not seen this relic before, but the tombs and dungeons below Callyn were eerier. The Crossing simply existed. He envied it, sometimes.

Hamsyn pushed off from the stone. "So where are we going? The message I received was not very detailed, and my sister may have issued death threats against the royal family when I left her alone with her harvesting."

Janto recalled the farmers' plants outside of Urs. "I nearly forgot! I learnt a bit about those seeds foraging in the mountains. The plant is called fallowent. I would be happy to tell her what else I know, though it is not much."

"She would love that." Hamsyn beamed, pleased at the offer.

"Fallowent?" Vesperi looked up with interest. "We have that in Sellwyn, though not much of it. Our herbalist uses it for . . . I am not certain he knows what it is for. I had some myself, but I ate it in the mountains when I ran low on food."

"She will be excited to hear you have it in Sellwyn already."

"How are her seeds faring with this weather?" Janto smiled at the memory of searching for dark seeds among the black sands of Braven.

"Thriving. Her stocks have nearly doubled since I left for the Murat. She cannot keep up, but nonetheless, she will not tell me where she plans to sow them all."

"She will not tell anyone where you went, either?"

"Oh no." Hamsyn clasped his arm. "You can trust me on that, Janto.

She would never—never—give away something that could endanger me. Though I hope I am not in too much danger?" Hamsyn's brow raised in question.

Mertina wore a well-practiced nonchalance, but she perked up slightly at Hamsyn's question—she had not been briefed on the details of their quest as yet. The fewer people who knew, the better for keeping their travels secret from the Guj's men, but this task required much of them both. Janto could not ask them to take it on blindly.

"You *are* in danger. So are we all. But that would be the case whether we stay at this Crossing forever or we continue on to Rall's home." He rubbed a hand over the Old Girl, the curve of her bow comforting. Then he looked up, sheepish. "We are saving Lansera. I hope you will come."

Hamsyn merely nodded his head before heading off to claim his horse.

CHAPTER 44
VESPERI

Five days. They had been traveling on horseback for five days, and as far as Vesperi was concerned, her companions needed to show more gratitude that she hadn't used her talent on a single one of them, nor even raised a finger their way. The last time she had used it, two nights ago, was to cleanse the shack Janto's friend had called a home. How was she to know the whole thing would flare up like a firecracker? Yes, she and Serra had barely made it out unscathed, so she understood the concern, she did.

But the princeling could only push her so much further.

He rode by her side, rambling on and on about how she should practice more, how they would deal with the Guj's men if they had to, but she needed to respond right away if Serra saw one of those creatures again—right away, without killing anyone. *Details.*

"Vesperi." Janto's frustration rose with each consecutive repetition of her name. "Vesperi, have you been practicing at all?"

"You have been blathering in my ear for two days straight. Maybe I would practice if you'd let me alone for a few minutes." She would not perform just because he asked, just because *anyone* asked. She had done enough performing to last a lifetime, and where had that gotten her? Riding on horseback for five days with a group of Lanserim, knowing whatever this companionship was would only last as long as it took for them to rid their precious towns of the claren.

And by Saeth's fist, that Serra annoyed her with her high-brow aloofness and her waifish charms. Janto wouldn't shut up about her on the ride to Callyn, and now she was here in the flesh, had been every day for a week, and Vesperi had expected someone a little more exciting. Even her clothing, that drab sheath, had no color to it. The way she cocked her head while scanning for claren trails made Vesperi want to knock a few thoughts into it.

That was not fair, and Vesperi knew it—the girl was smart. But Vesperi hated the glares she sent her way. They only intensified with Janto nearby, demanding Vesperi pay attention.

"I did practice," she finally admitted. "During my watch when the rest of you slept." She was surprised Janto had given her a watch last night, but he insisted on it over Serra and Napeler's protestations, because he wanted everyone as well rested as possible. Vesperi hoped they'd sleep for a week once they reached the temple up ahead.

It was so different from Mandat Hall. A few rows of huts curved around its northern side, but the whole thing took up so little area. Mandat Hall loomed over the hills of Qiltyn, like a koparin waiting to pounce from the heights. How did Lanserim priests inspire awe and obedience with such a simple dome and no one around to see it?

"Rynna Gemni," Serra called to a slender woman running toward them from the temple. She wore the same boring clothes as Serra. *Great, more thrilling companions.* But there must be something else at hand, because Serra dismounted.

"What's wrong?" Serra handed her reins to Nap, the cocky Wasylim, and began toward the other woman.

"No, no, get back on!" The woman spoke firmly, and Serra obeyed. "You have to go to the lake. We have had word of more bodies like the ones you described. Lourda confirmed it. You are needed there, Serra. Ryn Cladio instructed me to send you as soon as I sighted your group."

"He knew we were coming?"

"Of course he did. Madel's hand does not grasp at air. Go!"

Vesperi liked her. No need to beat around the bush with that woman. But she was tired, and more riding was not welcome. The others felt the same based on their slumped stances.

Janto sighed but nodded. "We will go. Serra, lead the way."

They secured handkerchiefs and masks and went, and though Vesperi's thighs would ache a while longer, being needed was a little thrilling. She blew a kiss to Esye, the moon full in the morning sky.

✳ ✳ ✳

The colossal lake was the most beautiful thing Vesperi had ever seen, including the expression on her father's face the day she told him he could stop holding her virginity over her head. The midday light reflecting off it nearly blinded her.

"They have to be in the village." Serra steered them toward an enclave of huts Vesperi could barely make out—they stood hardly taller than the reeds. The seer spurred her horse to a faster pace. They reached the first of the huts about ten minutes later. "I don't see any traces of claren here."

There was no one outside, and the day was so humid, Vesperi would not have forced herself inside for anything.

"Ryn Cladio?" Serra yelled louder than Vesperi would have thought the waif could manage. "We're here!" She galloped to the nearest hut. "It's me. It's Serra. Where are they? Where are the claren?"

A door opened several yards away and an ancient man dressed in another of those sheaths stepped out. White hair fell past his waist, and he held a cane. *Definitely not an adver.* None of them would dare hold a cane.

"Serra! Thanks be to Madel." His voice was pleasant.

"Ryn Cladio," Janto greeted the man with raised elbows. "I hate to meet you this way, but are the villagers here all right? Where are they?"

"Most of them are fine, slayer"—Ryn Cladio raised his elbows as well—"boarded up in their huts to keep the claren out. The Rasseleri-ans know what to do when such things stir. They brought the body of an elder who had fallen silent yesterday morning to us at the temple. "

Serra examined the huts intently. "Which one is his?"

He pointed to a far grouping. "You need handkerchiefs wrapped around your faces. And the weapon. His home is the—"

"Fourth one from the end. I see their trail." Serra beckoned Vesperi to follow. "You heard him. Let's get this over with, Meduan."

Shock shone plainly on the ryn's face. He must not have known his cherished weapon was a dirty Meduan. This Madel did not explain things to Her people very well.

Janto rode up beside her, speaking softer than Serra had. "Come on, you get to play. Let's go."

"But you don't need to come. I do not know if I can control—"

"If you think for a moment I am leaving you and Serra alone in another room full of the creatures that did that to Mar Pina, you're crazy." He shook his head, but fondness lit up his features. "Besides, you have been practicing. I trust you."

"A bigger fool you are for it." She laughed and trotted her horse after his. They paused to dismount, and Serra and Janto pulled scarves over their faces outside the front door. "Here." Nap, the nubbin, drew close. He extended a clean gray cloth to her. She had burnt her last one at Rall's home. "Take mine."

Vesperi was already tying the cloth before she realized she'd uttered a "thank you" in reply. *These people have made me weak.* The aggravating thought sparked her skill into life, and she rushed inside as Janto pushed the door closed behind them. The air was stifling and smelled worse than soured milk wine.

Serra's fingers clasped her arm, and her nails dug in to Vesperi's arm, sharp as thornberries.

"Focus. Channel. Aim." Janto's whisper gained him a huge eye roll, but Vesperi did as told. She had grown used to his particular brand of obnoxiousness.

"Fast." Serra's eyes were vacant. "They have not sensed us yet."

Focus. There was no window left uncovered in this place, so Vesperi imagined the moon instead, how it appeared at Sellwyn through the rusted metal bars of her tiny window. Serra shifted her arm to the left then a smidgen to the right.

Channel. Vesperi drew on the imagined moon's silvery light within her mind. Eyes closed, she grabbed at the energy that spilled from it, pulled it as though the reins of a troublesome horse until she could feel it inside her, flowing beneath her skin. The curls of her hair lifted up and straightened into tight barbs, and she knew she had it.

Aim. She unrolled her clenched finger, pointed, and released.

The strength of the magic's expulsion forced her eyes open, and only Serra's hands on it kept her arm up and finger pointing in the right direction. She steeled herself again and felt immense satisfaction at the crackling that filled the silver-tinged air. Energy whirled in her palm, and Vesperi released enough to extend to where the claren smoked and no farther, Serra nudging her arm back and forth all the while. When Serra finally let her hand fall away, Vesperi nearly jumped for joy. There were no scorch marks on the opposite wall.

"You did it." Janto inspected the same wall, disbelieving. In a moment, his arms were around her, pressing against her, and it felt almost as good as the energy fading to a hum in her ears. "You did it, Vesperi!"

She had. She really had. She sunk into his arms and hugged back. Her view was obscured, but she did not miss Serra's quick, hurried exit from the hut, her eyes flying anywhere but back at Vesperi and Janto, except for the moment when they'd glanced on hers.

Vesperi had seen that expression once before, when one of the advers had taken her to court from the convent. She had been deposited in a waiting room with the other playthings. The man left her there and Vesperi had grown livid, having expected to be paraded on his pasty, floppy arm for at least a few minutes. She had wanted to see the king.

"Ralion has thirty women lying at his feet," she had screamed at the adver's retreating back. "Leave me in that pile—I will gladly stroke his cock if I'm not good enough for yours!"

A nearby courtier was on her in an instant. The leather of his gloves left a red mark that did not fade for two days. He was a tall man in tight black pants and a crimson tunic, wavy hair the color of dried chicory. His manner had been composed, but his eyes swam with anguish in the moment she glimpsed them before he disappeared in the same direction the adver had gone.

"I'll suck yours too, if you bring me in," she had yelled at his retreating form, not caring if it bought her a matching mark on the other side.

"Not an appealing offer for him." One of the other women in the room had spoken up. "That was Rapsca Unger." She said his name as though it was all the explanation needed.

"The king's advisor?"

The woman laughed and patted her stomach in merriment. "Something like that."

Vesperi understood, once she'd been long enough at the convent to hear more rumors of court, but why Serra would feel the same torment as Rapsca Unger was a mystery, especially when Vesperi's every cell reverberated with victory.

CHAPTER 45
JANTO

I anto held a glass shard up to the sunlight and wiggled his blurry fingers behind it. The shard was dark blue, about an inch thick, and the sunlight exposed a pearlescent sheen on one of its faces. Tilt it any other way, and the sheen disappeared. That was how he knew this shard came from the oldest days, the ones when only Rasselerians had lived in Lansera and Madel's hand had not needed to reach so far. The Rasselerian sorters had described its qualities when they brought a barrel full of glass and emptied it at his feet no more than a day after they had rid the elder's hut of claren. Many piles of glass surrounded Janto now, the colors as varied as the feathers had been on Braven.

He sat on a bench in the sticky air, grateful for every wind gust from Lake Ashra, a mile to the north. Each breeze dispelled the jocal flies, if only for a moment. His party had traveled throughout the marshlands for the past four days, following news of other villagers who had been subsumed. Janto's patience with flies and the wet heat wore thin. The hut he sat in front of was a meeting place for the Rasselerians who scoured the swamps for the glass and other artifacts. They had more chances to hear news and rumors here than anywhere else the marshfolk gathered.

Their team was six now. Flivio had arrived last night with two rynnas guiding him. He sorted glass now with Janto, Hamsyn, and a handful of Rasselerians. He peppered their silence with the occasional insult at Vesperi's expense, although she was not around. "Practice," Flivio had called it, admiration for her laced in with his sarcasm. It had taken all of ten minutes after his arrival to begin a heated exchange that had brought a genuine smile to Vesperi's face.

She and Serra were a few miles away, investigating another report of a villager gone silent, with Sar Mertina and Nap as their guards. Janto had resisted when Vesperi insisted she try to control her magic without him there to prod her, but he acquiesced. Just yesterday morning, she had destroyed a tiny swarm. Ten charred shells had fallen from the sky, and no thistle on the surrounding reeds had so much as sparked. So he agreed, knowing with the surety that fixed his frown to his face that they would be fine without him. At least sorting glass to pass the time was something useful he could do.

"This piece is the sickliest green I have ever seen, aside from that Meduan's disposition." Flivio tossed the offending glass onto a pile of old, but not old enough, shards. A Rasselerian picked it up and nodded before letting it fall back down again.

"And apparently, I am not trusted to tell if these things have a sheen or not." Flivio brushed specks of glass dust from his pants, making the mud beneath him sparkle. Janto lifted another shard from his own pile to the sun, pink with a pearlescent surface. It also bore a broken sigil of the distinctive Xantas heraldry, a bear raised on its haunches. The shard went in yet another pile, hopefully to be reunited with its mates that held the rest of the sigil from when it had once been a vase or a plate.

"Come on, Janto." Flivio tossed another shard onto the pile from which it had come. "There has to be something else we can do while waiting for your women to come back—"

"They are not *my* women." His voice came across bitterer than intended. One of those women *should* be his, and he hated that she wasn't. They should have been doing this together as husband and wife, and he did not understand why they weren't. Serra would not speak with him for longer than courtesy allowed, and she avoided it half the time regardless. Vesperi, on the other hand, was not his woman at all.

"Calm down, *little child*." Flivio mimicked Sielban's voice so perfectly both Hamsyn and Janto laughed. "All I meant is you three are in this together, from what I understand. Your bedroom is none of my concern."

Janto rolled his eyes with good humor, refreshed to be around his friends again despite the circumstances. Three weeks of living in a forest with them during the Murat made this almost seem normal. And it would be for quite a long time if the claren had spread nearly as far as they feared. Janto was not certain they would ever gain the advantage. They could ride through all of Lansera for years eradicating them, but if the claren kept breeding in Medua, his people would never be safe. Janto's face fell again, and he reached for another piece of glass.

As he did, the Rasselerians among them lifted their heads in unison. They turned toward each other then rose and walked off in the same direction, away from the hut and toward the road that led north from Wasyla.

Hamsyn, Janto, and Flivio exchanged glances.

"They *are* little Sielbans, aren't they?" Hamsyn blinked with surprise. "Do you think they have been in our minds, too? I hope I haven't thought anything too offensive."

"Right." Flivio snorted. "Like you have worries. I only grace you with the tamest opinions that run through my head. I am fairly certain I was pondering the sex lives of frogs a few minutes ago."

Janto was too fascinated by the Rasselerians' movement to give Flivio the shove he deserved. Two others approached from the road, and they wiggled with what might have been excitement, one of them reaching into a bag slung over his shoulder. The Rasselerians leaned in as one, and an excited hum spread between them.

"What are you staring at?" Someone breathed into his ear then laughed mercilessly as he jumped.

Vesperi's amusement lightened her face, then she smiled. "We did it."

His pride soared, and he forgot the Rasselerians entirely.

"And she only lit a curtain on fire." Serra sounded just as satisfied, coming around the cabin's side.

Janto dropped the glass in his hand and pressed an arm around each woman in a hug. "That's amazing." He had been so focused on the Rasselerians, he had missed their party coming up behind them.

Janto directed his next statement to Nap, who was helping Mertina tie up the horses. "Come now, Nap. They left a trail of burned huts and reeds in their wake, did they not?"

Nap startled, the color draining from his face. "No, they speak the truth, of course."

Janto laughed. The Wasylim had yet to develop a sense of humor, but in a group with Flivio in it, that might be a survival instinct. The Meditlan had enough *humor* for them all.

The Rasselerians made their way back, and the new arrivals came to stand before Janto, the others gathered behind them. The colors of their suits shifted in fast succession, no attempt at camouflage made though the coarse, carnelian hair on their heads matched the reed tassels around them.

Janto took a deep breath to steady himself. It was time to be an Albrecht again, and that he knew how to do. "How can I aid you, fellow Lanserim?"

"We have spoken." The woman did not need to explain she meant all the Rasselerians with them. Their eyes were trained on Janto with the same intensity. "And we believe this finding is meant for you."

"It is rare," one of her companions took over. "From the days before the divide when Madel's reach went over the mountains. It is not so old as glass, but it is costlier. Wood breaks down when glass does not."

"I will gladly accept this gift on my father's behalf. I am certain he will be pleased. But I am afraid I don't know when I can give it to him. Madel's plan may be to keep us far from Callyn for some time." Not even his destination was his decision, or at least it didn't feel that way.

The Rasselerians sucked air through their teeth with a *tuuut*. "No, slayer, you need this now." The man unfurled his webbed fingers, revealing a box of petrified wood, dark and streaked with red on its edges as though blood had stained it.

It may well be blood. When he saw the insignia it bore, he took Serra's hand with what he hoped was reassurance. The moment she recognized it, he knew. Tension gathered in her limbs. The sigil was carved masterfully. After centuries caked in mud, every scale of the snake's raised hood could be counted.

"That's a Sellwyn chest." Vesperi took the box and rubbed her finger over the symbol, yet no gooseflesh rose on her arms like it had on his. She put it aside thoughtlessly, and the lack of heft in her action felt grotesque. "But we have not made these in at least a decade. We stopped harvesting rosewood for craft when they grew too thin. My father thinks using malnourished wood would reflect badly on our name."

She laughed to herself for a moment, a cynical sound that had grown rarer the longer they'd traveled together. Yet her tone was pleasant, happy even, as she addressed the Rasselerians. "That is what you found in the marshes? It does not seem like much to get your lot so excited." She shrugged.

"How do you know?" Janto feared the answer. "How do you know this is from your family?"

"It is our sigil—the forest viper. I have always been rather taken with it. Suits me, don't you think?" She smirked.

His mind filled with ashes, remembered the greasy residue they had left on his fingers when he had reached to pull a ring engraved with grapevines out of a box such as this. Anger wound itself up inside him, a coil of metal wire pulled tight.

He said nothing but gripped Serra's hand. She trembled. Whatever anger he felt, her body reflected it back tenfold. Silver flecks flashed in her green eyes. Yet she kept her voice calm as she spoke.

"Is it? Does it adorn all your boxes back in Sellwyn?"

"Oh yes," Vesperi answered. "I use one whenever I have something important to send."

He held tight to Serra's wrist. She jerked her arm, but he did not let go, did not want her to provoke Vesperi or to see what would happen if she did. Vesperi struck first, thought second, no matter what control she had learned, and Esye was rising this time of day, its moonslight amplified in the heavy air by the lake's reflecting waters. Serra would not consider that right now. Her vision was clouded, and Janto could only stop himself from choking on the same rage by keeping her from stumbling into the crosshairs.

Her tone was ice when Serra spoke again. "How does it feel when you use the flame? When you smite something?"

Vesperi frowned at the abrupt subject change, but her usual smirk came back fast. "Exhilarating. Like I have all the power in the world."

"What did he do?" The love of Janto's life had never sounded so frightening before, but he recognized a flickering hope in her words, a chance for Vesperi to explain. "What did he do to make you kill him? He was stupid, sometimes. I lived with him my whole life, Madel knows. Did he make an advance on you? Maybe he was trying to fit in?"

If they were wrong, then Vesperi would pretend confusion. She would look at Janto with unspoken questions, maybe cast a concerned glance toward Serra if brave enough to let herself show it.

Instead she flinched as realization dawned. Then she drew herself up tall and haughty. "He called me a lady. I could not let that go unaddressed."

All the color but red drained from Serra's face. "You killed my brother."

Janto held on tighter.

"You filthy Meduan, you killed my brother." Her voice was calm no longer.

Several glass shards fell to the piles with a tinkle as someone dropped them.

"Madel's hand," Hamsyn gaped. "Is it true?"

"Should I bind her, Janto?" Nap's voice was unsure. Janto did not know the answer.

The Rasselerians did not react, though they scrutinized the trio, if Janto read the meaning of their flicking tongues correctly.

Vesperi spoke next, disdain laced into her words. *Venom*, he thought. *Her speech is always venomous.* "Yes, I killed Agler. He was a spy and not a very good one."

"He was my brother!" Tears rushed over Serra's reddened face, hot lava down a mountainside. Fists clenched, she lunged at Vesperi with enough speed to escape his grip. The Meduan jumped back and began to raise her hand—

No, no, no. Janto slid between the two women, raising his arms up. "Nap, Flivio, please hold Serra back. Please." The Rasselerians had thrown themselves to the ground, but they were not his concern right now. There was nothing more important than the brown pair of eyes before him, filling with a silver glow.

"Vesperi," he said calmly, "Block it out. Block out the moon."

"Why should I?" Her hair lifted. She was close. "I have no choice. I know what happens to women who kill men."

"Block it out. Breathe. Focus. Send Esye back." It was pointless. Vesperi would not listen. She did not need to hide her magic anymore. Too many people knew the silver flame had returned, the weapon been reborn. She would strike. She was a killer.

"Breathe. Focus. Pull it back."

She lowered her arm. Relief flooded him but only until Serra yelled. He spun around to find her staring up at the heavens, fists raised as high as they could reach.

"I cannot do this! I cannot do this!"

Nap and Flivio released her when he gestured to, and then Serra ran far from them all. Sar Mertina made to follow, but Janto waved her back.

"She will be back." He tried to sound certain, but her cries as she disappeared into the miry forest to the east reminded him of his own the day she had not returned for him. If she did not return again—

"Never mind, Sar Mertina. Trail her, but give her space?"

The guardswoman mounted up in an instant.

Janto had to have faith something greater was happening here. Madel required the three of them to stop the claren, and that was what mattered most. Protecting their people. He would be damned if he let anything get in the way of that. Even his anger.

"You are not our prisoner, Vesperi." She sat on the bench beside him, silent and perhaps as shocked as he that nothing had changed when everything felt different. Her mouth was tight but the silver was gone from her eyes, leaving only the brown of a doe's.

He averted his gaze. "But I do not think I can look on you right now." He picked up a purple shard of glass and held it to the light.

CHAPTER 46
SERRA

Stomping off into the woods wasn't what she wanted to do. *That* was reaching her hands around Vesperi's neck and squeezing until no air came through it ever again. The Meduan had not murdered Agler—she had eviscerated him. Serra knew what that was like, had seen it with her own eyes no more than an hour ago when they had found a claren swarm in front of the missing candlemaker's hut. The creatures had sizzled, shells turning to ashes as they fell.

Agler pleading and burning in front of that woman who knew pity but not compassion—it was all Serra could imagine. The tears would win if she stopped moving, so she kept on. *Madel's hand, I do not know if I went east or south.* She would be lost if she kept this up, and Janto would come hunting for her. She did not want to see him, did not want to see the murderer with him who she knew—she knew—would be free. He would not kill Vesperi, would not even restrain her. Janto Albrecht *believed.*

Unrelenting tears made Serra's eyes sting, but no amount of rubbing could make them stop. She did not want them to, did not want clear vision.

A mangrove root spilled her onto the slimy floor of the forest. Crushed libtyl leaves clung to her sandals, and she closed her eyes to take in their sharp, minty tang. She looked on the familiar sight of water-logged forest floor and spindly branches. Also familiar were the blue lights beckoning like fireflies.

She shook her head violently. Oh no, she was *not* going to come when they called, not after this. But her feet moved to follow, and her reasoning soon caught up to them. She needed answers only the Brothers could give, and she'd be damned if she had to face Vesperi again without them.

The drop took her unawares when it came, but Serra knew enough to brace herself this time, landing on bent knees. Only one wraith waited in the cave, its gray robe illuminated by a faint blue aura.

She threw a stone from the cave floor at the Brother. "What right do you have to force me to do this?" Another thrown stone pushed into the fabric before it fell.

Her arm hair raised as the Brother cackled, "Serrafina Gavenstone, you are the seer. You must guide the weapon. You have accepted this."

"You left out a few details when I said yes."

It faced her, orbs flickering from the darkness of its hood where eyes should be. "They were insignificant."

"How dare you! He was my brother." She leapt toward him, hitting the packed dirt wall instead. "He was not insignificant!"

The Brother reappeared at the other end of the cave. "You must guide the weapon."

She should have known better than to think this would get her anywhere.

"You must guide the weapon." Its monotonous tone did not make the Brother's words any easier to hear.

"I cannot. I cannot do that." If she said it enough times, perhaps he would believe her. "I cannot work with *her*."

"She is the one who was chosen."

"I thought I was the one who was chosen. That's what you . . ." *No, maybe not this Brother, specifically, but does it matter?* They were all the same, all loathsome, inhuman spirits who would make her do this. ". . . what you told me. That is why I am here, is it not?"

"You were chosen because you made the choice to come. The slayer and the weapon, too, must keep making the choice to do what they must. And the weapon cannot do it without you to guide her."

The thought of anyone guiding that spiteful Meduan was ludicrous. Maybe months ago Serra could have, before she had become this other person. Before her brother had been taken from her, and Janto, too. Maybe when her life had been filled with practicing her courtesies while Bini braided golden threads through her hair, and she had wanted a future of leading couples to dance, her arm looped through Janto's. Maybe then she was someone who could have forgiven a wrong this horrific.

But she gave that life up because these creatures said it was her fate to do so, her destiny. What sort of goddess was Madel if She asked for sacrifices like this? "You are wrong. The prophecy is wrong."

"Madel's intent cannot be mistaken. Her hand touches us directly. You have seen it. You know it is true."

"I do not care!" Serra tugged at her hair. "I am the seer. I cannot deny that. You float three inches from the ground yet I am the only person who notices. But maybe the weapon isn't *her*. Maybe you are mistaken and there are others with the flame. It cannot be her. She is Meduan! How could Madel put our fates into one of their hands?"

"You are the seer, Serrafina Gavenstone, and you must guide her. You must work together to defeat them and save us."

But she killed my brother and has stolen Janto. She wanted to scream it. She wanted to find a way to grab onto the Brother's invisible body and wrest that truth from him.

"The slayer cannot realize his destiny without you. The stag has been caught, but he must find the right place to release her."

"You pilfer thoughts from my mind now? Then listen to these." She would find some other way to serve Lansera, become an herbalist and tour the afflicted cities where the claren spread, bring aid to their suffering where she could . . . if the claren left anyone to soothe.

Pressure built in her jaw as she clenched it, and her stomach gnawed with pain that had no relation to food. It hurt, realizing her commitment was unchanged. Knowing Vesperi had killed Agler did not change the evil preying on Lansera. Serra had to keep doing this. She could not punish innocent people because her heart and soul were broken.

The Brother shimmered as though a chime in a breeze. "Our time grows short. We forget, sometimes, how it was when we lived. How it feels to be human." It laughed again, and she could almost call it a chuckle, if it did not make her shiver. "You are ready?"

"I am."

Its hood dipped in assent, and the cool, dry ground beneath her returned to slick libtyl leaves and moss.

"There she is!"

The gruff voice startled Serra, and she stumbled backward as two unknown men advanced from the mangroves. They held swords aloft and wore strange that looked more like silver vestments and veils. The closest one spoke again. "You're a tricky one, whore. Thought you didn't have the sense to know we were trailing you."

The Guj's men. She'd run off, not thinking about the danger when—

The one farthest back screamed as the tip of a blade went through his flesh, slicing through the chainmail just as easily. The blade rotated and pulled back out, leaving the man to fall to his knees just long enough for a sure stroke to take his head off.

Sar Mertina spurred her horse into a charge, yelling, "Get down, Lady Serra! Roll aside!"

Serra dropped to her knees, heart pounding.

"That's a—that's a woman." The other man barely had time to finish before Sar Mertina slashed through his chest from shoulder to hip bone. His blood splattered on Serra's arm as the guard withdrew her sword. Part of his chainmail dropped into her lap. She rubbed the soft, malleable metal between her fingers in a dazed wonder.

"Lady Serra, are you all right?"

Serra let the metal drop and raised her head to her rescuer. "I am. Was that all of them?"

"All that I've seen since Janto sent me after you. They were nearly on you before you gave them the slip. That gave me enough time to plan an advance. Can I take you back now?"

Serra took her extended hand without hesitation. "You can. We need to tell the others that we've been discovered here."

It was time to move on in more ways than one.

CHAPTER 47
VESPERI

When Serra returned, she resolutely avoided the spot on the bench were Vesperi sat. Mud and blood splotched her arms and stained her sheath, but the seer left the explanations to Sar Mertina, disappearing inside to change when Napeler confirmed there had been no new claren reports.

Vesperi was fine with that, more than fine. In truth, she waited for shackles to be clasped around her wrists. But the only restraints she felt were ones of silence from everyone in their group. News of the attack on Serra subdued them more than they already had been, each preferring their own thoughts. More of the frog people brought them dinner, or perhaps it was the same ones; Vesperi could not tell the difference. Soon after, she went to bed, the hut's straw floor more welcoming than the others' wary glances.

Whispers rose up as soon as she went inside, and a muffled, heated exchange followed. Janto's guards disagreed—nay, argued with him. In Sellwyn, they would have hung for the gall of it, but Janto let them speak as though their opinions mattered. His tenor countered their voices, and Serra joined hers with his. Vesperi could not make out what they said, and she did not care to as long as her hands remained unbound.

There is no rope, but I am not free. Janto and Serra could not look her in the eye, yet they fought to keep her with them. It made no sense, but she was grateful they felt tied to her. Her hand traced the line around her neck where Janto or one of his men should have sliced the moment she confirmed killing the Raven. She should have denied it, but she was so tired when Serra had asked. It was easier to say yes, and she had felt lighter at once, as though she had lost her head after all by admitting the guilt.

She dozed until she heard footsteps walk from the doorway to where she lay. Vesperi sucked in her breath, bracing for the blow.

"You will cramp up in that position," Mertina's soft voice chided. The female guard stood tall, one hand resting on her sword pommel.

"Why are you speaking to me?" Vesperi cringed at her own tone. She hadn't meant to sound as though upbraiding a servant. Sar Mertina was certainly not one of those.

"Because I did not want you to wake up screaming. This will all be more difficult if we aren't well rested tomorrow. We'll have to move soon."

"No, I meant why are you in here at all? Has Janto changed his mind? Am I to be a prisoner again?"

"Then you should say what you mean, not sling barbs with your tongue at a friend." The older woman shifted her tight black braid from her left shoulder to her right. "I am guarding you. That fight—the prince's companions needed reminding of how great the threat is, even after seeing it every day. You are safe, but they do not trust you. Janto had to compromise."

"But you know what I can do. None of you could hold me."

The warrior laughed, and Vesperi wondered what her mother would sound like if she had ever done the same. This woman was no larger than Lady Sellwyn, but they could not be more dissimilar. Her mother would keel over from the weight of a sword, and Sar Mertina swung hers like a feather.

"You strike me as a woman who knows the performance is sometimes more important than the script." Mertina's smile was sly but genuine. "They need me here watching you so they can pretend sleeping next to you is not betraying themselves."

"And you are not so concerned with your conscience?"

"The king trusted you enough to send you with his son. And the Lady Serra is willing to work with you despite your crime. I have served the Albrechts nearly all my life and definitely all of hers. Their judgment is enough for me."

Vesperi was unused to loyalty that did not stem from fear of a noose. Mertina's came from the right to weigh one's rulers and serve them if they proved their worth. As she slipped back into sleep, the soldier's smile dominated Vesperi's dreams.

* * *

Her "guards" the next day were not so understanding. Hamsyn waited by the door when she rose to break her water. She gave him a pleasant "Good morning" without a trace of sarcasm, and he said nothing in response. Most of the others slept, but when she had finished, she spotted Janto leaning against a pile of glass shards, speaking with one of the Rasselerians. He had supported her, had convinced the others to let her stay with them rather than kill her on the spot. But when she placed a hand on his arm, he shrank back from it. The frogman stopped talking, flicking its tongue into the air between them instead.

"Good morning, Janto." She tried to sound as innocent as she had with Hamsyn. She raised her elbows to the frogman. His tongue withdrew into his mouth.

"Mer Hallorn here has informed me of another attack close by. We need to move fast—the villager fell silent only an hour ago, so the claren will be there in mass." No greeting, only business. *It doesn't matter.* She could do this without camaraderie. It was how she had always lived her life.

"Should we get Serra and go then? We could be back before anyone else woke."

Janto disturbed the ground between them with the toe of his boot. "No, we will all go. They would not like it if we split up. I will wake them. Just—" he waved his hand "—just wait right here."

Hamsyn took a few steps closer to her as Janto went into the hut. His eyes never left her, watching and waiting as though she were a hare hoping to flit away. It was almost funny, considering what she *would* do if trying to escape.

"Here." The Rasselerian offered her a corn cake that looked more appetizing than Yarowen cheese, at least. "You must keep your strength up as you travel. The need is great." She tried not to touch his webbing as she took it. No one in their group was apt to offer her food this morning, and Serra kept the store. There was no request she would ask of Serra presently.

The seer came out of the hut just then, and the first thing she did was seek out Vesperi. Their eyes connected long enough for Vesperi to feel the hatred. It felt worse than it had been yesterday. Yet Serra had defended her last night, had fought alongside Janto to keep her alive and working with them.

I should have escaped when only one of them was awake to guard me. But the disappointment it would cause the king and her companions kept Vesperi rooted to the spot no matter what her survival instincts said. *Curse Mertina and her talk of loyalty.*

She scowled. She did not have to like it.

During the ride to whatever hovel had been attacked, Vesperi readied her talent. Napeler rode beside her, and the disdain rolled off him in waves that she used to strengthen her tie to Esye, scorn that she could channel when she received the go ahead from Serra. All that power waiting right there for her to pull it and then release. The air thrummed, and she drummed her fingers on her thighs in anticipation. When the frogman Hallorn stopped them, she dismounted and scanned the horizon, impatient.

"Let's go," she said to the nearest person when she spotted the low-lying roof. "We have bugs to kill."

"Maybe you could sound less excited about what you do." Flivio cocked his head. "We might find you more tolerable if you did not take such obvious joy in it. I bet killing gets you off better than an orgasm."

Amusement and cruelty mixed in his face, a combination she had last seen when her father laughed away the hopes she had dared to harbor. She responded to it the same way she had then. But this time when she ran, it was into the fray. These people might never trust her, but she would make them respect her regardless.

CHAPTER 48

JANTO

Serra watched as Vesperi took off at full-speed toward the hut. "What does she think she's doing now?"

Janto shrugged, more worried about them coexisting than her escaping. The claren report this morning signaled the shortest time between reports they had yet received. Who knew how far the pestilence had spread? And on Janto's team was a murderer he could hardly endure and an ex-fiancé who barely acknowledged him.

"I cannot do this." Serra sounded as though she spoke to herself, but Janto knew better. "I thought I could, but every second near her, I relive it again. Reading the letter, opening the box—"

He dared to grab her hands and press his own against them for a moment. "I know. Believe me, I know. But you are strong enough, Serra. I . . . I don't entirely understand why you left, but saving our people was enough for you to put aside our love. It has to be enough for you to put aside hatred."

She tilted his face toward hers. "Can you set aside hatred to find love? I don't want you to stop it for me, you know. I want you to be happy."

"What are you talking about?"

His confusion surprised her. "You mean you do not know—"

A silver flare demanded their attention a second before the hut exploded into radiant flame.

They were running before he knew it, already halfway there before Vesperi released another wave of flame. A loud crackle of claren followed.

Nap caught up to them, dismounting with sword in hand.

Janto touched his arm in restraint. "That will do no good. She will only strike you instead."

Nap frowned.

"Keep everyone outside the hut, no matter what you hear. Serra and I have to do this alone."

Janto should have been more concerned. Fire consumed the walls of the hut. Vesperi was a loose cannon, but still he did not think she would harm them unless threatened. She had waited until now to release her magic, and Madel knew she'd had plenty of reason to unleash it in the past day. He pulled his handkerchief up and stepped inside.

Silver energy engulfed Vesperi, illuminating the hairs on her body. She faced east, eyes jumping wildly, straining to see what she could not and shaking with frustration.

With no hesitation, Serra pushed Vesperi's handkerchief up her face and took hold of her left arm. She guided them around until they faced the wall to Janto's right.

"Now," Serra said calmly and Janto ducked.

After the stream of energy rushed past him and the air combusted with blackened red shells, he felt its heat, so cool it burned. The hair of his left arm curled and disintegrated. He leapt toward what should have been the other side of the structure, but there was only the bright of day and piles of ashes. Everywhere he turned, ashes. Janto kicked them, grunting and yelling as the piles exploded into clouds that spread over the floor. *Why did she have to go off on her own?* Vesperi had lost control, destroyed this home. The Rasselerians could have used it for another family. Her lack of discipline and selfish anger had almost killed him and Serra. Janto had defended her to the others, said he trusted her not to harm them and that she was with them for the right reasons, not to avoid the dungeons again. But that defense felt thinner than the granfaylon's façade when she acted this way.

Both women gaped while he leveled the piles to the ground. Nap, exposed by the burned out walls, gave them the courtesy of looking away.

"We cannot do this," Serra repeated. Janto shared her exhausted frustration. "I know our people need us. The claren have to be stopped, but how we are to do it with *her?*" She did not sound angry but resigned, displaying a resiliency he had never known she had. He was both proud and pained he had not been there to watch it develop.

Vesperi's armed crossed. "I know that was not . . . restrained. But I did not ask to be here, either. I never thought I would be in Lansera, stuck with a pair of lovelorn dolts and shooting at invisible insects. But I am committed to this, I pro—"

"Your promises mean nothing." Serra's nostrils flared. "You are Meduan. You know nothing but lies. It is your way." Still, her voice was calm and her drawn face had color in it again—her formerly constant flush that Janto found adorable. It had been missing since she'd reappeared in Mar Pina's kitchen. The graceful lines of her sheath made her far sexier than she had ever been when wrapped in yards of glistening fabrics, metallic threads, and feathers.

Vesperi's dark curls, limed with receding silver, were just as fetching. *Am I twelve that all I can think of is a woman's shape, even now?* It was below him, below them, but his mind could grasp at nothing else. He slid to the ground and pulled his handkerchief over his whole face. These two women held the fate of his people in their hands, and he weighed which was prettier.

"Janto," Serra's voice broke in to his thoughts, "how are we supposed to continue? She is as untrained as a newly birthed colt in Eddy's stables."

Worse than a colt, he thought, remembering how she spat at the sandwich roll that day in the mountains. Yet his impulse was to defend her. *She was so proud yesterday.* Vesperi was despoiled, vain, and utterly power hungry, but he had a hard time holding it against her. Medua was not Lansera. She had not been raised by people who knew kindness.

"I have never pretended to be other than I am." Vesperi faced her accusers while trying to dust ash from her gray tunic and matching pants, a hopeless cause. "But I am honest when it benefits me. I do not care what happens to your kind, but *I* want to live. The king and those Brothers of yours have made it clear I will not if we let the claren multiply."

Janto rose. "They already multiply. Every day their numbers increase. We have been here for a week, and how many dead have we found?" His voice trembled. "And Ryn Cladio has had more reports of fallen Wasylim, of bodies drained and shriveled beneath their citrus trees. We cannot stop their spread, not like this. The Lanserim will only suffer."

Realization hit as memories cycled through his mind: a shimmering fish in deep river waters, a stag bleeding invisible blood. Some things, like the claren, straddled the line between two worlds, impossible to fully grasp—or defeat—in only one of them. Then he spoke with conviction.

"We must defend all Lanserim, including those on the other side of the mountains. We must do it for them *first*, if we hope to stop the claren. The pestilence is born from the Meduans' actions, and we have let it fester too long."

Serra frowned, but Vesperi laughed at his words. "We will never again be Lanserim in Medua. It is quaint you harbor such hopes. But it I had crossed your path in Sellwyn, do not doubt I would have stricken you down the moment you stepped across my father's terrace, bursting with all your polity and concern." She twisted her lips around that last word. "I would have done that without the promise of a place at my father's side. I would have done it without thinking at all."

"You have a place now, you know." Janto held her gaze as he spoke fast, excitement building. "Your place is here, helping us get rid of the claren. Serra and I do not dispute that, though it is difficult to understand why you did what you did to Agler. But that act does not change the existence of the claren. This evil should not exist, but it does, and we three must stop it. We have to do whatever is needed to make that happen."

Serra agreed. "But like you said, for every claren horde we strike, a hundred more are likely created by the Meduans. If Vesperi's experience is typical of that land, they will never stop breeding."

Janto's mind was back on Braven, standing beside Jerusho as he held a creature that was never meant to be in his net. "It's their source of course!" He clapped his hands together. "Medua is sick, and we must go to the source of that malady to cure the symptom, defeat the claren. There is no other way."

Serra shook her head in disbelief. "You are crazy."

"No, listen to me. If we stand any chance, we need to stop the claren from birthing. We need to cleanse the temple in Qiltyn."

Vesperi laughed. "You two would never last on the road from Sellwyn to Qiltyn, much less inside Mandat Hall. Only Saeth's priests and invited guests are allowed there by the Guj's decree, and nothing happens in Medua without his consent. He is untouchable. His wizards alone would see right through you."

Janto bounced on one leg, his half-formed plan solidifying by the second. "Which is why we need you—besides your magic, of course. You can guide us through Medua."

Vesperi paled.

Something softened in Serra's face. "You don't want to return. I did not realize that."

Vesperi looked away.

Serra placed a hand on Janto's arm. "I do not think we should go. They killed my brother, Janto."

The implications of her wording pleased him. *She's beginning to understand as well.* Vesperi was not fully responsible for Agler's death. Serra placed a hand on her head and shook her finger at him. "I will never go into that pit. Isn't it enough that I can . . . that I can stand to be around *her*?"

Janto sighed and kicked up more ash that clung to the moist air. He'd found the right path, or at least the beginnings of it, but the women were right, too. Sneaking into Medua and finagling their way into its stronghold would be no easy task. The Meduans had never been fool enough to assault Callyn by force and he, Vesperi, and Serra were no army. They were three heads of Madel's bird, and they fell back to the ground every time they caught air.

Serra twirled an unscathed feather in her hand, watching the patterns it made in the light. "You are right. I wish you weren't, but you are. There is no other way we can defeat them. You did not kill the stag by pricking it with darts—you pierced its heart with an arrow."

"And watched its blood drain out." He had her in his arms instantly, hugging her. The smell of her clove necklace filled his lungs, made him ache for what might have been while he nonetheless felt joy she understood him so well. He did not want to let go. She pulled away first, her attention on the oddly quiet Vesperi.

"Will you come with us, then?"

He could have hugged Serra again for the tenderness in her voice. He had never seen Vesperi this way. Usually a kill brought her satisfaction, not this palpable trepidation. The Meduan quavered almost imperceptibly, a cattail in the breeze. But she nodded, then lifted her head and placed her hands on her waist, reclaiming her usual stance.

Good. They were agreed. Janto was nearly giddy as he called the rest of their group over.

"Are the claren gone?" Nap spoke first.

Flivio rolled his eyes. "Do you have to ask after the show the Meduan put on?"

Janto chuckled. "Yes, we've destroyed the claren here."

"Is that why you're so happy?" Hamsyn speculated. "It has been a rough day or two. Another culling is worth a celebration. We are one step closer to safety for all Lanserim."

"That's true, but our steps must be bigger than we thought, and now they face east." Janto should have been nervous, but he felt peaceful instead. He hoped it a sign he had made the right choice.

"Back to Callyn to tell the king Ashra's been purged, then, and send a company after any more of the Guj's men?" Hamsyn plucked at the Old Girl's bow.

Sar Mertina offered a different guess. "Or to Wasyla, to investigate the reports from Ryn Cladio?"

"No, no. We travel to Medua."

Their smiles slid away faster than leaves over the falls of the Call.

CHAPTER 49
SERRA

It took near a week to reach the mountains, pushing their horses as much as they dared without drawing attention. In another two days, they had crested them. The near-constant riding had brokered a begrudging peace within their band, a peace with which Serra was not entirely comfortable. But it was necessary, so she held her tongue when Sar Mertina spent an evening showing Vesperi how to properly build a fire. She let herself be entertained when Flivio began a bantering match with the Meduan over the edibility of barools. She ignored the feeling of defeat that grew each day Janto's anger boiled off. He was enraptured with the woman, always touching her without reason though he barely acknowledged it. Serra wanted him to hold on to his anger on her behalf, to resist the curve of Vesperi's breast and sultriness of her laugh, but she was not the one who had been left at the altar. Janto did not owe her anything.

But did she have to see it all the time? It was barely day, and Janto was already by Vesperi's side, struggling not to chuckle as she rearranged the items in her saddlebag again and again, dropping her smallclothes in the dirt every time she tried to squeeze them in.

"Morning." Elbows raised, Hamsyn addressed Serra from his night's watch post a few feet from the ladies' tent.

She returned the greeting. "Anything on the horizon?"

"Trees. A grove, much thicker than the ones we passed in the mountains. I think we have found flat ground at last."

"That is a relief." The horses had stumbled too many times on the slick downhill passes. "You will have to excuse me. I need to break my water. I will be right beyond those prickly bushes."

She returned to a scene of near domesticity that would have comforted Serra under different circumstances. Janto was helping Flivio make breakfast porridge over their morning fire. Vesperi sat nearby, smoothing the tangles in her hair. Nap had replaced Hamsyn on watch, so Hamsyn curled up on his bedroll to get some sleep before they set out again after breakfast. Sar Mertina sat back against a log, sharpening her blade.

Work did wonders for distraction; Serra had learned that during the initiation. Standing over the boiling water, she picked up one of their hardened corn cakes. The cornmeal grit was rough against her fingers as she crumbled it to a fine powder that drifted into the pot.

"I could do that." Vesperi put down her brush. *She would have more room for her smallclothes if she left the brush behind.* They did not need more than a comb between them.

The Meduan jammed a corn cake into her fist and squeezed. Ungainly chunks of yellow- and white-speckled biscuit plopped into the pot.

"Not that way." Janto chuckled. "You have to be gentle with it. Rub it between your thumb and middle finger or it will never break down right. Here, let me show you."

He placed his hand over hers, using his fingers to guide her own.

"I can think of other things that roll like this." Vesperi laughed.

Revolting. "By Madel's hand, Janto, why don't you just take her up on the offer?"

Flivio snickered, and Janto flushed purpler than a thrushberry.

"We are talking. Now." He dropped Vesperi's hand and latched onto Serra's arm. The corn cake plunked whole into the porridge.

"No, we are not." Serra jerked her arm away. "Just because you cannot admit how you feel—"

He clapped his other hand over her mouth, reminding her of the first time he had done it when she had gaped after seeing her first Rasselerian. "We are. This is overdue." Dragging her along, he called back to the others, "We will be back in a little while, I promise."

"Can I watch from a distance?" Flivio slapped his knee with merriment.

As if. Janto had never regarded her with the sheer lust Vesperi drew forth.

They remained quiet until well out of both earshot and eyesight.

Only then did Janto loosen his hold, the action almost a dare for her to run, but she merely crossed her arms and glared.

"We can't keep doing this. We must have this out."

"Have what out?" Maybe it was that woman's defiance he was so keen on. Serra could give him that.

"You. Me. What is wrong between us. We have to fix it."

"There is nothing to fix, Janto. There is no *us* anymore."

Disbelief punctuated each of his statements. "And why not? This destiny of ours is a shared one. The prophesized bird has three heads and we are two of them. I have learned nothing, experienced nothing that would make me think we have to remain parted. Why do you insist on shattering our dream when it is there for the taking? Why are you so convinced I cannot be your betrothed again?"

Because you are already hers. "You know why not."

"No, Serra, I do not. That is the problem. You say we cannot be together. But we *are* together. You say our time is over, but I say it does not need to be. Our people would accept a wedding postponement in the middle of a plague. There is no reason we have to go on like this, sniping at each other and tangling Vesperi up in it. She has no place in our relationship."

"You really don't know, do you?" Who could blame him for deluding himself when the person he yearned for was Vesperi? It was not his fault the stag had so ensnared the slayer, that he could not resist the pull between them. "You are falling in love with her."

He scowled, taking umbrage at the charge. "That's impossible. Vesperi is a Meduan. She killed your brother. I would never do that to you."

"We are masters of our fates but not of our hearts."

When he spoke, his voice was barely more than a whisper. "You have always been my heart."

How could she hold onto her feelings of betrayal when he was so crushed? "You stare at her as though she hung the moons sometimes. When she and Flivio let their insults fly, you regard her with awe. I have never seen you that infatuated before."

"That is a lie. I have only ever loved you."

"Even if that were true, we could not go back to what we were." The realization cut through her like a storm front through humidity. It did not matter what Janto felt for Vesperi. That was not the core of the matter. Maybe they *could* work at it, rebuild their relationship, move past what had happened. But she did not want her life back as Lansera's princess. Too much had changed within her. No matter how deeply she loved Janto, life held more than festivals and ladies-in-waiting. Talks with Ryn Gylles, learning herb lore, braiding feathers into Lourda's hair—that was what she wanted now. There were so many places in Lansera she had never been, that she had never considered visiting when she had lived content within Callyn's walls. How could she know that path was for her when she had never traveled another?

"Janto, it is too late for our relationship to be what it was. I am so sorry, but marrying you is not what I want anymore. This is about me, not you—it could never be you. Agler's death, the sight . . . I am a different person now, and I need to figure out who Serrafina of Lansera is before I could ever become Serrafina Albrecht. Please understand. Please." She let the tears fall. He needed to know this was not easy for her, needed to know how much he meant to her.

And he did. His face, awash with tears like her own, hid no anger. A few months apart had not wrecked their bond. It had been forged through years of shared hopes, dreams, and fears.

A woranbird sounded loud and clear as he drew her close. "I could never hold that against you." He rubbed her shoulders, knowing how it soothed her. "Your aspirations have changed, even if our love has not. I wish—I wish you could have told me this before, but I understand. I truly do."

"Thank you." His chest muffled her words. "It would kill me if you didn't. I cannot lose you, too."

Time passed as they held each other. The repetitive flex of Janto's hand on her shoulders comforted as it always had. Janto separated from her with reluctance and a smile. "But none of that means I have feelings for Vesperi."

Serra laughed, covering her mouth. "Trust me."

"Trust you?" His incredulous tone demonstrated that things between them were not fully healed yet. "You did not trust me enough to understand you had to go back to Enjoin. You left me at the altar rather than take the risk I might talk you out of it, rather than trust *me* enough to know I would not stand in your way."

"I have traveled far enough on your rather flimsy convictions about the claren's breeding grounds for you to accuse me of distrust, Janto."

He grimaced, knowing it was true. "What do you want to know?

My plan is not perfect. I know we will never defeat the claren if we cannot stop them from multiplying. I know the claren exist because of how horribly the Meduans treat each other. I know the advers and their choke hold on the people are the reason such a society persists, the reason someone as strong as Vesperi could believe she is nothing. So journeying to Mandat Hall, to strike the claren where they proliferate, might deal an effective blow. And I have a theory about how we can do it."

"Which is what? I have little patience for veiled speech after dealing with the Brothers. Explain what your theory is plainly." This was progress. Janto needed to talk his plan through with someone, and she needed to understand his intentions so she could properly do her part.

"I think . . . I think there is another realm than ours. Maybe a realm of spirit? I do not know, but it is there. On Braven—Serra, I have wanted to tell you about the Murat for so long." It warmed her heart to know he wanted to share anything with her. "All sorts of magic happened there, but the magic was more a shifting of things between places, here and . . . and elsewhere, that other realm. Sounds carried straight into our minds rather than through the air. Our paths shifted constantly, making distances unknowable. And the animals . . . the stag and the granfaylon, and there was something on Mount Frelom . . . they did not exist solely in our realm. They fluttered between the two, sometimes visible, sometimes not depending on which one they were in. I think maybe Braven is a doorway between here and there. Ryn Cladio mentioned fissures and you have traveled through them. Maybe they are rips between our existence and whatever the other realm may be. Or portals? Maybe . . . maybe that other place is where Madel resides. Maybe She reaches Her hand to us from such doorways."

Janto's brow furrowed, but Serra clasped his arm. "I have seen it. Her hand—Madel's hand—I have seen it. The day when I first saw the claren. Under the temple in Enjoin was a room filled with Brothers, and She was there. Her hand was surrounded by a blue mist, a field of energy maybe. I do not know. But it was there, and streams of it flowed from Her hand like the licks of Vesperi's flame do from hers. They entered the Brothers' hoods and renewed their life somehow. The Rejuvenation, they called it."

She kissed his cheek and grinned. "I think you are right, Janto. I think there are openings between our worlds, and we must send the flame into them. If the claren spawn in that other realm, then we must destroy them there before they can find a portal here."

He hugged her again, releasing her fast enough to avoid any awkwardness. Then Serra realized something else, something that made her clap her hands with relief. "But if there are other places where the worlds meet, then why must we seek the one at Mandat Hall? We could go back to Enjoin where it is safe. There has to be one in that temple room. We could use Vesperi's magic there. Or we could go to Braven and Sielban could guide us to another."

"No, we have to go to Qiltyn. The weapon could be used at any fissure, but that will only kill them when they are young. It won't stop them from hatching in the first place. Cleansing the temple will be a first step toward renewing Medua. With the head cut off, the body cannot stand."

"And how do we cut off the head?"

He busied himself with wrapping an arm around her and beginning the walk back to camp. "I am not certain yet. I am praying Madel will show me what we can do. Going there feels right to me, so I have to believe the rest will come. I have a few ideas, but nothing is set in stone."

"And what are those ideas?"

His eyes focused on their path instead of her. "I'd rather . . . I'd rather not share them until I am certain they may work."

Fair enough, though she would encourage him later to tell the others and get their feedback. If there *were* openings between the realms at Mandat Hall, then his plan stood a chance. They needed to figure out how to approach the Guj and his underlings, but they had a few days yet to do so. In the meantime . . .

"You really should pursue Vesperi, if you want to. I cannot promise I won't be jealous, but I want you to be happy, Janto. Who knows how much more time any of us have to be happy."

"Shh." He kissed her forehead. "I have yet to receive those blessings Madel owes me—*blessed will he who binds it be*. I am owed those before I will believe any of us three are in danger."

But we are seven. Serra pushed away the thought. Their guards had also chosen to come, placing their fates in Madel's hand the same as she, Janto, and Vesperi had. And Madel protected Her children, didn't she?

Chapter 50
Vesperi

apeler paraded like a rooster as he paced the outskirts of their camp. Vesperi understood him least of all the Lanserim she had met. A wealthy man of his regrettable stature should spend his time in books if he hoped to survive. A poor one ought to have mastered snatching purses by his age, with a healthy sum holed away somewhere wizards could not divine. Yet there he walked, one hand on his sword's pommel, the other shielding his eyes from the sun. His stance projected a man twice his height, one proud to be on this journey simply because a prince had asked him to come.

She considered ignoring him—his dutiful reserve more obnoxious than Lokas's leering had ever been—but Serra and Janto were gone, and Vesperi hated how nervous that made her. They had managed the journey to Medua without incident, though she doubted she had the others' trust without Janto and Serra to demand it. But nerves were for weaker women than Vesperi Sellwyn. And the others in their little band were playing that obnoxious game again. She would never understand these people's fascination with feathers. They would toss them in the air for hours, grabbing at the falling fluff like lunatics batting away jocal flies. Those were the people she was supposed to break into Mandat Hall with.

She targeted Napeler with her sultry eyes. Maybe she could play a game of her own. "Why are you here?" Other than a little jump in his adam's apple, he did not react. *So behaved without a lord in sight.*

"We need someone to guard the area, Lady Sellwyn." The hard line of his mouth twisted downward.

Decency was a bore. "I meant here at all, with us. Janto told me you might have joined your town council if you had stayed. That must have taken you a lot of time to arrange."

A brief wistfulness took over his features. "There was no *arrangement*. We vote for our council members. But yes, I had hoped to join them. The vote was in a week when Rall found me. I had to bring him to the prince, so I withdrew my name."

"You gave up your spot that easily to accompany him to Callyn?"

The guard nodded. "It was not a choice. My fellow Murater needed help. We must be there for each other or we would not be worthy of our training."

"There is always a choice, is there not? You people make strange ones." As had she, traveling with them into Medua, so close to home. Meeting her father again with them would be a disaster, but it had to be done. She wished she could shake that conviction, but whenever she tried, she only saw the king bathed in a blue light more luminous than any magic she could wield.

Napeler jerked suddenly toward a grove of trees off to the east. *Rosewood.* So close to Sellwyn already? She took a step in their direction, but he held her back.

"I heard something. Best let me go first."

These nitwits were welcome to risk their necks rather than hers. Their willingness to do so was their best quality. Napeler waved her over after a brief inspection of the grove. The scent of the trees reached her first, nectar and talcum. She pulled back a low-lying branch, careful to avoid the sandy brown leaves tinged with pink around the edges. *Definitely rosewood.* Gooseflesh rose on her arms.

"Did you see something, Lady Sellwyn?" Her face must have paled. "Is something wrong?" She probably appeared as shaken as any Meduan noblewoman would be if found outside their manor. Father would be glad to see it, if she were unfortunate enough to see him.

She stroked one of the oval leaves from stem to tip. It was covered in miniscule thorns, rough as the spikes of a cat's tongue. If she rubbed the opposite way, they would prick her finger.

"What's wrong"—another voice sounded loud and clear from the tree directly above her—"is that we are almost at the *Lady* Sellwyn's home."

Napeler drew his sword and pointed it upward faster than Vesperi could register the movement. Hamsyn, Flivio, and Mertina took only a few moments to join their swords with his, leaving feathers fluttering in their wake. She followed the line of their weapons up the tree. If she had not already recognized the voice, she would have recognized those legs anywhere, though she had no idea how they could have grown longer—and more lascivious—than when she had last seen Lorne Granich. He stretched them out, testing the weight of the branch beneath him.

"Stay right there." Both hands gripped Nap's sword tightly. "Do not come down."

Lorne sighed. "I am one man to four. Surely, you could handle me on the ground if you needed to? I would have to be a fool to challenge you." He placed a toe on the branch, and Mertina scowled, raising her weapon arm higher.

The toe was withdrawn. "Whose leave do I need to get out of this tree? There are already too many thorns in my ass. I don't fancy picking up more."

With Serra and Janto gone . . .

"You need mine." Vesperi hoped the guards would support her. "And I'm not inclined to give it."

He laughed, tossing his considerable blond hair back as he did. "Let a woman out of Medua for a month and she takes on all sorts of airs."

"What are you doing here? Shouldn't you be suckling my brother?"

"Oh, your whelp of a brother is boarding with my family in Granich. My lord father thought it would help to have a Sellwyn under his wing when the advers put your manor up for sale."

"Are you mad?" *Nothing like idiocy to calm my nerves.* "My father would never sell Sellwyn." Then she realized Lorne was alone, and something clenched at her heart.

Lorne *tsked*, ignoring the swords precariously placed beneath his feet. "You have been gone, but surely your brain has not addled in all the sweet Lanserim air? I always admired that you knew you had wits—the other women have never figured it out. Now think, would your father have sent only me for a welcoming party?"

Lorne was right. Lord Sellwyn would have sent fifty men or more to hunt her down and bring her home in shackles if he knew of her return. But he never left the manor lands; he would not risk anyone making a play for them in his absence.

Her skin went cold beneath the gooseflesh. "I do not know what game you play, but I am not going to bat at feathers as these mummers do. Tell me what has happened. Uzziel—"

"Is at my father's house, as I said. Must have been all the fallowent that saved him. He did grow quite a taste for it. I had been developing a scheme to get you to consume it, too, when you ran."

Hamsyn's ears perked at that. "Fallowent? You think that protected her brother from something?"

Vesperi doubted the rancid herb had done anything. If it had, she would have to believe that Lorne had been protecting Uzziel all this time. What good did it do the Graniches to keep her brother alive, unless her father—

Serra's tinkling laughter drifted over from beyond the camp, a welcome distraction. She and Janto crested a hill, walking arm-in-arm. Vesperi embraced the jealousy that leapt up at the sight. It felt good, familiar. Unlike Lorne's lies.

"Another woman?" Lorne raised an eyebrow. "Surely you can satisfy these few men on your own?"

He does not know about Serra. Perhaps the Guj did not know the seer had been found either. But Lorne knew far more about their movements than he should. She recounted his words . . . and then laughed. He must not have realized one of the guards holding him captive was a woman, probably had not considered it possible. Mertina's hair *was* in a bun today.

"Let him down." Vesperi hoped they would listen. "I need to look him in the eye as he speaks to me."

The guards complied, except for Napeler who thrust his sword forward an inch or two then called out to Janto.

"What's going on there?" Janto yelled back, and Vesperi heard him trampling dry leaves in his haste as Lorne descended.

Once Lorne's feet were firmly planted on the ground, the jerk raised his elbows to her in mock respect. "Thank you, my *lady*."

The guards encircled him with their swords, and Vesperi narrowed her eyes, imagined fixing him with a stream of thanks—fiery, burning thanks. *Oh yes, that would make me feel better.*

A hand wrapped around her arm, the touch making her realize her hairs stood on end. Her hand had lifted toward Esye.

"You are trembling." Janto placed his other hand on her waist, pulling her around to him. Serra stood beside them yet did not grimace at their contact. She had always done so whenever they'd touched before.

"What's wrong?" Janto's concerned bronze eyes soothed her. Vesperi focused on them and her anger faded, at least enough to stop picturing Lorne consumed in ashes. For now.

A perplexed Lorne pointedly stared at Janto's arm wrapped around her. *Let him stare, the slimy bastard.* Though in truth, she was as confused by the action as he. But she could not deny how calm it made her feel.

"So you fled," she addressed Lorne, the rage controlled. "Leaving my father to die."

Serra and Janto gasped in unison.

"Like you would have done anything different." The confirmation of her father's death stung, no matter how much she'd deny it. "We are Meduans, Vesperi, not fools. Our selves are all we have. And I did get your brother out of there."

Did he think she cared about Uzziel?

Janto withdrew his arm. "What is going on here? Who is this man?"

Lorne raised his elbows with only a hint of irony. "Lorne Granich, son of Cavallen, a lesser lord at Qiltyn who is hoping to use this woman's brother to become a greater one. I hope you don't mind honesty. I take it you are the prince? Of course you are. Only an Albrecht would sound so offended to have something occur in their absence."

Janto looked to her for corroboration, and she gave it. "And your father?" His speech was gentle.

"Appears to be dead." Saying the words brought a disquieting relief. "If he were not, we would be outnumbered by my father's guards, not questioning this moron all alone. Something has happened at Sellwyn." A gurgle of emotion threatened again, but she pushed it back like her talent. "It is no matter. It will make our task easier."

"Of course it matters," Janto said, but she ignored him, prodding Lorne to continue.

"Not until you introduce me to this lovely creature." Lorne swept Serra's hand into a kiss. Vesperi would have punched him. "I assume that's the proper way to greet you? If you are Meduan, I will gladly get to know you more personally, perhaps a few trees away from this rabble."

Serra flushed and jumped back as the sword circle around Lorne shrunk. Janto added his weapon, his face red with anger. "You do not speak to her that way. You do not speak to any woman in that manner."

Idiot. Don't let him know she is so important to you.

Lorne lowered his hand to his side, likely considering the disadvantages of pissing off a prince, even one far from home and in enemy territory. Vesperi would think the same in his place. His eyes lingered on Serra for a moment, but then he turned back to Vesperi, his features softening.

"I had no choice but to leave, you know. Once people started . . . collapsing . . . I had to move fast." *The claren.* "One of the sweepers fell first, and luckily, I was in the hall to see it. I had been alerted they might be near, so I pulled out my handkerchief and ran to get Uzziel."

"You were warned?" She said it the first time, confused, but then her voice rose. "You were warned and you did not tell my father?"

"There was not time." He sighed. "You *know* that. You wouldn't be here if you yourself had not seen them attack. They move too fast."

"You know nothing of why I am here. I know nothing of why you are. If you have my brother, then why dangle from a tree, hoping for sight of me? I should have you killed. You have already admitted to plotting against my claim to Sellwyn."

"Lansera has either made you brave or reckless. Your claim to Sellwyn? I could kill you for saying that out loud. You honestly think I don't know your business here? Maybe Lansera *has* made you stupid."

She lunged at him, but he was fast, and Janto's free arm lashing out to restrain her was faster. Lorne ducked back toward the trees, and the swords moved with him, offering no escape. But if he was here for her, he should not want to escape.

He did not try to. Instead, he raised his palm to her. She flinched, bracing for a slap although she knew swords and the length of Janto's arm separated them. But he did not try to do that either. Silver energy swirled in his hand. It was fainter than her talent, and it only lasted a moment before sparking and dissipating. But it had happened. She was certain of it, and not merely because her companions were speechless.

"You have the flame?" She felt buoyant but not with surprise. With hope.

"Yes, I have it."

"But that means I am not the only one. There are others." *I don't have to do this.*

Lorne's smirk returned. "Oh, you don't get off so easily. What I have is an echo at best. What you are is the real thing. The weapon."

"How do you know about that?" Serra spoke for the first time since she had returned with Janto.

"The Brothers told me." The Brothers had been in Medua? In Sellwyn? None of this made any sense. "They were the ones who warned me of the claren."

"But the Brothers cannot be in Medua." Serra's words gave voice to Vesperi's thoughts.

Lorne's smirk deepened. "You know that's not true, woman, if you are who I think you are. The Brothers told me of you, too, but they did not say you were a woman. I had assumed the prince was the seer. Regardless, the seer surely knows Madel's hand extends everywhere. It is not limited to Lansera."

Vesperi had never heard a Meduan utter the name of the Lanserim goddess, not even as a curse. It had been wiped out entirely. She trusted this boy less than she had before. He knew too many things for a courtier. "We do not know what you speak of, Lorne. Are you one of Ralion's bards, spouting tales of men who can keep it up all night?"

"The truth, darling Vespy, is that I already know why I am here, but I would enjoy hearing you explain why *you* are."

"Because I have—"

He waved a finger, chiding her. "Do not answer 'because I have to be.' No one ever has to do anything. Besides, we both know there is more to it than that."

"I do not know what you mean."

"The king. You are here because of what you saw King Albrecht do one afternoon." *How can he know* . . . it did not matter. She could not explain the electric blue light that had wrapped around the king in that dungeon, so much purer than the stream in her veins, or how she had known he spoke the truth more certainly than she had known anything before. Who believed in such things? She scarcely did and she had seen it.

"They had hoped you would be further along, but frankly, I don't know what they were thinking. I suppose thinking might not be involved with the Brothers." He stroked his chin. "But they have been right so far. I will answer for you, then, if you refuse to speak. Though the whole thing is painfully dull for me to recount at this point."

"No!" Vesperi panicked.

Janto was confused. "We know why you are here, Vesperi. There's no harm in letting him talk. Maybe we will learn why he is."

"No!" She could not let this happen here. She was already too exposed so close to Sellwyn even if her father's wrath was no longer to be feared—maybe especially because of that.

Lorne kept talking, his gaze fixed on her, and she ignored him until she noticed his glow. It was feeble, as much an echo of how the king had appeared as Lorne's talent had been an echo of hers. Even so, it was arresting.

"You are here because there are some things you cannot deny, no matter how much you try. You are here because you have a job to do, and you are doing it because it is *right*."

She cried. Saeth's fist, she had been crying since she'd crossed this path in the opposite direction eons ago. Fleeing had destroyed her, had destroyed the Vesperi Sellwyn she used to be.

Lorne's words kept rolling. "Vesperi is here because she's the weapon, chosen to rescue Lansera from the claren's blood thirst. She's here because she knows she is supposed to be, and though everything in her screams to run, she has walked back into her worst nightmare—her home—to face that destiny. Because Vesperi wants to take part in it. She wants to be better than me and all Meduans who think only of power, lust, and greed. She has seen that life is more than that, and she wants everyone else to see it too. Vesperi is here because she is a hero, a servant of Madel, the true god. And Madel's heroes do what they know is right."

Never in her life had she wanted to smite someone out of existence so fervently.

CHAPTER 51
SERRA

Vesperi slept in the early morning light, arms clutched around her waist. The Meduan captive—Lorne—had unnerved the weapon, and Serra had not thought that possible. But she never thought she would journey into Medua, either. Nor would she have thought she would grant Janto freedom from their engagement, from her, and do it with only a few tears shed. Yet here she was.

When Vesperi muttered from her blankets in dreamt fear, Serra did not take the satisfaction she would have felt a day ago. Instead, she ran her hand down the woman's back to soothe her. Vesperi jumped at the touch, reaching toward a phantom dagger at her ankle. Yellow-green crusts of sleep nearly glued her eyes together.

"Shh," Serra said. "You were having a nightmare. I meant to calm you."

Vesperi nodded then closed her eyes and shifted onto her other side. Serra watched until her breathing normalized and wondered at the concern she felt. Perhaps it was because Vesperi's father had died. Serra knew better than most what it meant to lose family, especially ones who had never been what she wanted.

Outside the tent, morning had broken with a shower of rain that left mist rising from the ground. Sar Mertina packed their belongings into saddlebags, blankets tightly rolled to fit in between straps. Hamsyn and Napeler were also awake—Serra was never certain Nap slept at all. She gathered an armful of the light wood the men had collected the night before and went to join them at the fire pit. They would only cook in daylight hours now. Serra did not need her companions to tell her that.

Nor did she need them to tell her they were scared. The guards would never admit it, but their faces were collages of worry lines.

Janto slept. Once upon a time, Serra would have worried what the others thought of her as she ran a hand over his hips, searching under his tunic, but it did not matter now. Her fingers brushed the hardened leather of the pouch she had given him. He did not stir as she undid the clasp and pulled out a bag of crushed tachery pods. Then she hung a pot over the blaze Hamsyn had built and poured water into it from the jug they filled each morning. These mountains overflowed with water. The grapes on the Meditlan side of them would have rotted on their vines if this wet.

The water would take time to warm, so Serra left Hamsyn in charge of it, telling him to call her over when it was done. Then she walked to the edge of their encampment where Lorne slept with nothing to cover him, his legs and arms bound in case he tried to flee during the night. Blond hair wrapped around his chest like a Nevillim shawl of braided corn husks.

Then Serra peered deeper. Her stomach clenched as she concentrated, imagining herself kneeling on a prayer rug in Enjoin, scratchy reed fibers bristling against her knees. Each drop of moisture from the fog hung heavy before she watched them fall. Then she focused the sight on Lorne. Her brow furrowed as her gaze narrowed in on his nose and mouth. The air around him illumined with an effervescent blue. Nothing else appeared but a few jocal flies that veered away when their tiny wings brushed his face, as uniformly black as the handful of fallowent seeds he had shown them yesterday. Not a spot of red on their wings. He was clean.

Lorne was the first person she had seen who had survived the claren's attack, except for those who had been in the kitchen when Mar Pina fell. If his story was true, Vesperi's brother would be the second.

"It was the fallowent," Hamsyn called from the fire, "and the water is boiling."

With the release of her breath, the world returned to the muted colors of reality. *The reality of this world*, she thought, *but not of Madel's*.

"How did you know what I was doing?" She walked back to the campfire.

Hamsyn laughed, a sound that warmed her after using the sight. The brilliant colors of the other realm were too harsh to live in. "We have been traveling together for weeks, Lady Serra. I think we all know what you look like when you're searching."

Of course they would notice. It amazed her how narrow she let her perspective be. She shook the tachery pods onto a flat stone then raised another stone over them. It hit with a loud crack, then she rocked the top stone over the other again and again. Satisfied with the size of the grounds, she brushed them into the pot of boiling water. Creamy brown foam ballooned within it.

Hamsyn stoked the fire. "My sister took up gardening when she was four. She had figured out that dillweed brought the prettiest butterflies to the fields. Took first prize for her squashes at Lady Gella's raccoon festival two years back. But last fall, she became obsessed. I took to calling her 'the Black Thumb' because she spent every daylight hour over those fallowent plants. They were tiny, no taller than my thumb, and the seeds could barely be seen without a lens. But every day, she harvested them, soaked new seeds in water, and planted them again in her hut of glass. She had hundreds of them."

"What was she doing?" Serra leaned over the pot, waiting for the smells of rich tobacco and sharp berry to rise up, but the liquid was not done steeping yet.

"Saving us." He grinned. "Don't ever tell her I said so—I would never hear the end of it. But from what I gathered, the fallowent saved the lives of Lorne and the little Lord Sellwyn."

"It did." The captive's bored voice sounded before he opened his eyelids. He yawned and stretched—until the ropes dug into his skin. Serra could practically hear him roll his eyes at the afflicting knots. "These are not necessary."

Nap, who Serra realized had positioned himself near their prisoner this whole time, frowned sternly. "They stay until Janto commands otherwise."

"I know, I know." Lorne tried to raise his elbows to indicate compliance but the ropes pulled tight. "When does he rise, anyhow? I thought Lanserim awoke with the call of the birds and the dew from a fairy's wings on their noses."

Serra laughed despite herself. Waking to a fairy on her nose sounded rather charming.

"What a pleasing noise, Lady Gavenstone." Lorne flopped and hopped until in a sitting position. "Your laugh complements your features. You ought to use it more often."

She blushed. "You do not act how Vesperi described Meduan men. I have a feeling I should not trust your words, though they are sweet ones."

"No, you shouldn't. But you should trust your charms regardless. We may have to cover you when we head to Qiltyn. Wouldn't want anything to spoil your tour of our fair country, and keeping someone with your beauty out in the open would certainly do that."

Janto yawned, his voice scratchy from sleep. "You aren't coming to Qiltyn. But you may be right. We will need to disguise all the women on our way there. The Guj has men looking for Vesperi. We encountered some in Rasseleria."

"Good morning, prince." Lorne lifted his hands in Janto's direction. "If it pleases you, have these ropes cut." Janto laughed sharply, and Lorne's exaggerated smile evaporated. "You will not need disguises on the way to Sellwyn. There is no one left to pilfer your women there."

A whole village gone? The claren grew. Serra shuddered. But Janto sniffed the air, and she found herself laughing for the second time that morning. His mussed strawberry locks stuck up like beetle ant antennae. Janto patted his pouch then smiled boyishly at her. "Did Madel's hand guide you to my tachery?"

The tent's walls swayed violently, and Vesperi's head of curls poked through the opening. "Are we leaving soon? I want to get this over with."

Janto's whole demeanor changed, thoughts of tachery dropping as fast as the smile from his lips. "If it's too much, we do not have to go to Sellwyn. I just—I thought you would maybe want to find your father." When she neared, he took Vesperi's hand, which the woman was careful not to acknowledge. *How hard it would be to live like that, never able to show how someone's touch affected you.*

"Touching," Lorne broke in, "but you do need to go. There is something in Sellwyn we must bring with us."

"You aren't going," Janto repeated. "We cannot take a prisoner with us."

"Then make me not a prisoner."

Nap tapped the man with his sword. "You do not address him that way. He is your prince."

"That wasn't necessary." Janto sighed. "We do not hurt our prisoners. And we are not launching an invasion here—we are quelling one."

Nap's features darkened with the correction, but he straightened more stiffly to make up for it.

Lorne *tsked*. "Wrong again, *my* prince. You may have cut us off, but we are Lanserim as much as we try to hide it. Only Madel could truly tear us asunder, and I am told She withheld Her hand at the signing of Turyn's Peace." He paused. "Really, you ought to have more ambition as royalty."

"Lorne," Vesperi whined his name as though it was nothing more than an irritant. Treating people that way, Serra realized, was a luxury Vesperi afforded herself. "Can you stop the cryptic messages and philosophy lessons? No wonder I never seduced you if you were always this insufferable."

"Like you could have—"

She strode over, draping herself over his prone body and spoke again, a purr full of poisoned claws. "Oh, I always could have. But what I want to know"—she walked her fingers up his tunic—"is what we need at Sellwyn and why. Will you not tell me? Please?"

Nap did not adjust his posture, but the men were swept up by her display. Sar Mertina's eyes met Serra's and she stuck a finger down her throat. Lorne, with great effort, lifted his torso off the ground, tossing Vesperi onto the dirt beside him in the process.

"I will tell you why we must go to Sellwyn, but only if you promise never to pin me down again, darling Vespy. You are not my type."

She did not stoop to glare at him. Lorne propelled himself up from the waist into a sitting position. "There is some sort of charm we need there. I do not know what it does, but I know it's not Meduan and it's somewhere in Sellwyn Manor. I have been trying to find it for months, but my charge—her brother"—he waggled his arm in Vesperi's direction—"had no idea what I searched for. When that invalid whelp is strong enough to keep them open, he does not have much of an eye for anything but weapons."

An invalid? Vesperi's brother was crippled?

"How do you know we need it?" Flivio said. "I would love to believe a man who has a tongue that makes my heart sing, but we met you yesterday and not under friendly circumstances. How do we know this is not a trap?"

"You don't." Lorne sighed. "The Brothers told me to find it, just as they told me to bring fallowent to Sellwyn and to wait here for your arrival. I do their bidding, whether it's clear or not what they want. Vesperi, a little help here?"

Janto rose, indignant. "She does not have to defend you."

Vesperi's voice was strong. "It's fine. I believe him, as loath as I am to say it. And I may have an idea of where we should search. My father had a box of jewelry from before the war. If it is something of value the Brothers seek, it would be in there."

"I will lead the way," Lorne offered. "But I will need the use of my limbs, I'm afraid."

"Can't you show us?" Janto looked to Vesperi, eliciting a laugh from Lorne.

"You did appear late yesterday, my prince. I had forgotten. Our enchanting Vesperi did not know she was within a day's walk of home. I am rather surprised she made it over the mountains in the first place. However did you manage, dear?"

Vesperi directed her fiercest glare at Lorne then shifted it to Flivio who snickered by the fire. A pity her disdain alone could not kill the claren. It was as potent as her magic.

"Let him walk." Janto nodded to Nap. The Wasylim swung his sword.

Lorne flinched as the blade connected with the rope. He raised his elbows once he could. "My thanks. Now let's get started. Inhabited or not, Sellwyn is a tenebrous place. If we leave right away, we can avoid nightfall there."

Serra spoke for the first time in what felt like hours. "Not until everyone has had some tachery brew. It's the last we have, and I know our prince would be distraught if we wasted a single drop. Besides, I depend on all of you for my protection. Your reflexes should be sharp."

Janto was at her side before she finished speaking. He held out his mug.

CHAPTER 52
JANTO

Sellwyn was lusher than Janto expected after such a long drought. In Meditlan, grapevines ringed the countryside, strung through poles as tall as he was. But this side of the mountains was a world apart. No bitter winds from the gulf beat back the bushes that covered the hillsides. Vines laced their way through the rosewood groves, but radiant pink flowers studded them rather than grapes. Janto could not have imagined a lovelier location for an afternoon horse ride. Reconciling the view with the first skin they passed was difficult.

It wasn't the last. Vesperi climbed off her horse each time they sighted another that looked human. Occasionally, she muttered a name under her breath. The last had been *Bellick*. She had shed no tears for any of the fallen she'd recognized. Most of them she hadn't known, making them likely to be townspeople or servants. Lorne knew a few of the latter.

Janto trusted the Meduan man. It was the way he spoke with Vesperi, the affection mixed in with the taunts. Flivio sparred with her, but Lorne made their banter an art form. Janto would have loosed his ropes last night, but instinct was not a sound rationale to give his guards. Those who obeyed his orders deserved to understand the reasons for them, his father had taught.

They passed at least twenty bodies before the trees thinned and the ground showed signs of wear. Puddles had formed from panicked footsteps left in the mud.

"How long"—Janto drew his mare close to Hamsyn's palmetto where

Lorne sat behind his friend—"long ago did this happen?" The bodies had not shown signs of disturbance from the elements or animals. Neither had the ones they'd encountered in Lansera, but his group had found those soon after the claren.

"A week before you arrived. I barely had time to take Uzziel to my father and return before you came." Lorne led them on a real path now. One-storied buildings appeared, many recently flooded, pools of water visible from doors hanging open. Serra kept a constant watch, her eyes so focused they appeared vacant. Her silence was all Janto needed to know the claren had left. Even after a feast of this size, they fled fast. Their hunger did not abate for long.

The buildings grouped closer together as they made their way through the town. So did the bodies. Vesperi no longer tried to identify them. She did slow her horse to pick up a broken, clay pot from a scattered pile of many, tossing it back a moment later.

Her nonchalance concerned Janto. "Don't you want to check for your father?"

"We will not find him here. Not among the townspeople."

"But if he fled—"

"He will not be here." The tone of her voice brokered no argument.

Sar Mertina called out from where she had ridden ahead of the others, not as trusting of Lorne as Janto was to guide them safely. That was another thing his father had taught him: surround yourself with people who are smarter than you. He joined her and took in the view.

Deadened ivy covered Sellwyn Manor. The stone visible through it was barely recognizable from decades of dirt and mold, half the rocks probably soft enough to crumble. The manor rose from within a fence of rosewood, as a body from a grave, all slumped shoulders and awkward angles where towers had begun to fall. The sunlight bounced off it rather than light it.

"That is where you live?" Janto tried to keep the shock from his voice as he addressed Vesperi. He could not picture anything thriving there.

She shrugged. "This is my inheritance."

Serra pulled her horse beside Sar Mertina's. Then she pointed toward the western wing of the manor, where a light gray bridge arched over what must have been the River Sell. It was the only part of the manor not covered in grime. But Serra had noticed it for another reason.

"Claren. They are circling the bridge."

"Finally." Vesperi sounded excited. "Let's go." She raised her scarf over her nose and mouth and tightened her horse's protective lace before kicking her spurs into its flank. Serra quickly followed. Janto watched them ride through an open gate, silver sparks already pulsing through locks of Vesperi's raven hair.

"Raise your handkerchiefs," Janto instructed the others. "There are claren past the gate."

Serra dismounted near the small bridge, dragging Vesperi off her horse by the arm. Two streams of energy released from the Meduan's outstretched hands. They were too far to hear the noise, but a cloud of smoke burst into being from nowhere.

Something nearby smoked, too, and Janto lurched away from it. Two little volts of electricity danced in Lorne's palms.

"Could you help?"

Lorne watched his hands, apparently surprised to see the magic held within them. It faded and disappeared, then he shook his head. "I cannot control it at all, not even as poorly as she does. It is never stronger than this mimicry of what the weapon is, truly. I had never seen what that could be until now."

They watched Serra guide Vesperi toward another swarm. She pointed up a tree, and shimmering flames consumed the budding leaves.

"It is amazing," Lorne said with awe.

Serra turned to face them and raised her hand to signal the group forward. Vesperi stood in the middle of the bridge for a moment before going into her home. *No, this will never be her home again.* Janto would not let it be.

Hamsyn held the Old Girl ready in his free arm as they walked the horses through the gate. "There may be other swarms lingering. We should not dwell here."

Janto agreed. "I will help Vesperi search for the charm. Keep the others close together in case Serra sees something." Hamsyn nodded, and Janto tied his horse beside the bridge. He grazed his hand over its marble as he walked. Halfway across, a strange warmth and the raised lines of a chiseled carving made him pause, taking him back to Braven and the cabin in the forest. This carving was much more detailed than that burnt outline, but the primary image was the same, a giant bird ready to take flight. A ring of hooded figures surrounded it—Brothers, Janto suspected. Ribbons of the old language bordered the carving, fanciful loops bearing words so familiar to him now: *When the silver stag runs free . . .*

Other carvings graced the bridge, but Janto knew this was the one he needed to see.

"The bird of creation." Flivio came up behind him. "My grandfather used to tell stories about it. Said it would rise up again when Lansera faced great peril. He never understood why it had not come during the war. What could possibly be worse than that, he'd said."

"*Rise up, ye treasured bird of three. Wing him what boons ye foresee.*" That the old adage applied to him still mystified Janto. "Everyone's always thought the boons were treasure, not magic, not the flame and sight returned."

"Who doesn't want treasure?" Flivio shrugged. "I wish my grandfather were alive. I wish I could tell him I served the bird of three."

"That might be the most sentimental thing you have ever said."

Flivio socked him. Then Vesperi cried out from inside the manor, and they raced through the door together. The handkerchief around Janto's face could not keep out the wall of incense that assaulted him. Vanilla, spice, and sandalwood so thick they could not be considered pleasant scents, not like the ghost of them on Vesperi's skin. How had anyone breathed in here? No one did now. Collapsed bodies lay everywhere.

Sobs echoed down the hall. "I will take the passage to the left." Flivio swung his sword in that direction. "You take a right at that bend."

Janto tried to keep calm, but he had never heard Vesperi sound like that before. More bodies waited in the next room. For a brief moment, he worried Vesperi might be one of them, but that was not the scream of someone under attack from claren. It was a scream of grief. Through a door off an outcropping, he saw her. Her tan clothes were easy to pick out from the dark gray shrouds around them, shrouds that had once been tattered rags when they held people rather than skin.

She held one corpse up. No torn fabric hung loose around it, unlike the others. It wore a dark green shawl and black clothes. A brass viper clasped the fabric, holding it together around golden sable skin, skin the same color as Vesperi's.

So she had found what she looked for. And she'd crumbled from how little it weighed.

When he placed a hand on her back, Vesperi clambered out of reach. Her hands flew to wipe the tears off her face. It hurt that she felt she had to, but being here, in this place, it made sense why she did. Why she had always hidden herself away.

"You can cry." Janto tried to sound soothing. "I will not use it against you. I am sorry everyone you loved always did."

Her nostrils flared. "What do you think I am? My *mother* would not cry like this. It's weak. And I *hate* him. This is not sadness . . . it is . . . it is relief." She stretched her lips into a thin line as she lied. Her dishonesty had never been easier to read.

"No. It is not, Vesperi. Those tears are from grief, and only Madel knows how you could feel that for a man like your father. It is proof, I think, that you are better than he was."

"I am *not*. I could never be, but I tried so hard, so hard . . ." She wiped furiously at new tears, her voice choking.

This isn't fair. No one should have to war with themselves like that, reason away a lifetime of pain and anger with lies so deep-seated they could not see the truth in front of them. Seeing Vesperi in this place . . . it had been her home. They had made it her home, all Lanserim, when King Turyn signed a proclamation they thought would bring peace. What it brought was this.

"I am so sorry we did this to you, Vesperi. I am so sorry that Lansera . . . my family . . . we failed you. It is our fault you are ashamed of what you feel right now." He reached for her hand, and she retreated, utter disgust on her face.

"I am not the product of anything but myself, princeling. I have lived my life exactly as I wanted from the moment I realized what was important. You have not shaped me. *Lansera* has not shaped me." She shook, and he could see the flame flowing beneath her skin. Each tear that fell had a silver sheen to it. It was beautiful. She was beautiful. He mourned that she could not see it, the fault of those who gave up on a war fifty years ago and each person since who had willfully blinded themselves to what darkness that peace had grown into.

Vesperi rustled through the drawers of the vast, onyx-colored desk in the room. She threw each on the floor in turn. The search focused her passions, though a faint silver remained within her.

He had to risk it. She had to understand. "Vesperi, listen to me. You may have chosen what to do with it, but you did not choose this life. You did not choose to be the daughter of a father who left you to his guards to beat." His voice cracked. "*We* did that. We abandoned you. We let you be born in a world where you never had a chance to be anything at all. It was Lansera's weariness, Lansera's willingness to end the fighting without a real victory that did this to you. That is what made you who you are. We are the feeble ones, and you have paid the price. All of Medua has paid it."

He could picture them, the future generations they had left to the fates, deemed not worth the effort it took to protect them from violent people who lived life by no rules but their own. Women and children huddled in dark rooms like this one, quivering when the door would open and commands be yelled with none of the respect they deserved. Thrown onto soiled beds, laces ripped and metal threads snapped. And the men, the men too, had been left to become monsters. How could they know true desire and ambition came from honor, that there was joy to be taken in hard work and earning the respect of those they protected and loved if they never saw it?

"There is nothing wrong with Medua! It's me, Janto. Don't you see? It's me." She languished down to the floor by her father's shriveled skin again. She caressed it, gave up on stemming her tears. "I could never be what he wanted. I could never be enough."

He did not understand how she could touch that shell of a man without shuddering. She was so strong. Were all women so much fiercer than he?

"Thank Madel you were not what he wanted." He knelt beside her then gathered her into his arms. She tensed up, dug in her fingers. He restrained her lightly. There would be no clawing here, no struggling, no fighting for her life. Only her soul. "You are not wrong, Vesperi. You have never been wrong."

She jerked within his hug, as though her whole body rejected his words.

"You were the strong one, Vesperi. Not us, not him, you. You found a way to make it through this life, to survive it. I cannot imagine the things you have had to do to save yourself. I am so sorry you have lived through them."

He had no more words. His throat choked with sorrow for her and for all the Meduans who had never had the chance to live a life of their own choosing, free from cages of fear and anger.

Vesperi's sobs calmed as she clung to him. "Thank you," she whispered into his chest.

He held her then. Not for long—they did not know if more claren were about. But if he could have, Janto thought he may have held her for hours.

"Are you all right?"

She nodded against him.

"Good. We need to keep hunting for the charm. It is not safe to stay here."

She rose, returning to the last few drawers of the desk. "It may be in the cabinet by the door." She pointed to a narrow, dark wood structure carved to resemble a snake's hide.

"What am I looking for?"

"It is about the size of an apple but shaped like a disc, a medallion. My father—he would wear it sometimes around his neck. I always thought it was one of our family heirlooms, but it is made of the same glass as those relics in Ashra. I do not know if it's hollow. I have never touched it."

Janto opened the cabinet door as another desk drawer clattered to the floor. He expected a haphazard pile of trinkets, but everything inside lay side-by-side with precision. A pen shaped like a serpent sat beside a number of metal clasps engraved with the sigil of House Sellwyn. The next shelf down had a reading glass, an inkwell, and a number of items with barbs coming off them. He had no idea what they were but knew better than to touch them.

The last drawer fell to the floor, and Vesperi huffed with frustration. "Is it there?"

Just as she asked, he caught sight of something with promise. The luminescent, opaque, green glass outshone the mundane trinkets surrounding it. He showed Vesperi, but he did not need her confirmation to know it was what they sought. The three-headed bird molded into the glass was answer enough. He took Vesperi's hand and they left, leaving Sellwyn Manor and its victims behind them.

CHAPTER 53
VESPERI

"We found it," Janto announced to the others as Vesperi led him back over the raised walkway. Her free hand grazed the marble carving it held. Flivio brought up their rear. Vesperi had no idea where he'd come from, but she knew where she wanted to send him when he smirked at their entangled fingers. She challenged Flivio with an air of nonchalance but did not move so much as a finger. Janto's hand was . . . nice. She was shaky after that embarrassment of a display she'd given at finding her father, and the pressure soothed. *Soothing—what an odd reaction to a man's touch.*

When they reached the courtyard, Janto extended the medallion to Lorne.

"You were right, Vespy." He flipped it over, inspecting its mark. "This is exactly what we needed. I never saw it, I am certain. How did you know it was this?"

She shrugged. "Father only wore it on special occasions. We didn't have any executions while you were here, did we? I sometimes lose track—"

The rest of the gathered group asked questions with horrified eyes. If she could see through their scarves and handkerchiefs, she would guess their mouths hung open with shock. *Again, our ways impress them.* For the first time, she appreciated Lorne's presence. At least he did not stare as though she had sprouted gills.

"No. He talked about hanging a few servants after you ran, but he never made good on the threat. In all honesty, he was too distraught to consider whom to punish."

"Too distraught? Are you certain you are talking about my father? He has never—*had* never—been sad in his life, not even when Uzziel was born. Quiet and calm when the advers pronounced my brother's ill health, but not sad. Maybe you mean disappointed?"

"I know the difference."

"Obviously, you do not. I knew my father."

"Enough of this." Sar Mertina whacked her gauntlets against the trough where the horses had gathered. Now *her* emotion was obvious. Anger. And Vesperi did not take pleasure in having brought it out of the warrior.

"As enlightening as swapping gossip on hangings is, we need to keep going," Sar Mertina scolded. "Qiltyn is a fortnight's ride from here."

"Fine." Vesperi moved toward the horses, surprised to find the trough full. The drought *had* been broken. Vesperi wondered why now, with no people left in Sellwyn to benefit from it. She unclasped the horses' lace masks one by one. "It's safe enough for the horses to drink. Then we'll ride."

✳ ✳ ✳

They passed the last rosewood and moved into hilly countryside about an hour later. Vesperi had only seen the region from inside the carriage that took her to Qiltyn at fourteen and returned her five years later. The rains had not made it there yet, leaving no signs of budding life as there had been in Sellwyn. The thought was hollow; there had been nothing alive except for plants. She had not thought to check for her mother, and Lorne had not mentioned her. He might not have known Lady Sellwyn resided in the manor at all. Vesperi knew it unlikely any women had escaped the kitchen.

Lorne rode ahead of her. His hair whipped freely as they went. He searched the hillsides as intently as Serra, though they each tracked a different sort of monster. They had agreed taking the direct route to Qiltyn was best, even with the risk of bandits and being seen by the Guj's spies. Armed men were not as serious a threat as other terrors. The more time it took to carry out Janto's plan, the more time the claren had to breed.

When complete darkness fell, Janto gestured for them to stop. As they made camp, everyone undertook their regular duties. They had never been designated, only filled. Napeler made rounds of the perimeter. Hamsyn and Flivio ventured as far as they felt safe to gather wood for the morning, finding only tumbleweeds in this terrain. Janto borrowed Hamsyn's huge bow and went off to hunt for rabbits or snavelins. Serra sifted through everyone's saddlebags, piecing together a meal. Lorne, of all people, rolled out the others' blankets. *When did he become useful?*

Everyone had made a job for themselves—everyone except Vesperi. She had not considered how little she contributed during this daily routine, but her habit of watching the others work, pretending they were her servants at home, fulfilling her commands unquestioned, was not as appealing this night. Not after seeing what home had become while realizing what it always had been.

Mertina unrolled the oversized canvas swatch they used as a tent for the women each night. Its material was a compound of Elstonian fabrics: tough, tan, and thick. The northern fisherman needed its protection when they camped near the Sound, Janto had explained. It weighed a lot, but Mertina handled it like nothing, lacing her rope through a brass ring sewn into the canvas. Vesperi walked over, needing to do something, anything. Making shelter for herself sounded appealing, as did learning from a woman who was so adept at so much that mattered. Her earlier consternation still weighed heavily on Vesperi as well.

"Can I help?" A rare shyness made Vesperi's voice soft and cheeks flush.

Mertina looked doubtful. "I'm not certain you can do that yet, but I can teach you, and maybe you can try tomorrow?"

Vesperi spent the next half hour holding the rope taut as Mertina pointed out every ring on the fabric, which ones needed the rope woven through them in a row, and which ones needed it knotted in place. Then she staked the canvas down on one corner, then on another and another, six times in all. Vesperi was lost by the time Mertina pulled a bundle of sticks broad as her thigh out of her pack.

"I skip this part when I can." Mertina bound the sticks together with ribbons like the multihued ones Queen Lexamy wore on her skirts, except these were the same tan as the canvas. "It is so much faster when there's a tree I can loop the rope around, but we don't have that luxury here." When she finished, the bound sticks had been formed into a single pole that rose about a foot taller than the warrior. Sar Mertina nosed the pointed tip of it into a metal loop at the fabric's center then slowly raised it high, creating a frame for the tent that enveloped her. From within, Mertina explained that she was inserting the pole into a hole she had dug before she had started the rest of the tent-building process. A moment later she emerged from its loose flaps.

Vesperi was dumbstruck. "I am trying to figure out what you meant by square knot."

Mertina laughed as she smoothed her hair back and retied it in a ponytail. Then she swatted at Vesperi's knee. "We will try again tomorrow night. Maybe you will have figured out which ones are the guide lines by the time we are back in Callyn." She winked.

Lorne watched them, amusement evident in the way he held his hands at his hips. He treated everything as a joke, but his eyes were sharp. How had she never realized he was different from other Meduans, that he had a mission? The Raven—Agler—had been easy to see through. Vesperi must have categorized Lorne as *man* and never given another thought to it beyond what it would take to get him in bed if needed. She had been wrong on that account as well.

"I was not playing a game with you, you know." He came closer once he noted her gaze. "Searching for a medallion and entertaining your brother while keeping an eye on you are not easy goals to pinpoint. Even I didn't know my task half the time. It's how the Brothers prefer it."

Serra laughed sharply from several yards away, chopping strips of dried tomato with a knife. Just then, Janto reappeared on the darkening horizon, and Vesperi smiled unbidden. He held two animals in his grasp.

Lorne pulled the medallion from his pouch. "You should keep this. It should be with one of you, I think. One of the bird's heads. I am a wing at best. Probably a claw on a foot."

Its green glass glinted orange with the light from Tansic above them. Two of the familiar engraving's heads faced forward. She had heard the confounded prophecy many times by then—Flivio harassed them with a less-than-harmonious rendition almost nightly—but Vesperi had not thought to connect it with this medallion or the carving on the bridge. Had she always been marked for this, by a charm her father cherished, but kept close to his chest only when the occasion called for it?

"I cannot take it." She shook her head more vigorously than she liked. "I cannot."

Serra's extraordinary hearing saved her from explaining herself. "I will wear it."

Lorne shrugged, pushing his hair behind his ears. "Fine by me. As long as one of you three has it, I think it's in the right place." He looped the leather thread around Serra's neck. "It looks good on you," he flirted, "but then, you always look scrumptious."

Vesperi stifled a laugh. If she weren't a few years older, she would have sworn Lorne was her twin. For the second time that day, she felt like less of an aberration. It was probably a good thing she had ignored him so thoroughly before she had run away.

Serra tucked the medallion beneath her tunic. It lined up with the necklace of braided cloves she always wore, the outlines of both barely visible through the fabric. Janto caught up to the camp then, and whispered something into Serra's ear as he laid down the snavelin he had killed. Serra nodded and whispered something back. The ease of their interaction made Vesperi jealous, she could not help it, but when Janto's eyes finally met hers, they were full of something she'd begun to recognize as a reason not to be.

Mertina joined them after checking the horses, having made certain their ropes were tightly knotted and their manes smoothed. "The fallowent," she said to Lorne. "Do you have more? I think we will need it at the temple."

He pulled a petite leather bag from the pouch on his belt then tipped it into his palm. A healthy amount of the black seeds poured out, filling his cupped hand. "We can each eat a pinch a day, but I am not sure how much it will help. I had been feeding it to myself and Uzziel in regular doses for weeks. I do not know if it works over time or immediately. I have only been told it works."

"Might as well give it a try," Mertina decided. "We need to make use of all our resources."

Janto knit his eyebrows together. "Hamsyn, how many of these plants did you say your sister had?"

The other Nevillim was breaking up tumbleweed into kindling for the morning. "When I left to meet you at the Crossing, she had at least two hundred of them. They grow fast. All they produce are those seeds, and their branches are laden with them."

Vesperi's spirits sank at Janto's next words. "Mertina, I need you to ride back and tell my father about the fallowent and Hamsyn's sister's collection. They need to be harvested and planted everywhere. If there is enough, then the people of Rasseleria and Wasyla need to start eating them now. We cannot let what happened in Sellwyn happen anywhere else."

Mertina did not hesitate, moving toward the tent. Janto stopped her with a hug. "You are extraordinary. Ride fast."

She nodded, tucking a loose hair behind her ear. "You can count on it, my prince. May Madel's hand guide you all."

"And you, also," the other Lanserim echoed.

Vesperi did not want her to go. She wanted to blast Janto for ordering it. But she said nothing, not having the words to explain how she took solace in watching Sar Mertina's straight form on horseback and her sword comfortably hanging at her side.

Serra was back to chopping tomatoes, and Janto cleaned the snavelins, his face blank by the time Mertina reemerged. Flivio helped her secure her packs to her horse, white as drapian dander, and held the reins while she mounted.

Their movement startled Janto from his thoughts. "One more thing! Tell my father to send a company of mounted men to Qiltyn as fast as possible. They must ride right away, and we will need at least a brigade on their heels."

"Soldiers?" Sar Mertina slumped with confusion. "But you aren't invading the city."

Janto smiled wryly, looking at Lorne. "Aren't we? If we succeed, we have to follow this act with a show of force, or the Meduans will not get the message. The claren will never stop breeding."

"You *are* the slayer." Mertina shook her head as though realizing it for the first time. "I never thought, not in my lifetime . . ." For a moment, wonder overtook her, but she did not revel in it. The warrior in her was too strong. "I will see you back in Callyn, my prince. Your commands will make it to your father in two nights at the latest." She patted the horse's flank and they disappeared into the darkness.

✳ ✳ ✳

Vesperi retired to the tent early. By her pack lay an unfamiliar bag. She loosed the string around its neck, and when she saw the extra tan ribbons it held, she did not care about the tears that fell. All her life she had hoped for this from her father, hoped for a suggestion of what this single act from a woman she hardly knew accomplished. The bag held the pride and trust of another person, and Vesperi resolved to deserve it. She fell asleep with hands scratched from stroking the fibers of a spare coil of rope.

* * *

Two nights later, they hashed out their final plans behind a group of cabins at the base of Mandat's hills, homes for men who would only now be returning after a full day of work. Lorne and Vesperi inspected the rest of their measly band, who stood ramrod straight, maintaining good posture though dressed in discolored robes they'd stolen from storage sheds. No one bothered to protect such ratty servants' garments, their dense material stifling this time of year. Vesperi wore one of her own gowns that Lorne had snagged while they scoured Sellwyn for the charm. His direct connection to the Brothers had to be why Janto agreed to let him continue with them despite his earlier protests. Or Janto was the same trusting dolt she'd always thought him to be. *Likely that.*

"This will never work," Lorne scoffed. "They hold themselves like bloody royalty, even the guards."

"They are bloody royalty," Vesperi corrected. "Even the guards. At least compared with us."

He considered her words thoughtfully. She had not known Lorne possessed that capability and mulled it over as she addressed the group. "Your clothing is fine, but you need to slouch. You also need to shuffle as you walk, as though barools cover the floor. And you cannot meet anyone's eyes. It would be safer to keep the floor constantly in your view. Servants don't speak much, either, or we whip the tendency out of them." She paused. "That means you, Flivio."

He made to speak but opted for a shrug instead.

"Lorne will lead the group because he's been here a number of times with his father—he will draw the fewest questions from the advers. I will pretend to be no more than his plaything for the evening. Serra, can you use the sight and stay low at the same time?"

She nodded, training her gaze toward the floor to demonstrate and casting lightning-quick glances toward the stars. "If I see any claren, I will cough. Raise your handkerchiefs then."

Hamsyn raised a hand, righting himself in the process. Lorne called out "Slouch!" before hitting his shoulders and the back of his knees with a stick.

"Will there be a lot of people in the temple this time of night? Should we expect interruptions?" Hamsyn maintained the meek stature.

Janto probed closer to the point. "Is night what the priests prefer for their . . . activities?"

"The dark will be fine. The temple will not be busier because the sun has fallen—advers come and go in the light of day." Such quaint notions the Lanserim held. "Oh, and do not be surprised when you see their robes. Most of them bear at least a few bones—the more there are, the more that man has ascended in the ranks. Some of them may also wear levere veils, shawls, or medallions. It protects them . . . well, it is supposed to protect them from magic, but if I am the only one with the flame, maybe the levere is only for show."

Janto spoke next, nervousness evident in his voice's quaver. "So then we move. Lorne, please guide the way."

Lorne crooked his arm, and Vesperi laced her own through it as she had seen the courtesans do the evenings she had been at King Ralion's hall. There was a stone path at the base of the temple mount that wound its way up the hill in a spiral, likely intended to tire out visitors to Mandat Hall by making them travel much farther than necessary before reaching the immense domed building at its crest. The temple's salmon-colored walls were difficult to make out in the dark, but Vesperi knew them well. She had spent five years gazing up at it from the convent in Qiltyn. It dwarfed all other buildings, was at least twice as huge as the seat of Suma. If the advers' aim in constructing it was subtlety, Mandat Hall failed spectacularly.

Its cavernous doors, tall enough for three men to walk through if they stood on each others' shoulders, were a new sight to her, however, because they were only visible from the south. The people in town, huddled in their small-spired buildings, saw only a smooth face.

"Should I avert my eyes, also?" she whispered as they rounded another curve.

Lorne nodded. "Do not speak unless I address you. But you don't need to hold your tongue after that—the advers who live here are used to my spirited girls. I get bored, you see." *Twins.*

Lorne raised a hand to signal a stop about halfway up near a stable. Flivio followed closest on their heels, then Janto, Hamsyn, Nap, and

Serra. The seer was a few yards behind the others; they would need to slow their pace if they wanted her to check the way but not get left behind. And stopping here meant Lorne had already picked up on that. Vesperi raised an eyebrow he could not see at the close attention he gave Lady Gavenstone.

Lorne ushered them inside a horseless stable to catch their breaths. The missing animals might explain why they'd seen no advers yet on their ascent. *Do advers take field trips?* Hamsyn disappeared into a dark stall, likely to relieve himself. *Maybe a group outing to the convent?* Vesperi's breathing evened out with each deep gulp of gamey air. *Best not think too hard on gifts.* When Hamsyn returned, Lorne led them out again, walking slower this time.

The steep ascent made her calves burn, but the spires of Qiltyn were a splendid sight when they reached the top. She tried not to stare as they moved past them, but the moonslit outlines of Qiltyn's numerous buildings seduced her. Impressively, the Lanserim restrained from gaping. *Maybe we* will *get through this.*

As they approached the doors, Vesperi noticed a slumped shape on a stone dais inside a ring of bushes. She tugged on Lorne's arm. With no priests about, she risked it and raised her eyes to Serra's. A simple shake of her head confirmed it was safe. No victim of the claren, then, or if it was, they had moved on.

"That's the feasting table," Lorne whispered, moving closer to the display. "The Guj has enemies tied to it when the whim strikes him. Sometimes they are dead, sometimes not. The pigeons from the roost peck at the deserving soul for days, until there is nothing left but a fading stench. Or at least that's what I've been told. I have never seen someone on it before."

The stench was certainly present, strong enough for Vesperi to guess the man had been there over a week. But birds had left no pockmarks where his robes had fallen away. She grimaced as she lifted his head. His lifeless eyes and the thin ring of white hair around his balding head revealed someone she had not thought of in many years, since before she left for the convent: Adver Garadin, her father's former priest.

"You know him." A familiar hand grasped hers—Janto's. *What is he doing, coming near me so close to the Hall?* She almost cursed him, but the gesture was sweet, if misplaced. She cared nothing for Garadin. The man had been an incredible dullard. That the Guj had not killed him years ago surprised her.

"Yes, he used to work with my father."

Janto gave her hand a squeeze then slid back into his place in the group so swiftly, she thought she imagined the warmth where his fingers had been.

Lorne started back toward the entrance, and she followed on his heels, not sparing Garadin a second glance. He had never shown her the courtesy of one.

The doors opened wide enough for two to enter side-by-side. Inside were high stone walls freshly painted white and lit torches on every column. It was a place of exposure. Fewer advers congregated in the Hall than servants on a typical evening in Sellwyn Manor, maybe two dozen of them. Each covered their faces with some form of cloth or metal. That explained the small numbers. They had been attacked. Yet Serra did not cough. If the claren were there, she would see them.

Vesperi reached for her scarf just in case, but Lorne caught her hand, silencing her with a stern look.

"Only if forced," he cautioned.

All eyes turned to their group, but Lorne did not acknowledge the priests. Advers outranked noblemen socially, but noblemen did not show it, one of Medua's unspoken rules. Lorne strode confidently forward, and she followed suit, keeping her hand on his arm. The foyer's silence was eerie. She had never come across an adver who could keep his mouth shut before, but maybe that explained it. Vesperi had learned ages ago that power did not automatically mean good sense. Ask Adver Garadin rotting on the feasting table. These priests were still alive. They were the smart ones.

Footsteps echoed around a corner up ahead, and a tall, thin man with a bit of a limp rounded it. He clasped his hands together as they neared, apparently sent to greet the visitors. Around his many-boned robe hung a levere shawl. This was a man who took no chances, and a rich one, too.

"Lorne Granich!" The adver pulled his scarf down while he spoke, his voice more jovial than the mood in the hall. "What brings you here?" Vesperi saw the man's eyes briefly before averting hers toward the floor. A Deduin, and something about those eyes unnerved her. The right shade of violet colored them, but they were dim. She suppressed a shiver.

"Adver Votan." Lorne's voice oozed with charm. "It has been too long." He clasped the man's hand. "I am surprised to see so few advers here today. Did the Guj have a temper tantrum again?" He chuckled. "The last one was the talk at court for months! My father was so relieved he had stayed home that day. He would have hated to have blood splashed on his new levere medallion."

The adver laughed as well, but Vesperi glimpsed no life in those eyes. Nor did he regard her at all, which would have offended her a few months ago. Now it was opportune.

"No, no tantrum. Tell me why you are here, Lorne. I have not heard anything of courtiers expected today. And you have this tasty morsel on your arm and so many servants following. It is most unusual. I would not want to miss whatever you have planned."

Vesperi put on her sultriest expression at being noticed. It was her most comfortable persona, and she did not know what Lorne had come up with for their cover. He would not have told his consort his plans, so he did not acknowledge her now. Instead, he whispered it into Votan's ear.

"Now tell me." Lorne took her arm again. "What is this new fashion? Why do all your brothers wrap cloths around their heads? If it is a fad about to take Qiltyn, I would love being the first to don it near the king."

"Not at all. It is a method we use to make it easier to discern Saeth's commandments." The adver leaned in, conspiratorially. "A waste of time, if you ask me. Saeth speaks when He wants, and we obey. We do not play at empty rituals as the Lanserim do."

Lorne scoffed. "By Saeth's fist, may we never be the Lanserim. The day we lie prostrate in meditation to some female god is the day we take swords to ourselves."

The adver nodded, his expression unreadable.

"Now, if you will excuse me." Lorne raised his elbows and waited for the adver to grant permission by returning the gesture. "I must be on my way."

"Of course." The adver stepped to the side, but Vesperi could feel those eyes on them until they turned the corner.

"This way," Lorne said once assured the hall was empty. "Walk fast and discourage any more conversation. Keep that scowl on your face, Vesperi. Advers are unused to addressing disdain in women. It confuses them."

Nothing could be easier.

CHAPTER 54
SERRA

Mandat Hall was not how she pictured it. Sellwyn Manor had felt dirtier and heavier, as though the dankness of its walls and its dense incense haze trapped silent screams. Mandat Hall was fresh and breezy by contrast, though no windows could be seen. But the thickest coat of paint could only hide so much. Horrors might not shout from its walls, but they resonated loudly from its people. She had found no claren yet, but it was obvious this place had been attacked by the fear the ryns—the *advers*—projected. No one should have to feel that emotion, not even in a place like this. She could not imagine what kept any of them there. Serra had not thought there anything greater to fear than a claren attack. But here they remained.

Dark, dull sheets of levere hung on the pillars like mirrors, which made using the sight tricky. Lorne kept them walking so fast, Serra was tricked by the torchlight flickering off the levere a few times. A reddish hue caught her eye in one, and she stumbled into Hamsyn, too focused on her measured breathing to realize they had stopped before a grand, wooden door with more metal panels screwed over it. It was sturdy and appeared strong. Whoever resided behind it was well protected. Lorne raised his hand to knock, and the sound echoed down the empty hall. Serra continued her measured breathing as she watched it slide open enough for the slipper-clad feet of another adver to slip through. Lorne spoke first, projecting confidence with every word and sounding as fake as Vesperi used to. The Meduans kept up such charades to survive.

The adver pulled the door open all the way, and Lorne led them through it into a narrow passageway more luxuriously decorated than the entry hall had been. She focused but saw only the extensive tapestries covering the walls. Serra could not guess what the images depicted. A giant man held a war hammer mid-swing in one. In the other, he addressed a group of men wearing the dark robes and polished bones of the advers. So much death enshrined in arras.

The adver hurried them through the corridor, entering a room at the end. It was bigger than the corridor, but she did not have the chance to consider how much so. A mass of red wings and overwhelming feeling of malice quelled any thoughts of caution.

"Cover now!" she yelled.

The room swarmed with claren, a dozen funneling hordes of them. All she saw were wings flapping in fast succession. To gather so many in such a tight space . . . they had to have been collected. This many claren would not migrate into one place on their own. It was their nature to spread out and infest as many orifices as possible.

Claren flew close, skimming her skin, but they were repelled. *The fallowent's effect?* Yet they flew closer each time, seeking passage past the scent. There were so many, thicker than flies over a spoiled wine vat. The need for escape assaulted her, and Serra lunged back toward the doorway. It slammed shut before she could reach it. She threw herself at the wood, bruising her shoulder with the effort. It was shut firm. There would be no escape.

And then Hamsyn screamed. *No, no, no.* She had warned them, but she had been last to enter the room. Tears brimmed as she dropped to the ground, reaching for him already slumped on the floor. She took his hand, felt the warmth and weight of it for as long as she could. Janto was there, too, pressing Hamsyn's cloth closer to his face as though he could force out what had already gone in. It was too late, but Serra did not stop him from trying. She couldn't.

Hamsyn's features collapsed in on themselves, a hair's breadth at a time. Through the haze of red, she could see the moment when his brown eyes, so kind and courageous, melted into twin puddles that oozed out of the sockets. A handful of claren flew from the crevices left behind. What used to be a hand weighed no more than a feather.

The grief in Janto's eyes was raw and angry. A low murmur drew her attention, and she prayed none of the others had opened their mouths to make the noise. It was then she realized their companions had formed a circle around them, tightening it as they inched closer together, swords drawn. When Serra and Janto stood, she saw why.

Three figures had emerged from the shadows of the room. They wore hooded robes darker than the Brothers' and levere veils that draped to the floor. The noise—the chanting—came from them, and Serra watched as something else entered the room from no door, something the others surely could not see or they'd be screaming despite the claren.

An energy force rose from the top of the chanting figures' heads, three strands of faint azure energy coming together to form a stronger beam, an echo of the glory of Madel's hand. The claren parted where the energy came through, and it congregated directly above the Lanserim's heads. The shape it formed reminded her of the stories her mother used to tell of the needlestorms outside Thokketh in winter. The three men's voices strengthened and the storm solidified. They had amazing control of the energy—it grew firmer with each repetition of their verse. Vesperi had never been able to direct her magic like that.

Vesperi. Serra grabbed at her arm and pointed her hand toward one of the men. She could feel the energy pulse through the Meduan's skin as Vesperi released it. The silver stream surged and hit the veil the closest man wore. It rebounded.

"Duck!" Serra pulled Vesperi down with her, and the rest of their group went to the ground as soon as she spoke. The reflected energy flew right over their heads before slamming into a wall. Hundreds of burned claren clattered to the floor, but there were too many and it was too dangerous to use the flame again. The levere was no farce. It was meant to keep *Vesperi* out.

The remaining claren grew more frenzied as the spell strengthened. Serra had no idea what to do. They could not run, could not use the weapon, had walked into a trap they had been too naive to consider.

Lorne reached his hand down the front of her shirt, his fingers grasping blindly. Serra was too confused to react as he jerked his arm, breaking the leather strap around her neck that held the medallion. Then he winked at her before hurtling the charm against the stone wall. It shattered, a dozen shards of green Ashran glass falling to the floor with a clatter. The only more satisfying sound was that of claren crackling as they burned.

For the first time in her life, Serra smiled when Brothers appeared.

They came in a blue mist that spread out from the fragments of the charm. The claren doubled up and flocked into their hoods only to buzz out again, more determined than before to find an entry point. She knew they never would. Dead men could not be drained of life. The claren, creatures that thrived on malevolence and viciousness, could never be one with the force that animated the Brothers, the same force the wizards could still sufficiently wield though decades removed from their last Rejuvenation.

It took only a few moments for the room to fill with Brothers in the flesh or as near to flesh as they could be. The wizards chanted louder, and she could feel the wind of their spell whirl faster overhead, could sense that in a few seconds more, the wizards would lower it to doom them all, but she could not pick them out in the sea of gray robes. She saw only red wings diving in and out of hoods like fireballs and orbs of dazzling blue forming at the center of each Brother's form. It felt as if the air in the room had been sucked out. Serra took the nearest hands to her own and squeezed them, Flivio on her left, Vesperi on her right. Then she waited.

"*Dispel.*"

The Brothers spoke with one voice so loud she swore the volume of it was what caused the needles of ice to burst with blue flames. She could see clear through to the stone ceiling above their heads, faded emblems of spears painted on each support.

"*Flee. Our task is finished. Flee.*"

The Brothers' forms flickered, fading, and through the remaining claren, Serra could see the wizards. They had not been destroyed as their spell had been. She could just make out the hum of their voices renewed.

The Brothers commanded again. "*Flee.*"

Nap was on the ground by the door already, shoving his dagger under it for leverage. Flivio dropped down to aid him, and Janto threw his body against the wood. With the loosening the other men's efforts produced, it creaked open an inch, and then Janto tumbled through into the hall full of tapestries. Serra hurried after them, Vesperi and Lorne on her heels.

There was no one in the narrow passage. The adver who had greeted them before must have run for help as soon as he trapped them inside. They did likewise, running and running and not stopping until the domes and spires of Qiltyn loomed up against the night sky.

✳ ✳ ✳

Janto called them to a halt when they reached the stable. The passages had been empty as they fled. Perhaps the advers had been warned in case claren escaped the trap room or . . . or . . . who knew why advers did what they did. Serra did not think it mattered. Any advantage they had was lost. And they had lost much more than that.

Napeler broke the silence first, going down on both knees and clutching his handkerchief to his chest. "To Hamsyn, whose death will go down in legend."

Serra laughed bitterly. "No, it will not. We have failed. We cannot succeed at this. There are too few of us and too many of them, both men and claren. And if we cannot do this, cannot stop them here, then we will be overrun."

Vesperi, of all people, placed an arm around her in comfort. Serra shrugged it off and kicked the stable wall instead.

"Serra," Janto's voice was as tender as it had ever been. "We cannot let his death go unrevenged. We cannot help Lansera, either, by giving up on this. We have to stop it. We have to go back—"

"Don't say it," she warned. "Do not say we are going back inside that temple. We are unprepared for this—did we not just learn that in the worst possible way? Who did we think we were that we could pull this off? Hamsyn paid the price of our idiocy."

She had spent the last three months being told who she had been was a lie, that she was called to a higher purpose. And following it had gotten her precisely nothing. It had gotten Lansera, the country she had supposedly given it up for, one less brave man to defend it. It was too much. *Too much.* They had believed they could waltz into this temple as though nothing were the matter, walk into a den of the worst Meduans that existed and expect to blaze through their portals unnoticed.

Lorne had convinced them of it.

She turned on him. "Why didn't you tell us what would happen?" She was angry she had begun to trust him, angry Hamsyn had died when Lorne knew there would be a trap. He had to have known it—he knew what the charm was for.

"I did not know." He leaned back against the wall she had kicked, crossing his legs as though this were a casual conversation taking place over a dinner table. It infuriated her that he had the gall to act that way so close to Mandat Hall and another suicide mission. *Hamsyn was dead.*

"You did not know? You reached right for the charm."

He chuckled, hugging his arms to his chest loosely. "All right, what I said was not entirely true. I knew we needed it with us because the Brothers told me that, but I did not know what it would do. I am not well versed on ancient Lanserim artifacts."

"They only told you to find it and bring it along? Why did they want you to come with us at all?"

His tone tempered. "I am not certain they did, and from the mess we made of things in there, maybe I should not have come. The Brothers aren't exactly forthcoming with their plans. They give enough information to give us a choice. What we do with that information is ours. I—I thought you would understand that."

And there it was. The reason she had trusted him after knowing him for only two days, and him a Meduan no less. She *did* understand. She understood so well, she had pulled her hair out a million times trying to accept it for herself these last hellish weeks.

Serra stopped pacing. "When did they first come to you?"

She knew from his downcast eyes that no further explanation was needed for his actions. He was only doing the same as the rest of them—doing what felt right, however he stumbled into it.

He met her eyes with astounding vulnerability. How had he ever perfected the persona they had first encountered? How had Vesperi? "I was nine."

She pressed his arm, encouraging him to continue.

"They appeared in our courtyard one evening. Not at the stroke of midnight—that would have been priceless—but close. I was scouring the yard for my drindem doll. My father had tossed it from my window earlier that evening. I was too old for it, you see, and he had never wanted me to have one anyhow. If he knew I was out there searching for it that night . . . I found it a few nights later, wedged between my mattresses. I guess—I guess I have the servants to thank for that. Though why they would ever waste the effort on protecting me, I do not know."

"Didn't they care for you?" She thought of Bini who had always been there for her. Bini, who would never have hesitated to keep her favorite toy safe.

He shook his head. "I wish I could say yes, but defeat is the only emotion I ever read from them. It made me determined not to end up the same. That, and the Brothers' visits. They would tell me stories when I was upset, wondrous tales about a goddess who cared more for me than Father ever could. I grew up certain there was something different and better than what I knew out there. My life has been one of pretending I wanted nothing more than craval steak while knowing granfaylon was out there somewhere, and I would do anything to taste it."

"I have been lucky, you know." He gestured toward Vesperi. "Most Meduans never had that knowledge, that hope."

Nap spoke up. "We have had granfaylon. Flivio, Hamsyn, and me. At our Murat. It is more delicious than you could imagine and worth every bit of the effort it takes to find it."

Lorne patted Nap's shoulder. "Thank you for that."

Nap barely nodded, weariness evident in his stature. None of them could hold out for long, not now, not with Hamsyn's death. But they could not dally here. They had to go back, to do what they knew was right no matter what else it cost them. With or without a plan.

"I do understand," Serra spoke quietly. "Although I do not want to, sometimes."

Lorne took her hand in his and squeezed. "Those are the times we have to remind ourselves it is Madel's plan, not ours. And it will turn out beautifully, if we let it."

Nap disappeared into the stable, the rest of them lost in their thoughts, trying to come up with something that might help them figure out how they could stand against the wizards long enough to seek fissures from the other realm and send Vesperi's flame through them safely. When Nap re-emerged, he had an enormous bow, nearly as tall as he was, steadily gripped in hand—Hamsyn's Old Girl.

"My prince, I found this inside. We must have forgotten a servant wouldn't carry it at first, so he left it here to go unnoticed." Nap held the bow out to Janto. "I think—I think it is meant to be yours now."

"I cannot." Janto's face fell. "I cannot use it."

"That's ridiculous." Serra let Lorne's hand fall back to his side as she reached for Janto's instead. "What would Ser Allyn say to hear you refuse this weapon?" Her voice was light and chiding.

"You should take it." Flivio sounded choked up. "He gave it to you on Braven—you slayed the confounded stag with it. You honestly think he wouldn't want you to have it?"

"I . . . I . . ."

"You will bloody well take it, that's what you will do. And you will use it to get your prey as you did then."

Janto gasped, but Serra doubted it was due to Flivio's acerbic tone—there was nothing remarkable in that. No, there was something else going on in Janto's mind, something she had not realized before. Something she should have.

Flivio filled in the pieces, rolling his eyes. "Oh, come on, Janto. You think we don't know what you intend to do? We are cleansing the temple to stop the breeding, and the best way to do that is to kill the Guj and the advers, not just use Vesperi's flame on those bugs. I don't know how you intend for us to do it, but we don't have any other options."

An assassination mission? The conflict in Janto's eyes confirmed it. It—it had always been his plan, loath as he was to go through with it. But at least he was not as blind as she, letting herself believe they were only after the claren. Killing the ones in the temple would only forestall them for a time. The advers were horrible men; she knew that before she had ever seen their robes covered in bones. But that did not mean she wanted to kill them, no matter how much they deserved it. She had sensed their fear. They were people, *their* people.

"Well, let us get on with it and plan this," Flivio finished. "We have a better idea of what will happen now. Maybe that will help us this time, so we don't lose someone else."

Janto clasped the Old Girl in one hand as he began to speak. Serra spared little attention to him, unable to come to terms with what they had to do. As Janto laid out a new plan, ironing out the details with Flivio and Nap, Serra tried to stop her stomach from heaving. She knew she would help, regardless. It was too late to back away now. But it did not feel right, not like following the Brothers' instruction always did, despite how she'd resisted them.

Lorne seemed to have none of the same concerns, concentrating fully on what the others plotted. Maybe she was wrong. Maybe slaughter *was* what the Brothers had intended. Vesperi would act as bait, they decided. The Guj considered her the only threat to his collection of claren. They would use no subterfuge this time, except a role Lorne would play at first. Serra muttered, "Of course," when Janto asserted her main task would be the same it always was, using the sight. They could not afford falling into another trap while setting one of their own. As they considered the obstacles, an image of Ryn Gylles speaking fast with amusement came to her mind.

"Then we are agreed." Janto's voice broke through her thoughts. "I think we should ascend right away. There is no point in waiting."

The others nodded in assent, and they again started up the winding path. But Serra grabbed Janto's wrist, holding him back. The words she spoke echoed Ryn Gylles's that day in the cave —"Your life is your own, child. And so are your choices"—and she knew only she could say them.

"There are always other options, Janto." Her vision steadied. "Everything we—and they—do is a choice. Madel gives us all the right to make them for ourselves. You do not have to take that away from those men."

When she saw the relief wash over him, she knew he understood.

CHAPTER 55
JANTO

It was locked. Janto refrained from kicking the ostentatious doors that had earlier stood so freely open. "I don't suppose we can knock?"

He didn't need Lorne's chuckle to know the answer. The door being closed against them should have been the first obstacle they considered. The Guj was not a man who made foolish mistakes—greedy ones, Janto hoped, but not foolish.

Flivio took an oddly shaped rod, nearly as thin as a pressed metal thread, out from beneath his robes. The Meditlan maneuvered it into the keyhole.

"You are a lock pick?" Vesperi's dark eyes shone with surprise. "But I did not think Lanserim need fear a thief. You are all too noble and busy singing about sunshine and . . ." She was utterly flummoxed.

"We all have our layers." Flivio finagled the pick farther into the hole. "Even prissy, gallant Lanserim. This 'talent' is why I was sent to the Murat. My town council thought it showed promise."

Nap grimaced, but the rest of them laughed, their voices blending together joyfully, this little band of six that had been seven a few hours ago. Then Janto laughed too. *If we are marching to our deaths, we may as well enjoy it.*

The locking mechanism clicked, and the doors shifted open by the smallest of cracks. It was barred from inside, and Janto heard a shout and feet rushing to shut it. The advers moved fast, but Vesperi moved faster, holding her palms up parallel to each other and sending a thin stream out of both. The sizzle and smell of burning wood came next, only enough to snap the bars free from their hinges. Janto was impressed. She had never done something that precise without Serra's hand to guide her.

Nap shoved his way through the doors before they could be closed, and the rest of them hurried to follow, raising their scarves. Subterfuge was useless now. *Well, almost.*

The Deduin adver waited for them inside the hall. More advers filled it than before, their whispering a trickling brook as it echoed. The ones who had not rushed the door hung rolls of pounded levere from column to column in haphazard lines as though decorations for a party. News must have spread that it had blocked Vesperi's magic. *Thank Madel, it does not absorb it.* Lorne spoke right away, wasting no time. "Adver Votan, I am sorry we left in such a rush earlier. We did not expect that sort of welcome." His tone was playful, and Janto hoped, convincing.

The adver waved a hand in front of him as though starting a ritual, but nothing happened. "You can give it up now, young Granich. Especially after that display at the door. You have a wizard with you. You will not gain admittance into this hall."

"But I thought only the Guj had real wizards?" Lorne laughed. "You must have been seeing things."

"Who do you travel with? These people are not servants. Their wretched garb cannot hide that."

They had given up pretense, no eyes skirting the floor. Better to be alert for whatever came their way. Vesperi's eyes flashed silver. *Good.* She was keeping ready.

"I travel with Lanserim."

The sounds of the advers' whispers rose from a trickling to a steady stream, and they broke off their work, ends of levere rolls dangling.

Lorne pointed at Flivio first, giving the introductions as they had planned. "A friend of the prince's, Flivio of Meditlan. And here"—he took Serra's arm, breaking off her gaze from where it had been trained down the hall—"is the prince's formerly betrothed and lady of Meditlan, Serrafina Gavenstone. Isn't she gorgeous?" Lorne pursed his lips in appreciation.

Votan clearly gaped at each introduction, though cloth obscured his mouth and those purple, dead eyes showed no reaction.

Lorne clapped Janto's shoulders next and made sure to speak loudly, enunciating each syllable fully through the cloth. "And here we have

Prince Janto Albrecht, heir to the Lanserim throne, ruler of all lands that fall under Madel's hand." A collective gasp rang through the hall, and the whispers' volume rose from a flowing brook to a rushing one. "I do hope you will treat him nicely. He has come a long way."

Adver Votan laughed, a hollow sound. "You have fancy friends. I imagine Saeth waits outside the door? Or mayhap the imposter god you dare to name? But never mind all that—I cannot wait to hear who this second woman is. Queen Lexamy, perhaps? I had thought she would be older by now."

The disbelief was expected, and Janto hoped Vesperi's introduction would also go as planned.

"No." Lorne raised his voice loud enough the whole hall could hear in case Adver Votan was not privy to knowledge of the weapon. Janto prayed someone listening was. They needed Vesperi to be as wanted here as his father had claimed. "This is Vesperi Sellwyn, and I am fairly certain the Guj will want to know who he had chased out of his hall earlier this evening."

One pair of feet waddled with great speed over the tiled floor, and by the time its owner reached them, the man was huffing. Rounder than Jerusho, his body slumped in a way Janto's friend's never would. The adver leaned in close and whispered, "You will come with me."

"What's this, Nouin? The Guj said I was to—" Anger almost made Adver Votan appear alive. *Almost.* What came next succeeded in proving it.

"Do you want a repeat of the last time you interfered, Votan? Complain again, and I *will* let you come with us."

The Deduin recoiled, and at last, Janto saw emotion in his eyes: fear—abject, terrified fear. It made Janto realize, along with the words Serra had whispered in his ear before they headed back up the temple mount, that he had to give this man a chance. He had to give all of them a chance—a choice.

Adver Nouin walked down the passage they had taken earlier, beckoning the group to follow. Janto held back, considering the few dozen men gathered in the foyer. The fact that he would be the first Lanserim most of these men had ever had address them only gave him pause for a moment. He cleared his throat.

"If you value your lives"—he glanced at Serra who stopped with the rest of their group at his voice, and she gave him a nod of encouragement—"you will leave this place." He had the advers' attention, whether or not they believed who he was. The hall was silent. "You don't deserve to live, not after what you have put my people through." He gritted his teeth, thinking of Hamsyn and Mar Pina, and of Vesperi also, on the floor of Sellwyn Manor cradling her father's skin. "But you deserve the chance to. Leave this place and this life behind, and you will live. Stay, and Madel Herself will destroy you."

He rejoined the others and the whispers behind him rose to a waterfall pitch. Then the advers acted. They *left*. The priests bolted toward the front doors, except for a few who stayed back, uncertain. Most disappeared in seconds.

"Did that happen?" Janto turned to his friends. "Did they really heed my warning?" So many people spared, and he had thought they would doom them all. He swung Serra around and placed a kiss on her forehead. "You are brilliant."

Lorne patted him on the back. "Don't think too much of it, my prince. You threatened the only thing an adver values when it comes down to it—his life. And after a claren attack and our display earlier, they may have realized Mandat Hall is not as unassailable as they've believed."

Adver Nouin's shock at the mass abandonment was the same as Janto's, but he composed himself more quickly. "We must not delay. The Guj is leaving soon to travel to King Ralion's court."

They reached the end of the corridor, and the adver unlocked the levere-lined door. The second door, at the end of the narrow hall that had trapped them before, was open. Janto's skin tingled in nervous anticipation. Serra stared intently down the corridor then shook her head no. If they were lucky, they had killed most of the claren earlier. But what of the wizards? They were being led straight back into the room where they had lost Hamsyn and nearly all been killed. *My masterful plan, letting us be pinned up like lamtas by a lake filled with sheven.*

Janto braced himself to see Hamsyn's body, but to his shock, Adver Nouin stopped well short of the room at the end of the hall. Instead, he lifted the corner of one of the hideous tapestries. There was a door behind it, painted to blend in perfectly with the white walls. *Clever.* The Guj was no idiot.

Adver Nouin knocked on the door, and it pulled open from the inside. A slight and hairless man held it, frilled ridges of skin bunched around the tops of his ears. His eyes darted fast as he took in their group. If not for the robe of bones, Janto might have believed him a brother of Sielban. The likeness amazed him, but not enough to miss the quiet clatter of Flivio slipping his metal rod on the floor to wedge the door open as they followed the Rasselerian through another passage. The advers did not notice. Maybe, just maybe, they would pull this off.

CHAPTER 56
SERRA

The adver led them to another room much more cramped than the fake quarters they had been trapped in earlier. Torches lit it dimly, and levere sheets layered the walls from waist-height upward. Two wizards stood in far corners and one hovered by a round table where another adver sat. They waved their arms in continuous circles, humming words together. No wind blew or ethereal ice shards whirred, so they were not attacking, at least not yet.

Serra focused her sight to peer more deeply at their movements, but as she made to do so, another pair of eyes bore into her from the adver with the Rasselerian features. He peered inquisitively, and she dropped the sight. Vesperi's magic was known, but they had found no reason why hers should also be exposed. This man's gaze pierced too sharply.

Lorne broke her out of the stare with a squeeze of her hand. *The gall of that boy.* Even now, he lost no opportunity to make a move. She glared at him until he dropped her hand again. Her eyes itched to sweep the room, but she couldn't, not with that Rasselerian in here. At least they wore scarves already.

The adver at the table wore a robe so covered in bones no fabric could be seen. When he stood, they clattered, and he towered over the others, making it obvious who he was. Nothing had ever bent the Guj's back, though he was the oldest person in the room. Adver Nouin whispered in his ear, and the Guj smiled, a ghastly effect against the backdrop of his robe.

"Vesperi Sellwyn." He walked over to Vesperi, clasping her hands unbidden. She jerked them back. "I am so glad you have come to join us. You are the spitting image of your father, though he has not come to Qiltyn in years. How is he?" He moved his eyes slowly up and down her form with obvious appreciation. It made Serra's skin crawl.

"He's dead." Serra admired the way Vesperi always kept her voice so steady. "The creatures you are keeping as pets destroyed Sellwyn."

"A pity. Your father was one of my most loyal lieges, never skimming off my tribute—"

"You mean King Ralion's tribute," Lorne interjected, playing at bored. "Or are we speaking freely? I did not think honesty your style."

The Guj frowned before quickly reasserting his smile. "Your group and I have moved past such particulars, don't you think . . . Granich, is it? That's the name Votan gave after you fled from my wizards. I would not have remembered it myself. Lesser houses are not worth bothering about, though I may need to reconsider that stance. They do not usually storm into my home."

"And this"—the Guj darted forward, taking Janto by the hair and shaking him—"this is an Albrecht. You look so like your uncle Gelus before I swung my axe through his arm at the plain of Orelyn."

Serra gasped. She reached to give Janto a touch of comfort, but the Guj had pulled him too far away. The man forced an expression of contemplation onto his face. "Is that what did it, you think? Why your grandfather finally gave up the war? I expected more of a fight from him, in all truthfulness. But then, I did not expect an Albrecht to walk into my temple with a Meduan for an escort, no more than two guards, and a pair of *women,* either. Nouin!" The named adver shuffled over. "I cannot decide if I should ask for a ransom for this little prince. Should I kill him instead? It would be easier."

At that, Nap rushed forward, raising his sword in a charge. He slammed into something unseen and landed on his knees before springing back up again. *A spell of defense then.* Serra hated that she daren't sight it.

The Guj frowned at Nap's display. Then he shoved Janto back toward the others with a hard poke of his finger and turned his attention to Vesperi. Menace emanated from him that reminded Serra of the claren's quintessence, though he was a baser beast.

"You cannot imagine how thrilled I am you escaped our silly trap earlier, Vesperi, though I think letting these others go was a mistake."

He sighed, wringing his hands together. "It would have been such a shame to ruin your potential before it could be harnessed. I suppose you know what you are now?"

"*From silver the weapon comes.* Or so I have been told."

"By those superstitious Albrechts, I am certain. You ought to have done us a favor and killed them when you met them. Can you imagine how galvanizing it would be to take the other side of the mountains? Meduans seizing whatever they want, whomever they want. It's always been a dream of mine, I'll admit. I think you'd enjoy making it come true—I have heard much about you, you know. When something of value appears, I pay attention."

He reached a hand to her, and for the first time, Serra saw his age. Liver spots covered him, like a congealed bowl of craval pudding.

"I have not come to join you," Vesperi said. "I have come to destroy you."

"Like you did my claren pack?" The Guj waved his arm around. "Do you know how much time it took to gather them? Invisible creatures are hard to trap, but the wizards and I managed despite the damage to my advers—why, Nouin here barely escaped with his life after first discovering their handiwork. You were not there when I sent my envoy to collect—invite you to be Ralion's bride, so I had no choice but to use the claren that appeared in your stead. It is a sign we are meant to work together, Vesperi, now that you have destroyed them. A sign from Saeth that now is the time to attack the Lanserim."

Lorne spoke, his voice haughty and sure. "Saeth does not exist. You don't need to pretend with us, remember?"

"He speaks, and yet no one hears his words." The other advers laughed at the Guj's pronouncement.

Lorne sputtered, but Serra watched him shrug a smirk back in place like pulling on a favorite pair of gloves. "*King Ralion* heard me when I told him your plans, I am fairly certain. 'The Guj seeks to wed you,' I wrote to him from Sellwyn." Lorne stepped away from the others to divert the Guj's attention. "You see, I overheard the adver you sent to fetch Vesperi—you know the one, he's lying on your dais at this very moment. I felt this overwhelming urge to contact my father's old friend Ralion—and our blessed ruler, of course; I must not forget my pleasantries. 'He will probably kill your sweet Rapsca to keep up appearances,' I wrote. 'Best decide whether to let that happen or take a stand for once,

you lily-livered pansy. Yours sincerely, Lorne Granich.' Penmanship is
so important, don't you think?"

Lorne raised his elbows in deference to himself as he finished, and
Serra nearly laughed at the pleasure he took in the show, eyes shining.
"I may be only a young courtier, oh glorious champion of Saeth, but I
have grown up at court, and we know things. We watch, we wait, and
we use what we see. Ralion Suma may be your puppet, but he would
never give up his man." He sighed and pressed a hand to his chest. "True
love. Sometimes it prevails."

"Take him out of here." The Guj's face reddened with anger, no tease
left in his voice. He gestured at the Rasselerian, and Serra tensed. "Find
out if there is anything else he knows."

The adver darted his tongue toward her as he walked past, but she
had eyes only for the scene in front of her, not what he hoped to taste.
Nap tried to bar the adver's way, but his arm jerked back against his will
as soon as he had raised it. The adver escorted Lorne out. All pretense
had fled from their friend's countenance, and he looked at peace, having
done the part the Brothers had trusted him with. Yet he reached in his
pocket and swallowed another sprinkling of fallowent anyhow. Serra
prayed she would get the chance to thank him.

The Guj zeroed in on the only person he prized in the room, not
bothering to keep his temper in check. "Enough of this, wench. You will
use your magic for me or I will kill each of your friends, and I already
have a head start. When they are dead, you will be tied to a pole, and
my advers will coat their dicks in levere dust and take you, every one,
until there is nothing left of you to resist, nothing left of you but the
power you should never have been given in the first place."

Vesperi bristled. "You think that is a threat? That was every meal
time in my father's manor."

Serra slowed her breathing as they fought—Lorne had made her way
clear. The image of a farrowbird's feather came to mind, and she focused
her will on it. It took less than a second for the reddish-brown of it to
divide into separate bands of color in her mind's eye—white, brown, red,
black all shining with the glint of unseen light. She opened her eyes and
swept the room, her breath catching from the change in it now. There
were no claren—that they had all survived so long was proof enough of
that—but something else was there besides the defense spell that hung
like a net of filigree around them. Wisps of a deeper blue seeped out of

what looked like a seam ripped open. More blue shimmered from the ether beyond the seam. The opening was slim, but it was there. *Janto is right. He is right! There is a fissure here!*

Her spirits soared, and Janto could tell, whether the attunement came from being heads of the same prophesied bird or from having known each other so intimately for years. Janto tilted his head toward her almost imperceptibly, and she shifted her gaze toward where the mist flowed out. The touch of his thumb on her arm was all the assurance she needed.

It was perfect, what happened next. The Guj pushed Vesperi over the edge all on his own, unused to a challenge from any quarter, much less a woman. "You think you have any choices left, whore? Look around you. My wizards have made these Lanserim useless to protect you, and have no doubt, when they are finished with your friends, you will have all their attention. Breaking you will give me more pleasure than I have felt since cleaving Gelus Albrecht's arm from his shoulder. When you have learned your lessons, you will pray for the day I finish draining that delicious power from you and toss you in the kitchens."

A spark appeared in Vesperi's palm, and it danced back and forth from her index finger to her thumb. Serra grabbed her arm and pointed it toward the fissure. "Let it go. Hold it steady for as long as you can."

What happened next was neither expected nor perfect.

Chapter 57
Vesperi

agic surged through her, and Vesperi's hair rose in the electrified air, jerking arrhythmically, a nest of eaglets trying to reach their mother's worms. Time passed, but she had no awareness of it, no awareness of anything but the unbridled joy of release, the flinging of her anger, her power, and the trust she had in the person holding her arm up and pointing her hand. Smoke poured forth from where she aimed, and it parted around a strange mist lit by the radiance of silver flames. The sound of claren dying was louder than she had ever heard it before, but it came at a distance, as though the thunderous cracking was contained in a glass house like the one Hamsyn had described in his sister's garden. All else was silver—brilliant, sparking silver.

Too soon the rush of energy slowed to the trickle the River Sell used to be rather than the raging water it had become in her absence. The Esye in her mind darkened into Onsic, and drained of power, Vesperi observed the spot where the smoke and mist hung thickest.

Claren bodies poured out from the empty air. The loud clattering grew softer and quieter as the effects of her talent died down. Ash and shell surrounded her and Serra in a room of shambles. The rebounded energy had warped the sheets of levere, leaving burn marks. No more than a few sticks of furniture remained.

"What happened to the others?" Vesperi was unsure whether to be proud or terrified of what they had done.

"Our men crawled out on their stomachs as soon as I lifted your arm.

They were out before the first magic bounced its way through the crack in the door. Their levere vestments protected the Guj and his men long enough to escape as well."

"Come." Serra pulled Vesperi toward out of the room. "And stay angry."

The passages were worse. Only the levere-draped door leading to the fake bedroom was unscathed, though dying flames licked its edges. No ghoulish tapestries hung from the walls, and the walls themselves started to crack. The pillars too, louder than Thokketh's ice walls at the end of summer.

"Run!" yelled Serra.

They did, finding no signs of their companions anywhere, nor of anyone else. For the first time she could remember, Vesperi prayed. Prayed they could run faster than the ceilings of Mandat Hall could fall, prayed the others had already made it outside. If she was responsible for any of their—she refused to think of it.

Around every curve, the sight was the same. The cracking of walls echoed through the deserted building. They reached the grand entry hall, but the walls fell in earnest there, everything not made of stone aflame with silver. The magic must have just repelled through it, from one levere sheet to another.

Someone screamed and Vesperi stopped to listen. It came again, from a door at the southern end of the hall. Then she slammed her hands against her ears as a huge fragment of ceiling tumbled down behind her—in the direction Serra had kept running.

"Serra!" *I cannot lose her. She is my sight, my guide. I need her.* She needed all the insufferable Lanserim, damn them.

A moment later, Serra rose on unsteady legs from the other side of the debris. "I'm all right. Come on!"

Vesperi breathed thanks to Madel. Then she heard the scream again. "I hear someone—I have to go find them. Keep going!"

Serra nodded and made her escape. Flivio met Serra at the door, taking her hand and jerking her through the narrow opening. Vesperi was relieved to see him. *This world would be darker without his wit to entertain me.* She ran toward the door the screams had come from.

The room she entered was more ostentatious than any other she had seen at Mandat Hall and vast enough to fit a few hundred men. Flames of silver danced along the long tables. They would be an inferno soon; she could not linger there. Then she heard the scream again.

It was the fat adver who had guided them into the Guj's true quarters, on a stage in the front of the room. The Guj himself caused the terror. He wore a levere helm, a clenched fist rising from its apex. Then the ruler of Medua swung a mace against his thrall's nearly torn-off shoulder from what must have been a many times repeated blow.

"Stop!" Vesperi called Esye back to mind, though the Guj's levere shawl lay flat against his body. She could not touch this man, not like this, and he knew it, but she could hold her talent at the ready.

"You destroyed my wizards, you know." *Good.* "They were not strong enough to survive your flare into the ethosphere, their tether to Madel too weak. They fizzled out of existence the moment your power went in." He swung lazily at the adver as he spoke, bashing in his head and silencing the screams. "It wasn't Nouin's fault, all this, but I had to blame someone, you see. I cannot punish you. You are too valuable to destroy."

"You will never use me."

The Guj laughed, dropping his mace in the pooling blood beneath the dead man's body. He knelt on the floor beside him. "Do you think it's so simple, changing the world order? Did you think you could storm a castle and suddenly everyone and everything would welcome you? The Meduan lords will never accept a woman over them. They will never see you as anything but a weak, powerless gnat."

Something snapped. The Guj held one of the man's fingers up to the flamelight and sliced the flesh from the bone.

"If you join with me"—he finished the work in three quick strokes— "they will fear you. By my side, you will rule Medua. Think of it. Think of all those people cowering before you, showing you the respect that is your due as the weapon, the respect you have always craved. Your father was blind not to see it."

She did not ask how he knew of her relationship with her father, remembering Garadin rotting on the dais.

"You can be their savior. You have removed the claren and you can bring them true peace, bind Lansera and Medua together with the might of your palm." The finger disappeared somewhere into his cloak, and he made his way toward her through the thickening smoke. His voice grew more assured with each step. "We could rule it all, from Thokketh's fortress to the snow-whipped shores of Elston. None can stand before you, unless they have one of these." He tapped his fingers against his helm, not breaking eye contact. His eyes were soft brown as

Hamsyn's had been, and she wondered what this man had been like as a boy, wondered why he clung to an existence he hated so fiercely. *Does power make it worth it?*

"With my guidance"—he had almost reached her—"you will be magnificent."

How small her ambition had been, limited to only one manor in one dusty, ruined province. She had been crippled by her infinitesimal worldview, a looking glass honed in on her father. The Guj promised her a wider target, but he wanted to extend it where he chose. He wanted her to bring him *his* kingdom. He did not know how far her aims had shifted when she watched a king gleam with hope and faith that outshone mere ambition. Besides, she knew better than to trust a Meduan.

"I will never join with you. We are not equals. Look around you." She gestured toward the disintegrating tables, the splitting stone walls. "Your kingdom is falling."

"You cannot do anything to me." He was close enough she could see the silver flames engulfing the room reflected back at her in those human eyes. *Does he see them in mine?*

"And as long as I remain, there will be a Medua," he continued, looming over her, but she could not shake the feeling he was so very, very small. Her father had influenced all Vesperi did, and she had given him everything she had, never receiving anything in return. This man, this cretin who had tried to control her from afar, to wed her to King Ralion, thought he could influence her now? Her talent pulsed, and she wished she had the facility to strike at the space between his helm and his shawl on her own.

And then she watched as an arrow flew right into it, cutting straight through his windpipe. The Guj's eyes widened, and he stumbled to the floor.

"*She* cannot kill you"—Janto jumped down from the urum drum he had climbed to take aim—"but the bird has more than one head."

A gurgle of blood came out as the dying jackass spoke. "You—you are—"

"The slayer," Janto laced another arrow onto the Old Girl's thread. "I tracked you by the trail of blood your last loathsome act left behind."

Vesperi laughed then, laughed with pure amusement, letting the rage driving her talent die down until it was nothing more than a flicker. "You had not realized it, had you? You thought they used me as a pawn like you wanted to. You never considered I might be part of a team. I am a woman, after all."

"And the other?" The Guj gasped, his face turning purple.

"The seer." Janto loosed the second arrow at close range into an eye. "But I don't need her to see the color of your soul."

The Guj was only a man in the end, and then he was not that any longer.

"If you two have finished gawking at your handiwork, we have a burning building to flee."

By a rounded door near the stage, barely visible through the smoke, stood Lorne. Vesperi couldn't see it but she knew he smirked. Janto took her hand and they ran together into the tight passageway Lorne ducked into. Smoke billowed in after them.

"How did you escape?" Vesperi asked as they ran. "Did you charm the robe off that froggy adver?"

His consternation made it plain he had higher standards. "He proved my number one rule about advers as soon as your little fireball ricocheted into the stairway he had pushed me through, no doubt on our way to a cell below the temple. We fell to the ground, and by the time it was safe to move again, he had already gone on. So here I am, rescuing you."

"This does lead out?" Janto sounded dubious.

"Patience, princeling."

Only a few more turns, and they tumbled through a rotting door and onto the grass of the hillside. Vesperi spoke between gulps of fresh air. "How—*huuunf*—did you know—*hunf*—about that passage?"

The taller man sprawled beside her, finding his own breath. "You expect all—*hasp*—my secrets?" Lorne winked and went up on his knees. "I think the others are getting worried," he wheezed. "If my squinting can be trusted, Napeler is about to hurl himself through a stone column to get back inside. We should probably let them know we survived."

Janto was already on his feet before Vesperi realized there were more people gathered on the hillside than just their group. Dozens of advers stood by themselves, shaken, as they watched Mandat Hall burn. Silver and blue mists rose from the smoke that poured out of it, reminding her of the waters of Call that Janto always went on about. She did not care what they resembled when he leaned over and kissed her on the lips. Then he grinned like a loon before pulling her off toward their friends.

CHAPTER 58
JANTO

Gnawing doubt grew in Janto as the flames from Mandat Hall died down. But it lessened when a unit of Lanserim arrived from the west within the hour. Brown- and gray-clothed dots on the horizon multiplied from one to five to twenty and many more as he watched them come. A whoop of joy built in his throat as the feathers sticking out of the vanguardsmen's caps sharpened into view, but he let it die away. The milling advers could not know he'd been uncertain his father's men would come. By Madel's hand, Sar Mertina had ridden swiftly, and Janto prayed the words he'd soon speak would do likewise throughout Medua, along with news of Lanserim soldiers who had met no resistance.

Their small crew sat together in an exhausted lump, far enough from the destroyed hall that they could tolerate the heat from its ruins. The advers granted Janto and the others a wide berth, which he would have found funny if he wasn't so tired. The prince of Lansera was in their midst, and the Meduan leaders did not dare harm him for fear of the female company he kept.

The people of Qiltyn had gathered on the eastern slope of the hillside as the tower burned, men coming from their quarters to the west, women and children from the rest of the town. The latter group was smaller than it should be, and they kept plenty of space between themselves and the men. The crowd watched as the largest presence in their lives dwindled to nothing. Heads poked out of domed buildings' windows, enraptured with the sight. No shouts came up the hillside along with the cool breeze, merely shocked silence. When Janto spoke, he would have the attention of all Qiltyn. Without the manpower to spread the message, it would have accomplished little. His tired, exhausted sortie of six could not do it on their own.

But a unit of his father's cavalry, nearly on them now, could. They were perhaps a hundred soldiers, but they would do. It was enough to show the Meduans below that the Lanserim had returned.

Lord Sydley dismounted, leaning on his cane, and bent his knee. "My prince." Janto did not normally entertain such formalities, but it was essential now, and he was glad Sydley had discerned that.

"Rise." Janto clapped the elder liege-lord on his shoulder. The advers regarded them intently, some daring to creep closer, the allure of news too much to resist. "How many men follow you?" Janto spoke loudly enough for all nearby ears to hear.

"A hundred at your command. There are three hundred more on our heels, and a company makes its way over the mountains now."

Better. Hamsyn's death would not be pointless but a lasting testament to peace, if Madel's hand was with them. "My command is for the cavalry to follow me down this hillside and spread the words I speak to every home in Qiltyn. There will be some violence, I do not doubt it, but I have a feeling it will not last."

Lord Sydley whispered his doubts, "How can you know that? These people have been our enemies for years."

Janto's gaze went to Vesperi, of course, and to Lorne also, who had proven as essential to Madel's plan as the fabled bird. "I think we will find most of our enemies died years ago. Lead our soldiers down the hillside. I will soon follow."

Flivio groaned when Janto insisted they get up to join him. "A speech? Janto, we just saved their asses and ours. Can't these 'inspiring' words of yours wait until tomorrow?"

"No excuses. We have to do this now if we have any hope of being heard."

With his friends behind him and the Lanserim cavalry around him, Janto did not need to fake his confidence.

"People of Medua."

Heads turned toward him in a wave, rippling inward instead of out.

"We have destroyed Mandat Hall, and the Guj is dead." The silence continued, but many mouths opened in surprise and stayed that way. "I am Janto Albrecht, son of Dever Albrecht, king of Lansera. And I am here to reclaim this land for Lansera. I am not certain what histories you have been told, but I know they are not truthful. Nor is the one we tell over the mountains, not entirely.

"During the war, your forebears, some who endure among you, decided they did not want to live within our society. They wanted to take rather than give, to dominate rather than abide in peace and justice. So they rose against us and fought to steal as much land and wealth as they could. Civil war came, and it was brutal and hard on our people. They grew tired of fighting, tired of losing brothers and sisters for the sake of forcing those who did not want it to stay with us. Because of that weariness, we did the worst thing we could, far worse than anything your people have inflicted on each other. We let you go.

"Thus, we sentenced you—the young, the not-so-young, and the old who did not truly understand the need to flee before those criminals were given these lands—we sentenced you all to servitude. You lost your rights, though you did not know it. You lost your self-worth, though your advers never let you learn it. You lost the knowledge you were Lanserim, and Lanserim need never fear the lash of a liege-lord, nor be forced to do anything they would not do freely. We let them blind you to those truths. The horrors you have had to endure because of it . . . we can never make up for that.

"So I am here today to say I am sorry. On behalf of the Albrechts, my family, and the Lanserim, my people, we are sorry. And we want you back. We want to help you remember you are more than shadows in a hall. My soldiers will aid you if you want to leave these lands and start afresh over the mountains. We will teach you how to make use of your skills, find you jobs where you can take pride in your work. But you must decide fast, because there are men who will want to take this choice away from you. They will rise up soon enough, some of them behind me on this hill, no doubt. They will try to reforge the hold the Guj and his advers had over you. There are always those who will yearn for that power, but I am telling you today, you do not have to submit to it. You are not less of a person than anyone else in this world, and we will fight for you to know it. All you need to do is come home."

There was no great stirring when Janto stopped talking. He did not expect one. This society and its sicknesses had been built up over

decades. It would not become healthy in a day. He instructed the soldiers to go out into the cobblestoned streets and repeat the message to
whomever they could find. When the first rider returned with a slyph
of a woman on his mount and a tiny child in her lap, Vesperi slipped
her hand into Janto's and they went to greet them. The child, a girl no
more than two, giggled when Serra came up behind her and tucked a
blue feather behind her ear.

EPILOGUE
SERRA

They had been back from Thokketh for a fortnight, but Serra still felt cold. It was nearly spring again, the second since the fall of Mandat Hall. Thokketh did not have a spring from what she could tell, though the guards had called it breeding season just as her mother had once done. The waters surrounding the ice fortress teemed with sheven and streaks of dark red blood eddied near the surface. The occasional fin or chunk of purple flesh had been flung onto the snow banks beside the moat as the fish frenzied. But the eyes of the Deduins who lived outside Thokketh's walls had been more unnerving. Serra had scanned the night sky over their encampment in her seekings, and many dots of plum-colored light stared back from the dark, reflecting the cold of their environs unlike the warmth she had felt from Ryn Cladio's gaze. Yet the Deduins had been friendly, at least friendlier than the other people who remained in Medua by choice. Still, interactions with them left a foul taste in her mouth. She would never understand the men who had banished their women to such places as Thokketh for the crime of not submitting to their will. She would never understand a lot about Meduans.

Including the one who lounged beside her on the flat roof of his one-roomed home in Callyn. Lorne was among the first to move back to Lansera. Many other Meduans had followed, though King Albrecht had no intention of making them vacate the lands on that side of the mountains. Yet most did not consider staying where they were. Who would want to live where they had been imprisoned? Only the older Meduans and those who refused to relinquish their holdings resisted rejoining with Lansera. Lorne's father was one of them. He had vacated Lord Ralion's court and retreated to their manor on the Yarowen plains, likely sculpting Uzziel Sellwyn to take Lorne's place as the Granich heir. He was welcome to it, Lorne often claimed, but Serra knew the arrangement sometimes made him jealous. Wanting power and a title was a hard habit to break.

Janto had offered him a room in the castle, of course, but Lorne rejected it. Living within the walls of influence was a temptation he did not trust himself to resist. He wanted to change, to become whomever it was the Brothers thought he was. Helping his countrymen do the same was his eventual goal, but Lorne was determined to prove he could become *civilized* first, as he put it. If the way he stared at Serra with roving eyes and open desire was any indication, it would be an arduous journey. Such attention flattered only when wanted, and Lorne did not restrict his appreciation of women to one. *But he will.*

Thousands of vinum blossoms waved their heavy peach heads on the banks of the River Call. Serra could smell them from where she stood at the edge of Lorne's roof, the scent of warm caramel, peaches, and home. She should have done this years ago, relaxed on a morning like this, close enough to the blossoms to make out each ragged-edged petal. From the castle, they appeared as a massive puddle of orange beneath the bridge. So much detail was lost from that vantage point.

The three-headed bird had migrated far in the last two years. After culling them at Mandat Hall, hunting the claren had begun to be sport. At least until they returned to Callyn, often finding their next assignment waiting for them in the form of another family with grief writ plain in their defeated statures. With the Meduans, the tells were more pronounced. Some people who had been attacked were so angry they quaked as they yelled, shaking fists at the sky and Madel. Others collapsed, not having the strength to do anything more than reach Dever Albrecht's court. It sometimes took days before they could describe what had happened. After trips to more towns than Serra had known Lansera contained, the reports grew less frequent. But each death was one too many. The murders all brought an ache to her chest that hurt like failure. Yet she knew they could not cover the realm from Thokketh to Elston or predict where the remaining claren, those that had survived the blast, would migrate. Three heads were no better equipped to see the future than one, and the Brothers had vanished.

Someday, though, they would track them all. She, Vesperi, and Janto would eradicate each and every one of the vermin. She dreamed of the satisfaction when the smells of burning copper and ash faded away for the last time.

The air was full of more pleasant scents today. Vinum blossoms, her necklace of cloves, and . . . lemon. *Lemon?* Lorne rubbed a cream into his arms then joined her, resting his elbows on the roof's wall.

"Citrus?" She watched as he ran a hand through his lengthy blond hair, wishing her own was as radiant. "That does not smell like Meduan perfume."

"It's a balm the other students have been using to soothe their skins in this dry weather. All the rage at market."

She laughed at him, though with fondness and a good deal of finger pointing. "You are following a Lanserim fad? Oh, I must tell Vesperi of this."

"I'm young." He shrugged. "My mind is malleable by my contemporaries. Did you think I could resist their suggestions?"

She laughed again, bringing a smile to his lips. "Oh no, I am quite certain you cannot."

He gave no defense but gestured to the blanket where he had poured them both glasses of wine. It came from a vat bearing her family's sigil. Under Aunt Marji's competent winemaking, the Gavenstone vines were on their way to their first good harvest in years, but older vintages were rare. It was touching he had sought one out.

He smoothed a spot for her on the blanket. She lay down and stared at the sky. All four moons were out, Esye the most visible.

"You should come with us next time." One hand shielded her eyes and the other played with the rope that kept her blue and green raiment wrapped. She stayed with Rynna Hullvy when in town, practicing meditation so her sight would remain sharp and clear. Returning to Callyn rather than Enjoin or Gavenstone allowed her to be close by so she could leave with Janto and Vesperi as soon as they learned of a new attack. Besides, Callyn's rynna dressed so much better than the others. Serra could not imagine going back to those boring old sheaths. "You might learn something about resisting fads. Some of the styles in the smaller villages—"

Lorne laughed this time. "I am past learning about resistance, don't you think? Our trip back from Leba last fall taught me not to believe in it."

Serra cast him a disapproving glance. "You are only eighteen. I'm certain you have plenty yet to learn on the subject."

"And you are only twenty," he teased. "Tell me again about my slowed maturity when you have proven to have none of this resistance you so cherish? You swore you would never come see me again after the last time."

She scoffed. "I was bored. There are only so many hours I can spend in meditation before I need a break. You are a distraction." *An incredibly attractive distraction.* "And you lack maturity in so many areas, it would be cruel of me to recount them."

"You should not expect me to get everything right, you know. I am not certain I ever met a real woman before I met you. There is a considerable learning curve."

Serra blushed over every square inch of her skin, having expected a quick retort full of the sarcasm she had grown used to from him and Vesperi. Sincerity was not their chosen mode of communication. But sometimes it sneaked in and caught her unawares. "That is ridiculous. Vesperi is woman enough for twenty men, and I know you are well familiar with her."

She waited for a chortle, but Lorne remained serious, taking her hand. She kept her eyes on the landscape, all too aware of the man beside her. He was one of them, one of the people who had killed her brother, who had victimized each other daily. But he was also Lorne, the man sitting beside her on a rooftop in Callyn, admiring a rainbow of reflected sunlight from the quartz bridge, same as her. And he *was* learning.

"You are right." He rubbed a thumb over her palm. "But she was not a true woman then, when I first knew her. I do not think any of our women could have been what you are, not how we treated them. They had no chance. Someday I may know what it is to be a man, but not yet."

His earnestness was breathtaking, and she had to look upon him. The pastel blue of his eyes spoke of new tomorrows, ones free of expectation, and she took his other hand. His skin was smoother than Janto's, warmer too. But that was the last thought Serra had of her former betrothed that morning. "Well then, I hope I have been a good teacher."

"The best," Lorne agreed, meeting her lips. She knew this was right for her at this time, this place, this now. She did not know what the future held. No one did. The Brothers had only known what could be, not what would be. Maybe the reunification would be a failure five, ten, a hundred years from now. Maybe the Meduans would again tire of tempering their desires and a new horror would arise from their actions. But it did not matter on a morning like this, with the taste of lemon and Lorne on her tongue and the scent of vinum blossoms in the air. It did not matter at all.

Acknowledgments

The first glimmer of a silver stag came to me in college, over fifteen years ago now. As you can imagine, a great number of people have contributed to *Wings Unseen* since, and I apologize in advance for everyone I'm about to forget. I also apologize for thinking *Feathered Heads* was a reasonable name at some point in the process.

I can never fully express my thanks to my husband, Ben, for giving me the weapon needed to chase my dreams. To my poet mother, Sue, I attribute a deep love of storytelling, stemming from the horror novels she age-appropriately retold me as a young child. Thanks to my father, Gil, for leaving a dusty collection of genre fiction in the garage, including the 1970s edition of *The Lord of the Rings*. I'm sure he'd be very proud to have a writer for a daughter; I know all my Gomez family is. To my sister, Christa, I forgive you for chasing me around the house with spiders in Dixie cups, as I put those tortures to good use now. I'm sorry I ate the toes off your Crystal Barbie (and He-Man!).

To my first critique partners in North Carolina, who saw many versions of Serra, Vesperi, and Janto over the years, and who were smart enough to know that Lanvel was not a good name for the prince of Lansera, thank you: Dee Marley, Sarah Woods Doolittle, Conni Covington, Liz Thompson, and Susan Olson. To Ben (again), Paul Richards, Jessen Langley, Sarah Woods Doolittle (again), Dan Campbell, J. L. Hilton, and Ada Milenkovic Brown, thank you for beta reading the full book, whether or not your notes survived the wilds of your vacations.

My thanks to Kevin Davis of the blog *Bull City Rising* for a particularly well-timed post on the different approaches Raleigh and Durham, North Carolina, take toward addressing their crime and poverty issues.

The tension between turning a blind eye and shining a spotlight helped me tackle the social and political dynamics at play in Lansera and bring them to a resolution . . . for now.

To Tricia Reeks, Bernadette Geyer, and the whole team at Meerkat Press, thanks for being a small publisher that kicks booty in terms of quality and author support.

To the mosquitos of North Carolina, thank you for testing the bounds of my hatred.

And final thanks to my cats—Loki, Mazu, and the dearly departed Verdandi—for being the best (and furriest) coworkers a writer could want. Please, no more congratulatory presents.

Rebecca Gomez Farrell

In all but one career aptitude test Rebecca Gomez Farrell has taken, writer has been the #1 result. But when she tastes the salty air and hears  the sea lions bark, she wonders if maybe sea captain was the right choice after all. Currently marooned in Oakland, CA, Becca is an associate member of the Science Fiction and Fantasy Writers of America. Her short stories, which run the gamut of speculative fiction genres, have been published by *Beneath Ceaseless Skies*, *Pulp Literature*, the *Future Fire*, *Typehouse Literary Magazine*, and an upcoming story in the *Dark, Luminous Wings* anthology from Pole to Pole Publishing among others. *Maya's Vacation*, her contemporary romance novella, is available from Clean Reads. She is thrilled to have Meerkat Press publish her debut novel.

Becca's food, drink, and travel writing, which has appeared in local media in CA and NC, can primarily be found at her blog, *The Gourmez*. For a list of all her published work, fiction and nonfiction, check out her author website at RebeccaGomezFarrell.com.

CPSIA information can be obtained
at www.ICGtesting.com
Printed in the USA
LVOW03s1814020817
543486LV00007B/8/P

9 781946 154002